A FACE AT
THE WINDOW

A FACE AT THE WINDOW

A
Home Repair Is Homicide
Mystery

SARAH GRAVES

BANTAM BOOKS

A FACE AT THE WINDOW
A Bantam Book / January 2009

Published by Bantam Dell
A Division of Random House, Inc.
New York, New York

Library of Congress Cataloging-in-Publication Data

Graves, Sarah.
A face at the window / Sarah Graves.
p. cm. – (A home repair is homicide mystery)
ISBN 978-0-553-80679-3 (alk. paper)
1. Tiptree, Jacobia (Fictitious character)–Fiction. 2. White, Ellie (Fictitious
character)–Fiction. 3. Women detectives–Maine–Eastport–Fiction.
4. Historic buildings–Conservation and restoration–Fiction.
5. Female friendship–Fiction. 6. Eastport (Me.)–Fiction. I. Title.
PS3557.R2897F33 2009
813'.54–dc22
2008030284

Printed in the United States of America
Published simultaneously in Canada

www.bantamdell.com

10 9 8 7 6 5 4 3 2 1
BVG

A FACE AT
THE WINDOW

Discovering that Marky Larson had brought a gun along on the trip to Maine changed everything for Anthony Colapietro.

"Shut up," snarled Marky. It was the hundredth time he'd said it, or maybe the thousandth, since the two of them left New Jersey in Marky's old dark blue Monte Carlo nine hours earlier.

"I didn't say anything," Anthony protested. Not yet six in the morning, they'd been on the road all night, and his eyes felt sore and gritty from lack of sleep.

"You don't have to," retorted Marky from behind the wheel. "I can hear you thinking. You think I don't know what a punk like you is thinking? Quit thinking, you punk."

Marky believed, because he was a hardened twenty-four years old to Anthony's wet-behind-the-ears twenty-one, that he could call Anthony a punk.

"Got your face stuck up to the freakin' window," said Marky. "What if a cop drives by, gets a load of your face?"

There were no cops around here. But there was also no sense trying to tell Marky that. Anthony had wondered how he got picked for this job, but now he figured someone must've thought he could put up with Marky without blowing a gasket.

He stared at the water that appeared intermittently between the tall trees as the Monte rounded another curve in the narrow blacktop. The ocean was blue and glittery, flat as a plate; as he watched, a big bird lifted from it with a slow rhythm of wings.

"I just never saw it before is all," said Anthony.

Marky glanced over at him in contempt. "Never saw the ocean? What're you, a dope? Lived a coupla miles from it all your life, you never freakin' even been on the boardwalk?"

Anthony shook his head. "Uh-uh. Ma wouldn't let me."

Not as a little kid, anyway, and by the time she died he'd been in the juvie home six months already. From there, visiting the boardwalk was about as likely as visiting Mars.

Marky grimaced, showing small, even, white teeth. He was a good-looking guy with thick, curly black hair, a small, tightly constructed body, and what the girls called bedroom eyes.

Anthony didn't call them that, though, not even in his head.

When he met Marky's gaze, which he'd already learned not to do very often, he got the strong, unmistakable sense that something unpleasant was in there, peering out at him.

Unpleasant and . . . different. Several times Anthony had looked over from the passenger seat at Marky and glimpsed something that chilled him. A lizard, maybe, cold-blooded and primitive, dressed in a Marky Larson suit.

But that must be just his imagination. Some jealousy too, maybe, because Marky was flash, Anthony had to admit. Thick gold chains hung over the white T-shirt he wore under a black leather jacket; stolen, probably, along with the fancy wristwatch. Crisp new blue jeans, new sneakers on his feet; Air Jordans, it used to be, back when Anthony was helping boost them off of trucks, the drivers standing by knowing the score.

But that was years ago. Anthony's own jacket was a Jersey Devils warm-up he'd bought at a thrift shop for a few bucks, only because it was warm and cheap. He didn't even know what the in-demand sneaker was now. He'd never read a map before, either, and it was this that had Marky so annoyed.

"I think we should turn here," Anthony said as they came up on an intersection.

Well, not a real intersection like he was used to. More like a crossroads. Intersections had street signs. Stop lights.

And traffic. Other cars and people, neither of which were in evidence here on this empty, tree-lined road out in the middle of nowhere. This crossroads only had an old stone mile-marker.

No wonder there were no cops. "Well, should I or shouldn't I?" Marky demanded. "I mean who the freak've I got navigating for me, here, Chuckles the Clown?"

"Turn," Anthony said quickly. "Right. Or no, left. That's right, left."

Marky sighed heavily. "You're a moron, you know that?" But he took the turn. Despite his map-reading inexperience, somehow Anthony had managed so far not to steer them wrong.

It wasn't the real ocean out there, either. According to the words printed on the blue area that represented water on the map, it was a bay. He sounded out the unfamiliar name in his head. Passamaquoddy Bay, it was called, and on the far side of it was Canada.

Anthony stared at the land, low and tree-covered, on the other side of the water, wondering if living over there felt any different than it did on this side. Better, maybe.

"They sure get up early around here," he commented. Boats puttered offshore, cranelike contraptions jutting from the backs of them. Dragging something, though he couldn't see exactly what. Nets made of chain, it looked like, and on the opposite shore he could just make out small houses.

Maybe the boat operators lived in the houses. Had wives and kids there, even. Anthony frowned. "It's a whole other country, Canada."

Testing the idea. Sounding it out. They'd taught him to read, back in juvie. And they'd taken his tonsils out, after they got infected. That was the sum total of what he'd gotten out of the juvie experience.

Well, that and an early warning system, a kind of alarm that rang deep in his head when things were going haywire. It was jangling now very loudly and unnervingly like the bell for a fire drill, but there was nothing he could do about it.

Marky expelled an exasperated breath, plucked a smoke from the pack in his T-shirt pocket, and punched the dashboard lighter with an angry stab. "Jeeze," he said long-sufferingly.

The road here was even narrower than before, with great big trees crowded up on both sides. They made Anthony nervous, these huge green living things all around with no fences or any-thing to keep them in.

No paths, no park benches. He'd have given his left nut for a coffee shop but he hadn't seen one of those in a while, either.

Animals, though, he guessed. Bears, and . . . well, he didn't know what else might be running around in these trees. Were there lions in Maine forests?

Marky might know, but another thing Anthony had figured out was that it was better not to ask Marky unnecessary ques-tions. On the Tappan Zee, actually, when Anthony was first confronting the knotty problem of unfolding the map, he'd realized it.

He'd asked Marky to say where in Maine they were going so he could at least try to start plotting their route. That was the first time Marky had told Anthony to shut the freak up, adding that if Anthony gave him any crap whatsoever on this trip, Marky would shoot him and dump his dead body by the side of the road.

To emphasize this he'd opened his leather jacket to reveal the gun's checkered grip peeping from his inside breast pocket.

"Marky, the guy said not to bring any–"

"Screw the guy," Marky had said viciously. "He wants to do the thing, let him do it his way. Hires me, I do it mine, okay?"

Marky had already showed Anthony the small spiral note-book full of instructions for the job: Do this at this specific time, that at the other. Backup plans, too, for different things that might possibly go wrong. And . . . a photograph of a woman.

An old snapshot, white crinkly lines on it from where it had wrinkled a little. In it, the woman smiled into the camera: dark hair, full red lips, eyes laughing and bright. The snapshot had come out of the wallet of their employer, Marky had said, but he wouldn't say any more.

Probably because he didn't know, although just try getting Marky to admit anything like that. Finally there was the heavy cardboard box full of equipment that they'd brought along, which naturally it had been Anthony's job to load into the Monte's trunk: two sets of night vision goggles, rubber-strap headsets to wear them with, a small recorder with an old-fashioned cassette tape in it, plus other things that Anthony couldn't take the time to identify because Marky kept yelling at him to hurry.

What's up with that stuff? he'd wondered, but now he just looked out the window again to where the underbrush crept up to and in places right out over the crumbling pavement.

No power poles, he noticed. Probably no lions, either. But he still wished there were fences.

"This better be right," Marky growled threateningly, spewing out a stream of smoke while casting another evil look at Anthony. "Or you're in trouble."

Anthony was pretty sure he was already in trouble. Coming up here with Marky had been a bad idea, and not only because of the gun.

The money was good, though. He decided his best course now would be to concentrate on the money. He rolled his window down to let some of Marky's smoke out and got an unexpected faceful of ocean smell, cold salt water and what he guessed must be seaweed mingled with a hint of wood smoke.

The smell triggered a hard, deep *I want* feeling, like when a pretty girl walked by him wearing some really nice perfume. Went right on walking, usually, because girls like that wouldn't give Anthony Colapietro a second look.

Jesus, he thought, having given up yearning so long ago that he barely recognized it. Then they were in the trees again and a different smell came in, like the Pine-Sol from the juvie home.

Training school, they'd called it. Yeah, training to be a loser. Every kid in there had grown up to be a knucklehead. The luckiest ones ended up running errands for actual tough guys.

Like me, he thought in a moment of bleak self-knowledge. *An errand boy.*

But since the unlucky ones were either dead or in prison, he decided that maybe this little field trip with Marky wasn't so bad, after all. And the smell, he realized, was coming from the trees.

Pine trees, they must be, growing wild here right out of the dirt. He let this idea sink in some more, finding it worrisome but also strangely pleasant.

Marky spoke up again. "So I gotta do everything," he snarled, "while you sit there playin' freakin' tourist? What're you, the Queen of freakin' England, now?"

Anthony jumped, then consulted the map again hastily. Marky was right. He wasn't keeping his mind on the job enough. A mean voice in his head added that this was why the losers were errand boys, that it was in fact why they remained losers.

The thought was so surprising, so different from anything he had ever come up with before, that he wondered for an instant if maybe it wasn't coming from some *other* head. Marky's, maybe.

But no. Marky was an errand boy, too. Just a meaner, more confident one.

An errand boy with a gun. "Okay, keep your shirt on. Turn here," Anthony said. Hoping he was correct, that he hadn't maybe started getting it wrong a hundred miles ago without knowing it.

Because Marky really would kill him. Even the "keep your shirt on" remark, lightly delivered and intended merely to mollify Marky, jolly him into a better mood, had triggered a dirty look.

Marky wouldn't care if Anthony's body was only half dead when he shoved it out of the car. And Anthony had a feeling that if you got lost here, shot or otherwise, you might never get found again; that the absence of paths, park benches, and cages for the animals was the least of it.

The very least of it. As he thought this, something moved way back there among the trees where sunlight angled in wavery golden patches surrounded by green gloom. Anthony tried to see what it was and especially if it was coming any closer.

But by that time they'd already gone by, and when he craned his neck to look back, it wasn't following them. Or if it was, it was hiding in the underbrush where Anthony couldn't see.

"Hey, whoa, what the freak is this?" Marky demanded as the pavement ended suddenly and the car began bouncing violently.

"End of the line," Anthony replied. "That was the last turn, back there. We should see the house, coupla minutes."

The news seemed to cheer Marky. "Man, we are definitely not in Kansas anymore," he said, his fingers wrapped tightly around the wheel, cigarette dangling from his lips.

Grinning, suddenly lighthearted. He snapped on the radio, a blare of country music filling the car. Marky sang along with the tune in a sarcastic falsetto, ridiculing the words and the down-home country twang, making stupid faces.

"Oh, she broke mah heart so ah broke her jaw," Marky sang in his curiously high, nasal voice. "Ah cut 'er up with a big chain saw."

Anthony wasn't comforted by the sudden show of good humor, though, because that was another thing about Marky, that you couldn't tell when he meant it: the grin, or the lizard look. As if to prove this, Marky snapped the radio off abruptly.

"Christ," he exhaled in sudden disgust. "People listen to this crap around here?" They rode in silence a little more until, in half a mile or so, the dirt road got worse.

A lot worse. Loose stones clattered against the underside of Marky's beat-up Monte as they jounced over the uneven track. The muffler banged a rock sticking up out of a pothole.

Bam! Anthony looked back, wondering if the rock had torn the Monte's muffler right off. Marky cursed eloquently, coming up with words and combinations that even Anthony had never heard of before, and his eyes grew cold and reptilian again as he glared over at Anthony accusingly.

Be there, Anthony thought at the house that was supposed to be hidden away around here somewhere, imagining Marky getting too frustrated and tired to be able to keep a lid on it. Shooting Anthony in the knee, maybe, just to let off steam.

He hoped it would be only the knee. But then around the next curve, a house did appear, first the roof and then the rest of it huddled there under the low branches.

"About time," Marky said grimly, as if it were Anthony's fault that the trip had taken so long. They stopped in a graveled turnaround and got out into an enormous, waiting silence.

In juvie, the noise had been constant, like living against a background of heavy demolition. And afterward, the rooms in the boardinghouses he'd lived in had been loud, too, right over the street in the kinds of neighborhoods where nightfall only got the quiet people to go indoors. Here, though:

Trees and more trees. Through them Anthony glimpsed the bay again, blue and glittering and . . . big. Much bigger than anything he was used to. The silence all around kept enlarging as well, as if it just might suck Anthony right up into it.

He'd never felt so small, so at the mercy of something. Battling panic he waited for Marky to decide their next move, while his gut churned sourly and sweat prickled his armpits. Then a bird cried out raucously overhead: *chukka-chukka-chukka!*

Anthony's heart hammered and his mouth went dry. The smell of sun-warmed pine needles filled his head again, flooding into it like the ether they'd used on him for his tonsils, clapping the mask harshly to his face.

If Marky killed him here, no one would find him. It would be like when he first disappeared into the juvie home, and then his mom died.

No one would know. No one would even ask. Pretty soon wild animals would come along hungrily and eat his body. His eyes, his ears . . . even the tongue he'd used to cry out with, at the end.

Leaving only bones.

Chapter 2

For fixing a sidewalk, use concrete, not mortar. For fixing loose bricks or stone, use mortar, not concrete.
—Tiptree's Tips

D o you suppose you could explain to me again why you think this Campbell fellow is coming after you?" asked Eastport police chief Bob Arnold in tones of barely repressed skepticism.

It was a bright morning in August, a week before Labor Day. The warm air drifting in off Passamaquoddy Bay smelled sweetly of chamomile and sea salt. A seagull soared lazily over the spot where Bob's squad car sat parked under the maple tree, in front of the big old white house on Key Street.

Two tourists pedaled by on rented bicycles. "I told you. I think what I said about him made him mad," replied the dark-haired, jeans-and-sweater-clad woman crouched by the jagged hole in the front sidewalk. "Wrote about him, I mean."

Her name was Jake Tiptree, and when she first came to Maine and moved into the huge, ramshackle old dwelling on Moose Island, seven miles off the downeast coast, she thought that at least the concrete walk from the porch to the street looked indestructible.

But ten years and hundreds of old-house repairs later, she knew she might as well have believed in the tooth fairy. Nothing was indestructible; not windows or doors, not plaster or flooring or plumbing or wiring or, God forbid, the furnace.

Not even herself, which was her other problem on this fine late summer morning in Eastport, Maine, three hours from Bangor and light-years from anywhere else.

Not far enough, she thought. She dug more crumbly concrete pieces out of the walkway, using a hand trowel to scrape at the edges of the already gaping hole. Later she would widen its base even more but for now she just wanted to get the loose stuff out.

"That's why he's vanished. So he can sneak up on me. I feel like I'm in a horror movie, waiting for the monster." Lately, the mere thought of Ozzie Campbell gave her the creeps.

Bob Arnold leaned against the squad car, an aging off-white Crown Victoria with the city's emblem, a stylized blue-and-orange sunrise, stenciled on the door. Beneath the few strands of pale hair stretched over his forehead, his scalp gleamed in the sun.

"Yeah. You told me that on the phone, Jake," he said. Plump and pink-faced, Bob didn't resemble the kind of quick-on-the-uptake cop who could nab up a bad guy so fast that the guy was deposited in Bob's squad car and locked behind the perp screen before he even knew what hit him.

But just a week earlier, a couple of out-of-towners had decided that Eastport would make a great export center for bulk methamphetamines. Right on the water and only a few hundred yards from the Canadian border, they rigged waterproof bait boxes and attached them to Styrofoam buoys, then went on "fishing trips" and left the boxes floating, to be picked up by their cohorts on the far side of the imaginary line dividing the two nations.

They hadn't figured on (a) an informant willing to trade his pals for a break on his own legal problems, and (b) Bob, sitting out there in a dory with two arrest warrants and a .410 shotgun in his lap.

Bob always said cop work was ninety percent knowing and ten percent doing, as if to imply that anyone could be good at it. "But you didn't say how come he'd be *that* mad," he told Jake now.

And you still haven't, he was obviously thinking. But he was a friend in addition to being Eastport's only full-time police, so he'd driven over practically the minute she called. Which in turn was barely a minute after Sandy O'Neill, aide to Manhattan Assistant District Attorney Lawrence Trotta, had finished telling Jake the bad news: that Ozzie Campbell was AWOL.

She shoved the hand trowel's tip in under the big chunk of concrete still lodged in the hole. Experimentally, she pried at the chunk. It shifted a little, but not enough.

"All I know is, I sent in my victim's impact statement two weeks ago, just the way they asked me to. And now it's been read, processed, and—"

This was the bad part. "—copied to the defense attorneys," she finished. "Ozzie Campbell's lawyers."

It had been Sandy's other news, on the phone from his tiny office in downtown Manhattan, overlooking the Brooklyn Bridge: that her "vic statement," as Sandy had called it, detailing the many negative effects upon her of her mother's murder thirty-five years earlier, had been placed in discovery.

In other words, revealed to the defendant, too, if he wanted to read it. "So there are no surprises later," Sandy O'Neill had explained patiently in his thick Brooklyn accent. "We got enough problems with this case," he'd said.

Listening, she had practically been able to see the sunshine glittering on the East River, hear the traffic's clamor and smell the cooked-hydrocarbon reek of lower Manhattan on a hot day.

"If we do get a conviction," Sandy had told her, "we don't want any grounds for appeal. We don't want them quibbling over one thing, saying how maybe it suggests that we didn't show them other things. Also, this guy's got a bad temper; we don't want him going off half-cocked for some wild-hair reason, screwing us up some way we didn't anticipate. So," he'd finished, "we're just showing them *everything* right up front."

Including her victim's impact statement. It was a development Jake hadn't anticipated, and now with Ozzie Campbell doing his thin-air act right afterward—well, Sandy could say whatever he liked. It was still too coincidental for comfort.

"Twenty years in the bar business in Atlantic City, he's as regular as a bank clerk," she told Bob Arnold now. "Never a break or a vacation, guy never even takes a sick day. Two weeks before trial, though, suddenly his lawyers get my thing and . . . poof!"

Gone. Like a magic trick. Or a plan. It was another thing Sandy O'Neill had told her, that Campbell was a detail-oriented, hands-on type of person who'd pored obsessively over every single filing, motion, and court memorandum in the proceedings so far.

Also, you didn't run a bar successfully for all those years without being a good planner, a guy with a sharp eye for the small stuff and a habit of not letting even the slightest thing slip. People like Campbell took care of business.

And finally, though she didn't know much else about Campbell–Sandy had offered to tell, but at the time the minutiae of the killer's life hadn't interested her–she knew that when people's routines changed dramatically, there was always a reason.

Thinking this, she gripped the concrete chunk's edges with her fingertips. Roughly rectangular, it was about a foot long, nine inches wide, and six inches thick.

Difficult, in other words, and in need of attention, like the rest of the place. She wondered briefly why she'd chosen to take on a massive old dwelling every inch of which required constant maintenance. It was what living on an old wooden boat must be like, always scrambling to keep it from going under. Only when left to their own devices, old houses sank into the earth instead of the sea.

But she knew why she'd done it, really. The constant needs of someone or something kept people from sinking, too; ones like herself, for instance, who thrived on something useful to do. And it hadn't hurt that she'd loved the place the moment she saw it.

Still did. But that concrete was *heavy*.

"Jake." Bob stepped forward, ready to help. "Just 'cause the guy's not down there where he usually is, that still doesn't mean he's necessarily up here, trying to get on your case. 'Cause like you say, where'd be the sense?"

"Yeah, right. Things always make sense, don't they?" she

retorted. "They just fall into place like jigsaw puzzle pieces, fit to-gether right off the bat. And nobody's following me, or watching me, either."

Because that was the worst thing, the crawly sense of being observed like a bug under a lens. Or a target in the crosshairs. She'd been trying to get Bob to take her seriously about it for a few days now, earning in return the kind of looks that the atten-dants gave to the inmates in the really securely locked-down asy-lums.

She hadn't told anyone else, though; not her husband, Wade Sorenson, for example, or her best friend, Ellie White. Because what could they do? And she didn't want them worrying about her; about her safety, or more likely, her sanity.

But back to the dratted sidewalk; for something that rocked so alarmingly when stepped on, that concrete chunk was solidly in there. Rising, she crossed the yard to the tool shed under the maple tree, returning with a garden spade.

"Jake." Bob's tone was excessively patient. "So you've got an odd feeling? That you're being watched? Because it's what you said. But what the hell am I supposed to do with that?"

Right, she thought again. Tell it to the judge: "Your Honor, the hairs on the back of my neck are prickling and I feel some-thing bad coming." Heck, half the world felt something bad com-ing, and mostly they were right.

But that didn't mean Bob Arnold could help them, shotgun or not. He went on:

"Anyway, you said yourself there's nothing in your statement that'll mean anything at the guy's trial. No reason for him to want to get you out of the way, no new evidence against him, that you can supply."

She frowned. He was correct on this point, also; even all these years later, what happened on that night in the brownstone in Greenwich Village was so clear in her mind, it could've been etched there with an engraving tool.

But the memories of a witness who was just three years old at the time, Assistant DA Lawrence Trotta had informed her, would carry little weight with a jury. They might even harm his case, being as there was absolutely no corroborating evidence for them.

"Nothing they can use, even though I was right there," she confirmed. "Basically, they're prosecuting him without me."

Juries didn't like feeling that they were being manipulated by emotion, Trotta had said. The wise prosecutor didn't even try it. "So getting me out of the way couldn't help him at all. More likely the opposite," she finished.

She slid the spade's blade deeper underneath the concrete chunk. The best she could hope for, Trotta had said as kindly as he was able—being a prosecuting attorney had put a hide like an elephant's on him—was that her victim's impact statement might sway the jury when sentencing time came.

If it came, because there could instead be an acquittal; in fact, that was the likeliest outcome. After so many years, most of them occupied by the FBI's search for the wrong man, the case was no slam dunk and Trotta had made no secret of that, either.

Especially since the one thing she hadn't seen clearly that night was the killer's face. "Probably Campbell doesn't like being reminded of what he did," she told Bob. And her statement, so full of vividly recalled detail even after all this time, would at least accomplish that much.

But Campbell wouldn't do anything so risky as harming her right before his trial, merely over hurt feelings. If he did he'd be the obvious suspect. So what was he up to?

"Back away, Bob, will you? If some concrete snaps off or the spade breaks, I don't want it to hit you."

He obeyed, stepping up onto the porch where a pair of blue canvas lawn chairs took up most of the space. Summer was nearly over, the temperatures on clear nights plummeting to the forties under stars turning hard and cold, but in Eastport, people clung to the last dregs. When she woke up to snow overfilling the blue canvas drink cups built into the chair arms, she would haul them inside.

"That looks like kind of a tough job, there," Bob observed. "You sure you don't want me to . . . ?"

"Bob, don't treat me like a little old lady." *Or,* she added silently, *what you think of as a lady, at all.*

He still seemed to believe she should be hiring help for this kind of thing, that she was somehow too fragile for fixing up an old house. Partly she imagined that it was because she was slender and five foot four, with small, regular features capped by clipped-short dark hair; overall, it was a package that made some people—not ones she liked—describe her as "pixieish."

And partly it was because, even though his wife Clarissa was the kind of tough criminal defense attorney for whom the phrase "junkyard dog" was invented, Bob just still thought that way.

She leaned on the spade; if you crossed Dirty Harry with the Pillsbury Doughboy and added a dollop of Miss Manners, Bob was what you'd get. In his mind, the womanly spheres didn't include any power tools or guns, two areas in which she actually had some hard-won expertise.

It was yet another way in which the house had repaid her for her work on it. When she came here the only power tool she'd ever used was an electric toothbrush, unless you counted the blender in which she'd made strawberry daiquiris. And heavy lifting had been out of her realm entirely.

As she'd hoped, the mechanical advantage of the spade's long handle lifted the chunk easily; so much for needing a tough guy. Nothing like demolition work to put hair on a girl's chest, she thought; harness anger, keep a leash on revenge fantasies, even squelch fears . . .

Some fears. Pivoting, she deposited the big concrete piece on the lawn under the maple, whose roots were likely what had caused the concrete walk to fracture at all.

"Look, it's not like I don't sympathize. It can't be easy," said Bob. "The trial, remembering it all and hearing it brought up again—"

She laughed shortly. "That's putting it mildly." Having your mother killed and believing that your father had done it was the next best thing to being an orphan.

Or next worst. Her own experiences with parentlessness had made Oliver Twist look like Rebecca of Sunnybrook Farm. But that was all over and done with long ago, she reminded herself as, sighing, she peered into the hole.

It was wet. Muddy, even. "Oh, hell," she pronounced.

Straightening, she wiped her hands on her jeans and turned. "Bob, the guy murdered my mother. Strangled her, set a fire, blew up half a city block, and basically framed my father for it all. Sent him on the run."

The authorities had been happy to suspect Jacob Tiptree. He was already the kind of guy they liked making an example of, the kind who built bombs and exploded them as loudly and pub-licly as possible to highlight social injustice. Not hurting people; never that. He and his associates had been careful, and anyway in those days a big bang and a mimeographed manifesto had been enough.

The old, golden days . . . "You don't know for sure," Bob be-gan again, "that Ozzie Campbell was really even the one who—"

"Yes, I do," she retorted. "Everyone does. Besides my dad and the man who finally ended up being my dad's alibi—"

The fellow he'd been selling explosives to when the fire began hadn't wanted to come forward. Only on his deathbed had he told authorities how he knew for sure that Jacob Tiptree hadn't killed his beautiful young wife, Leonora:

Because the fellow had been planning a demonstration of his own, in support of an antipoverty group he'd been a part of. At the rally he meant to blow up an enormous statue of a pig wearing a business suit, and in return for black powder, fuse cord, and the blasting caps to do it with, he'd just finished handing ten thousand dollars over to Jacob Tiptree when the murder occurred.

"Ozzie Campbell was the only other adult in the house," she finished. He'd even had a motive: his love for Jake's mother, which afterward he'd never bothered keeping a secret.

So as soon as the cops stopped thinking Jake's dad had done the deed, Campbell was the clear next choice. Add a Manhattan ADA who badly wanted that word "assistant" lopped off his title and presto, instant prosecution.

Campbell would get Trotta's name and his brand-new slogan—"Justice Never Forgets"—into the newspapers and onto the blogs.

Win or lose hardly mattered; it was the name recognition Trotta would get out of it that counted.

"Jake, you were just a little kid," argued Bob. "You don't know who all might've been there with your folks in the—"

"Oh, but I do." Why was it so hard to make people understand this, that the facts of the case were clear? "Everyone saw who all went in and out of our house. In those days in the Village it was just like it is here, a neighborhood."

She waved at the other big old white wooden houses on the block, their front steps bright with potted chrysanthemums and blowsy late-season geraniums, many of their inhabitants taking advantage of the fine late summer weather and busy with chores: painting porches, washing windows, tidying dooryards.

A red muscle car rumbled by, thudding down the street to the deep bass thump of its oversized stereo speakers. An ice cream truck tootled in the opposite direction, jangling out its simple tune like a brain-dead Pied Piper.

"Still," Bob began again, wanting to reassure her.

He was like that. "Trotta has witnesses," she interrupted him. "From back then. People on their front stoops gossiping and watching the kids play. It was," she added, "a nice day."

Or so she'd been told. "And there's plenty of testimony that no one else went in there that afternoon. No one but my dad, the guy who was buying stuff from him, and Campbell."

ADA Trotta had hinted recently about new forensics evidence, stuff that hadn't been possible back then, though she'd yet to be told anything definite. He was tight-lipped both about potential new lab results and about his trial strategy. But even if new scientific evidence came in, getting a jury to care would still be a challenge, everything faded by years and by the brighter contrasts of newer, more sensational crimes.

Bob relented a little. "So you think Campbell's nervous."

"Yeah. About me. And if I knew why, maybe I'd feel better about this little thin-air maneuver he's pulling."

Or maybe not. She dropped to her knees again by the muddy hole in the front walk, scowled into it.

No wonder the concrete had finally broken. There was nothing underneath to hold it up. All the dirt down there had washed away.

"I don't know what might've set Campbell off," she said, "but I don't care what the ADA's aide says about him maybe just wanting a vacation, a little peace and quiet before the you-know-what hits the fan."

A swiftly set bail requirement of two point five million had been no bar to Ozzie's gaining his freedom, a few days after the indictment. Defendants only had to put up ten percent; still, it was a lot of money. On the telephone, Sandy O'Neill had suggested Campbell's absence was probably no big deal, just on account of the potential forfeiture of so much money and property.

That Jake shouldn't be alarmed. But Jake thought O'Neill was alarmed himself on some level, or he wouldn't have called her.

"Campbell's a slime toad," she said. "A thug, with thuggish connections." Everyone knew that about him, too; the indictment, along with a brief profile of him, had appeared in the papers as Trotta hoped. "And no one knows where he is."

Looking around for the possible cause of the muddiness in the hole, she found it a few feet away in the metal downspout of a gutter still dripping from showers the night before. "Damn."

"What's the trouble?" Bob asked.

A half-hour repair job had just expanded to the better part of a week. "That," she replied, pointing up in disgust.

New aluminum gutters gleamed at the roofline of the house, an 1823 white Federal clapboard with three full floors plus an attic, three tall red brick chimneys, and forty-eight old double-hung windows each with a set of old green wooden shutters.

And a collapsed front walk. Squinting, Bob frowned. "Looks okay to me. The rainwater used to come down there—"

He pointed to where small rust stains betrayed the earlier presence of metal. "But you rearranged it so it comes down here." He aimed an index finger at the relocated downspout. "So . . . ?"

Inhaling deeply, she pressed the pad of her thumb to the spot just between her eyes where her head was beginning to throb.

"So when I redirected the rainwater runoff, I didn't take into account where the water would run once I got it away from the foundation, that's what. And where it would go turns out to be under that sidewalk."

"Oh," Bob said, nodding comprehendingly. "Then, when it got under there, it caused . . ."

"Erosion. And then the concrete cracked. So the other day when my dad stepped on it, it collapsed and so did he."

"He's okay, though? Your dad?" Bob asked solicitously.

The lean old man with the stringy gray ponytail, big work-roughened hands, and pale blue eyes was a favorite of the Eastport police chief, even though Jake's dad wore a ruby in his earlobe and Bob believed firmly that earrings on men were against the laws of nature.

"Yeah." Jake eyed the hole. "Cast on his foot, but he and Bella went on their honeymoon anyway, just the way they planned."

Her dad and her housekeeper Bella Diamond had been courting for years behind a smokescreen of quarrels and spats. Underneath all the friction, though, they were as made for each other as a pair of Siamese fighting fish.

"Going to be interesting," Bob remarked. "Got the first-aid kit stocked?"

A laugh escaped her. "Yeah. And one of those bells they ring at boxing matches to make them get back to their corners. I guess I'm the designated referee."

She looked up. "Seriously, though, if she doesn't nurse him to death after his foot injury, and he doesn't get so cranky he ends up swatting her with a rolled newspaper, they'll be fine."

Behind Bob, the house soared solidly into the sky, its proportions—from door height to window width to the arc of the leaded-glass fanlight over the massive front entry, right down to the lap of the clapboards nailed precisely upon one another—as satisfying as a mathematical equation.

That more than anything was what had attracted her to the old structure, she supposed, the idea that if you stayed in such a place long enough, you might come to resemble it. That a person might eventually learn to live by its dignified example.

So far it hadn't happened, but one could hope.

Just then a car pulled up alongside her and a familiar hoot issued from its open window. "Ja-ake!" called Eastport's closest equivalent to a human foghorn, Billie Whitson.

Reluctantly, Jake turned. Billie was a recent arrival to the area, fresh from the sunny climes and even sunnier financial prospects of Carmel, California. She was full of marvelous plans for turning Eastport into a Maine island paradise.

That it already was one seemed not to have occurred to her. "Now, Jake, I want you to tell me I can put you on the list," she declared.

The California sun had turned Billie's short, straight hair to yellow straw, and her face into a leathery mask of bright paint, jangly earrings, and black-rimmed eyes. "If people see how beautifully you've rehabbed *that* old monstrosity," she went on with a wave at Jake's beloved antique dwelling, "they'll be more likely to buy one of the truly good old homes that *I'm* in the business of selling."

Feasting her eyes upon Internet photos of cheap shoreline property and unaware that in Maine what you saved on land, you spent on heat, Billie had wasted no time getting a Realtor's license and setting up a Web site of her own. Now she wanted to put Jake's place on her virtual home tour, "just to show what you can do with even the worst old heap," as she so flatteringly put it.

"Maybe after the sidewalk's fixed," Jake told the clueless real estate maven, not quite meeting her avid gaze. When Billie fixed her sights on you it was like being stared at by a bird of prey that had spotted something edible.

"Don't wait too long," Billie advised, letting her face show what she thought of Jake's efforts with the fractured concrete. Where she came from, home-owners had staff to take care of things like that. "You wouldn't want it to fall down any more than it has already, before people get a chance to see it."

Unless it falls on you, Jake thought as Billie's red-tipped fingers twitched in a farewell wave.

"Bella and my dad are due home in a week," she told Bob once Billie had zoomed off in her silver MG convertible, her trailing scarf provoking a final, thoroughly uncharitable thought. "When he comes up the front walk, it would be good if I could keep him from breaking the other foot. So I'd better get started."

She faced Bob squarely. "But about Campbell. He's here. Or on his way. Mark my words," she added as Bob started to object again.

True, she had no evidence. But she didn't want to look back someday on her suspicions and say *if only.* Not about a man who, thirty-five years earlier, had strangled a woman with his bare hands while her child looked on, then ripped one of the earrings from her ear and taken it away with him.

He'd worn it ever since, brazenly insisting she'd given it to him as a love token long before she was murdered. "And you see most everything that happens around here, so . . ."

"Yeah, yeah. Keep an eye out for weirdos." Bob got into his car, settling onto the torn black seat. "I always do. Although I still don't get why you and Lee can't come and stay with us for a few nights."

At his words, a new unease struck her. But that really was just paranoia, surely; Campbell had no way of knowing about

the three-year-old girl staying with Jake while her parents, Jake's
dearest friend Ellie White and Ellie's husband George Valentine,
were away on vacation.

Nor would he have any reason to care. Still, Jake wished all at
once she hadn't decided to keep Lee here, that instead she had
taken up Ellie and George's offer to bunk over at their place for
the duration.

Bob seemed to read her thought. "We've got plenty of room,"
he urged, "and you know Clarissa would love it."

Jake didn't doubt it. When she wasn't in a courtroom bash-
ing holes into prosecutors' supposedly watertight arguments,
Clarissa was a peach. He squinted around, suddenly seeming to
realize what was missing. "You don't even have the dogs here, do
you?"

"Nope." No dogs, no people, just herself and a little girl who
would likely go early to bed. Jake had been looking forward to
the solitude, actually.

Until now. "Sam's starting school in Portland in a couple of
weeks," she went on. "He's in a brand-new apartment there, has
a new job; he's getting himself settled."

At twenty-one, her son was trying yet again to make a life for
himself. "Wade's at work," she added. Her husband, Wade
Sorenson, was Eastport's harbor pilot, an expert at getting big
cargo freighters in and out of the tricky local waterways.

"And the dogs are away at training camp," she finished.
Wade sent them out there each late summer to get them ready
for turkey season, partridge season, duck season, grouse season,
deer season, moose season, rabbit season, and any other season
that he and his hunting buddies could come up with. If he
could've taught the animals to play cards and drink brandy, he'd
have taken them ice-fishing, too.

"They'll be there a few more days. I still think I'll stay here, though." A quiet house, a bathtub available for long, hot soaks, plus glasses of wine, a free hand with the TV's remote control, not to mention its Off button—

"Thanks anyway, Bob. Tell Clarissa I'll call her, will you?"

"Yeah, all right," he gave in. "Anyway, I gotta go. There's a lady out near Dog Island complaining that kids were partying on the Knife Edge last night. Like that's anything new."

Beer parties on the cliffs at the south end of the island were a perennial problem. Only a few town kids attended out of the many who lived here, but when they got going, it seemed like a lot. "Trust teenagers to want to get drunk at the edge of a hundred-foot drop," he added resignedly. "So I need to go calm her down, I guess. And there was an accident a little while ago out by the causeway, car hit a deer."

No surprise there, either; car versus deer incidents were a dime a dozen around here. "Anyone hurt?"

He spread his hands. "Only the deer. Venison for the food pantry. And the car's totaled, belonged to a guy staying out at the campgrounds for a week. He's from Connecticut, and he says he's suing the city for not putting up Cyclone fencing to keep the deer off the roads."

He glanced heavenward as if praying for relief from visitors who thought they'd be swaddled in cotton wool here, just the way they were at home. "They're still clearing up the broken glass on the road and so on; guess I'd better have a look," Bob said.

Then another thought occurred to him. "Kid still biting?" He rubbed the side of his head in remembered pain.

Lee, he meant. "Unfortunately, yes." It was the toddler's only seriously bad habit, but it was a doozy; just that morning, Jake had nearly lost the tip of a finger.

"Mistook your ear for a chew toy, did she?" Jake asked Bob.

The pediatrician said Lee would grow out of it, eventually, but Jake wasn't so sure.

"Few days back," Bob confirmed, grimacing. "You ever find a way to make her let go?"

"Nope. Pry bar, maybe." His radio began sputtering just as, back in the house, her phone began ringing. With a wave he drove off to check on the deer-car mishap; she stepped over the hole in the front walk on her way to answer.

Inside, the house shimmered emptily: silent, serene. Solitude was a rare luxury for her, and as she picked up the receiver she thought again about the ways in which she planned to enjoy it.

"Hello, Jacobia," the voice on the phone said, and then it struck her, just exactly how alone she really was here.

Once they found the house at the end of the dirt road, Marky settled down some and on account of that Anthony felt better, too, less worried and more able to size up the situation. But as soon as he lugged the heavy boxful of gear in from the Monte's trunk, they'd gone into town to get the lay of the land.

As they crossed the long, curving causeway onto the island– *Welcome to Eastport!* said the sign–Marky remarked sourly that if he had to live way out here in the boondocks like this, he'd just kill himself and get it over with.

But Anthony wasn't so sure. To him the town's big old white houses with green shutters and red chimneys were like dwellings out of a child's storybook, one of tales simpler and luckier than his own. Even the less well-kept places here looked better than his crummy room and hotplate back in New Jersey.

Marky turned the car away from the neat clusters of houses, following small hand-painted signs with arrows on them that

read *See the Old Sow Whirlpool!* The signs led to a grassy bluff end-
ing at a gravel turnaround, perched on a high cliff.

From here you couldn't see the town, only water in a
nearly 360-degree panorama, churning and swirling. *Danger,* an-
nounced the placard posted by the weedy, crumbling edge of the
cliff.

No kidding, thought Anthony as Marky got out of the car and
slammed the door, striding away. A chilly feeling hit Anthony as
he let his gaze stray to where a section of cliff stuck straight out
over the waves like a big stone bridge to nowhere.

Dizzyingly high and narrow, the craggy stone trail over thin
air widened suddenly at its very end to a tablelike platform big
enough to stand on, but not much more. Yeah, like you could
even get out that far, he thought. It made the pit of his stomach
feel hollow just looking at it.

Scattered beer cans and the blackened remains of a small fire
said the *Danger* sign was regularly disregarded, probably by local
kids. But Anthony had no problem obeying it, as Marky made
his way to the last bit of solid ground before the precipice and
stood there staring.

"What?" called Anthony, but Marky ignored him, squinting
out into the morning brilliance over the foamy, turbulent water
as if gauging directions and distances while Anthony watched
uneasily, then crept to the edge of the cliff himself.

Cripes, but it was a long way down. A little to his right, a
path snaked through the loose stones and strangled-looking
bushes down to a narrow beach. At the foot of the cliff, a steel cable was clipped to a big bolt in one of the boulders down there.

He let his eyes follow the cable out to where it ended on an
enormous black rock jutting out of the water fifty yards distant.
On the rock stood a concrete pyramid, maybe four feet high;

from a construction job he'd done manual labor on once, he recognized it as an old U. S. government survey marker.

The cable was to help you get out there, he knew. Clip a
safety line to the cable, it would keep you from getting washed
away. Or worst case, you could go hand over hand. . . .

Watching the waves batter the rock and fall back again, gey-
sers of white foam hurling themselves skyward and subsiding,
Anthony was glad he didn't have to get out to the survey
marker. Meanwhile, Marky made a point of examining a small
red-and-white replica of a lighthouse set a dozen yards back from
the cliff's edge, walking around it, frowning and looking from
the lighthouse to the water and back, as if fixing their relationship in his mind. Then, seemingly satisfied, he returned to
the car.

What new wrinkle was this? Anthony wondered. He didn't
know Marky well, but he'd seen him often enough around the
bar they both hung out in back in Jersey. And the only scenery
Marky was ever interested in there wore tassels and a bikini
bottom.

If that. "Never mind," Marky rebuked him before he could
ask. "You don't have to know everything."

Anthony had snappy answers for this; plenty of them. But he
didn't offer any because for one thing, Marky still had the gun.
Besides, why bother? It would only start another whole big
thing.

Slamming the car into gear, Marky spun out of the parking
area near the cliff and headed back toward town, where
Anthony wanted to go, too. Maybe there'd be coffee there.

Eastport's single short market street opposite the harbor was
composed of two- or three-story brick or shingle-fronted old
buildings with benches and flower boxes arranged out in front of
their wide plate-glass windows. Mostly they housed restaurants

and souvenir shops but there were a few offices among them, too, including several for lawyers and real estate agents.

Anthony wondered idly what the deal was, anyway, buying a house. Did you have to apply somewhere, were there papers to fill out? Was there a background check? He was curious, too, about what use people around here had for lawyers. None of the faces he saw on the street had the pinched look he associated with crime.

Mostly they were tourists, their pocketbooks and expensive cameras dangling off them like ripe fruit dangling from low trees and their big SUVs just begging to be raced to the nearest chop shop. Back wherever they came from he supposed they could be up to plenty of shenanigans, but here they were on vacation from it.

Opposite a long wooden pier with two tugboats tied up to it, Marky pulled into an angled parking spot. When they got out of the car Anthony smelled that ocean smell again, fresher than before, seagulls crying distantly in it as if trying to tell him that nothing at all in this life was as he'd believed it to be.

That he could just walk away, preferably into the diner that beckoned from across the street. The smell of bacon and eggs wafting from it made his stomach growl hungrily. Washed down, he thought wistfully, with a gallon of coffee . . . But he didn't walk there or anywhere else, because Marky was waving impatiently at him to quit gawking and hurry on up into the hardware store.

Inside, with the morning sun slanting yellow onto a window display of garden tools and a key machine whirring busily at the back of the store, Anthony picked up a tourist map of the town and folded it into his pocket.

"You really think this'll work?" said the kid operating the key machine. "Copyin' some other key, replace the one you lost?"

The big man in bib overalls waiting for his key to be made nodded. "Yeah, mostly all the backhoes use a single key. 'S why it's so easy to steal 'em. Hell, you'd think the manufacturers want people to take 'em," he went on. "I could just as well leave the bent nail I got stuck in the ignition now, keep usin' that."

Anthony tried to listen without seeming to be, arranging his face so that it looked as if he were perusing a bin full of half-inch steel bolts. He hadn't known that heavy machinery was easy to steal, and the information might come in handy, sometime.

The kid turned the machine off, handed the man his pair of replacement keys. "So why don't you? Leave the nail?"

"Prob'ly will, for now," the man said. Under the enormous Carhartt coveralls he wore a red pebblecloth sweatshirt big enough to serve as a tent, and boots the same size as the three-gallon buckets on sale at the front of the store were on his feet.

"But when I bring the backhoe back to my brother-in-law he's gonna want the real thing," the giant guy finished.

Anthony would've liked to hear more about backhoe theft; a lot more. But his attention snapped back in alarm to his partner when, after the big man had paid for his key and departed, Marky showed the snapshot of the woman from the blue spiral notebook to the clerk behind the counter, and began asking questions.

Why the hell are you doing that? Anthony wondered. He hadn't read the whole instruction notebook—Marky hadn't let him—but this move with the photo was way too ballsy, in his opinion. And as he'd feared, it didn't go well, the clerk giving them both the fish-eye as soon as the first words were out of Marky's mouth.

"Don't know anything about her," the clerk said, looking at Marky with a get-lost expression and then turning it on Anthony. So they got out of there, not even stopping at the convenience store for anything on their way back out of town, as Anthony had been hoping they would.

Presto, one wasted trip, he thought. Or worse, if Marky's stunt blew up in their faces. Annoyed, he decided the first thing he would do when they got back to the house was find a percolator and something to brew in it. Acorns, maybe; they must have a lot of those here, and to hell with what Marky wanted or didn't.

But once they reached the place, Anthony just stood looking at it again. It had about a million wooden shingles on it, a tan silvery color, and its different rectangles were stacked unevenly atop one another but still flowing together, the opposite of the aluminum-sided three-deckers he was used to back in New Jersey.

Big clay pots of dead flowers out front, leaves matted on the stone walkway leading around to the rear . . .

The guy who'd sent them here had found this place and made sure nobody would be in it, Marky had informed him. One week in July and another in autumn was all anyone ever used it.

What a life, Anthony thought. An envious pang struck him as he imagined the ritzy cocktail parties the owners probably held here when they did come, with beautiful women in sparkly dresses; fancy, unfamiliar snack foods on trays; and tinkling music played on a real piano.

Nice, he thought; the women in dresses, especially. And if he ever got a chance to try any of those strange snack foods, he decided, still staring up at the house, he was going to.

The last of his earlier panic faded as he imagined himself all dressed up in a tuxedo—smelling like Cleopatra, as he dimly remembered his mother saying once—slurping down an oyster and chasing it with champagne, or maybe a martini.

But then a small, brownish-red creature ran practically across Marky's feet on the front steps, chittering angrily. Marky let out a high shriek and jumped back fast, glaring furiously at Anthony as if to say it was his fault.

Anthony knew Marky was mad because of the shriek, which had sounded like a little girl's. But he also knew better than to say anything about it, or to let his face betray anything.

"C'mon," he said quietly, stepping past Marky.

The key had been right where the guy who'd hired them said it would be, under a certain rock. A bunch of dark, many-legged insects had been squirming under there with it when Anthony first looked, but these hadn't bothered him. He understood insects. Ignoring them once more, he retrieved the key again.

The cardboard box stood in the entryway where he'd left it. "Just a chipmunk or something," he said, flipping a light switch.

Nothing happened. Hurrying to keep Marky happy, he hadn't tried the lights the first time he'd come in. But now he recalled suddenly that he hadn't seen any power poles along the dirt road.

"The freak you know about chipmunks?" Marky demanded. "You some kind of freakin' nature expert?"

He stamped his feet hard as if coming in from the cold. "And where're the freakin' lights?" he demanded. "I drive all the way up here, you're just sittin' there playin' with your . . . Come on, make me a cup of coffee or something, will you? I mean, what am I now, your freakin' baby-sitter?"

Anthony knew this was meant to make him forget the chipmunk embarrassment. But worse was to come as soon as Marky discovered what Anthony had already figured out.

Marky stopped in mid-tirade, seeing Anthony's face. "What?" he asked scathingly. "What is it now?" He reached past

Anthony to snap the wall switch up and down a few times himself.

Still nothing. But the light dawned inside Marky's head, all right, and then he really went ballistic, pulling the gun from his jacket pocket and waving it as he stomped around cursing and threatening, spit drops flying from his mouth.

"Guy freakin' didn't turn the power on!" he bellowed. "Guy freakin' thinks we're idiots, doesn't even trust us to close the blinds, fer freak's sake!"

But it was worse than that, Anthony realized. The house had electricity; why else would there be light fixtures in it? But . . . where did it come from?

Back in juvie, guys had tried to teach Anthony things, guys who were plumbers, electricians, or carpenters. They took kids out to job sites, showing them how it was to be a working stiff, that maybe it was okay: getting up early and breaking their asses for a few lousy bucks a week. Carrying their lunches and kissing up to bosses; beers after work, maybe, for a treat.

Big whoop, Anthony had thought back then. He hadn't seen the attraction, and kowtowing to Marky now only reminded him how much he hadn't seen it. But he'd picked up a few facts on his outings with working guys, one of them being that everything in a house either came from somewhere, or went somewhere, or both.

Water, sewer . . . power. You could run it in underground, but the driveway was way too long for that. So it was a mystery, but if he didn't want Marky going batshit, Anthony knew he'd better figure it out fast.

Moving through the house, he kept searching for the answer. There weren't any blinds at the windows; no shades or curtains, either. It wasn't that kind of place, the walls all painted a clean, pale tan like a bleached paper bag, floors polyurethane-shiny and the woodwork white as a polished skeleton. And all the windows faced the water, as Anthony had noticed right off, so no one would see any lights.

He crossed through a large, sparsely furnished living and dining area—cream-colored sofas covered in nubbly cloth, pale wooden tables and chairs, huge framed art prints—to stand by a wide plate-glass sliding door leading out onto the deck. Through the trees, he could see a flock of birds flying low across the water, all turning at once this way and that as precisely as if the flock were a single well-trained acrobatic troupe.

Or a single bird. Behind him, Marky ranted and raved some more; Anthony tuned it all out until a thunderclap sent his heart into his throat, the shot from Marky's pistol whizzing past him to punch a small hole in the plate glass with a sharp *whap!*

As slowly and gracefully as a waterfall in a slow-motion nature film—they'd run a lot of nature films in the juvie home, those and John Wayne pictures—the window collapsed, cascading a shower of shining, greenish-white bits down onto the deck hanging off the back of the house, and the polished wood floor inside.

"Freakin' guy," Marky pronounced, tucking the gun back into his jacket as if he'd accomplished something useful with it. "No lights, no coffee, what the freak we're gonna do, now?"

Turning to Anthony as if he expected an answer.

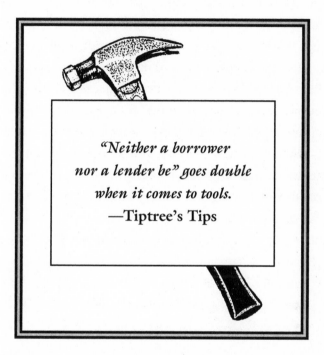

Chapter 3

"*Neither a borrower
nor a lender be*" *goes double
when it comes to tools.*
—Tiptree's Tips

The night before, they'd all had dinner together in
the big old house on Key Street: grilled salmon with mustard
sauce, wild rice pilaf, and Swiss chard from the garden. Dessert
was a pie of wild blueberries picked locally, earlier in summer; in
the dining room with candlelight reflecting in the gold-medallion
wallpaper, dusk purpling in the wavery-glassed antique windows, and a birch log flickering on the hearth—for in August the

Maine evenings already hinted insistently at winter—Jake basked contentedly in the presence of her nearest and dearest.

But then in the noisy confusion of everyone leaving at once, she'd wished them all gone immediately, if only to get some peace and quiet around here.

"Don't lose her Raggedy Ann doll," Ellie White entreated at the last minute, gazing around a little wildly. Lee was already upstairs in the child's bed they'd set up for her in Jake's room.

Ellie's husband, George, waited in the car. "Or forget to pick her up from day care," she added.

"I won't. Ellie, come on, now, we've talked about this. You know it's going to be fine." Jake would've happily kept the child home with her all day but Ellie wanted the little girl's mornings to go exactly as usual, and Lee, a precocious, outgoing toddler, adored visiting her baby-sitter.

"I know, I know." Tall, slender, and ridiculously pretty in tailored slacks, a white blouse, and a black cashmere cardigan that she'd plucked out of a sale bin—on her, it looked as if it had been designed for her in Paris—Ellie pushed pale red hair off her forehead uncertainly. "Oh, what am I forgetting?"

Outside, George touched the car horn lightly. "Go," urged Jake. "It'll be okay, you'll see."

Ellie hadn't ever been away from her daughter for even one night, and now here she was going off to Italy for a whole week. "I guess," she said doubtfully, glancing around as if she might just stay home after all. But at last with a tearful embrace she fled, and then the rest of them were going, too.

"See ya," said Sam, easing out before Jake could grab him. With dark, curly hair, a rakish grin like his late father's, and way more physical agility than one human being had any right to possess, he was a man now, his attitude seemed to say, no longer available for random hugs from his mother or anyone else.

"Bye," she said softly. He'd spent the last few days trying to teach her how to handle a boat, using his own wooden dory out on Passamaquoddy Bay for a classroom. But she'd spent most of the time on the water with him just memorizing his face; if things went well for him in Portland, he'd be away from here all autumn and winter.

"Where," Bella Diamond demanded fretfully, rooting through her handbag as Sam's car backed noisily out the driveway, "are my spare packets of antiseptic hand wipes?"

With her henna-purple hair twisted into a knot on her skinny neck and her ropily muscled arms poking from the sleeves of a red silk dress, Jake's housekeeper resembled a rawboned male prison inmate put forcibly through a department-store beauty makeover. Bella was a clean-freak, but she was also the kindest, funniest, hardest-working person Jake knew, and her marriage to Jake's dad just put the cherry on the cake as far as Jake was concerned.

"Now, now, old girl," the old man groused comfortably to his new wife. "No soap shortage where we're going." He was dressed for the occasion in new jeans and suspenders, a new plaid flannel shirt with the creases still in it, and leather boots.

Or rather, one boot. The other foot was encased in a plastic cast. He saw Jake looking at it, waved her concern away.

"Now, if both feet were broken," he began, wrapping an arm around Bella's skinny, silk-clad waist.

Slipping away from him, Bella ran for the door, her voice as usual the squawk of a rough stick scratched over a violin. "Come on, you old fool, or we'll be left on the dock the way I nearly left you at the altar. And I'm still not sure I shouldn't have."

But it was in their faces, their happy triumph at having found one another; her dad's, especially. The ruby stud glinted in his earlobe as, taking Bella's hand, he hobbled out.

Which left only Wade. Tall and solidly built with blond, brush-cut hair, pale eyes that were blue or gray depending on the weather, and a confident grin whose ability to make her heart do flip-flops hadn't lessened in the slightest since the first time she saw it, he wrapped her in a farewell embrace.

"You going to be okay here without anyone to boss around?" he wanted to know.

"Don't worry, I can boss you around from any distance."

He chuckled into her hair. "Guess so."

He was headed out to help stabilize a freighter that had lost propulsion in the channel on its way into the harbor. The radio call had come in about an hour ago; the vessel had dragged one anchor and was in serious danger of dragging the other.

So it was an emergency. "I'll be fine," she told him as he stepped away from her to shoulder his backpack. "Lee's going to keep me busy. Watch out for the sidewalk hole," she added as he went out and descended the porch steps.

Through the gathering fog-wisps of evening he'd strode away toward the harbor, whistling as he went. Bath, book, bed; she'd thought contentedly of the solitary evening ahead of her.

But now only a little over twelve hours later she clutched the phone in one suddenly icy hand. Around her the house stood empty, the phone alcove scented by the boxes of spices she kept there, morning sunlight lying motionless in pale squares on the varnished hardwood floor.

Couldn't be him, she tried telling herself. But it was; she hadn't heard the voice on the phone in decades, yet its harsh, distinctive rasp was as familiar to her as her own. Anxiously she punched in Sandy O'Neill's New York number and cursed when it connected her to his voice mail.

"Sandy, listen, Ozzie Campbell just called me. I don't know

where from, the number was blocked. But . . . tell Larry Trotta, and get back in touch with me as soon as you can, will you please?"

She wondered what else to add. But there wasn't anything. "Thanks, Sandy," she said finally, and hung up.

In the kitchen she gazed around indecisively, barely seeing the high, bright windows, pine wainscoting, and venerable old soapstone sink, her glance lingering instead on the dogs' dishes lined up by the stove.

She should have kept the animals here. The old black Lab, Monday, would be no help against an intruder, but the Doberman would be; Prill was a rescue dog with some very bad history Jake was better off not knowing, but whatever it was made the dog a mailman's worst nightmare.

Or an intruder's. And even Monday could still bark. But when she tried calling the training center's number she got a message reminding her that hunting-dog refresher training took place on a remote lake way up-country. Ham radio was the only voice access, so unless she got in the car and drove the ninety or so miles to the center to claim them, the dogs were gone for the duration.

Frustrated, she poured cold coffee, dumped it after a bitter sip, then spied the note she'd written to herself, reminding her to pick Lee up from the baby-sitter's at eleven-thirty.

It was now ten forty-five. She touched her fingertips to her lips; should she even bring Lee back here at all?

But then she frowned. "All right. Get hold of yourself," she said aloud. "Call Bob Arnold and let him know what's happened."

So she did, getting put through first to the dispatcher and then to Bob's voice mail because it wasn't an emergency.

Keeping her voice even, she described Ozzie Campbell's call, then phoned the baby-sitter, Helen Nevelson. Her machine picked up:

"Hi! This is Helen. If I'm not answering, I've probably got my hands full with your kid. So leave your number, call us again later, or come on over and join us . . . bye!"

The girl's cheerful voice made Jake feel better, and the day-care place itself, set on a hidden cul-de-sac in Eastport's North End section, would be nearly impossible for Ozzie Campbell or any other stranger to find. Besides, three hours from Bangor and light-years from anywhere else . . . Eastport was surely too far for even that creep Campbell to come, just because he was in a snit.

Wasn't it?

In Jake's old house, the previous owners did repairs with what-ever materials they had handy. Wooden windows got fixed up with bathtub caulk, pictures dangled crookedly from hammered-in metal screws, and sticking doors were rejiggered by the simple method of hacking off a rough quarter inch or so at the bottom.

Thus the neat, well-organized bins, shelves, and racks of Wadsworth's Hardware Store on Water Street had the same ef-fect on her as photos of delicious food might have on a starving person, especially if they were accompanied by scratch-n-sniff cards for turpentine, leather work gloves, and sweeping com-pound.

"Morning, Jake. What's the project for today?" Tom Godley poked his graying head from behind a stack of cardboard car-tons in the delivery area of the store.

"Concrete," she replied as the scent of 3-IN-ONE oil joined the other perfumes wafting into her head. "That sidewalk."

He nodded silently. "I need a couple of bags of sand, one of gravel . . ." Tom had already begun writing on a yellow pad. ". . . one of those plastic mixing troughs, but not a trowel, because my dad has one of those—"

Tom looked up. "If your dad's anything like my dad you don't want to mess with his tools."

"Right. A mixing trowel, then." She hadn't intended to come to the hardware store at all, but as she was hastily setting up wooden sawhorses to guard against anybody else falling into the sidewalk hole, the baby-sitter had called back.

And all was well, not one single unusual thing had happened, and anyway, Helen was a capable girl, Jake reminded herself. Lee was having her snack, no strangers had phoned or visited . . . and the call from Campbell had been distressing, but nothing worse. So Jake had decided to leave well enough alone and pick the child up at the usual time.

Finished with her order, Tom Godley went back to unloading cardboard cartons: claw hammers, whisk brooms, fuses, saw blades, a nail gun, two coal scuttles, and a box of mothballs were noted against a packing slip, priced with a label gun, and placed on the shelves with the other essential items Wadsworth's carried.

"We'll send the stuff up on the truck this afternoon, okay?" he said. "Too heavy for you to haul."

"Yes, thanks." Once dubbed the empty-building capital of the world, Eastport was now full of old-house fix-up folks who liked good architecture and relatively cheap real estate, both of which the town had lots of, so the work truck went out twice a day.

"Follow the instructions," said Tom. "Don't rush. Build it up in layers like interior plaster. Too thick and it'll crack so don't slop it on all at once. But you know that by now, I guess."

She did, but Tom could never resist. "Once you get it laid in there, spray it and lay a tarp over it. You cut the concrete out wider at the bottom already?"

She nodded, but apparently not firmly enough. "It should be like a pyramid, lots wider at the base," he said. "So the shape locks the new material in place."

He plucked a wide chisel from a shelf. "Masonry tool," he said. "Your dad's probably got one of these, too."

Over his years of being a fugitive from justice—or in his case, injustice—Jacob Tiptree had become an expert stonemason; it was a job he could travel with, never staying more than a few weeks or months in any one place, and best of all, a stonemason often got paid in cash.

She let Tom add the chisel to the list. "Keep it all nice and moist, but not wet," he added.

Pocketing her change, Jake planned to attack the sidewalk hole again later in the day, when Lee was down for a nap. As for Campbell's call, she'd be hearing from Bob Arnold and Sandy O'Neill soon, and now that she'd had the baby-sitter's reassuring report she decided to wait and see what they both thought before getting into any kind of a panic.

A decent plan . . . but what Tom said next threw a monkey wrench into it. "Coupla fellas in here asking about you, earlier."

At the end of the fish pier across the street the red-sailed schooner *Sylvina Beal* was taking on a party of whale-watchers for a trip out into the Bay of Fundy. Hampers full of lunch got handed over the rail, and coolers full of refreshment followed.

"Really?" She turned in alarm. "Asking what?"

Through the big plate-glass window behind the cash register, Tom watched the landlubbers make their way gingerly down the steep metal gang toward the *Sylvina*'s foredeck. "Whether or not I knew you, anything about you. The one guy had a snapshot of you."

She swallowed hard. "Who were they? And what'd you say?"

"Told 'em what I always do," said Tom, "when someone I don't know comes snoopin' around asking questions about somebody I do."

He mimed zipping his lip. "Young fellas. Sam's friends, at first I thought. But they didn't mention him."

"What'd they look like?" Campbell was in his early sixties.

He shrugged. "Twentyish, in T-shirts and jeans. Didn't pay 'em a lot of attention at first. City boys. Gold chains and some fancy wristwatch one of 'em had on. I do remember that."

It was still just barely possible that this was nothing. "Thanks, Tom. I appreciate your not telling them where to find me. I like a heads-up before I get company, you know?"

Tom nodded, turning his attention to a woman buying a lot of paint scrapers and sandpaper as Jake rushed out.

On the street, crowds of tourists lent a holiday atmosphere to the brilliant day. Folks dressed in new-looking L.L. Bean gear peered into shop windows; cars bearing out-of-state plates eased slowly along, searching for parking spots, and kids wearing tiny baseball caps skipped back and forth atop the granite breakwater.

"Excuse me, but do you know where I can find a restaurant that serves–?"

Lobster, the pleasant lady in the white straw hat was going to finish; tourists here always did. And the answer this late in the season was nowhere; August was molting season for the clawed delicacies, their shells thin as paper now and the meat beneath unappetizing. But Jake didn't give it.

"I'm sorry, I'm in a hurry," she interrupted, getting into her car; the nice lady looked affronted. *So much for that famous downeast Maine hospitality.*

Jake didn't care, and was about to punctuate her rudeness with a squeal of tires as she backed out of her parking spot. But instead Billie Whitson's silver MG pulled up fast behind her and stopped, blocking her exit.

"Hoo-hoo!" Billie called, getting out and hurrying to Jake's driver's side window. "I mean it, Jake," she said, hooking her long, red nails atop the partly open car window as if she could claw her way in.

"I'm showing properties nonstop," she added impatiently, "and I know you think you don't want to sell. But what if you got a great offer?"

Which was the main thing Billie had figured out about Eastport: that it *wasn't* Carmel, California. People here had lost just about every possible way to make a living: fish, factories, shipbuilding. They needed money, and Billie convinced them their only hope of getting any was to list the family home, at a price that to them looked like oceans of cash but was really a joke.

Then she promptly sold it out from under them to people from away, pocketed the commission plus "expenses," and left the sellers to the coldly dawning realization that what they'd gotten for their place wouldn't even make a down payment on a home anywhere else.

Or here, either, now that Billie was jacking up everyone's expectations. "Get your fingers out of my window," Jake grated, stabbing the Up button with one of her own.

When Eastport's other real estate agents discussed Billie, they wore the sour expressions they usually reserved for visiting looky-loos who had no real thought of actually buying any land or houses, but just wanted to kill time by getting shown around.

"I mean it," Jake warned the sun-shriveled opportunist.

Startled, Billie jerked away just in time to avoid losing a few of her claws. Jake's reversing her own car to within a few millimeters of the tiny MG's silvery fender further convinced her of Jake's seriousness; backing out fast, Jake spied the straw-yellow hair and bright scarf zooming away, already half a block distant.

All the way down Water Street, past bright banners snapping crisply in front of shops selling pottery and jewelry, postcards and crafts, Maine-made foods and boat rides, Jake kept reciting a single phrase to herself: *Let her be there.*

She punched in Helen's number again. "Hi! This is Helen . . ."

Past the corner convenience store and the old granite post office building, past Rosie's Hot Dog Stand and the big new Coast Guard station on the breakwater, leaving the fishing boats in the boat basin behind and hurrying uphill:

Let her be there, and let me be an idiot who worries about nothing. Just . . .

Let her be there.

And . . . let her be okay.

Past the Chowder House restaurant and the ferry dock, Water Street curved between old wood-frame houses in various stages of repair. Jake turned left on Clark Street and soon after that into a warren of packed-earth lanes that tourists never got to see.

Pulled up close to the lanes were tiny house trailers with built-on rooms and small, neat vegetable gardens fenced by big pieces of driftwood. Whitewashed stones edged the flower beds; odd sculptures clustered around some of the iron-railed front steps.

Earlier that summer, Ellie had brought Jake here to visit

Ellie's cousins, Charlotte and Edwina. Both their husbands were away with the National Guard, so the sisters were living together in Charlotte's trailer with their kids, all under age five.

Lee had come, too, to play with her young relatives, and Bella had arrived to help; passing the place now, Jake recalled the afternoon, full of diapers, sippy cups, and a steady procession of toddlers by turns either laughing or bawling their heads off, as one of the pleasantest of her life.

By the time they left, under Bella's hands that trailer had been so clean you could eat off any surface anywhere in it, even under the sink. While Jake fixed two leaky faucets, a loose door-knob, and a broken bedpost that in childish hands had threatened to become a deadly weapon, Ellie sang the kids to sleep. In the calm that followed, the pair of young moms sat looking shell-shocked, each with a glass of wine in one hand, a romance novel in the other, and a box of chocolates on the table between them.

A wonderful day; Jake wished it back as the lane narrowed, curving around an ancient apple tree shading a trio of leaning gravestones in the oldest section of Hillside Cemetery. At last the lane widened before the only house in the cul-de-sac beyond the burying place.

It was a small factory-built Cape with gray siding and white shutters, set on a concrete slab. Green-coated Cyclone fence made an enclosure of the backyard; inside it were toys and play-ground equipment. Jake shut the car off and got out.

"Hello?" But she could already tell that no one was around. Her heart rate quickened. "Helen?"

The baby-sitter's car wasn't here, either. At the top of the poured-concrete steps Jacobia shaded her eyes with her hands to peer through the screen door. No sound came from within.

The spicy aroma of a scented candle mingling with the sharp

smell of bleach drifted faintly through the screen's new mesh. On the wall over the kitchen table hung a framed sampler embroidered with the motto *No Matter Where I Serve My Guests It Seems They Like My Kitchen Best.*

Crayon drawings were stuck haphazardly to the front of the refrigerator. A khaki cap with a Maine Guide badge stitched to it hung from a hook. A stack of manila folders imprinted with the legend *Maine Literacy Initiative* lay on the counter. Helen's mother, Jerrilyn, volunteered in the program, which gave individual—and, most importantly, confidential—tutoring to local adults who couldn't read and wanted to learn.

"Anyone home?" Jake tried the screen door: unlocked. It was possible that in the half hour since Jake spoke with her, Helen had managed to get Lee down for a nap, then fallen asleep, too. Maybe her mother had taken the car. But it was wildly unlikely.

Sturdy as a fireplug, with Ellie's gold-dust freckles and strawberry-blond hair, little Leonora White-Valentine was cute, charming—except for her biting habit—and so precocious, she'd already taught herself to read. But when it came to morning naps she was approximately as manageable as a Tasmanian devil.

Jake went in, crossed the kitchen to the back door, and peered out into the fenced yard: empty. Besides volunteering, Jerrilyn did hands-on outdoor work—Jake wasn't sure what—while Helen's stepfather, Jody Pierce, was a registered Maine Guide who made his living taking visitors on hunting and fishing trips. He also taught wilderness survival to folks who aspired to be Guides themselves, and he repaired electronic gear—global satellite positioners, depth finders, and radios—for working fishermen.

A note on the kitchen counter said milk, bread, margarine. Jake pressed the blinking red button on the phone machine.

"Helen? Hi, it's eleven o'clock and I just wanted to confirm you can take Madison this afternoon. At one o'clock and I'll need you to keep her until four, so call me, okay?"

No other messages. But this one had come in . . . Jake glanced at the black cartoon-cat clock whose pendulum tail ticked off the seconds, over the stove. Twenty minutes ago, right after Helen had called Jake back.

Don't panic. There are plenty of explanations for . . .

But there weren't. One reason everyone loved leaving their kids with Helen was her reliability. Other girls, even women, could be dicey: have a boyfriend over to your place while caring for your kid. Or worse, take your kid to their boyfriend's.

Helen, though . . . Safe as houses, everyone always said. So why wasn't she here with Lee? Where was her car? Had there been some sudden medical emergency? Or . . .

Jake entered the family room. Blue shag rug, woodstove on a brick hearth. A granny quilt lay on the oversized recliner sofa, in front of the big TV.

A *TV Guide* and a pair of reading glasses lay on the cherry-veneer end table. A family portrait—Helen, Jerrilyn, and a man Jake recognized as Jody Pierce, Jerrilyn's second husband and Helen's stepfather—hung over a bookcase containing textbooks for the adult reading lessons Jerrilyn taught.

On the wall over the TV hung a 1960s-era clock in a gold-plated metal sun-ray frame. Eleven twenty-one, only nine minutes until the time Jake had promised she'd pick Lee up from Helen, and neither of them was around.

Okay, Jake thought, still trying to quell her fright. A good look at the place just to be sure they weren't playing hide-and-seek in the closets, or something. And then she'd summon her old pal, Bob Arnold, again. . . .

Yet another cry-wolf call this morning would kill her credibility with him for weeks, not that it was all that great in the first place. And her sweaty palms notwithstanding, it was still a fair bet she was getting all nervous for something that would turn out to be a false alarm, she tried convincing herself.

So two guys in the hardware store had been asking about her. Big deal. And Campbell had called. But that didn't mean there was any connection to this situation, or that Campbell was nearby. So why was she still standing here uncertainly in the family room, frowning at the hallway that led to the two bedrooms, spare room, and bath at the rear of the house?

Taking a deep breath, she padded down the hall on the soft, silent, green wall-to-wall shag carpet. Bathroom: pink tile. She snapped back the plastic shower curtain, finding nothing behind it but a worn soap on a rope.

The first bedroom held a queen-sized bed, neatly made up with a white chenille bedspread and matching throw pillows. The curtains, like the ones in the family room, were heavy brocade with fringed tie-backs, only in here they were blue.

No one behind them; she let out a breath she hadn't known she was holding. The louvered closet door opened with a creak.

Packed full of clothes, some zippered into garment bags; Helen's mom and stepdad obviously shared this one closet. A pair of plain dressers, one with a mirror hung on the wall above it, made up the rest of the furniture in the small bedchamber.

In the hall again, Jake paused. So far she'd found nothing amiss in the house, except that Helen and Lee weren't anywhere in it. Just a few more places to check: Helen's room, which took but a glance—its tiny dimensions and single, miniature louvered window would've made it more suitable for a sewing room, or in a pinch maybe a baby's bedroom—and the spare room Jody worked in, plus an added-on room that was more like a glorified sunporch.

Jody's room was windowless, closetless, and full of the kind of gear he repaired. A police-band scanner sat on a small work-bench, its case off and its insides out. Plain wooden shelves held other jobs with paper tags bearing the owners' names. A very pretty old Crosley radio in a silver Bakelite case stood on a low shelf of its own with a bill of sale and packing material stuffed in next to it.

But nothing more. She was hurrying toward the screened porch when she heard the crash. Glass breaking . . .

A quick glance outside showed no other car in the turn-around except hers. But intruders didn't necessarily come in cars, or if they did they might not leave them nearby, in plain sight.

She hesitated again in the family room. A glass-fronted gun case in the corner, built of fine tiger maple and holding half a dozen rifles plus an over-and-under pump shotgun, offered a next move. Having a gun-expert husband came in handy some-times, she reflected as she approached the case.

But its door was locked, and the weapons were probably all trigger-locked and unloaded, the shells kept securely somewhere else. A fellow whose stepdaughter did child care for a living would take special precautions, unless he was a complete idiot.

And nothing about this place—neat, clean, comfortable and beautifully maintained, with not a single needed repair any-where to be seen—suggested that anyone who lived here was an idiot or anything like one.

No sound from the sunporch. Helen kept the kids she sat for out there in good weather; Jake tiptoed toward it. The crash had been like a drinking glass breaking, not the bigger shattering of a window or door.

She swallowed past the hard lump of fear in her throat, well aware that she'd left the door open coming in here, wishing hard for a pair of eyes in the back of her head. Then:

Oh, screw it. There's no one there. No more strange sounds, no small betraying eddies disturbed the silent air, no alien smells of sweat or cigarettes floated warningly. Steeling herself, on the count of three she lunged through the door to the sunroom.

As she'd thought, no one was in it. But the room itself . . . Jake gave herself a mental shake, trying to make sense of it.

A small easeled chalkboard, overturned and with its colored chalks scattered across the floor. Child-sized plastic chairs all scattered around, a giant beanbag seat flung against a wall.

A china coffee cup—Helen's, Jake thought distantly; she'd never have let Lee drink from anything that might break—lay in shards, a few drops of tan milky liquid spilled around it. It had stood on a shelf, gotten bumped maybe, then teetered and settled. Until a breeze toppled it . . . but what shoved it to the edge of the shelf in the first place?

Helen wouldn't have left it there. One thing was for sure: either a fight-to-the-death struggle had happened here recently, or someone had gone to a lot of trouble to fake one.

Then she spotted the worst thing: a pair of miniature six-guns in holsters, part of a child's toy cowboy outfit, lay tossed into a corner along with a matching hat, neckerchief, and fringed black-and-white imitation cowhide vest.

Lee . . . It was the outfit Jake had dressed the little girl in that morning at the child's stubborn insistence, atop a turquoise sweatshirt, navy blue overalls, and nylon anklets with ruffles.

Plus cowboy boots. The morning had been warm; Lee would've shed the extra clothing once she reached Helen's place. Probably she was still wearing the boots.

"Where are you?" Jake whispered. Scared, now.

Really scared. She dug her cell phone from her bag to call Bob Arnold, but before she could, it rang in her hand.

"Hello?" Her voice was shaking. "Listen, whoever this is, I can't talk now. I've got to—"

Then something about the silence on the line alerted her. A waiting silence . . .

"Who is this?" she demanded.

"You know who it is. I want something. Now you do, too. So let's make a deal, Jacobia. I'll call back."

Click.

Ozzie Campbell had hung up.

"You didn't have to hit her that hard," said the guy in the passenger seat sulkily.

He was young, twenty or so, with dark hair and a big nose, spotty skin just starting to clear up. Bound hand and foot with harsh rope in the backseat with an oily-tasting rag stuck in her mouth, Helen Nevelson tried to memorize her abductors' features. But her left eye was already swollen shut, and her head ached so badly she could barely see out of the right one. Struggling to breathe, she fought back the impulse to gag on the filthy cloth.

"Hey," snapped the driver in reply. "What do you think, I should maybe just've let her win? Oh, sorry, honey, you fight so good I guess I'll just give up my whole plan, here?"

He made a sound of disgust. "How the hell was I supposed to know the chick'd turn out to be a freakin' Amazon?"

He glanced in the rearview at her, his annoyance turning to humor. "Man, they really feed 'em here, though, don't they? Outta my weight class, for sure," he added.

Helen felt her face flush with humiliation even through her pain. The younger one was a bastard, but this guy with his gold chains, manicured nails, and strutting attitude—

This one was mean. A surge of fear went through her, so bad that she almost couldn't feel her body. The way they'd come in so suddenly, rushing into the house without a word, the young one grabbing her and holding her while the other one snatched Lee—

Lee. The child lay motionless on the seat beside her. Once they were out of town they had given her something to drink, forcing it down her throat by holding her nose, yanking away the Raggedy Ann doll the child tried swatting them with and pouring the stuff into her mouth while she kicked and struggled.

Minutes later, the little girl had fallen asleep. With tears streaming on her cheeks, Helen managed painfully to turn her head enough to see that Lee was at least still breathing, her bowl-cut blond hair fallen over her flushed, feverish-looking face.

But the doll was gone. A sob rose painfully into Helen's throat. They'd left the island, speeding over the causeway into Pleasant Point, where the Passamaquoddy tribal land spread out on both sides of the road.

As they did so she'd had a moment of hope that since neither of the men was from around here—that much had been clear to her right away, from their accents—they might just keep on speeding through the reservation. If they had, they'd have been caught by one of the reservation's black-and-white squad car's radar guns.

But her captors had slowed obediently for the speed limit sign, and although she'd tried raising herself up high enough to be seen through the car window, nobody had spotted her.

"So now what?" the passenger-seat guy wanted to know.

The driver looked in the rearview mirror at Helen again, then glanced at his partner significantly, patting something in the inside pocket of his black leather jacket.

Gun, Helen thought, another bolt of terror running through her. Beside her Lee muttered fretfully and slept again.

"She saw your face. And my face," the driver said as if trying to explain something to a not-quite-bright person. "Now, I suppose if we want to, we could just let her go."

"We could've covered our faces," said the passenger guy. "We could've waited, gotten the kid out of there somehow without the baby-sitter getting a look."

Helen could still feel his hands gripping her, smell his breath and the reek of his clothes. When she'd screamed, kicking viciously backward in hopes of getting his shin, the short one had turned curiously, like a scientist observing a new species, then punched her hard in the side of the head with his fist.

She didn't remember anything else until they were out of town, when they'd pulled over briefly to give Lee the drug-laced drink. But she had the strong feeling that more time had passed than she knew about, and when she craned her neck again to squint sideways at the Timex she wore, she saw that it was true.

Quarter after twelve . . . she'd been out cold for an hour. "But we didn't, did we?" the driver said reasonably to his buddy. "We didn't screw around with masks and so on."

Her clothes weren't disarranged, nor were Lee's. So in the missing time at least they hadn't been doing anything disgusting.

Yet. *Why?* her brain screamed at them. *Why are you doing this to us?* But the slightest movement of her throat sent waves of nausea sweeping over her once more. Then the driver's eyes found her in the rearview again.

"We got on with it," their owner said flatly, and from the remark and his expression she understood that, from his point of view, anyway, omitting the masks had been deliberate.

That if she hadn't seen their faces, then they wouldn't have to do what he was hinting about doing. And driver-guy, his gaze chilly and unblinking like that of a snake identifying its prey—

She didn't know yet what passenger-guy thought about killing her, she realized as she fought back panic. But the driver guy—

Slyly he eyed her, his tongue flickering out over his thin lips in anticipation.

Driver-guy wanted to.

Chapter 4

*Wet cement can give you
a chemical burn. Don't get it
on your skin, and wash it off
right away if you do.*
—Tiptree's Tips

I don't understand," said Jerrilyn Pierce, gazing around at the assembled Washington County Sheriff's Department officers and Maine State Police investigators.

It had taken only about an hour to gather them here. Her own house had been designated a crime scene, so they'd taken Helen's mother to a room at the Motel East where they'd set up a sort of preliminary command center.

The room had a coffee maker, a small refrigerator, a sizable bathroom, and a table with chairs pulled up to it. The draperies and big sliding glass windows were open, letting in a spectacular view of the bay and Campobello Island beyond.

Nobody was looking at it. "Somebody . . . *took* Helen and Lee?" Jerrilyn seemed unable to comprehend this. "And her car? But why?"

"I don't know," said Jacobia, seated across from the woman with the wad of unused tissues in her hand. Tears might come later, but for now Helen Nevelson's mother was simply in shock.

Me, too, thought Jake. "Just answer their questions," she went on. "Anything you can think of that might help."

Jerrilyn nodded shakily. She was a tall, ruddy-faced woman with thick, wavy salt-and-pepper hair pulled back in a rubber-band-wrapped braid, wearing a man's plaid shirt, faded jeans, and tan steel-toed boots. Fit and muscular-looking, it turned out she worked on a landscaping crew over on the mainland clearing brush for new house lots going in on the north end of Boyden Lake. After Jake's call, Bob Arnold had driven to the site to get Jerrilyn, to break the news and bring her here. Next, he'd begun calling in help and organizing search teams.

"They'll go from one end of the island to the other," he told the girl's mother. "Every house, every shed, they'll cover every inch," he assured her.

Which at first sounded as if it might be fairly easy to do; Jerrilyn nodded, attempting a grateful smile through lips pressed together in the beginnings of panic. The whole island, after all, was only two miles wide and seven miles long.

But that added up to fourteen square miles, some of it in streets and sidewalks but a good deal more in fields, forested areas, and stony beaches that lay straight down a hundred or more feet below the cave-riddled and precipitous granite cliffs.

Not to mention the whole of Shackford Head State Park, a big wooded peninsula near the airfield, whose many off-trail portions could take days to investigate thoroughly.

"Mrs. Nevelson," said one of the State Police officers. "If you could perhaps just try answering a few questions for me."

"Pierce," Jerrilyn corrected him. "Nevelson is Helen's last name. I've remarried."

It was just past one in the afternoon and by now every cop in Maine had fresh descriptions of the two missing persons, plus recent photographs. The one of Helen Nevelson showed a tall, broad-shouldered girl with fair hair piled up in a braid atop her head. Round-cheeked and smiling, like most Maine girls outside of the cities she didn't appear to put much stock in the current fad for emaciation.

Or stylish clothes; jeans and a sweatshirt were her usual garb, and the snapshot of her was no exception. Handing over one of Lee—pale Dutch-boy bob, baby-toothed grin, blue eyes— Jake had thought for an awful moment that she might vomit.

Now she walked out onto the motel room's small deck for some air, then turned back as Jerrilyn got up, too, pressing her hands together. "Maybe it's a mistake," Jerrilyn began, "maybe Helen just decided to take Leonora somewhere. For an outing, or . . ."

But her voice trailed off as she remembered the chaos in the screened porch. "The little *bastard*," she snapped suddenly.

"Who?" Jake asked, puzzled. There was no way Jerrilyn could have known about Ozzie Campbell.

"Tim Barnard," Jerrilyn said, accepting a glass of water from one of the officers. Her voice strengthened slightly after a swallow of it.

"That little pissant from Topsfield that Helen was going out with for a while," she said. "He thought he could push her around and he got ugly when she let him know he couldn't."

She looked at Jacobia, the only other woman in the room. "He *hit* Helen. Can you imagine?" Even in her distress, she seemed to find this idea amusing, her lips twisting in a near-smile.

"Not really," Jake agreed, peering again at the snapshot of Helen. Big-boned, with a fresh pink complexion, generous figure, and yellow hair, she resembled a Nordic goddess. And Tim Barnard, if Jake recalled him correctly, was indeed a little pissant.

"She fixed him, though," Jerrilyn said grimly. "He thought she was flirting with someone—they were at the Crab with some other young people?"

The Happy Crab was a downtown Eastport sports bar, a popular hangout for local twenty-somethings, with a large-screen TV, pool table, and finger foods, hot wings and onion blossoms and so on, plus lunch and dinner for all ages.

"Helen turned around and slapped the taste right out of that boy's mouth," Jerrilyn went on. "Right there with all his buddies watching it. And then she put the five in the corner pocket, just like nothin' ever happened."

For a moment Jerrilyn looked happy. But then: " 'Course, that wasn't how *he* felt about it. He starts yellin' at her, how she can't do that to him, he's going to fix her. And when her stepdad heard the story—"

The cops' ears, already alerted at the mention of a violent boyfriend, pricked further.

"Stepdad's Jody Pierce," Bob Arnold put in quickly. "Some of you might know him, registered Maine Guide, runs a hunting and fishing service a little ways up-country, out of Grand Lake."

Bob looked around at the group. "Rest of the time he fixes all kinds of electronic equipment, in that shop of his out at his house."

A couple of the cops nodded and glanced at each other, the tone of Bob's remarks having put them on notice that going after Jody for any of this would be barking up the wrong tree, in Bob's opinion.

"Jody found the Barnard kid, the night after the events Mrs. Pierce, here, just described to you. Found him in that bar out on Route 214, there, in Meddybemps, 'bout eleven o'clock."

Some of the officers looked impatient, as if wondering what this part of Bob's narrative had to do with missing persons. Jake wondered, too, and she didn't like the way this was going anyway.

Ozzie Campbell had called her, once before the kidnapping and again afterward, as if to make sure she understood he was behind this, nobody else. Taunting her, daring her to do anything about it. But when she'd told that to the officers all they wanted to know was had she seen anyone, and when she made it clear that she hadn't, they'd pretty much dismissed her story.

"What about the parents?" asked one of the county deputies. "Where are they?"

"Europe," Bob replied. "Italy. I already called the airline; they got off the plane early this morning just like they planned, right around the time we were all finishing up our breakfasts."

"Look," Jake began impatiently again, "you don't understand. I know who did this, and—"

"Anyway, Jody Pierce seized Tim Barnard by the collar," Bob went on, ignoring her, "hauled him out of there, put a beating on him like you wouldn't believe."

The cops were all listening to him. "So where's Tim Barnard now?" asked the county sheriff's deputy.

"In traction," spat Jerrilyn. "Too bad Jody didn't put him in a coma." Or worse, her tone clearly expressed.

"And now poor Jody's got a warrant out on him for assault," she went on aggrievedly, "all because he stood up like a man and took care of his family. Which *you* guys didn't. None of you did."

She fixed Bob in an accusing gaze. "I called, you know. She called, too. Helen did," she added to the men standing around in the motel room. "Called Bob, here, to say she was a-scared of Tim. It wasn't even the first time he'd decided to knock a girl around. Nobody ever stopped him, till Helen."

"Now, Jerri, you know we did all we—" Bob began.

"Sure. All you could do. Which was *nothing*," she accused him bitterly. "And now look. He's got some rotten friends of his, put them up to it from his hospital bed to take it out on poor Helen, when you couldn't even be bothered to . . . you couldn't even . . ."

She bit her lip to try stopping the flood of tears that was finally coming. Jake got up and put her hand gently on Jerrilyn's heaving shoulder.

"So this boyfriend, this Barnard guy, he's in the hospital. We're sure?" said one of the state guys. "He's still there? And the stepdad, where's he at?"

"His *name*," Jerrilyn managed angrily through the tissues she clutched to her face, "is *Jody*. Not 'the stepdad.' "

"Fine. That's fine, Mrs. Nevelson. We're just trying to—"

"Pierce. And you're *not* trying!" she shouted, looking around wildly at the men. "You're just standing around with your thumbs up your butts. Why aren't you out finding the little bastards who took Helen?"

"And Lee," Jake said quietly. Jerrilyn stopped shouting.

"Yes," she whispered, glancing over apologetically. "Her, too."

"All right, then," Bob Arnold said, taking charge by his voice and his body language once more. The other men, all with more authority than he had, let him do it, too, because around here the guy who knew the territory got to plot the course, and never mind how it got written up in the reports later.

"Let's get going on what we do know," he said. "The missing car, the girls' descriptions, the boyfriend and *his* friends . . ."

Not mentioning Jody Pierce. But it was clear that in the others' minds he was still on the agenda, if only long enough to get him definitively off it. Once upon a time, stepfathers had come in two flavors, heroes and villains, and it was obvious from the start which kind a particular one was.

Nowadays, though, anything might go on behind closed doors. And a guy with a warrant automatically came under suspicion.

Bob looked around. "Anyone mind if I go up to the hospital, talk with Tim?" he asked mildly. "He knows me," Bob explained, "so I might be able to get more out of him faster than if . . ."

Nods from the other men. "And Jerri," Bob went on, "I think these guys'll be done with your house pretty soon, so you can go back there for the rest of the questions if you—"

"Wait," said Jake. No one was talking about Ozzie Campbell. Or Lee. They seemed to assume this was just about Helen. But in that case, why take Lee? "What about the phone calls I got?"

She searched for something else, something to convince them that they shouldn't jump to conclusions. "And what about the guys who were asking about me?" she added. "Who had a picture of me?"

This better be good, their faces said as they all turned to her. Suddenly she was even more aware of how weak it all sounded.

"In the hardware store earlier. Tom Godley said two guys were in there with a photograph of me, asking questions about me."

Her face burned under their skeptical looks. "Strangers," she added. "And then the calls. Two strange phone calls, and I'm sure I know who—"

"Why don't I handle that, too?" Bob cut in smoothly as the rest moved toward the door, no longer listening.

Bob was getting her off the hook, Jake realized, saving her from looking any more foolish than she already did. Jerrilyn was frowning oddly at her, as well.

As if, Jake thought, the thin-sounding story about strangers and phone calls was an attempt to grab the spotlight, somehow. But clearly to the others Helen's violent boyfriend was the whole focus of the investigation, now; him and his friends.

And maybe Helen's stepfather, Jody Pierce. "Jake," Bob said when the rest had gone outside, "I know you're upset. I am, too. But we're going to get Lee back. And Helen," he added hastily at Jerrilyn's sharp look.

Last chance, Jake thought. "Bob, he called me. Campbell . . . I can't prove it, but I know his voice."

"Yeah," Bob said. "I heard you. Thing is, how you *feel* about it doesn't guarantee it *means* anything, does it? And we don't know where this Campbell guy's gotten to but what we do know is, he's not from around here."

She took his point; she'd thought it herself, earlier. How would Campbell have even known about Lee, much less found her at Helen's secluded home? The street Helen lived on didn't even have a name, much less a sign.

And Campbell was a big strapping guy with thinning blond hair, bushy eyebrows, and a face like a rotten orange, all swollen nose and blown red capillaries. She'd seen a brief New York news clip of him that Sandy O'Neill had e-mailed to her, just after the indictment was handed down.

No way did he resemble either of the two guys Tom Godley had seen. "You'll talk to Tom, though? At Wadsworth's, about the—?"

"I will. I'm not ignoring you, Jake. But what I want from you now is phone numbers where you think we can maybe get hold of Ellie and George, in case the airline doesn't manage to."

"Oh," Jerrilyn breathed sorrowfully, looking up from the table where she'd been cradling her face in her hands. "Oh, that poor little baby's mother and dad, they're going to be so—"

Fresh misery swamped Jake. "Do we have to call them right away? Maybe it is just a mean trick, Tim Barnard getting back at Helen, and in a couple of hours they'll be—"

Her voice trailed off. Ellie and George, away on the very first trip they'd taken alone together since Lee was born—

To Italy, no less, George acting unimpressed but as excited as Ellie, really. Rome and a rented villa on the Riviera . . . jet-setting, Ellie had called it while she'd packed a pretty sundress and new swimsuit, more daringly cut than any she would wear here.

Worrying all the while about leaving Lee. *I swear,* Jacobia had told her friend earnestly while they pored over pictures of the exotic destination. *Nothing bad will happen.*

And now . . . Jake tried to think what she would say to Ellie, how she could possibly break the news to her that her child had been taken.

Bob shook his head. "We have to get them back here; they'll both have to be questioned," he said. "It could be someone with a grudge against George, or mad at Ellie—"

Neither of which things Jake could imagine. "Get the numbers and call me and give 'em to me. And that's all I want you to do," Bob finished firmly. "I've got squads of guys out there—"

Jerrilyn frowned again. "—and girls, too," Bob said. "Women. And I don't want things going on that I don't know about, next thing you know I've got to spend a whole lot of time and energy, rescuing a rescuer. You catching my drift, here?" he added. "Stay home, sit tight, and call me if anyone calls you."

Sit down. Shut up. Stay out of it. "Yes. Yes, I understand," she answered obediently, keeping her voice low. Because feeling the way she did, suddenly—scared, angry, and frustrated in the extreme—if she raised it even a little bit she might scream the whole place down.

"I'll get the numbers for you," she said.

Back in the bad old days, Jake Tiptree had been a hotshot Manhattan money-manager with a brain-surgeon husband, a son just entering puberty, and an Upper East Side penthouse looking out over Central Park in a building so exclusive that you practically needed an FBI background check just to deliver pizza there.

Unfortunately her husband had turned out to be even better at adultery than at surgery, which was how she reached the point one day of standing alone in her fancy kitchen with a broken wineglass in her right hand, frowning thoughtfully at the skin of her left wrist. But then the phone rang and it was a client needing to be talked off a financial ledge, and by the time she got done handling him she'd also crept back down off her own.

Months later, though, driving home alone from New Brunswick, Canada, after a stockholders' meeting, she'd stopped overnight in Eastport, Maine. And although until then she'd had no interest in old houses, home repair, or (God forbid) power tools, she'd fallen in love.

With the house: enormous, antique, and to her unskilled eye

charmingly dilapidated. With the town, salt-scoured and severely lovely, set by the water's edge at the end of a curving causeway so low that she could almost reach out through the car window to dabble her hand in the ice-cold waves.

And with the idea of a life that did not include a husband whose brain was habitually occupied so far south of his cranium, it was a wonder he remembered how to operate on anyone else's.

Also, in Eastport Sam might just possibly not grow up to be a monster. No guarantees, but for one thing the apparent absence of exotic, lab-quality pharmaceuticals seemed like a good omen; even then, he'd had a worrisome taste for illegal substances.

So she'd moved from Times Square to fresh air in one dumb jump, as her by-then-ex-husband criticized the decision. But it had, as Sam told her much later when he'd been clean, sober, and halfway rational for seven whole weeks, made all the difference.

Since then she'd worked on the old house through moments of extreme happiness as well as through turmoil and disruption: her marriage to Wade, Sam's relapses and recoveries, her father's return to her life after so long, her ex-husband's death. Even the news that Ozzie Campbell was finally to be tried for her mother's murder went down easier with a paintbrush in her hand, and the breaks she took from working on her victim's impact statement had been oddly soothed by the creak of a prybar or slam of a hammer.

Thus, by two-thirty in the afternoon on the day Lee White-Valentine and her baby-sitter Helen Nevelson were taken, Jake was back at the sidewalk hole in front of her old house. Bob Arnold had called twice; once to get the number of the villa where Ellie White and George Valentine were to be staying, and again to ask if she wanted him to get hold of Wade, and ask him to come home.

"Don't bother him. He'll call when he can," she'd replied, thinking that if their situations were reversed, Bob would not be asking if Wade wanted his spouse summoned in off the disabled freighter currently stalled in the Bay of Fundy, where despite the bright day a line of thunderstorms was forecast for tonight.

Bob meant well, though, she reminded herself as she frowned at the bag of concrete mix. By his renewed invitation, too, to stay the night with him and Clarissa and the kids. He just didn't realize that now, even the touch of the warm late summer air on her skin made her want to howl.

The harmless chatter of his children, and Clarissa's gentle concern, would only be fresh torture, reminding her of Ellie and Lee; if she could, she'd have crawled down into a hole much deeper than the one in the sidewalk, pulled the cool, dark earth in over herself, and wept.

But she couldn't. She had to stay calm, keep her mind clear for when Campbell called again.

Which he would. Otherwise, what was the point to him having done so in the first place? She had to figure out what came next, too, Bob's order to sit tight and do nothing being sensible, but impossible to obey.

At the moment, though, all she knew how to do was work. So she forced herself to continue on with the sidewalk project while her cell phone kept ringing, each time making her throat close with anxiety and each time not being Campbell.

As if triggered by her thought, it rang once more. "Ma, d'you want me to come home?" Sam asked when she'd told him what was happening. "I can be up there in a couple of hours. I could help with the . . ."

Search. Half of Eastport was already out knocking on doors, stomping through bushes, and peering into sheds and boathouses, while the other half made sandwiches and brewed coffee. She'd have been, as well, but she needed to stay near the house phone, not just her cell, in case . . .

"No, Sam, thanks for asking." His new place in Portland was a tiny apartment near the water where he would share a small yard and a big dog with the woman who owned the house.

"I'm fine," she lied, hoping he wouldn't get bored and decide to find someplace livelier. He was in a sober phase, now. But that could change any minute.

"Why don't you just go on doing what you're doing? That way you'd be fresh if they ended up—"

Needing you. But from the remainder of this thought her mind recoiled. Surely they'd be found soon. "And when your grandfather and Bella call later, I know they'll decide to . . ."

Come home. For a moment she allowed herself to imagine the comfort it would bring, having Sam around. But—"I won't be alone for long. Gramps and Bella will want to get back right away when they hear. And it helps, knowing you'd come if I did ask."

"Okay," he said reluctantly, and when they'd hung up she turned back to the concrete mix bag. If the hole you were fixing was small, you were to clear it thoroughly, then wet its edges. But this one was a crater, big enough to swallow a dog or cat. Or a small child . . . *No. Don't think that.*

She considered calling Sandy O'Neill again, but she'd tried several times already and gotten either a busy signal or the infernal voice mail. She'd tried Ellie and George's cell, too, but either it wasn't working or they'd turned it off.

Kneeling, Jake dug away more soil and stones. The concrete bag's instructions echoed Tom Godley's advice to make the hole a lot wider at the bottom than at the top . . .

Her phone rang again. "Hey."

"Wade . . ." At the sound of his voice, even distant and tinny sounding as it was over the Comsat system the freighters used to communicate ship-to-shore, she felt her resolve buckle.

". . . anything?" The connection was crackly.

"No." Any hint of panic from her and he'd be here right away, never mind what kind of emergency anyone else was having; she straightened, gripping the phone. "Everyone's looking. Cops from all over the state are here. Bob's going to try to get hold of Ellie and George; I can't seem to. Wade, this is all . . ."

My fault. But it wasn't, and anyway that was another thing that if she said it, he would come home despite the freighter out there wallowing helplessly.

"I miss you," she told him instead. "But I'm all right."

Much more of this and her pants would catch fire. She pictured him high up on the freighter's comm deck, the other men waiting for him to get back to work.

". . . you . . ." The connection was breaking up.

"I love you, too." Static in reply; reluctantly she pressed Disconnect, as another wave of fright hit her hard. *Where are they?* But that way lay disaster; if something happened she had to be ready for it.

Which meant she should eat something, whether she wanted to or not. Inside, the afternoon light slanted through the kitchen's tall, bare windows, brightening the jar of red dahlias she'd picked and placed there only that morning. As she was putting a slice of cheese onto a slice of dry bread, the phone rang again; this time it was the cordless in the phone alcove, not her cell.

"Jake? You okay?" Another crackly connection.

"Yes, I'm fine," she said as her heart rate slowed.

Not Campbell. "Who is this?" she began, annoyed. But then with a guilty start she realized. "Dad. Hey, sorry about that."

He'd planned to fix the sidewalk himself; doing it without

telling him made her feel suddenly like a naughty child. "You heard about Lee and Helen?"

"Yes." Around here, news traveled almost as fast between is-lands as on them. "Mail boat came, fellow runnin' it had the story. Listen, I don't like your being there alone."

If anyone understood Ozzie Campbell, it was Jacob Tiptree. The two had been longtime friends until one blasted the other's life to bits. "I'm fine, Dad," she said.

For an instant it was as if he were right there with her, smelling of Old Spice, brick dust, and Tom's of Maine toothpaste while planning how to attack the hole in the concrete.

The ferry could have him and Bella home tonight but his next words dashed this hope. "Ferry's down. Repairs. To-morrow, too."

Her heart sank. "Oh. That's too bad." She forced confidence into her voice. "But look, you and Bella don't have to rush home. There's nothing to do but wait."

The back door stood open, and while she was talking a squad car zoomed by, driven by a uniform cop but carrying men in suits.

"How's Bella?" she asked. Keeping her voice even; she hadn't known how much she had been counting on their return until the prospect was snatched away.

"She's fine." He chuckled drily. "Gave the poor fellow at the ferry dock the wet-hen treatment when she found out the boat wasn't going, but that didn't do any good."

Jake imagined Bella Diamond dressing down the unfortunate ticket agent. With her big, bad teeth, her grape-green bulging eyes, and her bony face twisted into the variety of outraged scowl only she could really produce properly, no doubt she'd gone right up one side of that poor ferry guy and down the other.

Still, when there was no ferry, there was no ferry. For an emergency, a helicopter could be summoned, but . . .

"'Copter's in St. John with a sick kid," Jacob Tiptree said as if reading her thought. "And for light air traffic it's a tad breezy. Gale flags're up."

Those storms coming tonight, she remembered. And the remote, windswept isle of Grand Manan where her dad and Bella had gone was no kiddy ride by propeller-driven plane, even in the best of weather. Not that he'd have been able to get Bella onto any such damn-fool gizmo, as she'd have called it.

"Anyway, she's got our room in the motel spic and span, and if I don't go grab her she'll be starting on the lobby area."

"I can see it," she said, managing a weak chuckle. But then the horror of what had happened came over her again. "Dad . . ."

"I'll take her on a tour," he said, not seeming to notice.

But he had. It was a sort of good-news, bad-news feature of their relationship that even after many years of no communication between them at all, he could still read her so clearly.

"Did you know," he went on in the deep, gravelly voice she used to hear in her dreams all the while he'd been on the run, "that New Brunswick was set up by Canada as a refuge for British Loyalists from America, after the Revolution?"

Tears prickled her eyes. "No," she said lightly through the tightness in her throat. "I didn't know that."

His ancestors, and hers, had taken great glee in picking off the hated redcoats with flintlock muskets, the equivalent of 12-gauge shotguns, from their hiding places in the Kentucky hills.

Another squad car went by, this one with its lights flashing although no siren was on. "Dad, I've got to go. Somebody might be trying to . . ."

Call. But she didn't want to discuss that with him. He was

fully capable of commandeering a fishing boat to get back here if he had to, and even the suggestion that his old nemesis Campbell was behind this—

"All right," he said. And then, "You remind me of your mom, d'you know that?" A rush of feeling washed over her; despite the long separation they'd had, his approval was important to her.

Or perhaps because of it, as if they were making up for lost time. "Not just because you look just like her, either," he said.

The spitting image, actually, although her mother had been barely out of her teens when she died. Same dark hair, lean face, and alert expression . . . sometimes it seemed Jake had inherited all her physical features from her mother, and none from her dad.

"She had your nerve," he finished almost tenderly, and Jake could almost see him reminiscently touching the ruby earring in his ear. He'd asked Bella if she wanted him to take it out, to which the housekeeper had replied *Of course not, you fool,* and meant it.

His voice regained its usual dry forcefulness. "Before I go, though, Jacobia, I wanted to remind you, that broken sidewalk's no amateur project. Don't let your eyes get bigger'n your toolbox."

Caught. He knew her, all right. And when he called her by her full name, the jig was definitely up. "Uh-huh. I'm aware of that, don't worry. How's your foot?" she changed the subject.

His fall on the fractured concrete had been so spectacular, it seemed the only one not still horrified over it was the victim himself. "The cast feels like it's made of lead," he groused.

In the background she heard gulls crying, and a foghorn's two-note hoot. "Soon as I get home," he went on, "I'm going to get a hacksaw, stick my leg out in front of me, and—"

He'd do it, too; yet another reason it was as well he stayed away. "Look, you just take care of yourself and Bella, okay? I'm fine, I talked to Wade, and Bob and Clarissa have invited me to stay with them. I might, or Sam might come up tonight, so . . ."

So she wouldn't be alone. It was only a small lie, she told herself, maybe not even entirely one since whatever he said, you never knew when Sam would show up for a meal and a night in what he still thought of as his own bed.

Silence from her dad, while he decided whether or not to call her on the fib. Then: "All right," he said finally, and hung up just as a third squad car raced by the house. In its wake came Tom Godley in the pickup truck with Wadsworth's Hardware Store stenciled freshly in white on the new, candy-apple red paint.

Tom slowed, leaning toward the passenger-side window when he saw her coming out.

"They've found something," he said.

She had to get away. And she had to get Lee away, too.

Helen Nevelson lay half on and half off the wide backseat of the old car they'd bundled her into, trying to think through the blinding pain in her head.

And the terror in her heart. They were on Route 1, heading toward the town of Calais and the Canadian border just beyond.

But they couldn't be trying to get out of the country; the border control officer would see her, gagged and tied back here. So they must be going somewhere else, but where?

Lee was still asleep, her hair fanned out over her smooth, pink cheek. Tears leaked from Helen's eyes; she hadn't protected the little girl. She'd tried, but she hadn't. They'd been too strong. And now, unless she thought of a way out of this, something awful was going to happen.

The gag in her mouth had compressed between her teeth so

it wasn't choking her so much, now. But it wasn't slipping off, and neither were the ropes around her ankles and wrists.

The guy behind the wheel hummed a tune to himself over and over. *By the sea, by the sea, by the beautiful . . .*

Bastard, Helen thought. Evil, cruel . . . She hiked herself up painfully so she could see out the front window. Cars went by in the opposite direction, coming from Wal-Mart or the Shop 'n Save. People on errands, not knowing she was in here screaming at them in her head.

Screaming for help, but there wasn't going to be any, she knew that now. Not unless she did something—and anyway, the best help, her stepfather Jody Pierce always liked to tell her, was the help you gave yourself.

A sob swelled in her chest as she thought of the look she'd always given him when he said things like that. Stupid Jody, boring Jody. Wanting her to do stupid, boring things, like fishing or hunting. Or hiking around in the woods, where he was always full of useless advice, like what to do if you got lost.

Yeah, she'd thought, slapping at a mosquito or smearing on more greasy sunscreen lotion. *Like that's ever going to happen. Like I'm ever going to be in the woods without you forcing me to go on one of these stupid outings with you.*

Like we're ever going to be friends. Now she'd have given anything to see him again, hear his dumb outdoor safety rules and the routines he made her follow. Such as wearing sturdy shoes or boots instead of sandals when you went out hiking, and right this minute she was barefoot. She hadn't been wearing shoes or socks when these guys burst in, and they wouldn't let her take the time to find some, just started hitting and grabbing.

More tears . . . God, she was so scared. But then just ahead she saw a cop car coming toward them in the southbound lane.

Coming fast. Quickly she slid sideways behind the driver's

seat. Then she bent her knees up tightly under her chin. If she shoved both feet hard into the back of the front seat, it might slide forward.

The driver guy might lose control and swerve, even if only a little. The cop would see. And then . . .

The driver guy glanced at her in the rearview. "You wanna die right now? Want me to put a bullet in your freakin' head?"

The cop car sped past. He might have seen her if she hadn't slid down below window level to get her feet up high enough to kick with.

But she had, so he hadn't. Then: "You ready for later?" the driver guy asked the guy in the passenger seat. His name was Anthony. The driver had said it earlier, dragging the name out sarcastically for some reason she didn't understand.

"You better be getting it straight in your head," the driver went on to his partner. "Wouldn't hurt, you have another look at the map, there. Make sure you remember the road by the thing, the whaddyacallit."

"Promontory," said Anthony distractedly. "They got it marked on the tourist flyer I picked up in the hardware store. And those whirlpool signs lead right to it, that we saw on the way there."

The cliffs, Helen realized; they were talking about the high cliffs back in Eastport at the south end of the island. She knew the area well; it was one of the places the kids went in summer, at night. Boys mostly, but girls, too, when their boyfriends talked them into it. For a while over the summer, Helen had slipped out at night and gone to the cliffs with Tim pretty often.

Once when she'd been there, a guy visiting from Bangor had clipped his belt to the big steel cable that ran to the survey marker on the rocks out in the water, trying to play Spider Man. There'd been a party there just last night, but she hadn't gone.

She'd had to get up early this morning to get ready to take care of Lee, and besides, after hanging out with Tim Barnard for most of the summer she'd had enough beer drinking and pot smoking to last her the rest of her whole life.

Now she wished she'd gone to the party and gotten stupid on booze-laced energy drinks, the big fad now among kids too young to be drinking at all, then stayed in bed this morning pleading a headache instead of doing what she'd promised to do. Maybe then she wouldn't be in this fix.

But she was, so now she lay tied up in the backseat of a speeding car, listening hard in hopes of hearing something else that might help her.

"Yeah, well, make sure you know how to get away from your big fancy word, not just to it," the driver said sourly. "It's the away part we want to be clear on, you dope."

He hadn't liked it that Anthony knew the word "promontory," Helen could tell. He seemed mean like that, as if he enjoyed getting the chance to make somebody else feel bad. Helen didn't know what his name was, and by now she was pretty certain neither one of them meant to give her the chance to find out.

Not that she cared. But she had to try to listen and find out everything about them so she could tell someone, later. Jody, the police . . .

If there was a later. "How far we gotta go?" the driver demanded. "Jeeze, these rural areas go on freakin' forever."

"Not far," Anthony said, frowning at the map spread across his knees. "Half a mile, maybe, on the left. Little dirt road; I think we gotta watch for it."

She hiked herself back up. On either side of Route 1 spread rolling fields full of goldenrod and black-eyed Susans. Here and there long driveways led off through fields of wildflowers to the treed hills on one side, or the sparkling bay on the other.

The trees were just barely beginning to turn, red and gold flaming amidst the green leaves. A herd of black-and-white cows stood in the shade of a cedar windbreak; on the mainland the sun still got hot in the daytime, although the nights were already bitter previews of the coming winter.

Half a mile . . . it passed in the time it took her to realize where they must be going, and then they reached the turn onto the old abandoned logging track that meandered around Money Lake.

The car bottomed out with a huge bang, then bounced through a series of holes and craters while the driver cursed loudly. He didn't slow down, though, as if he were in a hurry to get deeper into the woods.

Lee whimpered fretfully in her sleep. "Freakin' place," the driver commented as they bumped along.

Nobody maintained this road, which was rarely used by anyone but hunters and, in winter, a few ice fishermen and snowmobilers. Logging trucks had beaten it into grooves that the weather and an occasional all-terrain vehicle's passage had only deepened.

But once all the logs were cut and hauled off, the trucks had gone, leaving the rough ruined land littered with stumps and piles of dead branches like blackened miniature mountains.

"You do that thing okay, with her car?" the driver guy asked his partner.

Anthony nodded. "Like it said," he replied, angling his head at a spiral notebook on the dashboard. "I don't get why, but—"

"Yours is not to reason why," said driver-guy. "Just that you got it where the book said to put it, wiped the prints out of it good and got it covered up enough. But not too much," he added cautioningly.

"Yeah. I did all that. That's taken care of," said Anthony.

They're talking about my car, Helen realized. Putting it somewhere; that must've been what happened during the hour or so
she couldn't account for, while she was out cold. Hiding the car,
but only partially, because they wanted it to look as if . . . what?

They bumped through more ruts and potholes. She'd never
been on this road with Jody, although in his attempts to befriend
her after he married her mother he'd hauled her down just about
every other lousy backwoods track in the whole county.

Too wrecked, he'd said of this swamp-pocked, mosquito-
ridden acreage. In fifty years, Mother Nature might fix it, but
now even the ATVers didn't like wilderness areas this rough.
Thin stands of popple and tiny pines pocked the tan soil, leaves
yellowing with the end of summer and the pines like baby
Christmas trees. Old gray cedar posts bore twists of rusted
barbed wire, marking pastures long gone.

No one would be out here. They were taking her here to kill
her, and Lee, too, for reasons she would never know, and there
would be no one to stop them. No one would know what had
happened to them until someday, some hiker or hunter found
their bones . . .

"Jee-sus!" Driver-guy hit the brakes in a sudden panic stop,
hurling Helen forward against the front seat. Beside her, Lee slid
limply to the floor, her head down and her neck bent so her chin
jutted into her chest and her body's weight kept her pinned
there.

A string of drool dangled from her lips, which began turning
blue. Helen screamed, slamming herself against the front seat
and jamming her elbow into it, shrieking against the slimy rag in
her mouth.

"Shut her up, will you?" driver-guy demanded, not taking his
eyes off the thing in front of the car.

Helen drove the top of her head against the seat back again, ignoring the driver's implied threat and the agony it cost her. A cut over her eyebrow opened, warm blood trickling from it.

Looking pained, Anthony twisted around and saw the trouble. Hoisting Lee up by the back straps of the blue corduroy overalls she wore, he deposited her on the seat.

The blue went out of her face. "Shut up," Anthony told Helen in a calm, unthreatening tone. But from the look in his dark eyes she knew that even if she obeyed, in the long run it wasn't going to make any difference.

He just didn't want her freaking out again. With her breath still coming in shudders she nodded shakily; he turned away.

Think, she could hear Jody saying. You get in a tight spot outdoors, you think about it and *do* something.

Don't just sit waiting to get rescued, he would tell her.

Had told her, about everything from an allergic bee-sting reaction to an overturned canoe. Because nature's a bitch. Not like in the cartoons, cute little talking animals you can reason with and they'll behave right.

Eat or get eaten is nature's motto, Jody had emphasized. Kill or be killed. Remembering, Helen peered out the windshield through a haze of renewed pain. The side of her face where driver-guy had punched her felt as big as a watermelon, and the ache in her jaw was like a hammer that was threatening to burst that melon open.

They'd stopped in a swamp, black water thick with rotting tree stumps bordering both sides of the road, which had narrowed to the width of a single car. Directly in front of them stood the reason that driver-guy had slammed on the brakes: a moose.

A big one, with an enormous antler rack. "Holy Christmas," breathed driver-guy.

It was about six feet high at the shoulder, with big, round, rolling eyes and a massively muscled, rust brown body atop long, improbably slender legs. Up close like this she could see the hide's coarse texture, ratty-looking from bug bites and from rubbing up against trees because the bites itched.

Those eyes were as big as tennis balls, and from his voice Helen could tell that driver-guy was a little frightened by the animal. *Good,* she thought at him. *I hope you have a heart attack.*

"Too bad we didn't bring a shotgun, huh?" he joked, trying to sound unfazed. "Bag ourselves some moose meat."

Rifle, she corrected him mentally; a shotgun would destroy too much of the meat and pollute much of the rest with buckshot. Jody would want to shoot it, too, though, if it were in season. Afterward, he would hang it for a few days to age the meat, then dress it out and butcher it into steaks, chops, and burgers.

All of which she hated, especially the days when the moose carcass dangled practically right outside her own bedroom window, strung up from a tree branch in the yard. Also, moose meat was gamy and tough. *Why can't we go to McDonald's?* she would complain when it appeared on the table, while her mother tut-tutted and Jody sat there, slowly shaking his head at her.

This moose stood calmly, white dripping roots of water grass from the swamp dangling out of the side of his mouth as he slowly pulverized them with his huge yellow teeth. Twitching his tail he brushed away some of the insects pestering his rear end.

The two guys from the city sat silently staring at the moose with their own mouths hanging open, forgetting about Helen and Lee for the moment. It was like the scene from the movie *Jurassic Park,* she thought, where the people in the cars sat waiting for the dinosaurs to spot them, and bust through their windshields to get at them.

She wished the moose would do that. But it wasn't going to. In mating season, the males were irritable and would charge you, and later in the year females would defend their calves.

This one, though, was just munching along placidly. "Honk the damn horn at it," Anthony said impatiently, reaching for the wheel.

Driver-guy slapped his hand. "What're you, nuts? Just wait. Maybe it'll . . ."

As he spoke, the moose ambled unconcernedly away along the edge of the swamp. After twenty yards or so, it stepped off the dirt road into the underbrush and vanished.

"There, see?" driver-guy snapped, and started the car. "You and your bright ideas," he groused as they moved forward again. "You'll get us killed out here."

Helen hoped so. Meanwhile, though, hearing them talk about shooting the moose—and knowing that Jody would really have done it—had given her an idea. The driver had a gun, and though Jody had never shown her how to shoot a pistol, she knew how to pull a trigger, all right.

She definitely could do that. "How much farther?" Anthony wanted to know. Then a partridge rocketed up from the road just in front of them with a loud whir of wings, startling him so he gasped.

Driver-guy laughed. "Hey, whoa, there, cowboy. It's only a freakin' bird," he teased Anthony, who reddened in silence.

The first time she'd fired a rifle, the sound had been like a thunderclap, the weapon's concussive kick against her shoulder surprising her and sitting her down hard. She'd started crying and when Jody tried helping her, she'd swung out at him blindly, hitting him in the face with the back of her hand.

Later, though, she'd sucked it up defiantly and let him show her. Being able to shoot the rifle, however inexpertly, felt like proving something, that she chose not to be the kind of girl who went hunting and fishing and ate moose meat.

That she wasn't a weakling, that she could do it if she

wanted. She'd learned a lot of things, in fact, just to wipe that "She's only a girl" look off his smug face. Cold-water swimming had come pretty naturally to her, kayaking was flat-out easy, and righting an overturned canoe wasn't so bad once you got past the fear of overturning it in the first place. Besides, and this she'd have never admitted to Jody, once she'd started dating Tim Barnard, being able to shoot a gun seemed only prudent.

But she still didn't enjoy any of those things. She just did them to shut Jody up. She liked clothes, music, hanging out with her friends, and kids.

Little kids. Lee's eyes drifted open, her lips moving. *Mama,* she murmured silently. Then her lids fell shut again under the effect of whatever they'd given her, some licorice-smelling stuff whose sharp, medicinal scent still clung faintly to the child's breath.

You poor little thing, Helen thought. *You're having a bad day, too, aren't you? First your doll and then this. . . .*

"Couple more miles yet," Anthony told the driver.

The gun was in the driver guy's inside front jacket pocket; she knew from the way he kept patting it every so often without seeming to know he was doing it. Reassuring himself, she guessed, that he had the upper hand.

But if she got the gun, which she thought maybe she could if she moved fast enough, then the shoe would be on the other foot, wouldn't it?

Soitanly! Jody would have agreed, imitating Curly from the Three Stooges. He had all their movies and shows on DVD and never tired of them.

She hated the Stooges. But thinking about Jody going Woo! Woo! in that silly way made things now seem a bit less hopeless. And she needed hope, because from the sound of it she had only a few minutes left to get her hands on that weapon.

By now the swamp was behind them, the track curving up-hill between huge granite boulders, then down again and over an old log bridge running across the still water of a beaver pond. A fat black snake sunning itself atop the lodge flickered its tongue at them.

If she did it fast, she could get the gun from the guy's pocket before either of them could react. Fire it right into the driver, maybe, pull the trigger as soon as she got her hand on the thing. But first—

First things first, she could hear Jody saying to her as she regarded her bound wrists.

First, she had to get out of these ropes.

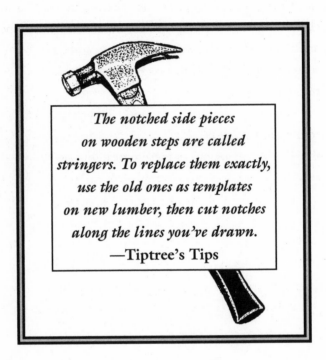

Chapter 5

*The notched side pieces
on wooden steps are called
stringers. To replace them exactly,
use the old ones as templates
on new lumber, then cut notches
along the lines you've drawn.*
—Tiptree's Tips

T his look familiar?" Bob Arnold asked Jacobia, handing over the sodden object.

Jake nodded dumbly, staring down into the painted, button-eyed face of a Raggedy Ann doll with yarn hair, a stuffed muslin body and head, and a red-checked gingham dress with a white apron tied around the doll's middle.

Black cloth shoes covered the doll's feet. "It's Lee's," she managed. "Who . . . who found it?"

They stood on the weed-strewn beach at the foot of Jefferson Street, with the old sardine cannery building to their right and a granite cliff shouldering out into the water on their left. It was almost high tide, waves lapping up over the stones nearly to where the lush patches of sea lavender and saw grass began.

"Tourists," Bob said. "Looking for beach glass."

A cloud bank sat motionless on the horizon, high and solid as if somebody had piled it there with an ice cream scoop. She looked down. There'd been a bonfire here last night, driftwood and charred chunks of old railroad ties beginning to float. Kids at the end of summer, she thought; school started next week.

The sand-polished pieces of antique bottles in aqua, green, and red littered some of the sandy stretches around Moose Island, along with bits of antique china and clay pipe stems. But not here; the tourists had come to the wrong place. By some trick of the current, only light stuff washed up on this stretch of the shore; buoys, Styrofoam pieces, driftwood. And cloth dolls . . .

"I guess even they'd heard about Lee being missing," Bob went on. "So when they spotted this . . ."

"Uh-huh," she said, still barely able to speak. Until now she'd been able to keep thinking that maybe against all odds she had it wrong. That Lee and Helen would reappear.

That it had been a misunderstanding. But no more. "Did Helen Nevelson ever bring Lee down here?" Bob wanted to know. "Trip to the beach, play in the sand . . ."

"There's no sand here," Jake pointed out. At high tide, there barely was a beach at all, and when the water was low the space between it and the shoreline was covered with rockweed, the kind you had to pick your way gingerly across to avoid slipping.

"Anyway, the answer is no," she said. "As far as I know, she never brought Lee here. Or any of the kids she took care of."

They walked through the waving, sharp-edged grasses growing between scattered heaps of old red brick rubble at the edge of the water. Once, workers summoned by a whistle had come here to start their shift in the cannery building, a long, low wooden structure built out over the water on a massive wharf.

Cutting the fish and packing them, sealing the cans, sticking the labels on . . .

"There is one other possibility," Bob said reluctantly.

Nowadays what fish processing there was got done in Canada, and the old cannery building was being remodeled for condos. Blue tarps covered the roof, their edges flapping, and pallets of new lumber loomed by the front entrance, covered with more tarps. A Realtor's sign tacked to a post advertised *Ocean! Views!*

Jake wondered why, when you lived on an island, you needed an ocean view, or in winter the gale-driven leaks and constant, howling winds that went along with it. People around here paid good money to get away from those things, and for the heavy-duty sheets of plastic that substituted so poorly for vacations in Florida.

"Anything that goes in the water up by the causeway ends up here," Bob said unhappily.

She looked up at him. "But that would mean . . ."

"Yeah. They got that far, they're not on the island, now."

She absorbed this in silence. It meant they could be headed anywhere. By now, Lee and Helen could be hundreds of miles away. Or their bodies could be in the water just as the doll had been. It meant that one or both of them could wash up here any minute.

Like the doll. "Did you ever get hold of George or Ellie?" she asked finally.

Bob shook his head. "I left a message at the hotel. They're already out on a bus tour of Rome. Turns out you need a special cell phone to get international calls, did you know that?"

Of course, Jake realized; no wonder trying to call Ellie on *her* cell hadn't worked. "They meant to rent an international cell phone over there," she put in. "Instead of buying one."

But maybe they'd forgotten, or the process had turned out to be more complicated than they'd thought.

"I said to have them call me as soon as they get in," Bob went on, "but the guy I told, his English wasn't so good, and my Italian—"

Bob speaking Italian was about as likely as one of those beach stones speaking it. He sighed heavily, pushed his thinning hair back off his forehead. "Meanwhile Helen Nevelson's boyfriend says from his hospital bed that he ain't got nothin' to do with the bitch bein' missing. Those are his words," the police chief added scathingly.

"And," he continued, "Jody Pierce hasn't said anything because I still can't find him. Although when he hears Helen's missing he'll turn up, Jerrilyn says. Jail's the least of what he'd go through for his stepdaughter, 'ccording to his wife."

They reached Jefferson Street near where it dead-ended at the back gate of the Coast Guard building. He got into his car.

"The ladies from the churches are busy printing up flyers. They're gonna post 'em around town, out along Route 1, everywhere they can think of. Jerri got a clearer picture of Helen for them to use, and I went in George and Ellie's house and found 'em a better one of Lee. Studio portrait, she's all face in it so you can really recognize . . ."

His voice trailed off while they both remembered the day the studio portrait was taken, Lee in a frilly dress she'd had to be coaxed and finally bribed into wearing. Then, "As for you . . ."

"I know. Stay out of it. It's okay to think of it, though, right?" she added, unable to keep the anger from her voice. "Sit around and torture myself about it, that's allowed?"

Thinking *Jesus. Her doll was in the water.*

The cold water. His face tightened, then relented. "Yeah, Jake. It's allowed. Required, I guess. Except the sitting around part, I don't think that's a very good idea. Which reminds me, Clarissa wondered if maybe you could do her a favor."

Jake never spoke that way to Bob. He was just trying to help, the way he always did. "Sorry. I just lost my . . ."

Temper. Composure. Mind. Choose one, or take all three. He waved her outburst away before she could even finish apologizing for it.

"Forget it. I hear worse'n that most days before breakfast." Bob looked out at the water and the long, low reach of Campobello Island beyond. "Sam get that dory hauled okay?"

The question was both an olive branch and a genuine inquiry; he was fond of her troubled son and well versed in the ups and downs of the young man's life, many of which he had witnessed.

Or been involved in, when the downs were really bad. "Yes," she said. "After the lessons he gave me, he thought I might use it when he's away. But I told him I need more practice before I take it out alone, so it's out at the boatyard under a tarp."

Bob smiled indulgently. "Still kind of a landlubber, aren't you?"

That was putting it mildly. "Yeah. I don't know where he got his seagoing tendencies from, but it wasn't me. And anyway, he's got lots of boats to think about in Portland. No sense him having to worry about the one here at home."

"I guess," Bob allowed. "Good move, him going down there," he added. "Plenty of work year-round in Portland for a fellow who knows boats. And even here, I never saw a kid take to the water like he does."

Bob paused. Then: "Going to meetings, is he?" he inquired mildly.

AA meetings, Bob meant. "Says he is. I mean, yes. At least once a day, sometimes more. But you know how that is."

That going today didn't mean he'd go tomorrow, she meant. Sam fell in love with being sober all over again each time he got that way. Sometimes she wondered if the falling in love part of it wasn't what he liked most.

"Yeah. He's going to meetings until he isn't," Bob said. Not disapprovingly, just realistically. "But you never know, Jake. It could be different this time. . . ."

She said nothing as he let the sentence trail off. Sam was at heart a good kid, and he was sober now, this minute.

She hoped. "So, this Campbell fella," Bob changed the subject again. "You still really believe he's—"

"I do," she cut in gratefully. "He does, and—"

"Not from around here, though," Bob interrupted. They'd been through all this already. But he wanted to be sure. "No local connections, no relatives in the area, nothing he's ever done or been in on around here, that you know of," Bob said.

"No. Not that I know of," she added. "His bar in New Jersey is called the Pig and Whistle. It's got a reputation for illegal betting, probably some money-lending . . ."

There were rumors about Campbell's place, Sandy O'Neill

had said; unsavory customers, a few actual mob types. But hey, even crooks had favorite hangouts, Sandy had added. It didn't mean the owner was involved.

Sure it doesn't, she remembered thinking skeptically. *And if you lie down with dogs, you won't necessarily get up with fleas.*

Maybe you'd get ticks. She went on, "And I know it's not easy to . . ." Thinking you could slink around Eastport for long was a fool's game. ". . . hide, here," she finished.

"Tourists're one thing, newcomers something else again," Bob agreed, gazing out across the water.

The tourists being as numerous and indistinguishable from one another as blackflies, especially late in the season, while actual newcomers, ones who intended to live here, were rare, fascinating, and subject to endless discussion among locals: Who? From where? And most of all, They paid *how* much for that house?

"Ozzie Campbell probably wouldn't stay in Eastport anyway, though, in the motel or a B-and-B," she told Bob. "He's sly, he'd know better than to—"

Bob's face remained skeptical. "Look, I know it's him," she finished stubbornly. "Helen and Lee didn't drown—"

Please let it be true. "—and no boyfriend of Helen's took them. Either Campbell did it, or he had it done, to get at me."

Although for what reason she still couldn't say, because she didn't know. "Look, Bob, I'm not asking you to take it on faith. Just don't rule it out is all I'm really saying to you."

He nodded slowly. "Okay. Believe me, I'm not discounting it. But right now it's a missing-persons situation and that's all it is. I know," he added hastily before she could interrupt. "A missing kid. Two, actually. Urgent as hell, sure, and that's the way it's getting handled."

He squinted at the Deer Island ferry pulling away from the

dock at the Chowder House restaurant. "But we still don't know. It still could be that Helen herself took Lee somewhere."

She started to object, but he held a hand up. "No, let me finish, Jake, you need to know this. Because if we're calling it kidnapping, that's federal. Next thing, it's out of our hands. And I'll call them in, you know I will, but if I do then it's a whole new ball game. They get here, they're more'n apt to get somebody scared. I mean, if somebody's really got them."

Correct, she realized bleakly. Because for a kidnapper the best way to get un-scared was to kill the victim and hide the body someplace where nobody would find it. And around here there were a lot of places like that.

More than anyone could ever search completely. "And then we might never know what happened?" Though she meant it as agreement it came out a tentative whisper.

Bob rubbed his pink forehead, glancing around the interior of the squad car as if surprised and not particularly pleased to find himself in it. "Yup," he said quietly, massaging the bridge of his nose between his thumb and index finger. "That is what I'm worried about. One of those open-ended things."

He went on as if to himself. "Bad enough when you do know, sometimes, if the outcome's poor. When you don't, though, it's just permanent hell for all concerned."

But then he rallied, put his hands on the steering wheel. "Anyway, what Clarissa wanted to know was would you check on Hoke Sturdevant today. She'd do it, but she's tied up in depositions all afternoon and she can't get out of them."

"Oh, Bob," Jake began reluctantly, "I'm not sure I–"

Hoke was one of the grand old men of town, well into his nineties; now that his wife was gone, someone went to his house out on the Harris Point road to visit with him nearly every day.

Jake liked Hoke. But she wasn't sure she had the patience for him today. "Bob," she began again, meaning to refuse, but when she looked up from the dripping cloth doll she still held, he was watching her carefully.

"I talked to Tom Godley," he said, surprising her. "And I went up and down Water Street, went into all the shops and storefronts. Two young guys, I said, asking questions. Told 'em what little else Tom remembered of 'em."

"And?" But she already knew the answer. The two fellows who had been inquiring about her in the hardware store sounded as if they'd looked unusual enough—gold chains and leather jackets not being at all the standard tourist garb in Eastport—that they might've stuck in people's minds.

But if there'd been other sightings, Bob would have said so already. "No one else remembers anyone like that," he confirmed, and started the car. "But I wanted you to know I didn't brush 'em off, like maybe you thought."

She squeezed water out of the doll's sodden body. Its red-painted muslin cheeks were beginning to smear as if with tears from its button eyes. "So," he went on after a moment, "what do you want me to tell Clarissa?"

She took a deep breath of the brisk salt air blowing in off the bay. Sunlight from the west was already beginning to turn Campobello Island into a long gold bar, sandwiched between blue water and blue sky. But behind the island loomed high, massively mounding clouds full of rain.

"Tell her I'll go." It was too late to mix concrete today; those clouds promised more water than she could keep off the repair with a tarp. Besides, checking in on Hoke would be better than sitting at home, going crazy.

And on the way out to his house and back, she could keep her eyes peeled.

• • •

The Harris Point road wound out to the end of a peninsula jutting into the bay, past cottages and summer homes clinging to the ridge under massive white pines. In Hoke Sturdevant's dirt driveway she parked between the battered, paint-peeling garage and a rusty Dumpster overflowing with broken drywall sheets.

Before his wife died, he'd been remodeling the house. Since then, though, he seemed to have lost heart for the project. The car door slammed loudly in the silence. "Hoke?"

She climbed the steps onto the pressure-treated deck running around three sides of the small ranch-style dwelling. Beyond it lay a yard full of raised garden beds edged by railroad ties, laid out at right angles to one another.

A few tomato plants still straggled in one of them. The rest were clotted with weeds overwhelming the few surviving flowers. She was about to call out again when Hoke came to the glass door leading out onto the deck, slid it open.

"Afternoon," he greeted her amiably. From inside came the smell of sausages frying. "Come on in."

He was a tall, gangly man with a wizened, winter-apple face and a shock of thick white hair hanging unkempt over his creased forehead, wearing old khaki pants and a white dress shirt open at the collar. He held a barbecue fork in one hand and a beer can in the other.

"Well, what a pleasant surprise," he said. "To what do I owe the honor?"

It was part of his charm that he accepted being checked on like this, greeting each visitor as if he didn't know they'd come to make sure he hadn't dropped dead since the last time anyone saw him. The sausages on the stove spat energetically.

"Care for a beer?" he offered, raising the can.

Be-ah: the Maine way of saying it. "No, thanks, Hoke. I was out this way and just thought I'd stop by and say hello."

His sideways look at her was cloudy with cataracts but full of knowing humor. "Good sausages. Don Jespersen puts up some fine venison, don't y'know."

Sassages. The ketchup bottle stood on the counter. "Hear you had a bit of excitement," he said mildly, forking the sausages onto a paper plate.

She glanced up, surprised that he knew already.

"Girl gone. Jody Pierce's girl, Helen, it was, correct?"

"Uh-huh," she confirmed. He bit off the end of a sausage, chased it with beer. "But how did you know about that?"

He waved at the kitchen counter where a small black box with a digital readout stood. As she followed his gesture it sputtered a burst of static, and a few garbled words came out of it.

"Scanner," he said. "Ain't supposed to, but I got it wired so it monitors police, fire, and emergency calls. Keep up on all the local doings that way."

He fished a slice of Wonder Bread out of the wrapper, folded it in half and took a big bite. "My great-granddaughter," he said when he'd finished chewing and swallowing, "was friends with that missing girl."

His daughter and son-in-law had moved away years ago; now the family came back for a month each summer. "Really? When? And did she ever say anything about her?" It hadn't occurred to Jake that Hoke Sturdevant might know anything about any of this.

He shook his head. A dot of adhesive tape on the side of his jaw showed where he'd nicked himself shaving. "Not about the girl. 'Bout the boyfriend, though. Piece o' work, he was. Saw it myself. He had himself some ideas."

Hoke put a wry twist on the final word; clearly he didn't agree with the ideas. "He was the type, if'n a girl wants a bit o' time with her friends he's gotta come around checkin' on her. Make sure she's where she said she'd be."

"And if she wasn't?"

Hoke nodded sagely. "Aye, that's when the trouble begins. I saw it here. Tiffany—that's my great-granddaughter—had a few friends out on the deck visiting."

Off Hoke's small, bright kitchen, a door led to his living room, which was furnished with an old black woodstove, a recliner with a red-and-black wool blanket thrown over it, and a dog bed containing a very old white springer spaniel, now sound asleep.

The other door leading from the kitchen was closed. He saw her looking at it, ducked his head a little embarrassedly.

"Old man's housekeeping," he said with a rueful grin. "Shut the door on the mess, clean it up another day. That way, at least my guests don't have to look at it."

He drank some beer. "Anyway, the girls'd play music, fool around in the boat a little. Jody's girl was with 'em that day."

She followed his gesture out the kitchen window. Below his yard was a stony, downward-slanting trail with a wooden railing, leading to the cove; he still kept a small dory down there.

"And while they were here, this kid shows up, him and some others in his truck, all put out an' wantin' to know how come *he* wasn't invited. Raisin' a ruckus, the whole bunch of 'em."

With a nod at the scanner he added, "They've picked up his pals, by the way. Few minutes ago, a deputy on Shore Road in Perry found 'em tryin' to break into a summer camp."

Against expectations, Hoke was turning out to be quite the useful little fountain of information. Out on the deck, a trio of chickadees found his bird feeder full of thistle seed.

"Put his hand on her, the kid did," said Hoke. "Tried to get her to go in the truck with him."

"And?" The top step of Hoke's deck was beginning to rot. A plank and a claw hammer lay by a box of nails on the deck.

From the rust stain spreading under the hammer, though, it seemed they'd been there for at least as long as the mess hiding behind his closed hallway door. Sighing, the spaniel stretched, turned, and lay down again.

Hoke put his paper plate in the trash bin, drained his beer and dropped the can into a turquoise plastic box marked *Eastport Recycles*. "I went out, told 'em if I didn't see their south ends goin' north in about two seconds, I'd be right pleased to drop-kick all their asses off'n the dock," he recalled.

His eyes brightened at the memory. "One at a time or all of 'em together, I told 'em. They chose skedaddlin' away."

"So you think this Tim Barnard kid could've gotten mad about something this morning, and decided to do something about it?"

Lying in the hospital, mulling over the beating he'd gotten from Helen's stepfather . . . that could make him angry enough.

"He could've told his friends," she went on, "they showed up and took her somewhere, maybe the child she was baby-sitting, too? To get back at Helen? Teach her a lesson?"

Her heart lifted briefly. Because if that was true maybe all her worry really was just–

"Nope," Hoke said flatly. "Bunch of babies, they were, an' Timmy Barnard the worst o' the crew. That big mouth o' his, and sure, he'll slap a girl around if he gets the chance. But in the real world, he's all net and no herring."

Hoke had been a fisherman before he retired. "Oh," she said disappointedly, wondering whether Bob Arnold had reached

Ellie and George yet, if they were rushing home in a panic right now.

Not that they could do anything when they got here, any more than anyone else could. Hoke regarded Jake kindly.

"No," he repeated, "I'm afeared that girl o' Jody's might be in worse trouble'n Tim Barnard could cook up," he said as he put his fork into the sink.

As she went out, he stopped her. "Listen, before you go I wonder if you could do an old man a favor?"

She paused unwillingly. "I got the tools out," he went on, "an' the prep work's all done. But my eyesight ain't what it used to be." *That deck,* she thought, *he's going to ask me to fix the step on the . . .*

But instead he waved at the far end of his yard where an old green canoe rested under the cedar trees, rails-down across two more of the railroad ties. Going back inside briefly he returned with two glass jars, one full of black, gooey stuff, the other containing clear fluid.

"I wonder if you could maybe mix this up for me, slap it on there," he asked, gesturing out at the canoe.

The tarry stuff was patching compound, the liquid the curing agent, to make the compound harden. "Hoke, I really need to–"

He regarded her gravely. She'd tried to be calm and polite to him but her fear hadn't escaped his notice, she realized.

He was way too wise an old bird for that. "You look like a levelheaded young woman," he said. "Don't need no advice on how to do things from me. But here it is anyway, for what it's worth: When trouble comes, keep your hands full and your mind on practical matters."

He waved a freckled hand at the device clipped to her belt. "I see you've got a cell phone." It hadn't rung in a while, and she couldn't decide whether that was a good or a bad thing.

"Anyone needs to call you," Hoke went on, "they can. Here or anywhere. I have," he added, "a fair amount of experience in the keep-busy department."

The dead wife, the silent house, the long, solitary decline of old age and its related maladies, the chores getting to be too much . . .

"Sure, Hoke, I'll do it," she gave in, stepping off the deck into the yard.

Minutes later, she finished mixing the black, tarry goo and the clear fluid together, using a paper plate for a palette and the wooden spatula that had come in the patching kit to stir the stuff with. Over the edge of the cliff, slanted afternoon light turned the water in the cove pale blue, so clear she could see straight down through it to the submerged rocks and weeds growing up from them, long dark green fronds waving in the current.

Hoke wrinkled his nose; even outdoors the mixture reeked of epoxy fumes, a sharp chemical stink.

"Just stuff it in there," he said as she began spreading the goo. "No need to be too delicate about it. Don't need pretty for this job, just watertight."

Years of use in the rocky cove had turned the boat's bow into a bumpy, mushy-looking mess. He'd cut away the worst of it, or had someone do it for him, so that now a long, narrow opening gaped like a dark mouth.

She used the wooden spatula to pack the deeper recesses with gunk, layered more on top and smoothed it as best she could; by tomorrow it would harden. Getting it down the stairs to the short wooden pier where the dory floated would be another matter.

But she wouldn't be here for that. Hoke watched, his wrinkly face impassive, as she finished smoothing the epoxy in.

"Thanks," he said. "That looks like a mighty fine job. I get that vessel back down in the water, she'll leak nary a drop."

They walked back toward the house. "Care for a soft drink? Or mebbe that beer, now? Reward for your hard work?"

She offered him a smile instead. "Thanks. But I've got to go. I've got to . . ."

What? Fright ambushed her again at the realization that she didn't know, her gaze falling once more on the deteriorating deck. The damaged step was rotted nearly through; sooner or later he would forget and put his weight on it.

The resulting fall wouldn't be at all like her dad's, though that had been bad enough. Hoke was a lot older, and would likely fracture his hip, and that would be the end of whatever peace he had out here, his long quiet afternoon at the close of day.

Next would come hospitals, painful convalescence, a nursing home. Probably they wouldn't serve fried sausages, there.

Or beer. And the nails and three-quarter-inch plank lay on the deck as if waiting for her.

She picked up the hammer.

Two hours later, Jake drove back out the Harris Point road toward home. The riser holding up Hoke Sturdevant's punky deck step had turned out to be rotted; she'd ended up cutting a whole new one out of an old length of pressure-treated lumber she found stuck away at the back of his garage.

What he didn't have was a power saw, or not one that worked. So the cutting had taken a while, pressure-treated lumber being about as amenable to hand-sawing as stainless steel was. Her arm ached, her hand felt permanently cramped, and there was a fresh blister swelling painfully on her thumb, which for good measure she'd also managed to hit with the hammer.

But she'd done her good deed, and Bob Arnold had kept his promise to keep in close touch, calling twice just while she was out at Hoke's. So even though there'd still been no progress in the search for Helen Nevelson and Lee, at least Jake didn't feel left out of the loop.

Truth was, she had the sense Bob was checking *on* her as much as he was checking *in* with her, but that was okay, too. Feeling that somebody right here on the island now cared about how she was doing wasn't much; it didn't get Lee back, or Helen, either.

But it was something. It helped. Meanwhile, though, the sidewalk-repair chore waiting for her at home was unavoidably on hold, and her hands had a not-quite-trembly feeling lurking in them. She thought that if she didn't do something useful and preoccupying with them again soon, they might begin shaking.

Her phone chirped again as she waited for an RV headed for the campgrounds to pass; she grabbed it as she turned from the Harris Point road onto Route 190. Maybe this time, Bob would have something good to report . . . "Hello, Jacobia."

"Who is this?" But she knew; the new blister throbbed as her hand tightened on the wheel.

"Don't talk. Listen." Campbell's raspy voice. "Now that you know who's really in control here, I think we should meet. Soon."

She fought to control her own voice. "What have you done with Lee? The little girl?"

"Nothing. I'm not in the habit of harming kids. Don't annoy me, though, or I might change that."

With an effort she bit back a retort. "What do you want?"

"Not so fast. You need to understand me, first. Get a real sense of our . . . special relationship."

I understand you, you murdering son of a bitch. She passed the old power plant, painted army green, at the rear of a field full of yellow goldenrod off Route 190.

"It's a stony road you're traveling, Jacobia," he said. "I think you should stay on it a while. See what you might find. And not to alarm you, but . . . you'd better hurry."

The connection went dead.. She cursed at the phone, pulled to the side of the road, and punched in Sandy O'Neill's number again, got his voice mail yet again—what the *hell* was he doing?—and left an urgent message asking him to call her back. Then she keyed in Bob Arnold's number, paused, and canceled it before throwing the phone down and pulling back out onto the pavement.

If she called Bob now and this was just another taunt from Campbell, a false alarm, then her credibility with Bob would be even more damaged than it already was. Having the phone meant she could still summon help in an instant, though, if she needed it. So . . .

Wait. Don't do anything until you know something. And then she saw it, opposite the airport driveway on her left: a street sign. Stony Road ran uphill past a wire-fenced pony paddock. Two brown-and-white Shetlands frisked in the neatly kept enclosure while a girl in boots forked out fresh hay.

Jake took the turn. The road climbed steadily around a field of sunflowers. At the end of it stood a ranch-style house with another horse fenced in behind it, this one a roan mare. A German shepherd dog got up alertly from his spot in front of the garage as she went by.

Past the house a sandy cut ran through raspberry cane and burdock. She slowed again, feeling the car's tires digging in as around the next curve the road opened into a gravel pit, behind it a wooded area with trails; she'd often brought the dogs for long walks here. She stopped when the track ended at a mountain of sand, the car door's slam loud as a rifle shot. A crow flapped overhead, cawing as it vanished into the trees.

"Hello?" Kids came here to ride ATVs and scramble around in the sand, though it was forbidden as unsafe, and it was another isolated place on the island where the older ones gathered to drink beer and hang out, as a litter of cans and other detritus showed.

But now it was deserted except for a yellow backhoe parked a few yards from a mountain of gravel near what looked like a brush heap. A loose rock clattered down the gravel pile; startled, she whirled, then felt foolish. Unless—

Better hurry . . . Around her, shadows lengthened; at nearly five o'clock the sky was still light overhead but to the east it was deepening fast, a few early stars coming out in it. The brush heap was larger than she'd thought, filling and towering up from an excavated depression at the pit's far end.

She approached it. Campbell had been hinting at something with his remark about the stony road; it couldn't possibly be a coincidence. But when she peered in, slash-cut brush was all that she could see in the pit.

She opened the phone, punched in all but the last digit of Bob Arnold's number, then crept to the edge of the brush heap. It smelled faintly of gasoline.

Puzzled, she peered through the branches, took a few steps back and approached the heap of cut greenery and tree limbs from the other side. A car lay half on its side, backed at an angle into the depression behind the brush heap.

Above and behind it loomed the huge pile of stones with the backhoe standing silent beside it, so that between the brush and the stone heap the car was hidden unless you looked just so. It was a black Ford sedan with a pink plastic barrette clipped to the right front sun visor.

Helen's car. The driver's side door was exposed, facing up. The windshield was intact, as were the other windows Jake could see, on the passenger side. Leaning against the car, she peered in. The keys hung in the ignition on Helen's beaded key fob. And something was in the backseat.

Not Lee. Don't let it be . . .

Stuffing the phone in her pocket to grasp the door handle with both hands, she pulled, braced her feet apart, and pulled harder. Opening the latch was easy but the car rested on a sharp slant so lifting the door up against gravity was a struggle. When the opening was as wide as her body, she slipped in and pushed up from behind it, until the door opened the rest of the way.

"Lee?" Heart thudding, she crawled in, releasing the door very carefully. It stayed open, and it would only take a moment to be sure about the thing on the seat. *Please not . . .*

Dark. Her weight made the car settle, branches scraping all around and beneath it. "Baby, are you . . . ?"

She knelt on the front seat, leaned over, and put her hands out, feeling around. On the backseat lay a lump of blankets. A sob caught in her throat as she shoved her hand beneath.

Nothing. She closed her eyes briefly. *Thank you . . .*

Behind her the car door fell shut with a thud. She jumped, bumping her head as the car settled a fraction more, seemed to hesitate, then sank abruptly another foot on the driver's side.

Very dark. But never fear, the door would open again and if worse came to worst, she still had the phone. . . . And the car was resting on piled brush, wasn't it? So it couldn't sink too far.

She felt for the door handle with one hand and gripped the phone with the other. *Don't lose it.* . . . But then a new sound made her pause, a loud, rumbling noise, like a dump truck or—

A backhoe. It was the backhoe's engine, starting.

Chapter 6

> *If you don't sweat the small*
> *stuff, you'll end up sweating*
> *the big stuff. Especially*
> *if it's plumbing.*
> —Tiptree's Tips

S o you're sure you did like I told you?" Marky demanded yet again. "You wiped off everything in that freakin' car? You didn't miss nothing?"

Bouncing along on the dirt road, Anthony kept the map open on his knees. It was a different map from the one he'd used while getting them here from New Jersey, showing more detail.

Anthony thought about the job of making the map, finding

the camping areas, boat ramps, and rest stops, and drawing the tiny picnic tables and tents representing these places. The road they were on now was a dotted line snaking around Money Lake, Havey's Pond, Fickett Lake, and Little Cranberry Swamp.

There were no tent or picnic table icons on this part of the map. "'Cause we still got somethin' to do out here and I ain't gonna till I know you freakin' stuck to the instructions," Marky continued.

He turned. "Hey. You listenin' to me?"

"I stuck to them." Anthony wished the map showed a rocket ship icon that he could get into and blast off to another planet. Something about the way he'd begun talking made Anthony nervous, as if maybe Marky's plan from here on out wouldn't be so good.

Or that it wouldn't be good for Anthony. Recalling how Marky had flung the kid's doll out the car window as they crossed the causeway, the surging water seizing the toy and hurrying it away toward the ocean, made Anthony feel bad.

Marky grinning as he did it, like a mean kid torturing some poor dumb creature that couldn't fight back. Like he enjoyed it.

Marky patted the gun in his inside jacket pocket again, not seeming to realize he was doing it. "You got your prints on file, y'know. Freakin' juvenile delinquent, they still go in the database. You screw up, anyone gets your prints off the car, you're the one—"

"Yeah," Anthony said flatly. "I know."

Marky glanced sharply at him. "Yeah, I know," he repeated in a sarcastic singsong. "You know, huh? What d'you think you know? You don't know nothing, you punk."

He swerved around a rock in the awful road, and then through a rut; the old Monte swayed mushily on its big, soft suspension before leveling out. "Freakin' punk."

The girl in the backseat wept steadily, her strangled sobs through the rag in her mouth making a steady counterpoint to the thuds and bangs of stones hitting the car's underside. Beside her the little kid still slept like the dead.

"Shut up, will you?" Marky snapped suddenly at her, glaring into the rearview. "Jeeze, we should've given her the freakin' dope juice instead of the kid."

"Yeah, maybe," Anthony replied. They'd already had to retie her wrists; somehow when they weren't watching her, she'd nearly gotten the ropes off, and Marky had blown his top over it.

At Anthony, of course. "Look at the map, there. Keep your mind on the job, will you, please? Are we there yet or what?"

When Marky talked this much it meant he was getting nervous, too, and Anthony knew why. He'd figured it out a while ago, when they turned onto this road and just kept going, into a wilderness that only got more desolate the farther in they got.

They weren't just going to dump the girl. They couldn't; she had seen their faces. They could've worn masks when they grabbed her but Marky had vetoed it.

So they were going to kill her. Marky wanted to; had wanted to all along, Anthony realized. The not-covering-up-their-faces thing was just his excuse.

And the girl knew it, too. Anthony could tell by her eyes, the one time he'd accidentally looked into them while he tied her up again, tighter this time, the way Marky had ordered.

Marky had also told him to hit her again, but Anthony had ignored this; he wasn't sure why. Because she was going to die soon, maybe. Although hearing her sobbing was like listening to an animal suffer, so maybe he should have knocked her out.

He didn't know. Staring out the window in the fading light, he just wished it was over and done with.

"Well?" Marky snapped.

Anthony squinted at the map. "I think . . . okay. Yeah, I think this is it."

"You think, you think." Marky looked disgusted. "Lemme ask you something. Do you ever know anything, or do you just think?" But he pulled the car into the grassy turnoff, gunning it through the tall weeds until it was hidden from the road.

In the backseat, the girl sobbed harder.

"All right. Both of you get out, now." Marky stared straight ahead through the windshield at a sky full of near-sunset colors: rose, purple, and gold.

"What about you?" Anthony asked.

Marky turned slowly, the look in his eyes unreadable. His right hand reached into the left inside pocket of his jacket, and Anthony went ice cold. But it was okay.

For now. "Take this. Do what needs to be done," said Marky.

Anthony stared. "What're you, nuts?" he blurted without thinking. Because of course Marky was nuts, everyone in the whole tristate area knew that. It was his stock-in-trade, being nuts enough to do things that nobody else would.

Crack skulls, crush a guy's fingers . . . It was what Anthony had thought they were doing, coming up here. That a guy owed some money and wouldn't pay, so they were coming up here to collect.

"I never did anything like this," said Anthony.

The girl had stopped sobbing. He could practically feel her listening back there, wanting to know if there was hope. Anthony could have told her there wasn't.

Murder, he thought, wondering for a wild instant if maybe the map still open on his knees had an icon for it, a tiny gun or a knife. And not even the result of a too-energetic beating on a guy who deserved it, for being a deadbeat or for some other sin.

In the backseat the girl began screaming again through the gag, kicking and struggling. Ignoring her, Marky looked serious, like back in the juvie home when one of the counselors would try explaining something to Anthony for his own good.

"Listen to me, you punk," said Marky, still holding out the gun. "This is gonna happen one of two ways. I am gonna drive out of here with you and that little kid back there, or it is gonna be just me and the kid. Because so far you have seen everything, but you ain't had to do much of anything. Get it?"

Anthony nodded, trying to come up with some way out of doing this particular thing and not finding one. Marky meant that if they got caught he didn't want Anthony rolling over on him, which he figured Anthony couldn't if Anthony pulled the trigger.

Which was probably true, but it wasn't the only true thing. Anthony thought of grabbing the gun right now and shooting Marky with it. Catching him by surprise, driving the girl home, letting her out; the kid, too. Then coming back here, maybe.

Here where it was quiet, the shadows lengthening all around and something—an owl, maybe—*hoo-hoo*ing in the woods nearby.

But Marky must've seen this in Anthony's eyes, or maybe he'd been expecting it. His own face relaxed into something like pity, mingled with contempt.

"You punk," Marky said softly. Kindly, almost. Reaching out, pressing the gun into Anthony Colapietro's unwilling hand.

She'd tried keeping her head on straight, tried getting her hands untied, tried kicking the seat back and screaming and begging through the gag in her mouth, and none of it had worked.

Now the young one from the passenger seat got a handful of

her hair in his hand and hauled her out of the car. She fell down at once, partly to make it difficult for him and partly because she almost couldn't feel her own body anymore, she was so scared.

He untied the rope from around her ankles and yanked her up again, shoving her against the car. Her head banged against the window so hard she saw stars, and through them the little girl's body limp and motionless on the backseat.

Lee . . . He seized Helen's collar, bunching it up in his hand so that it tightened chokingly around her throat, and with his other hand he put the gun to her head.

"Walk," he said.

The gun was like an ice-cold fingertip on the back of her neck. It was cold out here, and nearly dark. The path was a deer trail, barely visible in the gathering gloom, but if she got free she could probably outrun him, and hide.

He tightened his grip, cutting off the shuddery gasps that were all she had left for breath. "Don't even think about it."

The one in the leather jacket sat in the car waiting. Soon the two of them would drive back out of here.

With Lee. But not with Helen. It hit her, then, that this was happening to her and there was nothing she could do about it. To stop it or make it happen any differently.

Or at some other time. Tomorrow, the next day. Any time but now. That death wasn't a thing that happened only to old people, an event she wouldn't have to worry about until some unspecified time in the distant future.

That it was real. That she, Helen Ann Nevelson of Eastport, Maine, was really and truly about to die.

Suddenly the world seemed so precious and good to her, she thought she must surely get another chance just for knowing it so certainly. That it was *good* to be alive. . . .

Under her bare feet the grass was icy cold and she was shivering uncontrollably, more falling forward with each step and catching herself than walking. And so afraid, more scared than she'd ever believed possible.

"Stop," the guy named Anthony said.

As if from a long distance and in slow motion she heard the trigger moving, metal sliding against metal. Then came a spring-loaded creak of the hammer and the cylinder's oiled whisper as it lined the charged projectile up between the firing pin at one end of the weapon and the barrel at the other.

Jody, she thought, because he had taught her all this. Her stepfather, who had wanted to be her friend. But he was far away, now, back there in the life she was leaving.

In the sky, early stars hung around a round, white moon even as the last bloodred shreds of the dying day hung stubbornly on.

Through her tears, Helen gazed lovingly at them.

Thwack! **A huge** rock smacked the windshield on the passenger side, starring it. Then the clatter of stones rose to a hammering roar as Jake sat in Helen Nevelson's car, cursing herself. The cascading gravel rose up past the windows with astonishing speed; within moments, the darkness inside the car was complete.

Damn, how stupid was this? She could've called, told someone where she was going. Right before she approached the car, even, she could have finished punching in Bob Arnold's number.

But no, she had to see for herself, first. Praying not to find Lee there, or if she was there that she was still alive. She would call the instant she knew, Jake had thought.

Well, now she did know. But she'd dropped the phone when the door slammed shut and now, in the darkness . . . She fumbled upward, snapped on the dome light. Searching around, she discovered that Helen's car held every safety item and piece of emergency gear imaginable, plus some whose usefulness she could not fathom.

Jody Pierce had put it all there, no doubt. Young girls didn't think of stuff like this. Flashlight, emergency flares, an ice scraper, hat-and-gloves combo with the price tag still on it, a tire inflator, matches, a blanket, a safety-glass hammer, a sheet of plywood the same size and shape as the backseat, placed on the seat as if to reinforce it—except for the flashlight, none of it looked useful.

And still no phone. But it had to be here somewhere. . . .

Fool, she berated herself. Getting in, she'd told herself it was reasonably safe. This of course had been an exaggeration, but what if Lee was inside? Jake couldn't very well just stand there ignoring the possibility that the little girl was mere feet away, perhaps in need of immediate first aid.

But then the trap had snapped shut. Someone out there waiting for her to investigate the car's interior—someone who had known she would; Campbell, probably—had started the backhoe and given the gravel mountain a shove.

Onto her, burying her here. Cross-legged in the front seat, she pressed her fingers to her lips and tried to think, turned the ignition on and ran the fan for a few minutes. Fresh air came through the vents, smelling of damp earth and tree sap from the broken branches all around and beneath her.

Stuck. Although on the plus side, the roof hadn't collapsed. She wasn't going to suffocate or get crushed, or at any rate not soon. Not unless whoever it was turned that backhoe on again . . .

The thought sent fresh alarm coursing through her, but the machine's rumble, she realized suddenly, had been stopped for a little while, now. She tried listening for footsteps but couldn't hear any.

"Hey! Hey, Campbell! I know it's you. . . . Hey, what's the point of this?"

Because he'd said he wanted something—but there was no answer from out there now, and little sense using up her energy by shouting. Struggling to keep her thoughts ordered, she turned her mind to more immediate concerns:

The car battery wouldn't last forever so she couldn't keep the dome light on, and she didn't want to waste the flashlight's juice, either. She shut them off, along with the fan, thinking *phone, where is it, I'm going to die without that. . . .*

But all right, now, calm down, she instructed herself. She would find it. Also on the plus side, the more time that passed with only silence from outside, the more it seemed likely that her attacker had gone away. If he hadn't, even after she escaped this makeshift tomb she'd still be up the creek. But not quite as far, and to find out, she'd need to *achieve* that escape. . . .

Gravel covered the doors, holding them shut. The car was an economy model, though, so it had crank windows she could roll down. There might be several feet or more of gravel between herself and the outside, enough so she couldn't push her way out a window and basically just swim up through the stones.

But maybe there was only an inch. She couldn't tell. Enough to shove through, or enough to hammer her flat and press all the breath out of her: which? If she cranked one of the windows down a little, she might be able to tell. If she could shove her hand through, into the air . . .

Well, then she could try to get out. If not, she would have to think of something else; find that cell phone, probably, and call someone on it, even though not having found it so far was making her feel more uneasy with each passing instant.

Waiting for rescue didn't seem like a viable option, since the gravel pit might be visited again later tonight, first thing in the morning, or not until next week. And even if someone did come, there'd be no way for them to know *she* was here. But that line of thought was for later.

For now . . . *Try. Just try something.* Sliding behind the wheel since that side of the car angled upward, suggesting that it was less buried, she sucked a few deep breaths in and switched the dome light back on. Still no phone anywhere; she shoved her hand into each upholstery crevice without success. Pale illumination flooded the car's interior with an illusion of safety. Until . . .

Uh-oh. In the few minutes since she'd last seen it the whole windshield had begun bulging inward, its expanse crazed whitely with the hundreds of impacts it had suffered. If it hadn't been for the first hard smack from that big rock . . .

But there was no sense worrying about that, either. It had happened, popping out a small hole at the center of the starred area and weakening the windshield's structure severely. Now greenish fragments puddled from small sections that were already beginning to let go.

From underneath the car came groaning and cracking sounds; sliding across the seat had been enough to shift whatever balance the car had found, apparently. So it was moving again, and tipping.

Or sinking. Biting her lip, she reached out and carefully rolled the window down a fraction. Gravel scraped the glass as it moved, but nothing else happened; she let out the breath she hadn't known she was holding. Now all she had to do was open it a bit more, enough to shove her hand through . . .

With a hideous metallic groan the car settled suddenly half a foot or so, the lurching jolt forcing a squeak of fright from her and popping more glass pebbles from the sagging windshield.

A sharp pain brought her hand to her forehead. Warm and

wet; a flying glass bit must've struck her, and the glass heaps on the dashboard were a lot bigger. Also, the holes in the windshield were enlarging, their edges curved raggedly inward like punctures in a cloth tent.

At last the groaning sounds stopped. Cautiously, she turned the window crank another fraction. Ideally she needed enough room to get her arm out, all the way to the elbow. But the moment she put her hand through, a lot of gravel began pouring in around it.

And then a lot more, surging like water . . . hastily she rolled the window back up, holding the invading stones back with her arm as best she could, frantically poking the last few from the gap between the window and the frame with her fingers before sealing it tight.

Now what? If she saved the car's battery tonight, tomorrow when people were likely to be around she might be able to honk the horn for a while. That might bring someone.

Or it might not. Simply starting the car and trying to drive it from beneath the gravel was an attractive thought, but it was not really an option; for one thing, it was unlikely to work, and for another, that windshield was obviously ready to fail.

A half-bottle of orange juice had been lying on the floor when she got into the car; it was still around here, somewhere. And in the glove compartment . . . she fumbled for it and opened it, grateful for the glow of the tiny bulb inside.

And for the unopened packet of peanut butter crackers Helen had stashed there, emergency rations, no doubt, in case one of her young charges got hungry and cranky. Jake ate one of the crackers and drank some juice, put the rest on the passenger seat.

For later. Because there must be a way out of this, but it might not be fast. Or safe. The car might shift again, or—

A deep, rolling rumble came from outside and above the car, followed by a heavy drumming noise . . . *thunder*. And rain, heavy by the sound of it. Gingerly she touched the fractured windshield.

Wet. She hadn't been paying any attention to the weather but the storms that had been looming out over the bay had approached just the same, and now they were here. She turned the flashlight on again, saw to her horror the trickles of water dripping steadily in through the crazed glass. Her chances of surviving this night had just dropped a lot, she realized bleakly, for in addition to water's other undesirable qualities—

It was cold and unbreathable, and in a massive downpour, why shouldn't the buried car just fill up?

—water was heavy. A pint is a pound, Bella Diamond would say. So waiting for morning no longer seemed practical, either. Outside, thunder rumbled and the rain fell harder; the trickles through the windshield freshened to torrents.

Don't panic. But without wanting to she began wondering how many pints of water per minute were pouring into the pit, anyway, and about how long they might keep on pouring . . .

Her cell phone rang. Startled, she nearly screamed, scanning around wildly—oh, dear God, there it was, on the floor wedged up under the gas pedal somehow, she must've kicked it there . . .

"Hello? Whoever this is, I need help—"

"Jake?"

"Ellie! Oh, my God, Ellie, listen to me—"

"Jake? Are you there?" The connection was crystal clear, as if Ellie were right outside the car.

But she had to be in an airport somewhere, or in a plane on her way home. "Jake, what's happened? Is Lee okay? We got a call from Bob Arnold, I mean a message, but I don't understand, we've been calling and calling, and . . ."

Her voice faded; Jake found her own. "Ellie, I'm sorry. I'm so sorry, I don't know, everyone's trying to find her, but–"

A piece of gravel popped through the windshield and struck her cheek. "Ellie, I'm in trouble. I need you to call Bob and–"

"Jake?" Tinny and mechanical, now, Ellie's voice came back briefly. "Say it again, please, I can't . . ."

Fighting panic, Jake recited her location and asked Ellie to call Bob Arnold, tell him where she was and that she needed help right away. But she didn't know if Ellie heard, and the lighted bar display on the phone dropped to nothing before she finished.

She stared at it for a moment. Surely the battery couldn't be failing, not now on top of everything else. She pressed the Off button, tried to connect again as a massive boom of thunder shook the car, sending yet another heavy slide of gravel rattling and thudding. Then the center of the bulging windshield ruptured abruptly with a sound like cloth ripping, a fist-sized gout of stones poured in over the dashboard ledge, and the rest of the windshield sagged, beginning to tear away from the frame.

This is ridiculous, she thought, her heart hammering; *things like this just don't happen to people.*

But the gravel said otherwise. The gravel said it was coming in, now, so if there was anything she wanted to think about, any particularly bad deed she wished to say an act of contrition for, or some pleasant moment she wished to review . . .

Whatever it was, she'd better take care of it, that gravel said. Because it was coming in, ready or not.

The phone chirruped again. She snatched it up and gasped into it. "Ellie? I'm not kidding, you've got to–"

With a loud, wet *r-r-ri-üp!* the windshield tore in, letting an enormous wave of stones pour through. Scrambling sideways, she lost the phone and found it again.

"Can you hear me? Ellie, I'm in a—"

The gravel just kept coming, hissing and banging, piling up on the seat as if it would never stop.

But then it did stop. Or maybe just paused . . . "Ellie?" she whispered, pressed against the driver's-side door, staring at the ragged spot where one edge of the windshield was still attached to the frame.

Only . . . the edge was *moving,* slowly but surely separating from the windshield mount, bit by tiny—

"Ellie!" No answer. Until . . .

"Hello, Jacobia," a man's voice said clearly.

Not from the phone. Slowly, she closed the instrument.

"Goodness, what a predicament," said Ozzie Campbell.

Right outside, only a few feet away.

Standing by the buried car. "Don't you hurt her. Don't you hurt that little girl, you son of a bitch," she shouted.

Knowing he could hear. That he was out there, laughing and waiting. "What do you *want* with her, you *psycho*?" she demanded.

But there was no answer, and there kept on not being one.

Minutes passed, then half an hour with no sound from him. Longer. She held her breath; nothing. Maybe he was gone. Maybe not.

When Anthony Colapietro returned to Marky Larson's old blue Monte Carlo after muscling Helen Nevelson into the woods, first Marky wanted his gun back right away and then of course Anthony got stuck having to take care of the little kid in the backseat.

Luckily she was still hung over from the tincture of opium they'd given her, a pharmaceutical mixture that Marky had scored from a guy he knew who worked in a drugstore. *Do not kill the kid,* the guy who'd hired them had told Marky very seriously, and Marky had conveyed this instruction to Anthony, as well.

Thus Anthony had been careful, dosing more of the brown, licorice-smelling stuff out in stages while the baby-sitter was still out cold, until the kid conked out, too. So when they got back to the hideout—

That was how he'd begun thinking of the big house in the woods, as a hideout, and himself as a sort of custodian of it and of this whole situation—

The kid was awake, sitting up. "Mommy?" she said, and then louder: "Mommy!"

A lot louder, and sounding pretty ticked off. Marky glowered into the rearview at the kid, then at Anthony. "Yo, do something about her, would ya? I'm tryna' drive, here, for freak's sake."

"Yeah, okay," said Anthony. If Marky hadn't taken the kid's rag doll and pitched it, maybe Anthony would have a better chance of quieting her down. But Marky would never think of something like that. Let Anthony handle it, was Marky's strategy, and if it doesn't go right, bitch Anthony out so you can feel better. That was Marky's whole plan, as far as Anthony could see.

Still, this was no time to complain. Get back home, get his money, after that maybe Anthony could develop his own inkling of what to do next. A new angle; heavy-equipment theft, maybe. That no-key-needed thing sounded good. Or maybe just plain old theft.

Robbery, even. Because he wasn't afraid of guns. He just had the idea that he might like choosing his own target for a change. And it had already occurred to him that he might need to, because Marky had started eyeing him as soon as he got back to the car, after dragging the girl into the woods. To see, Anthony supposed, whether killing somebody had taken the piss out of him.

Which it hadn't, but not for the reason that Marky thought. It was because Anthony had put a pair of bullets into a tree trunk instead of the girl's head.

Heck, the shape she was in, she probably wouldn't make it out of the woods anyway. And even if she did, they'd be long gone by the time she emerged. She'd seen their faces but not the plate on the Monte; Anthony had muddied it up before they grabbed her, cleaned it off again afterward so as not to get pulled over by some random cop who happened to pass.

Better make sure, Marky had probably been thinking. But he'd also been thinking about something else, Anthony knew: that pulling the trigger on the girl was the he-who. That's what they called it in the juvie home, as in, he who did the deed took the punishment.

Like for instance if a kid there just suddenly snapped and beat another kid nearly to death with a metal chair leg, even if the other kid started it by saying the first kid's mother wasn't really dead. That she'd dumped him in the home, didn't even try to get him off the bogus burglary charge he was here for, 'cause she was sick of him, sick of his stupid face.

That she was a doper and hooker who'd run off with some man and wasn't coming back, and *that's* why she never visited him. He wasn't orphaned, he was abandoned, the soon-to-be-beat-up kid had gone on *nyah-nyah*ing tauntingly at Anthony. That he tried to act so tough, but everyone knew his mom had kept him locked in a–

Quit it, Anthony told himself, yanking his mind back to the important thing: that he who pulled the trigger got prison time, maybe even a needle. He didn't know whether Maine had capital punishment, but whatever they had, he knew he wouldn't like it.

So screw Marky, Anthony thought rebelliously again as he leaned over the backseat. Marky thought he had all the angles figured. But what he didn't know wouldn't hurt him. "Hey, kid," Anthony said, putting his hand out to the little girl as Marky pulled the car up to the house in the woods.

No lights, but they'd left it that way on purpose. Anthony had finally gone down into the cellar and solved the electricity mystery by flipping a half dozen circuit switches and pressing a button marked On. The power in the house, he had gathered from the markings and instructions on the equipment down there, came from solar panels.

In other words, from the sun. He'd seen this before, when he was out with the working stiffs, so it wasn't even a new concept for him. The collection panels were outside somewhere; the cellar room held a wall-mounted control box with digital readouts on it, an exhaust fan that went on when he pressed the On button, and a dozen golf-cart-sized storage batteries.

"Took you long enough," had been Marky's only comment when Anthony got back upstairs. "So where's the coffee?"

As if somehow Anthony was in charge of keeping Marky fed and comfortable. Like he was running this hotel.

But to his surprise Anthony had found he didn't mind that assumption; for one thing, anything he did to keep Marky happy he could also do for himself.

Besides . . . well, he wasn't sure exactly what else he didn't mind. Being in charge of this kind of nuts-and-bolts thing might help him, that was all, somewhere down the road.

"Hey," he repeated now to the kid in the backseat, as Marky got out and strode away. She seemed unharmed by the tincture of opium he'd given her, forcing her to drink the first big dose but putting the rest in a juice box he'd grabbed in the house that they'd taken her from, a few hours earlier.

Marky had pooh-poohed it in his usual sarcastic, you-idiot way, but Anthony remembered from the juvie home how children had to be tricked into taking medicine. Now the kid eyed Anthony's hand mistrustfully but didn't start howling or anything.

And that was good. That was progress. Maybe this whole I'm-in-charge-of-the-kid thing wouldn't be so bad. Keep Marky out of his hair, anyway. Marky hated kids.

Anthony tried touching her on the chin, maybe get her to smile a little. But instead with a lightning-fast move she ducked her head and sank her teeth into Anthony's knuckle.

"Ow! Hey, let go, you little—"

Anthony yanked his hand back, trying to get his finger out of the kid's mouth. But she wouldn't give it up.

"Ow, ow, ow!" Halfway over the seat, he grabbed the straps of her overalls, trying to pull her off him. But the harder he pulled, the harder she bit.

Marky yanked the back door open and the dome light went on. "Hey, what're you, tryin'a' wake up the freakin' dead out here?"

Then he saw what the problem was. "Oh, jeeze. You're lucky she didn't getcha by the balls, you stupid punk. Here, lemme."

Marky reached into the car, conveying by his manner that he knew just how to handle this. Anthony thought right then that the kid was history, and never mind what the guy who hired them might say about it. But instead of making quick work of her as Anthony expected, Marky just grabbed her by the nose, squeezing it.

"Here, ya brat, how d'ya like this, huh? You like this, a little a' your own medicine?"

The kid's eyes widened and her mouth dropped open abruptly. Anthony yanked his finger out and put his bleeding knuckle into his own mouth, tasting licorice-flavored·orange juice. "Jeeze," he mumbled around it.

Marky glared scathingly at him. "You're useless, you know? Freakin' useless." He walked toward the house.

"Now get the kid outta there," he called over his shoulder. "Get her inside, then find us some freakin' food. I'm starvin,' for freak's sake."

Helen woke up hurting. Her head, her jaw. Her throat raw and aching. Everything just hurt so bad.

And scared. Oh, Jesus God so scared. But alive. . . .

Alive. The guy had shot her, held the gun to her head and shot her, and that was the last thing Helen Nevelson remembered.

The only thing, really. Dying. But now . . .

The rest all came back in an awful rush, being at the house, them showing up, getting shoved roughly into the car, and–

Lee. What had they done with her? Helen began to cry, tiny whimpers that hurt worse than anything she'd ever felt before. Curled in a ball on the cold, wet ground, her hands tied before her, she lay in the darkness where she'd fallen and wept for the baby she'd been supposed to safeguard.

And for herself, because it hurt so much. *Please. Please, somebody come and help me.* . . .

But nobody did, and after a long time, when it sank in that no one was going to, she stopped. Cold, it was so cold here . . .

And wet. Mist dripped from the trees, soaking her. Chills rattled through her bones, her teeth chattering hard, muscles spasming with agony. And her head . . .

"Oh," she groaned, shifting slightly to get her weight off her leg, cramped beneath her. A bolt of pain shot cruelly through it, but she sat up anyway.

Listening. Shivering and listening, because they might still be here. Shoving her wrists to her mouth, she held her breath, still wondering if maybe she actually was dead, and this was . . . purgatory?

Or hell. But the sounds from the woods all around her were merely the ones she expected: leaves rustling, droplets pattering from them in a breeze that only made the cold more penetrating.

The low, breathy *hoo-hoodoo!* of an owl came from somewhere in the trees. Far away, a coyote yipped. A loon's maniac laugh on a lake nearby told her that it wasn't very late, yet, despite the darkness—

Suddenly from just above her came a deep, urgent moaning; the leaves rattled sharply and she gasped, rolling into a ball as small as possible and never mind how it hurt. . . .

Ungh, mmungh, ungh . . . Were they there, those guys, sitting up there in a tree just waiting for her to wake up? So they could shoot her again and get it right this time, maybe, like a game? Playing with her for a while, until they killed her for real. . . .

Fear drilled through her until it came to her, finally, where she'd heard that sound before: with her stepfather, on one of his damned nature walks. It was a porcupine up there on that tree branch, talking to itself.

Or maybe even two of them. She'd seen them hanging out together in the branches of a young tree, chewing twig ends and having a grand old gabfest, the slender tree swaying under their weight. She'd been out in the woods with Jody and seen it.

A porky party, Jody would've called it. A laugh that was half a sob forced its way up her throat as she remembered that day;

Jody wasn't like any other fathers she knew of, football or barstool-sitting their only regular interests. He always had to be out somewhere, on a boat or in the woods, herding tourists around or guiding visiting hunters, and if he wasn't doing that he was fiddling with electronic stuff, fixing something or taking it apart just to find out more about it.

Or with her, making her walk for miles on dirt roads so far from the beaten track, she sometimes wondered how even he ever found their way out again. Silent, mostly, especially when she got so mad at him that she wouldn't talk, either. He didn't get it, that it just wasn't the kind of thing she liked, boots and blisters and warm black coffee out of a metal-tasting thermos.

Or he didn't care. Either way, if she wanted to keep peace she had to go, and after a while she'd given in and done it when he asked, stomping around with him, listening to his endless talk about the disgusting things that were edible out here, and which side of the tree moss grew on, and other useless information.

God, how she wished she were out here with Jody right now. He'd know what to do. Sniffling, she sat up again. The pain was still so awful, and her fear of those guys was even worse. She couldn't get over the idea that maybe it was a trick, that any instant one of them would jump out of the dark at her, and then . . .

Boom. It would be all over. As it should have been already. She'd seen the gun's muzzle flash, so why wasn't she . . .

But then she paused, frowning in the darkness. Because wait a minute, if the gun really had been pressed to the side of her head when the guy fired it, how could she have seen that?

Puzzling over this, she brought her tied wrists to her lips, began rubbing at the cloth gag in her mouth with the knot of the rope the guy had used for binding her hands together. A massive boom of pain thudded in her jaw each time it shifted, but she moved it anyway because the gag made her feel she might throw up.

And if she did that, she definitely would die here. *Get the airway open* was practically the first thing Jody had ever said to her about outdoor survival tips and wilderness safety; trust him to get to the worst stuff first. Like out in the woods you were ever going to meet someone who couldn't breathe, she'd thought scornfully.

But now here she was, and wouldn't it be stupid to survive a shooting only to choke on her own upchuck? Except that the more she thought about it the more certain she was that the guy *hadn't* shot her. Rubbing the gag up over her nose and past her eyebrows, she rolled the disgusting thing off the top of her head.

There . . . She sucked a breath in. The air tasted like lake mist, fresh and weedy and with a faint tang of minerals. Then she began using her teeth to work at the knot on her wrists.

The side of her jaw where she'd been punched felt like a tennis ball had been stuffed into her cheek and set on fire in there, and when she'd been working on the knot a while, biting into it and pulling, one of her back teeth on the hurt side fell out, or broke off. Spitting it out, she probed with her tongue and found a raw space that tasted warmly of blood.

Fresh, vigorously pulsing blood . . . She spat again, resisting the renewed urge to throw up and wishing desperately for a drink of water. But it felt better, the tennis ball in there shrinking suddenly to the size of a walnut. A throbbing walnut, but still, and now the knot around her wrists came free, sending twin pulse beats of agony into her hands from where the circulation had been cut off.

Cold, scared, hurting, and alone, Helen sat rocking back and forth and rubbing her hands together for what felt like hours, weeping quietly, lurching in terror at each new sound—a fox's rusty-hinge cry, that loon's last evening giggle, the mutter of distant thunder, and an accompanying flare of lightning overhead.

Waiting: for her fear to back off a little. For her teeth to stop chattering, sending rat-a-tat bolts of fresh anguish through her head every time her poor aching jaws clacked together.

And for somebody to show up and save her. None of which, she began realizing as the thud of her pulse dulled and deepened to a low, ominous drumbeat of despair . . .

None of which was going to happen.

Thinking this, she forced herself up. She could die, here. She would, unless she did something. And . . .

Get away. They might come back.

He hadn't shot her, the guy with the gun hadn't shot her, but what if he changed his mind? Or if the other one, the really mean one, found out that he hadn't?

The thought sent her flailing through the darkness, whippy branches slapping her face until she fell, gasping and trying to hear through the booming pain in her head.

Were they out there? Were they? Was this part of it, just a sick prank, let the girl flounder around for a while and *then* shoot her, pick her off like a wounded bird or a deer?

But when the thundering in her head faded she heard only the loon once more. Louder. Or . . . nearer?

Wretchedly, she struggled up. The thunder she'd heard hadn't sounded again, but it still might, and now the moon was rising higher, shedding a pale glow. That meant once the rain passed it would probably get colder out here tonight, maybe a lot colder.

Freezing, even. It was why you could get in real trouble way up north like this, even in summer, if you didn't have the right gear. But loons meant lakes, and around here lakes meant camps, the small primitive places that people went to in summer to fish, swim, and relax.

And camps, even the simplest ones, meant woodstoves, caches of food, candles and kerosene lamps. Some of them had generators, and a few even had ham radios.

Standing unsteadily, she prayed to hear the loon's lunatic call once more, and did. Hearing it, she looked up at the moon; keeping the white, cold orb in the same position overhead as she walked would help her to avoid going in circles, just as Jody had taught her.

Or so she hoped.

Chapter 7

*Label every shutoff valve
in your cellar* **before** *you have
to stop a big leak in a hurry.*
—Tiptree's Tips

Eat!" **shouted the kid once they got inside the house.**

Anthony was worried that she might not have bathroom skills. Back in the home they'd had kids like that, older ones who should have but either couldn't or wouldn't manage their personal tasks for themselves, and sometimes he'd had to deal with them.

And right now, he wasn't in the mood. But after he'd carried her in—making sure while he did so to keep all his parts well away from her teeth—she demanded at once to use the facilities, then did so very competently and efficiently.

Marky didn't say anything about that, or about how good it was that the lights worked now that Anthony had figured out about running the solar power, or that he had also found and turned on the built-in propane heater set into the living room wall.

All Marky did was complain. "Jeeze, what a dump," he groused irritably, rubbing his hands in front of the flame while waiting for Anthony to do something about dinner.

"Yeah," Anthony said, still shivering. He would have built a fire in the big stone fireplace that was in there, too, flanked by rustic baskets filled with small, splintery sticks on one side of the hearth and big, bark-encrusted log quarters on the other.

But he'd never built a fire before and wasn't sure he knew how. Besides, if he did build one, somebody going by out on the main road might smell smoke and call the fire department or something, to the house where nobody was supposed to be and so why was there a fire going out there?

"Yeah, it's a drag," said Anthony, peering into the kitchen cabinets. They should've brought things to eat, but they hadn't done that, either.

"Buncha yokels," Marky had said after their visit to town. But even Marky must have noticed the eyes of the guy behind the counter in the hardware store. Not yokel eyes, and that wasn't any yokel brain looking out from them, either. Marky gave up pretty fast, too, when the hardware store guy didn't co-operate in talking about the woman in the picture.

After thinking about it, Anthony had concluded that maybe they weren't even supposed to get any information about her. Just show it around, get the word out that they'd been asking;

make her nervous, maybe, for some reason that Anthony didn't
know the whys or wherefores of.

And at the moment didn't care. "Eat, eat . . ." the little girl
chanted as she marched around the kitchen.

"Shut that kid up," Marky ordered from where he gloated
over the gear on the dining table. The goggles for night vision
looked to Anthony like the eyes on monsters in science fiction
movies.

The kid kept yelling. "I mean it, Anthony," said Marky.

Yeah, yeah, Anthony thought. *You mean it; what else is new?*
There was a small telescope-type thing on the table in there, too;
he didn't know what it was, but he didn't like it any more than
he liked the goggles. *A gadget guy,* Marky had said of their employer when Anthony had first begun loading all the items into
the cardboard box, back in New Jersey. *Likes all this stuff.*

But all it had meant to Anthony was loading things into a
box, carrying them, and carrying them again. *Anthony do this and
Anthony do that,* he thought as the kid stomped up to him now and
stood there, so close to him that the toes of her little cowboy
boots nearly touched the toes of his big sneakers.

"Eat!" she demanded. And that probably would shut her up
at least for a while, so he grabbed whatever came first to hand
from the kitchen cabinet. Saltines, jar of applesauce, canned ravioli . . . He hunted for a can opener, then looked down to find the
kid pulling at the tab-top on the can.

Unsuccessfully; she thrust it at him, her gaze expectant.
Opening it, he slopped some into a saucepan and turned the gas
stove on.

"Hey! What's the holdup out there?" Marky yelled.
Anthony guessed he'd found the liquor cabinet, because the next
thing he heard was Marky grumbling to himself about no ice in
this dump.

The ravioli began sizzling. Anthony turned the heat down and stirred the stuff around a little, emptied it onto a plate with a dollop of applesauce and some of the saltines.

"Here," he said, holding the plate out. But the kid just looked at him, like, *What are you, stupid?* Then after a moment she marched over to the kitchenette set, yanked a chair out for herself, and stood there waiting, eyeing him kind of pityingly, he thought.

For a flaring instant he considered dumping the plate on the floor. She'd already bitten him, he had Marky on his case about dinner—and canned ravioli was not going to cut it with Marky, Anthony knew that much for an absolute fact—and now she thought she'd pull the old wait-on-me, I'm-a-princess act?

"Hey!" Marky yelled again from the other room. "What're you, playin' with yourself out there?"

His tone was noticeably uglier this time, as if never mind the ice, he'd been pouring himself doubles of whatever he'd found in the booze department, on the shelf with the fancy glasses and so on. Next, Anthony heard a lamp's chain being yanked over and over.

Just like he's yanking mine, Anthony thought clearly. "Yeah, yeah," he muttered under his breath, meanwhile deciding to humor the kid. Because what the hell, if he'd gone through all that she had today, he'd be doing bloody murder by now, not just nipping people with his teeth.

"Okay," he said, putting the plate on the table and the kid in the chair. She still wasn't high enough so he found a big flat kettle in one of the lower cabinets, set it upside down on the chair, and sat her on that.

She waited patiently while he did this—arms crossed, not quite tapping her booted foot at him—then began forking the ravioli hungrily into her mouth. No milk; kids drank milk, he remembered from the juvie home.

Although back there it was powdered milk inadequately mixed into not-very-cold water, a concoction the mere memory of whose taste threatened to gag him, not to mention its gritty texture. But there was a case of root beer in the pantry, so he opened one of those plus another one for himself, and she swallowed some of it without protest.

When she'd washed down the final ravioli with a gulp of the stuff, she plunked the bottle down in businesslike fashion like a guy drinking beer out of one and began scraping up applesauce, holding the spoon in a clumsy, overhand way but getting it in there all right.

She sure knew how to put away the groceries, he thought with grudging admiration; she might be little, but the kid had stones. Figuring it would take her a while to finish, he turned back to the kitchen cabinets. Canned stuff was all they held, that and dry staples: rice, macaroni, freeze-dried potato mix with what looked in the picture like melted cheese, but it was really only powder in a packet. Something called Instant Breakfast lurked at the rear of the top shelf; it looked like some kind of chocolate drink and the kid might like it.

So mix it with water, maybe. Fill up her little belly, maybe she'd fall asleep soon, although he was not opposed to breaking out the sedative bottle again if that proved necessary. Or even just convenient, because from the sound of things in the living room, Marky was getting drunk in there.

"Shoot," Marky snarled thickly, only that wasn't what he said, exactly. "Shoot, shoot, shoot," he recited, slurring the *sh* sound a little more each time.

Then came the sound of something hitting the wall hard and

shattering against it, plastic pieces clattering to the floor and scattering. A TV remote, maybe; there was a satellite dish in the yard but most likely that service hadn't been left on.

Marky appeared in the kitchen doorway. "What the freak?" he uttered unpleasantly. "Where's the freakin' food?"

He narrowed his eyes at the child still seated at the table, finishing off the saltines. There was an orange smear of ravioli sauce on her face and a root beer dribble stained the front of her overalls. "Hi!" she greeted Marky brightly.

Uh-oh, thought Anthony, whose experience with Marky didn't lead him to believe the kid's chutzpah would impress Marky very much. Or at all, actually.

But Anthony had found a bottle of olive oil, another can of ravioli, some unopened Ritz crackers, and a jar of peanut butter plus a can of Cheez Whiz. While the kid ate, the ravioli had been sizzling in the olive oil on the stove and he'd made cheese-and-peanut-butter snacks.

"Here," he said, thrusting a full plate at Marky, hoping the food would distract him.

"What the shoot is this?" Marky asked sourly, but he took it and went back unsteadily into the living room with it.

Anthony wished the TV worked, because Marky with a snootful was not exactly going to be a joy to be around this evening, Anthony could already tell. Also, he was pretty hungry, himself. But the kid was done eating and starting to get antsy, pounding on the table, her plate, and her empty root beer bottle with the side of her fork.

"Down, down, down," she chanted in time to the clinks and bangs. "I wanna get down, get me *down,* I wanna get *down—*"

"Shaddup in there!" Marky yelled. "What do I hafta do to get a little peace and . . ."

"Quiet," Anthony whispered to the kid, who stopped in mid-chant, her eyes widening. She was, he realized suddenly, scared out of her little mind; that, not some freaky adult fearlessness, was why she was being so good. Holding herself together, waiting for this to end, waiting for things to go back to the way they'd been before.

Waiting to go home. Good luck, Anthony thought, feeling the same way. In fact when you got down to it, he couldn't remember a time when he hadn't felt it.

Maybe there'd never been one. He put his hands around the kid's middle. "I hear you," he said, lifting her, remembering to keep her teeth away from himself. Her booted feet started moving even before they hit the floor.

"Yayyy!" she shouted, running away. *Oh, jeeze,* he thought, *now we're in for it.* But in the doorway she stopped short.

"Ssshh," she whispered, turning back to the kitchen with an elaborate finger to her lips. "Man is sleeping."

Sweeping: the kid way of pronouncing it. "Yeah, he is," said Anthony, moving up beside her.

Peeking into the living room, he saw Marky sprawled on one of the sofas with his empty plate on his lap, a cut crystal glass with an inch of whiskey still in it on the floor beside him.

"Come on," he said, reaching his hand down to the kid. He didn't want her running away from him again, yelling her head off and maybe waking Marky up early.

Couple of hours yet, before Marky needed to be up and doing. "He's taking a nap," Anthony said. "So we should be very quiet."

The kid considered this. Slowly she nodded, then wrapped her small fingers deliberately around his and let him lead her toward a small room off the kitchen. It was set up like an office with a desk, swivel chair, and two-drawer filing cabinet.

But there was a daybed in the corner, a table and a lamp,

and a low bookshelf that mostly held reference books. There were a few kids' books in it, too, though, some even with pictures.

"Lie down," Anthony said, and the kid climbed onto the bed obediently. He handed her a book. "Stay here," he said, turning. But when he got to the doorway a whimper stopped him, and when he turned her eyes implored him, huge and tear-filled.

"Aw, jeeze. What is it now?" He hadn't made her take the boots off, which she probably expected at bedtime. But the night was young and there were a lot of things left to do.

Like Marky, she'd be up again in only a few hours. And that, Anthony hoped, would be the end of this mess. "What do you want?"

She held the book out. "Read. You read."

Christ. "Listen, kid, I don't have time for—"

"Read!" she insisted, and he could tell from her quavering tone that despite her weird, calm self-control so far, she was getting ready to lose it.

Bottom line, the only thing keeping her cooperative was her desire to stop anything worse from happening. Which it could, and not just to her. If she didn't keep quiet, she'd wake Marky. Then Marky might start asking questions, wanting to know for instance how Anthony felt after killing someone for the first time.

On the way here he hadn't asked, because all he'd wanted was to get out of the woods and back to the house without incident. After that he'd been hungry, then drunk, then asleep. But when he got up he would ask, and if Anthony couldn't come up with a good, convincing answer, Marky really would go apeshit.

Anthony bent to the kid. "Okay, I'll read to you. But I'm hungry. You had your supper, right?"

She nodded reluctantly. "Well, see, now I want mine. Look,

I'll be right back, you just lemme go get a buncha crackers an' some root beer for myself."

Her lower lip thrust out mutinously. She was going to start bawling, and Marky would shut her up if Anthony couldn't.

"All right," he gave in. "You can come with me. But *quiet*. Okay? Leave the book here," he instructed as she slid off the bed to follow him. "I mean it, now, we gotta *tiptoe*."

"Quiet," she echoed softly, padding along behind him with exaggerated care. "We be vewy, vewy–"

"Hey!" yelled Marky from the other room, stopping them both in their tracks. "Hey, what the freak? You said the lights worked and now the gee-dee light don't work. The freak's the problem?"

Damn. The lights did work, but one of the lamps was broken and of course Marky would choose that one to fixate on. Yet again came the sound of its chain being pulled repeatedly, and then the crash of the lamp hitting a wall.

Finally came footsteps, Marky stomping angrily through the house. "Hey! Where the freak are you? I'm callin' you here, an' when I call for you, you punk, you better answer me. *Capisce?*"

Yeah, Anthony thought. *I* capisce, *all right.* Marky liked to use the old Italian words he'd learned from the gangster movies. *I* capisce *that you're a nut job and I never should've come here with you at all. But now here I am.*

He looked down at the kid, who stood with one cowboy-booted foot held theatrically up in mid-tiptoe while Marky kept charging around out there. Yelling, and coming closer.

"Hide," Anthony told the kid.

Buried alive . . .

Jacobia crouched in the car's pitch-dark front seat, in the

gravel pit on Stony Road. By now, someone had probably seen that her house was dark, too, but they wouldn't have begun looking for her. A casual passerby would simply believe she hadn't come home yet this evening, and anyone who habitually paid closer attention to her whereabouts was away or busy.

So here she was; screwed, blued, and tattooed, as Sam would've put it. She hunched against the car door with her arms wrapped around her knees. It was cold in here.

Cold and miserable. And silent, except for the creaks and groans of the vehicle as it went on settling.

Collapsing, she amended bitterly as somewhere outside in the night, the distant *whap-whap-whap* of a helicopter sounded; not looking for her, though. Why should it be? No one had missed her.

At least Campbell wasn't still out there, or at any rate she hadn't heard him lately. Probably when the rain started he'd gone back to wherever it was he was staying. Because after all, why be uncomfortable when you're committing murder?

Another murder, she reminded herself bleakly, aware of the faint, constant noises of the car giving in to the weight on it. And that *thrumming* sound . . .

She sat up, little patters of gravel falling to the floor; she'd stopped bothering to brush them off. It *was* a new sound out there now, a deep, rumble-and-crunch sound, faint but definite.

Getting louder. Or . . . nearer? Panting with anxiety, she shoved her fist under the section of windshield that had collapsed in over the steering wheel. The horn, where the hell in this godforsaken vehicle had they put the–?

She found it, heard its muffled bleat. Three long and three short, the universal distress signal–not that the sound of a car horn from under a rock pile wouldn't signal distress clearly enough all by itself. *Hear it, please let whoever it is hear. . . .*

The thrumming sound became a growl. Suddenly she was aware of how bad the air in here had become, sour and evil-tasting.

Her clothes, stinking of fear-sweat, clung wetly to her. She hit the dying horn again, heard its wavering *wonk!*

"Hello? Hello, is anyone out there? Can you hear me?"

No answer. No sound of an engine anymore, either. So what was it, or who? A teenager on an all-terrain vehicle out buzzing around the gravel pit in the dark? Or could it be Ozzie Campbell come back to taunt her again? Taunt her, or . . . worse?

Then came a sliding metallic clank, fast and rhythmic. She recognized it: Someone was trying to dig her out with a shovel.

But it wasn't going to be enough, because the gravel had begun pouring in thick and fast again. Each time whoever it was hit the pile with the shovel, more shifted and came inside.

Please let this get better somehow. But instead things got terrifyingly worse as the digging sounds stopped and the car lurched suddenly backward. *Tow chain, someone's hooked a tow chain to the—*

With a loud, wet, ripping sound the windshield fell in. She dove away as the car's rear end rose abruptly; her neck twisted, her arm and shoulder sliding down into the foot well.

She couldn't breathe; her chin was jammed too hard into her throat. Light strafed the car's interior as it went vertical all at once, her face jammed in between the accelerator and the brake pedal, until with a bone-jarring thud the vehicle slammed down onto its tires and the driver's-side door opened.

Someone grabbed her shirt. Her head hit the steering wheel, the door frame, finally the ground. There was an awful whooping sound from somewhere; her mouth, she realized, sucking in air.

She struggled to her knees, stomach heaving. A voice came from nearby but she couldn't understand it or see whose it was;

after the darkness in the car, the light was violent as a hammer blow. Hideously, she began to weep.

"Jake. Hey, you're okay. We've got you, now, you're out."

Hands gripped her shoulders, lifting her.

Breathe. Breathe. "Jake? Look at me, now, come on."

She looked. Breathe. Again. Disbelievingly. "Wade?"

It was Wade Sorenson holding her tightly, whose strong hands had seized her, dragged her from the death trap she'd blundered into. Over a thick sweatshirt with the Federal Marine anchor logo stenciled in white on the chest, he wore an old denim jacket that smelled of diesel fuel and engine lubricant.

She pressed her face into it. "Wade," she whispered. "She's gone. Lee—and Helen, too—they really are *gone.*"

Chapter 8

If you want fluorescent lightbulbs but don't like the spiral-shaped ones, try "A-shaped" bulbs.
—Tiptree's Tips

Never mind how I found it," Jake told Bob Arnold shakily, three hours after being dug out. She'd been through the story a dozen times already with a grim-faced State Police detective whose chilly manner had unnerved her more than anything else so far.

"I told you, Ozzie Campbell called me and told me about it,

or hinted, anyway, and if you don't believe it, there's nothing else I can say. What I want to know is how you found me."

But the Eastport police chief wasn't having any of her own questions or theories, and especially not the one about Campbell being right outside the buried vehicle.

"Jake," he persisted doubtfully. "You're sure? It wasn't . . ."

She'd had a shower, forcing herself numbly through it; now the familiar old overstuffed chair in the parlor of her own big old house seemed to gather her in. She resisted the urge just to close her eyes for a minute.

"It wasn't what?" she said tiredly. "A hallucination? Like I was hysterical with fear? Or so oxygen-deprived that I–"

"Hey." Wade put a calming hand on her shoulder. "He doesn't mean it like that. There's a lot going on; he just needs to be sure."

Yeah, yeah, she thought resentfully. Bob thought her getting trapped in the car was on account of a dumb notion she'd gotten and hadn't resisted. Which was partly true; in hindsight, she should have called him sooner.

But if Lee *had* been in there . . . "What did Tim Barnard's pals say?" she asked, deliberately changing the subject. Clearly she wasn't getting anywhere with this one.

"Did they know anything? D'you still think one of them took Helen and Lee?" She sipped some of the hot, sweet tea Wade had made.

Not knowing she was missing, he'd hitched a helicopter ride in with a diesel mechanic who needed a part made for the crippled freighter's broken propulsion system. At the machine shop Dana Weatherby ran on the Toll Bridge road, the job would take about an hour once Dana got everything warmed up and running–which the old, retired machinist would, at Wade's personal request. And out on the water the tide was turning, so Wade and the mechanic were going back later tonight.

"No," Bob said, "I don't think the boys did it. They've got good alibis for the whole day. Turns out Jody Pierce didn't just beat up Tim Barnard, he put the fear of God in all of 'em."

At her questioning look he went on, "When they got picked up on Shore Road, they weren't breaking into a camp like we all thought at first. Jody had got 'em a job workin' on it; they was just clearin' stuff out of there so they could start painting."

Bob shook his head regretfully. "And I heard from George and Ellie. They're on their way home."

So Ellie must've been calling from the airport or even from the plane. There was a message on the machine here in the phone alcove, too, the little red light blinking urgently. But Jake had no stomach for listening to it; not yet.

Bob glanced at his wristwatch. "It's a long flight to New York, though, and after that they need to get up here, so . . ."

He shrugged. "They might not be home until tomorrow. In the meantime the state and county guys've been working overtime, news bulletins are out and people've been plasterin' 'em everywhere, and every cop in the U.S. and Canada's been told," Bob said.

He stopped and sighed deeply. "As for Lee and Helen, though, they could still be anywhere. There's not been a single sighting of either one of 'em."

He peered at Jake. "There's something else, too, and you'd better hear it from me."

He got up from the sofa and began pacing the rug unhappily. "State guys've called the feds in. It's gone on way too long for this to be a misunderstanding, Helen maybe going somewhere with Lee and not telling anyone. Or running away on purpose. Not," he added, "that there was ever really any possibility of it."

"And now that her car's been found . . ."

"Right. Now we know she didn't have car trouble, get stuck

somewhere, something like that. Somebody hid her car in the pit."

But not all the way, Jake thought. Just enough so you'd only see it if you were specifically directed to it. "So what's he up to?" she murmured, and both men looked at her.

"It's as if he put the car there on purpose for me to find," she explained, "as if he set it up so I just wouldn't be able to resist crawling in, and then with the backhoe, he—"

Bob met her gaze squarely. He'd already informed her that there was no way of proving that the backhoe had been moved. If it had, it was back in its proper place when he and the rest of her rescuers arrived.

"Jake, that rock slide could have happened by its own self. All those piles are pretty unstable; it's why we tell the kids to stay out."

He frowned, then added, "And that's just one way of looking at it. Another is—and that's what I need to talk to you about— another is that you put her car there, tried hiding it, maybe the slide happened when you were rocking it farther down into the hole."

"What?" She shot up from her chair, spilling tea. "That's crazy, you can't be—"

"Bob," Wade objected, coming back from the phone alcove, "you know better than to think she'd do anything like that."

"Yeah. I do know," he replied. "But the feds won't. Even the state guys're starting to think your behavior's a little hinky."

She stared as he went on. "I mean look at it their way for a minute. All they know about you is, you had Lee before she went missing. You say she went to Helen's but they don't know that. What else happened and when is anyone's guess as far as they are concerned. And," he continued, "now there's this."

He faced her. "You were out looking for Lee. You think this Campbell guy's got something to do with it. I get that, but to them it looks like you keep on showing up in the investigation in ways most people wouldn't."

She kept her mouth shut tight. Because they were right; she was involved. Just not in the way they thought.

Or would believe. "And this time, you messed up a lot of evidence," he continued. "When they start working on that car of Helen's, your fingerprints are going to be in it. Hair and skin cells, blood that might've come from a struggle, only now . . ."

Now they'd think maybe Jake had deliberately obscured those things, to cover her own involvement. "So you'd better get ready for it," said Bob. "Get used to it, that until you're ruled out you're on their persons-of-interest list, just like anyone else."

Or more so. Bob turned to Wade. "And don't you go all righteous on me, either," Bob told him. "You read the papers, see TV. You know the ugly stuff that happens to kids."

And, he didn't have to add, the kind of people who ended up being the culprits. As often as not they were the ones who'd been closest to the child; the ones most trusted.

Bob's voice penetrated again. "As for you," he said, "I'm glad you're all right. And it's a good thing you had a cell phone to get me with is all I've got left to say on the subject."

He headed for the door. She hurried after him. "Bob, wait. I don't get it. What about the phone?"

Because that made no sense, it made *absolutely* no—

"The text message you sent me," he explained impatiently. "Without it you'd still be in the pit, so that was smart of you. But if you'd called earlier, I'd have already had my supper, now, 'stead of my nice, rare burger sittin' on the counter at home, turnin' into a hockey puck."

"Thanks, Bob," said Wade, joining Bob at the door. "We owe you one, for sure."

"No!" she blurted when she was finally able to speak. They

both looked at her, Wade curiously and Bob with an unmistakable, not-quite-hidden "Oh, hell, what is it now?" expression.

"Campbell had called me to hint about where the car was, I told you that," she said.

She rushed on past Bob's here-we-go-again look. "And I got a minute or so out of the phone in the gravel pit, when Ellie called me. But in there, the reception was pretty crappy."

Surrounded by the pit's high sand walls and by a mountain of gravel . . . no wonder the signal had been weak. And then she'd lost the thing.

"But I most certainly did not text-message you from inside the car. I couldn't have, I told you, and even if—"

She took a deep breath. "The only things on that phone that I actually use are the numbers and the redial. I no more know how to text-message somebody on it than I could jump off a building and fly."

Back in the city she might have had some practical reason to acquire such a simple skill. But in Eastport, she'd just never found a reason to.

"Bob, what did the message say?" Wade asked.

Bob looked from Jacobia to Wade and back again. " 'I'm in the gravel pit, come get me, ha ha ha,' " he recited. "And then the one word, 'Jacobia.' "

Wade looked taken aback. "Ha-ha like laughing?"

"Yep. I figured it was a joke at first. Somebody having fun with me, I thought. Rotten sense of humor but hey, you can't get a message like that and not check on it, can you?"

He turned to her again. "But the phone—it does have a text-messaging feature on it, right?"

She nodded. "Sam bought it for me, so naturally it's got all the bells and whistles." And her protests about not knowing how to use most of them could be lies, of course. She couldn't prove they weren't.

"Can't someone trace the message?" Wade asked. "Find out who–?"

"Maybe. Maybe not." Bob shook his head vexedly. "My phone said 'anon,' on the sender line, though, which I know stands for anonymous. So . . ."

So forget it. Campbell was smart, she realized; he'd have figured out something. Abruptly she came to a decision. "Bob, when that federal team gets here, you tell them I will take a polygraph, give fingerprints and hair samples and saliva, anything. Anything they want."

Her voice trembled; she let it. "In fact, I insist. Also you need to tell them I'll answer any question they ask me, no matter how embarrassing, impertinent, or even potentially incriminating, about absolutely anything. Got that?"

Because the idea that she'd done anything to that child, and then done something else to cover it up, was what Bob was talking about. And soon a lot of other people would be saying it, too.

People with badges. "But I want it all as soon as possible. No, wait," she added as he started to answer.

She held up a finger. "I get it that no one believes me. That no one else has any reason to think Campbell is involved in any of this. I get it, and I understand it."

"Jake," Wade began, "no one thinks you–"

She whirled on him. "Why not? Bob's right: I'm the only one who's heard from the guy. Nobody else can back me up on that. So even Bob's got his doubts, and why shouldn't he? Besides," she added, feeling her shoulders sag in defeat, "it's usually the nearest and dearest, isn't it? That's just the way of the world."

She heard her tone turn bitter, didn't care. "Never mind that my name's Jake. That's what I go by, and everyone knows it."

She saw Bob register this point, that the text message had used her full name, Jacobia. Only a few people in the world would do so and she wasn't one of them. But so what? From a cop's point of view, maybe she'd just been trying to confuse things further.

"So let's get it over with and get me ruled out. Jerrilyn, too. And Jody, if they can find him. The stepfather," she finished, putting an acid twist on the final word.

If *you* can find him, she meant, and saw Bob register that, too. "And then when they finish doing everything by the book, when they're done with their rules and procedures and regulations and when they're done grilling me—after all that, *then* maybe we can all get our heads around the crazy idea that just maybe I'm telling the truth about everything that happened. And we can get back to the business of *finding that baby*."

A sob swelled her throat but she would not weep in front of either of them, not now. She absolutely would not.

"Yeah," Bob said quietly into the silence that followed her outburst. "I hear you, Jake. I'll tell them."

He pushed thinning hair off his forehead with a tired hand. "Media's got this now, by the way. Evening news went with it, had a camera truck up here. They even ran a shot of your house."

Great, just what she needed. Although any publicity would be good publicity now, everyone seeing pictures of Helen and Lee and hearing the awful story . . .

Bob looked out the door past the sawhorses and caution tape she'd set up over the front walk—Had it been just hours ago?—to the silent, empty street.

"They've given up for the night," he said. "I saw 'em all pil-

ing into the Motel East. But it won't be long before they show up
again and when they do, the best idea is 'no comment.' Tell them
I said so if they get pushy. Which," he added, "they will."

"Yeah," she agreed, resigned. Whether or not being on the
news would really help Helen and Lee remained to be seen, but
if they stayed missing much longer, Jake and this whole mess
would end up being the top story on the Nancy Grace show.

For a brief unwelcome moment she imagined herself the tar-
get of the cable show host's sharp, skeptical interrogation style.
But I'd do it; at this moment I would literally do anything, she thought as
Wade went with Bob out onto the back porch.

She let them go, hearing Campbell's sly laughter again in her
head, each separate syllable a short, sharp exhalation like a raspy
cough or a dog's bark. She remembered it well, just as she recalled the explosive rumble of the backhoe's engine starting.

Perfectly well; *exactly* like that.

And the question was . . .

She wandered into the kitchen and sank into a chair, staring
at the slow drip-drip of the kitchen faucet and listening to its
plink. She should fix it: screwdriver, pliers, faucet washer.

Slowly she rose and went to fetch the tools, their familiar
shapes in her hands as always a remedy for disordered thoughts.

. . . the question was *why?*

Nobody came out here in the woods at night, not this late in
summer. On the weekend, maybe, if the weather was sunny and
warm, a few Labor Day picnics might end up happening on the
shores of nearby lakes, but even those folks would go home
when the shadows began lengthening.

After dark, it was just too cold. Helen put her hands up in
front of her face to keep the branches she blundered into from

poking her eyes out. She'd tripped over a fallen tree limb, then found a rotten branch from it and carefully put it between her teeth, so when they chattered it didn't hurt quite so much.

She hoped no poison mushrooms had been growing on it. Jody had warned her about them, not only the red death caps and white, innocent-appearing destroying angels but also false chanterelles, as sweetly yellow as real ones, and the little brown mushrooms that looked so harmless but could turn your liver and kidneys to runny mush if you didn't get to a doctor in time.

God, it was dark. She pushed through another thicket, biting her lip to keep from crying out when her bare foot went into a hole. A shower of ice water came down off the leaves every time she moved and her arms stung from shoving them into bramble thickets.

She hauled herself up, pushed the leaves to one side, and found the road suddenly. It must lead to a lake, she realized as a breeze chilled her wet clothes and hair so that she began to shiver uncontrollably again. Sooner or later all the dirt roads out here did.

Or away from one. Overhead, the moon still shone frigidly, a few last tags of cloud blurring its edges as the sky cleared for the night. *The man in the moon,* she always told the little kids she took care of, *is your guy in the sky. He's your buddy, you can tell him your secrets, and if you're very, very good, once in a while he might even answer you.*

So you're never alone, she'd told those little children, but now she knew it had been a lie. In the moonlight, the dirt road looked nearly white. If it didn't go to the lake, it would lead back out toward the tar road, where there were houses, and people who would help her. But she had no idea which way was which.

If you're lost, stay in one place and let people come and find you, Jody always said. You roam around, you turn into a moving target and that's harder to locate. But he'd also told her once that if nobody knows where to look for you, you'd damn well better keep moving, especially if it's cold. You lie down or give up and you can die out here just as easy as falling off a—

But in the midst of this thought something *moved* in the bit of branch she had wedged into her mouth. Convulsively she ejected it, her whole body spasming in disgust; next came everything she had eaten or drunk in, it seemed, the past five years or so.

Gasping, she struggled up from her hands and knees, thinking hard to herself: *Don't freak out.* It was a bug or a grub, that was all. Disgusting, but nothing dangerous. If she got hungry enough, she might find a few of them on purpose and gobble 'em down fast, so she didn't have to think about it.

Hey, if those skinny, silly girls on the reality TV shows could do it . . . Wash 'em down with puddle water; there you've got your protein, calories, and enough fluids to keep you alive for a little while, Jody would've insisted.

Grinning at the look on her face when he said it. But then he would take pity on her, toss her a Slim Jim or maybe a piece of chocolate, let her sip the brandy-laced black coffee he kept hot in his own silver thermos. She'd have killed for some of it now.

But shivering . . . shivering was good. It kept you warm; if you were shaking, you were still in the game. It was when you stopped that you were in real trouble, your body shutting down so that it couldn't even try anymore. Swirling around the old bowl-o-rama, as Jody would've put it. And puddle water . . .

That was a good idea, too; wincing, she dropped to her knees again, felt around with her hands for water. The earlier downpour had been brief but very intense; probably in one of the road ruts there'd be a—

Suddenly from somewhere in the distance came the roar of

an engine, getting louder. Panic seized her; they were coming back. The guy who had nearly killed her had changed his mind; they knew where they'd left her and that she was still alive, and . . .

Hide. Weeping again, she scrambled to the side of the road just as a pair of yellow headlights appeared from around a curve. Pulling wet branches down in front of herself she crouched there, shaking more from fear now than from the awful cold, holding her breath and praying not to be spotted.

It wasn't a car, though. The engine's unmuffled roar said it was an all-terrain vehicle. Out here on the remote dirt roads, local kids raced around on them sometimes at night, whooping and hollering. Tim did it, and his friends, though she had never wanted to go with them. He said she was a pussy for not wanting to. But *was* it just local kids, or . . . ?

As the lights and roaring engine drew nearer, she came to a decision. Those guys wouldn't be on an ATV. "Help," she cried as she staggered from between the branches. "Help me, please. . . ."

But too late. By the time she managed to drag herself onto the road, the small, chunky vehicle with two people on board had gone by, and the engine roar was too loud for them to have heard her calling to them.

She took a few staggering, hopeless steps in the direction they had gone, then stopped. "Please," she whispered. "Please."

But the man in the moon was the only one watching, the only one listening. And now Helen guessed that sometime or another in the recent past, she must not have been good.

Nope. Not very good at all. Because no matter how she wept, begged, bargained, or pleaded, her face turned to the sky . . .

The man in the moon wasn't talking. Or helping; she was all alone out here, her mouth was bleeding again—a lot harder, she realized as she spat out a hot, copious mouthful of fresh blood—and if she didn't get warm soon, in the shape she was in she was probably not going to survive the night. Already, all she really wanted to do was crawl back into the branches and sleep.

The idea sent a needle of fright through her.

Don't you lie down, girl. Don't you do it.

Jody's voice, in that tone he used when he wasn't kidding. Like when she tipped over the kayak because he insisted, saying it was safety training. *I'll drown,* she'd wailed at him, and he'd said *Okay, drown, then. Go ahead. But just try swimming a little while you're drowning, will you?*

Just try. So she had. She wasn't a bad swimmer, actually; they both knew that. And of course in the end she hadn't drowned.

But she was drowning now. *Swim a little,* his voice said, so she did, moving through the night air like a person underwater. The road went both ways; no telling whether the ATV had been heading into the woods or out.

Knowing as if from a distance that she really was badly injured—otherwise why would her mouth still be bleeding this way?—she took a swaying step.

And then another, shakier still, not really aware in the end which direction it was that she had irrevocably chosen.

"You didn't tell me you were worried about Campbell."

Wade set the heavily laden tray on the coffee table in the parlor. She looked down at him from where she teetered on the top step of a stepladder at the center of the room.

"I wasn't. Not then. Just a funny feeling I had, that something wasn't right."

She looked back up at the old brass chandelier overhead. "It wasn't until after you left that Sandy O'Neill called to say Ozzie Campbell was missing."

The most recent message on the machine in the phone alcove had been Sandy again at last, saying there had been developments, Larry Trotta had new plans, and that she should call Sandy back once more as soon as possible.

But when Wade tried he'd been treated to yet another round of telephone tag, either because Sandy was urgently involved in something else, or just because it was late. Jake unscrewed another lightbulb, resisted the strong urge to hurl it against the wall, and tucked it into her sweater pocket instead.

"You could," Wade offered mildly, "try keeping your hands busy with this food."

He waved at the coffee table: eggs, toast, browned slices of Canadian bacon. A tall glass of orange juice glistened. "Mm-hmm," she said. "In a minute."

The lightbulbs weren't energy-efficient. She had a whole bag of the less electricity-wasting kind, and if she took the time to insert them now, life would be a lot more . . . a lot *better* . . .

"Jake," he said kindly. "You do know how ridiculous this is, right?"

"Right," she responded, gulping back tears. She knew. But it was too dark outside now to work on the sidewalk hole, and if she stopped working altogether, then the idle hands that were the devil's tools would just . . . would simply . . .

Wade just stood watching her until without wanting to she gave in and climbed carefully down off the ladder. "It wasn't me, you know. The text message."

"I know. I know it wasn't. Now get over there and eat some of that stuff I just cooked for you. Or I might get the idea you don't appreciate me."

It got a weak laugh out of her, which was why he'd said it. "Yeah, like there's a chance of that."

She sat, and ate a bite of the egg to placate him. Half an hour later, having cleaned her plate, she lay on the sofa with pillows shoved in behind her and an afghan that Ellie had knitted in happier days spread colorfully over her legs.

Another mug of tea, this one with whiskey in it, steamed in her hands. "So that's the story," she finished unhappily.

She'd laid it all out for him: Ozzie Campbell's going AWOL from his usual haunts, the guys at Wadsworth's who'd had a photo of her, Helen and Lee's disappearance, and the doll on the beach, followed by her visit to Hoke Sturdevant's place and her venture into the gravel pit.

"Campbell text-messaged Bob Arnold," she said. "To get me out of there, I'm certain of it. He didn't want to kill me, just scare me, just to show me what he's capable of. Because he wants something and he doesn't think I'll cooperate so he's scaring me to death, to soften me up."

She heard her voice rise, controlled it with an effort. "Sorry. Anyway, that's the story."

Wade nodded. "Tell me again why this guy's not in jail?"

Sighing, she looked around at the comfortable room. Antique rugs, heavy fringed draperies, and velvet upholstery all combined with the crocheted doilies and painted lamps to give the parlor a nineteenth-century feeling. Dark woodwork, varnished floor, and old gold-medallion wallpaper increased the back-in-time atmosphere.

"Well-known businessman with roots in the community," she replied finally. "Like the roots on a rotten tooth, if you ask me." But nobody had. "And a thirty-year-old murder case doesn't exactly spell imminent danger to the public," she added.

She looked up at Wade. "You believe me, right? That Campbell did call me, that he—"

"Of course I do." He'd made tea for himself, too, minus the booze. "I'm just wondering . . . I mean, I've got to assume that just calling you voids his bail. Why he would take the risk of leaving the jurisdiction? Because that—"

"Is even worse," she agreed. "Which is why I just do not see what he could possibly hope to gain by . . ."

"He knows something we don't know," Wade said thought-fully, almost to himself.

"And it's made him desperate," she agreed. "But . . . what?"

He got up. "I don't know, but whatever it is, he's sure gone to a lot of trouble over it. Accomplices, details, timing—that back-hoe couldn't have been planned, but the location must've been. You don't just happen upon a handy gravel pit to stash a car in."

The cell phone lay on the coffee table. "Did you put fresh batteries in that?" he asked.

"Yes. It's working fine, now. And I set the speed-dial up, again, too, Bob Arnold and the state cops. And the Federal Marine number. Not," she went on hastily, "that I'm going to need any of them . . ."

"Uh-huh," Wade said, looking unfooled. He was not the kind of husband who asked for assurances: that for instance she would lock the doors, stay on the couch, and watch an old movie on TV while she waited for news of Helen and Lee.

He knew better. Also, he was about to take a helicopter ride out over the ocean, get himself lowered onto a ship's deck on the same rope ladder they'd hauled him up with hours earlier, then pilot the disabled ship in through the ferocious tides, murderous currents, and treacherous granite ledges with which the local wa-terways were so plentifully furnished. So in the risk-avoidance department, he was no one to talk.

"Wish I could stay," he said, massaging the back of her neck with a big hand. But they both knew he couldn't.

"Me, too." She let her head rest in his palm. "D'you think they'll come anymore tonight? The FBI guys, I mean, to . . ."

Question me. "No," Wade said. "I asked Bob, outside. He said they won't even get here until early tomorrow morning. And it'll take them a little while to get set up and organized, probably."

"Oh." Then: "Wade, tell me the truth. Was it stupid of me, going in there?"

He shrugged. "Don't know. I'd have done it, I can tell you that much. If Lee was in there, hurt, and you just missed saving her life because you waited for Bob to get there and help you . . ."

"I could've called him and not waited."

"There's that. But if you did, and she wasn't there—which as it turned out she wasn't, remember—then you're right about that, too. I mean, there goes your believability with Bob."

She laughed humorlessly. "Which is gone anyway, or nearly. Oh, he's trying to be nice about it," she allowed, "but you know what he really thinks of all this."

Wade nodded slowly. "That you're upset about Campbell's trial. That it's brought it all back to you, all the memories. Of your mom, and . . ."

That her judgment was clouded. Which maybe it was; how could it not be? A pair of earrings gleamed bloodred in her mind's eye briefly and vanished as Wade went to the hall, returning with a small, red-smeared cloth object.

"Here. It was in your car. I put it on the radiator to dry."

Lee's doll . . . Jake smoothed the tangled yarn hair and gingham skirt whose red dye had run until it was pink. The buttons at the centers of the painted eye-triangles had come off, and the cheek circles stained the face a feverish-looking crimson.

"Poor thing," she murmured. "I sure wish you could talk."

Wade stood over her. "Listen, do you think Campbell's still around somewhere, watching all this?"

Watching you, he meant. "I don't know what to think."

The food had helped, and the hot whiskey made her blood feel less like iced sludge. "I know he was in the gravel pit. Where he might be now, though . . ."

She let her voice indicate uncertainty. "I don't know," she repeated, and saw Wade take that for what it was worth.

Torn between going and staying, he knew her too well. But there was a four-hundred-foot container vessel full of cargo and fuel out there in the bay right now, and if it didn't get back under way very efficiently it would be floating around like a bathtub toy, soon.

A large, potentially very destructive bathtub toy . . . "Maybe I should ask a couple of fellows from the marine terminal to come over," he began.

"No!" At her tone his eyebrows arched interestedly. "Please don't," she added more quietly. "I'll be fine," she assured him.

Lonely as hell. And scared; no denying it. But there was an astringent comfort to be had in such solitary anguish, and at the moment it was the only sort of comfort she could tolerate.

"Okay," Wade relented. "Need anything from my shop?" Bigger guns than she already had access to, he meant, from among the ones he had stored under lock and key up there.

"No. I've got the Bisley and the twenty-two in the lockbox in the cellar." Her own guns, which she took care of herself: The .22 was only a target pistol but the Bisley was a .45-caliber six-shot revolver that Wade had given her and taught her to shoot.

She stepped into his embrace. "Which I won't. Need them, that is. You just go on and get the job done out there, and come home."

Safe, she didn't add aloud. Because to anyone who worked out on the water you never even whispered the idea that it might turn out otherwise.

You just didn't. "She'll be okay, Jake," he reassured her. "Both of them will: everyone in town is working on it, and now the feds. . . . They'll find Lee. Helen, too, I know they will, even if . . ."

Even if you're right and Campbell's got her. She swallowed hard, held him another moment, and stepped back.

"Sure. Sure they will," she managed to reply.

In the hall she watched him pull on his windbreaker and grab his duffel bag; waving him out, she waited for him to go down the porch steps, then locked the door behind him. When the knock came a few minutes later she thought he'd forgotten something and returned for it, and hurried to answer.

But it was Bob Arnold, holding a flat, rectangular object in his hand. A VCR tape.

"Hey," she said. "What's—?"

Before she could finish he stepped inside, closing the door and waving the tape at her.

"You need to see this," he said, but what he really meant was that *he* needed her to see it.

She slotted the tape into the VCR in the living room, in the big TV where Wade watched sports, usually. But there was nothing sporting about what this tape showed: gray and grainy, shot from a high angle, like a security tape from a store camera.

Only it wasn't from any store. Instead it had been made out-side Helen Nevelson's house. "Do you recognize either of those two?" Bob asked.

"No." The action was difficult to watch, first as Helen was

muscled roughly into the driveway, her wrists bound. Next Lee was carried out struggling and tossed into a car behind Helen.

Then one drove away in Helen's car while his accomplice took the one the kidnappers had come in. "Where'd you get this?" Jake asked.

The worst part of the tape was the last few moments, Lee's small, white face pressed for an instant to the car window.

Scared. Frantic, even . . .

Bob looked grim. "It was on my desk when I got downtown. I'd just stopped in to check with the state cops on my way home, see if there were any new developments. Which there weren't."

He waved at the TV in disgust. "Look again." He hit the rewind button on the remote.

"Stop," she said. He paused the tape; she squinted hard at the men on it. One was smaller, with dark, curly hair, wearing a leather jacket . . . a cocky-looking guy with a strutting walk.

"Bastard," she whispered. The other one, tall and beak-nosed with a pointy Adam's apple and big ears, wore a jacket with . . .

"What's that?" Bob asked, pointing. "Some kind of a logo?"

"Yes." Excitement seized her; she leaned toward the screen. "It's the logo of the New Jersey Devils. Supposed to be a linked N and J. Plus a stylized pair of horns and forked tail . . ."

"A hockey team," she added; Bob wasn't a sports fan. "Run the tape again, will you? That's right, keep it going until—there. Watch the car, now. When it goes around the circle on its way out you can see . . . oh, my God. Did you get it? Run it back."

"The plate," Bob said, but not happily. He'd seen it before, she realized. "You can almost read the tag number."

He ran it back and forth a few more times, but with the same result. The license plate on the old blue Monte Carlo was unreadable. "You want to see it again?"

She felt her shoulders sag. "No. You're right, it's just not there, and looking at it over and over won't make it be."

If the numbers weren't visible, they weren't. "But why would Jody and Jerrilyn Pierce want to be taping their . . . oh. On account of Tim Barnard?"

Bob nodded. "Jody worked on video gear sometimes. I'll bet he set this camera up. Figured like we did, that even with Tim out of commission his buddies might be trouble."

Jake recalled Jody Pierce's workroom, the electronics in it. "So once Jerrilyn calmed down, she remembered it?"

"Nope. I already asked, she says she never even knew about the camera."

He rolled his head around, trying to work the kinks out of his neck. "I think Jody must've slipped into town while we were all out at the gravel pit, left the tape for me, and vamoosed."

He ejected the tape from the player. "So I couldn't arrest him for assault, not to mention those state boys'd like to talk to him, too. Anyone else, I would not believe it was possible."

Jody sneaking into what Sam would've called the cop shop, he meant, right under everyone's nose. But Wade had gone out hunting with Jody once and when he came back he'd said Jody Pierce was so smooth in the woods, he could've walked right up to a moose and pinned a target on its hide, and the moose wouldn't have noticed.

"So what're you going to do with it? The tape, that is?" she asked.

"Copy it, show it around to everyone. And when the feds get here, maybe they'll be able to enhance it enough to . . ."

Maybe. But probably not. The numbers weren't just blurred, they were absent, as if someone had deliberately smeared them up heavily with mud.

Bob slid the tape into its cardboard holder. "Listen, Jake. I'm sorry about before. I mean, the way I . . ."

"What, that you didn't treat my story like it came on stone tablets? Forget it."

She got up. A few months earlier when Sam was deep in his most recent troubles with the bottle, Bob could have arrested him any number of times. Drunk and disorderly, public nuisance, all sorts of things—But he hadn't. Again and again he'd delivered Sam into the care of his family.

Sometimes he'd even sobered him up first. She thought for a moment. "This tape doesn't get me off the hook, though, does it?"

"Nope. It does not." He zipped his jacket; the earlier rain had dragged a cold front in.

"Just the opposite, 'cause a guy from New Jersey that you think's got a grudge against you either has showed up, just the way you say. Or he hasn't, and you're putting yourself in the middle of this for some reason. Putting a story together."

A story some bits of which now had confirmation, courtesy of a videotape and a guy in it wearing a Devils jacket. Because Campbell was from New Jersey, too, so there was a link.

But it was still a flimsy one. At the door Bob asked, "Jake, have you given any thought to who might be helping this fellow?" He moved his shoulders around in his jacket. "I mean, if Campbell is here and he is doing these things like you say, somebody's got to have shown him around. So have you given any thought to that at all?"

He looked out to the silent street, where one by one all the neighboring houses were going dark. "Somebody local, giving him a place to stay and so on. Or suggesting one. You thought of that?"

"Sure, I have." *When I wasn't busy thinking about getting crushed to death in a buried car,* she added silently. "But I haven't come up with anything. It's hard to imagine anyone from around here doing that knowingly."

"Yeah. Yeah, I guess it is." He stepped outside. "All right, then, but if you get lonesome, later, come on down to the house. Never mind what time it is. Meanwhile, if you get any more calls, you call me up right away on Clarissa's line."

It was the only phone their household answered twenty-four seven. "But if I get yanked back here tonight for anything else," he finished, "there'd better be a burglar coming in the window. You got that?"

"Yes. Thanks, Bob," she said again as he made his way under the maple tree to his car at the end of the blockaded sidewalk.

She waited until he'd driven away, then closed and locked the door and returned to the kitchen. She was spooning in the Maxwell House—if Bella were here now, she'd be grinding fresh beans and rubbing the already sparkling carafe with a suds-laden scrubber—when the telephone rang. Dropping the coffee scoop, her heart clamoring painfully in her chest, she scrambled to answer.

"All right, now," said a voice. "You better freakin' listen to me 'cause I ain't sayin' it twice. Got it?"

Not Campbell this time. Someone else. Her throat closed with fright. "Yes. Are they all right?" she whispered.

"Shut up. You do this thing the way you're supposed to, you won't have to worry about that."

The voice told her where to be and when. Alone, of course. "Don't be early, don't be late. You tell anybody, I'll know. Had a chat with your dad, today? And your kid? That was your husband, I guess, with the cop there, tonight. Both of them gone now."

He paused to let it sink in, that he knew who'd called and who'd been at the house.

And that she was alone. "So, you understand?"

Before she could reply, a shriek of mingled pain and fear erupted from the phone, so terrible it forced a sob from her.

"No! Stop, please don't hurt her—"

"Do. You. Understand?"

"Yes," she replied dully. "I understand."

Click.

Chapter 9

Some wood putties clean up with
water, others with paint thinner.
If yours requires thinner,
buy it when you buy the putty.
—Tiptree's Tips

Anthony Colapietro had eaten an oyster once, on a dare. One of the working guys had taken some kids from the ju-vie home out on a job, to a restaurant out by the airport. To work on the air-conditioning, the job was, and while they were in the cellar the joint's owner came down with a platter of raw oysters.

White fluted paper cups full of the hot sauce that went with them were on the platter, and some lemon slices. "Don't just gulp it," the HVAC guy had told Anthony. "Bite in."

So Anthony had, finding that a raw oyster tasted like what he imagined would happen if he fell facedown on a beach like the ones he'd watched dreamily on TV shows, and let the water roll into his mouth. The rich, somehow primitive-tasting saltiness of it seemed to explode in his head, scouring it from the inside.

He'd laughed in surprise, and the working guy had laughed, too. But Anthony wasn't laughing now, in the doorway of the small room with the empty kid's bed in it.

No kid. Not under the bed, or in the closet . . . Well, he'd told her to hide, hadn't he? But he'd thought she'd do it in the room, not—

"Check the boat," Marky yelled. He'd started yelling it as soon as he hung up from making the call, on the cell given to him to use just for this by the guy who had hired them.

"What boat?" Anthony called back to Marky, playing for time, Marky pacing back and forth in front of the sliding glass door he'd broken earlier. Marky didn't know the kid was missing yet; Anthony had only just now discovered that worrisome fact.

Anthony moved to the hall, peeked out just as Marky pulled the cell phone from his jacket, glowered at it, and answered. He listened briefly, saying, "Yup. Yup. Got it. Okay." Snapping the phone shut, he shoved it back into his pocket.

"Nobody told me anything about a boat," Anthony said.

"Yeah, well, now I'm tellin' you." On the earlier call it had been Marky doing all the talking. It hadn't sounded as if whoever was on the other end gave Marky any argument, either.

Which was, Anthony thought, smart. He hoped whoever it was went on being smart. But all the brilliance in the world wouldn't save this situation if he couldn't find the kid.

"Down by the water, there," Marky said now, "tied up to a freakin' rock. The life jackets and oars, too. We'll be needin' 'em on our voyage."

Marky's mouth twisted viciously on the word, causing Anthony further alarm. "Now? We're going on a boat in the . . . ?"

Dark. "Got a problem with it?" Marky inquired. " 'Cause if you do . . ."

Eyeing Anthony darkly, he fingered his black leather lapel in a suggestive manner. Suggestive of the gun . . . Anthony noticed that the tape player he'd seen on the table earlier was gone, as was the telescope-ish item whose purpose he'd decided not to pursue.

He had enough on his plate. "No problem," he said hastily. "Good idea with the sound effects," he added, hoping to get Marky into a better mood.

The scream, he meant. It had come out of the little tape machine while Marky was on the phone, the first time. Marky grinned. "Yeah, huh? I thought of that. Got my sister's kid to do it, my niece. Kid screams like you're murderin' her."

Then he saw Anthony's expression, which Anthony had not been quick enough to hide. "What, you don't think I got a family like anyone else?" Marky asked insultedly. " 'Course I do; everyone's got a family, you moron."

Anthony changed the subject. "So they're gonna trade for the kid? Money, or–?"

Because that had to be it, didn't it? Some kind of a ransom thing. But Marky's eyes narrowed at this, too.

"Hey, Anthony? Why'n't you mind your own freakin' business? You just go do exactly what the freak I tell you, then you don't have to worry."

"Okay, okay," Anthony replied resentfully. For one thing, he didn't see why he couldn't know as much as Marky, being as Marky was obviously no genius. And for another, he was already worried.

Very worried. But since the kid still wasn't showing up, he might as well go find the boat; probably she was hiding somewhere like he'd told her and would show up when she realized he'd quit looking, that she was no longer the focus of his attention.

On his way out he heard Marky cursing the broken lamp again, shouting obscenities like he could scare it into doing what he wanted. Which was another thing starting to frost Anthony, the amount of cursing Marky seemed to feel it was necessary to do.

Freaking this, freaking that and the other as if he couldn't think of any other words to use, and so had to rely on that one. Anthony wondered if Marky knew how stupid it made him sound.

Anyway, the boat. Waving a flashlight he'd grabbed out of the cardboard box—Marky scowling but not saying anything about it—Anthony spotted a boatlike shape down on the beach. Making his way to it carefully, because the stones here were slippery and he didn't want to break his neck, he found it tied by a rope looped through an iron ring that was bolted into a boulder.

No lock. Just the knot. Seeing that made him wonder again about how different it must be living here, if you could leave a boat sitting around unlocked. All anybody had to do was untie it.

But that turned out not to be quite as easy as he expected. Time and moisture had compressed the sodden rope until it was as solid as concrete. He had a junky little jackknife in his pocket, though, so he used that to saw away at the rope until he felt frayed ends separating.

The boat was a wooden one, pointy-shaped at the front end, broad at the middle, and flat at the rear, with three wooden seats and a pair of oarlocks. The flat rear end must be so you could mount an engine on it if you wanted, Anthony figured. Along with a large coffee can that he supposed uneasily must be for bailing, the oars and life jackets were in a wooden lean-to nearby on the shore.

He figured out how to get the oars into their oarlocks and did it. But they weren't going to be rowing anywhere tonight, he knew right away, no matter how mad Marky decided to get about it. Only a little ways out from the beach, the water moved violently, racing like a river. Shove that boat in there and you were going where the water wanted to go, nowhere else.

But it would be better to let Marky come to that conclusion himself. Anthony hauled the boat around until the pointed end aimed at the waves, then crouched to examine its flat end. Deep grooves on it said an engine had been clamped to it at some time or another, but no engine had been in the lean-to.

He hoped it was locked up somewhere up at the house, and that they would find it. Then without warning he found himself wondering about the girl he hadn't shot, whether or not she was still alive out there in the woods.

He'd felt bad about even leaving her there, but he hadn't had much choice. Shoot her. Or not shoot her. Those had been his choices, and of the two he wasn't sure now which one had really been better. A cold, salty wind off the water cut through these musings, filling his head with the same scoured-clean sensation that the long-ago raw oyster had given him. But he didn't know now what to do with the feeling any more than he had back then.

Suddenly his foot slipped and the next thing he knew, both feet were in the air; landing hard on his back he felt the air get smacked out of him with a thudding whoosh while the side of his head connected painfully with the boulder the wooden boat had been tied to.

"Ugh," he said, mostly just to see if he still could. Cold, wet, and hurting, he lay there for a moment gathering his wits and processing what had happened. Then he tried struggling up, discovering that the slippery seaweed all around him made this difficult, too. But at last he managed to crawl.

Amazingly, nothing felt broken. Through the damp, chilly darkness he heard Marky ranting and raving again, up in the house. Anthony couldn't hear the words, only their tone, like an engine revving uncontrollably higher and higher. It meant that once again, Marky was angry about something.

And that he was nuts. Listening, Anthony felt a needle of fear dig into the place in his mind where the oyster memory had been. From the needle's tip came a shining drop of clarity:

Marky really was crazy. Loony tunes. Wackola. And what they were doing here—the girl, the kid, most of all the idea of going out there on that water in a boat equipped with a pair of wooden oars and a couple of life jackets—all that was crazy, too. And there was nothing Anthony could do about it.

He hoped to hell Marky hadn't started looking for the kid. She couldn't get outside; the chain on the only door she could get to without being seen immediately was too high. So if he was methodical about it he would locate her, Anthony felt certain. If Marky found out she was missing, though . . . well, he'd better get back up there and eliminate that possibility, Anthony decided as he struggled miserably to his knees. But into the midst of this thought came a bright, sharp *crack!*

An instant later, the burning pain in his arm told Anthony that he had been shot.

. . .

"**Come on, it's** only a flesh wound," said Marky.

Anthony wasn't sure how he'd made it back up to the house. His scraped hands suggested that he'd crawled part of the way; a bump on his forehead said he'd fallen at least once.

Marky slapped him hard on the back; the pain nearly made him faint. "See? Hardly even any blood," Marky said cheerfully.

The telescope-type thing was a telescopic sight, Anthony realized now; an eyepiece, like, for a handgun. You held it up to your eye with one hand, the gun with the other.

The living room smelled of fireworks. Anthony guessed Marky must've been trying the thing out.

On Anthony. Or for the hell of it. Or maybe Marky'd shot him by accident, never used the eyepiece at all.

Whatever. "Freakin' bullet went right through you," Marky said. "Lucky you, it'll heal by itself."

Yeah, lucky. Anthony glanced down at the small, purplish hole in his upper arm, like a little mouth. Or an eye, winking slyly at him, sending a wave of nausea through him.

He didn't feel lucky. He didn't think the bullet had gone all the way through, either; if it had, where was the hole that it had come out of?

"Here, lemme tie a bandage around it for you, you'll be fine in no time," said Marky, yanking on a strip of bedsheet he'd torn up for the purpose.

"Right. Now you're a first-aid expert," said Anthony through clenched teeth. He could still leave here. He could get in the car and . . .

"Why'd you have to shoot the gun off, anyway? You already broke the window, why d'you have to—ouch." He took a shuddering breath and held it, as Marky finished tying the bandage, Marky's face gone suddenly as hard as stone.

"Jesus. That hurts," Anthony said, inspecting the strip of cloth. Blood seeped through it already.

"Yeah, it hurts. Big deal, you freakin' baby. Ask me any more of your stupid freakin' questions," Marky said, "I'll make all your pains go away, shoot you through the freakin' head. You got that, you little punk? Right. Through. The head."

On the word *punk,* spit drops flew out of Marky's mouth. He flicked Anthony's skull hard with his fingers.

"Do you? Get it?" He shoved Anthony in his wounded arm.

"Y-yes," Anthony replied, staggering partly from the roaring pain and partly from the blackness that kept threatening to close in over his head. "G-got it."

If he left, Marky would find him. Marky would catch up with him sooner or later, or the guy who'd hired them would. And what happened after that wouldn't be good.

Marky turned away. "Now go get the freakin' kid. We haven't got much time, we're already running late. It's your own fault," he added petulantly. "If you'd left her out where I could get her ready, none of this would've happened."

So that was it. Marky had been searching, and he hadn't been able to find the kid, either. *Hide,* Anthony had told her, to keep her from driving Marky any more crazy than he already was.

And she had. She'd done it real well. But that might've been a mistake, he realized now.

The hiding part. Not the crazy part.

Standing in the kitchen at a few minutes to midnight, Jake tried washing the dirty dishes still sitting in the sink, gave up after only a few cups had been rinsed. *That scream . . .*

For the hundredth time she banished the sound from her head. But it came back; it was in the water running over her hands, the night outside. It was in each breath she dragged in and forced out once more, only to have to do it again.

She threw the sponge down, cranked the faucet off. Without even the dogs here, the house was incredibly silent, their steady breathing—her usual remedy for nighttime worry—now painfully absent. She let herself look at the clock on the kitchen mantel again, found that the minute hand had moved only a fraction since the last time she'd checked.

Four o'clock. You can't be there until . . . Three whole hours, or better yet, three and a half, would have to pass before she could take any useful action. Until then, she had to stay clearheaded, keep her courage up, and most of all, stay silent.

Because if she didn't do this right, if she messed anything up or she broke down and told someone . . . Her cell phone lay on the kitchen table. The urge to pick it up and call someone on it was nearly overwhelming. Without looking at it again she snatched it up, dropped it into her sweater pocket, and left the room, shaky as someone newly recovering from a serious illness.

In the parlor she paused, pressing her fingertips to her lips. Somehow these next few hours must pass, and at the end of them she had to be focused, purposeful, and calm. And although it felt absolutely foolish, irrelevant, and out-of-this-world silly, there was really only one way to accomplish that.

Straightening, she regarded the fireplace mantel. Andirons and a set of fire irons stood on the hearth; these she moved from their places into the hall, setting them on a pad of newspapers to keep the soot off the carpet.

Careful, competent, step-by-step: In this way, she knew, she might manage to keep her mind working competently, too, even though everything in her shrieked insistently—overwhelmingly,

almost—that what she really ought to do was panic, fully and ir-
retrievably.

She clipped a work lamp to the mantel's thin top board and
by its good, strong light examined the repair job she hoped
would rescue her state of mind. Somewhere in the back of her
head that child's scream replayed itself; grimly, she let it, because
right now there wasn't a single thing she could do about it.

Nothing but wait . . . and work. From her toolbox she se-
lected a razor knife and with it began carving away the loose
paint and splinters from in and around the deep, uneven gouge
in the mantel trim; painting the ceiling in here a few weeks earlier, she'd swung the stepladder around clumsily and taken the
ragged chunk out of the old wood.

The fix was much like patching up Hoke Sturdevant's canoe,
only in the case of an architectural repair like this one, it was a
multiple-step job; now, with the flaked paint chips and other
loose material cut out and the ragged gouge trimmed clean with
the razor knife, she spread more newspaper sheets on the hearth
to protect it, then pried open the half-pint tin of architectural
primer with the tip of a flat-headed screwdriver.

Around her, the old house creaked and sighed, shifting and
settling, expanding a little with the warmth of the daytime and
shrinking with the chill of night. She used a cheap, disposable
brush to paint the raw wound in the wood—it was, she reflected,
the first time in almost two centuries that wood had been out
from under a coat of paint—to swab the clear liquid primer on.

Otherwise the repair would look good at first but eventually
it would fall out. And she meant this to be a permanent fix. *Let
dry,* the instructions on the primer tin said.

Nuts to that, she thought, and went upstairs past the clock in
the hall, its white face sneering, for the hair dryer. Back in the
parlor she set the dryer's handle into a coffee can half full of peb-

bles so it wouldn't fall over, then set the can on the top step of the stepladder. Twelve thirty, twelve thirty-five . . .

With the dryer aimed at the repair, she set the heating element to Cool and the power to Low and turned the thing on.

The elegant fireplace trim was original to the house, like the medallions in the door trim and the carved wooden baseboards. As she left the dryer to do its work, she noted distantly that her heart's frantic thudding had eased, even though actually doing the tasks one by one instead of running screaming from them had taken all the restraint she possessed.

Twelve forty-five. One o'clock. Under the rush of lukewarm forced air, the epoxy primer dried swiftly while she spent the interval selecting her clothes—warmer sweater, thick corduroy dungarees, heavy socks, and her good pair of sturdy hiking boots—and putting them on.

At last, she went to the cellar and unlocked the lockbox where she kept the .22 and the Bisley. Through the floorboards held up by massive two-hundred-year-old beams, hand-cut with the ancient bark shreds still hanging from them and the adze marks in them, she heard the hair dryer whirring steadily. In another half hour, she could go on to the next step. Meanwhile, though . . .

The smell of gun oil drifted sweetly from the opened lockbox as she removed the .22, checked to see that it was loaded and in working order, then zipped it into the pocket of the new, warmer sweater and closed the box again. Putting it away behind the one loose brick remaining in the fireplace foundation—she'd rebuilt the rest—she climbed the old, unpainted wooden stairs again and returned to the parlor.

One-thirty. The gouge in the mantel was a deep one, she saw when she examined it again; worse than she'd believed at first. But the hair dryer had dried the primer completely, the old wood paling even in its deepest recesses from dark gold to champagne. Behind her the hall clock tick-tocked the desperate moments away as, opening the second tin, stirring and scooping out some of the thick, gray glop inside and pushing it into the gouge's depths, she reminded herself again that even quite serious harm to an old house—and to other things, she told herself very firmly—could be repaired.

That is, if you were willing to do what it took. The epoxy tin's instructions said to pack the stuff in there as if it were putty, so she did. Two o'clock, and at last two-thirty . . . At a few minutes past three in the morning, Jake tapped the top back onto the tin, washed her hands very thoroughly to get the epoxy stink off them, and left the house.

Her car sat in the driveway; one of the fellows who'd helped get her hauled out of the gravel pit had driven it here. Striding toward it, she gripped her car keys tightly enough to hurt; if this wasn't the dumbest thing she'd ever done in her life, it was close. But she didn't see much choice. If she wanted Lee and Helen back, she would have to go out there to meet with Campbell as he demanded, humor him and at least try to find out what it was he wanted so badly from her.

Around her, Eastport was silent, the moon a small iced disk and the sky around it deep, velvety black, prickling with stars. Crossing the dark driveway she shivered despite the thick clothing she'd pulled on; still August, not even Labor Day yet, but on a clear night like this it was already cold as a twitch's wit, as Sam would've said.

If she went back for a jacket, though, she was so thoroughly nervous about all this that she might not be able to force herself out here again, she realized bleakly. Because for the very first time, though she'd gotten her tools out and applied herself fully to the task of keeping her hands full, her mind clear, and her nerves at least minimally unjangled . . .

It hadn't worked. None of it had; she felt absolutely scared witless and as if she might chicken out at the slightest excuse. So she didn't go back, and she'd managed to get herself nearly to the car when a voice came out of the darkness at her.

"Going somewhere?" Not Ozzie Campbell's voice, and not the one that had been on the phone when the screaming happened. *The screaming, dear God, the–*

Someone else. "Get in the car. Turn the dome light off and start it." As she did so a man's shape slipped into the backseat and pulled the door shut. "Take it easy."

She glanced over her shoulder, felt relief wash over her. It was Jody Pierce, Helen Nevelson's stepfather; she recognized him at once from the portrait she'd seen in the family's living room.

He slid below window level as she backed angrily out of the driveway. "What are you doing here? I could've shot you if–"

A dry laugh came from the backseat. "Yeah, I worried about that. But Wade says you're pretty decent with a gun, so I figured you probably wouldn't."

The .22 was still zipped into her sweater pocket. "Great. I'm flattered."

The Bisley .45 was a lot more powerful; the difference was between sitting a man down, and leaving him there for good. She'd decided against it only because the bigger gun couldn't be hidden as easily on her person, and carrying a purse would've been flat-out stupid. "You didn't answer my question," he said.

No following car was in the rearview mirror, idling on a side street, or lurking by a curb. She crossed Washington Street, the pavement still gleaming from the earlier rain, passed the Mobil station and the Baptist church with its vast flat parking lot shimmering wetly under the backlit marquee: *All Welcome!*

"I'm going to a meeting," she said tightly. "You could say it's a command performance. But you're not invited." She thought a moment. "How'd you know I'd be going anywhere?"

Because he had known; it was why he'd been out there waiting for her. "Did you know a person can eavesdrop on a cordless phone with only a baby monitor?" he asked, seemingly in reply.

At which she felt like smacking the heel of her hand to her forehead: *Fool.* Get a digital phone, Sam always said, not that old analog cordless; anyone who wants to can hear your business.

But she never had; why bother? After all, this was Eastport, where everyone already knew your business. "So you just—?"

"Easy as pie," he confirmed from the backseat. "I sat," he added confidingly, "in your backyard."

Of course; out there where it was dark. But . . . "How did you know you wanted to listen to me at all, though?"

She glanced into the rearview again; still no one following. On every telephone pole flapped a white 8½-by-11-inch flyer with two photographs on it. *MISSING,* shouted the top of the flyer.

"I didn't," he said. "But I was scanning cop radio traffic and your name was getting a lot of attention, for somebody who wasn't directly involved. That said that maybe you were."

He paused. "And anyway, by then I didn't know what else to do," he admitted. *Join the club,* she thought as he went on.

"I know all Helen's passwords, for MySpace and Facebook and so on, on her computer. And there's no plot to run away from home and be a movie star, no chat-room boyfriend who's pretending to be a nineteen-year-old and is really a forty-two-year-old ex-con."

He sounded frustrated. She kept driving, letting him talk.

"So after I made sure of all that, I figured I'd have a look at you. A listen, rather," he amended.

Uphill past the recycling center and the dialysis clinic: no one else on the dark road, more flyers everywhere. "Which," he went on, "is what I think this other guy must be doing, too, the one you're worried about."

Past the clinic came the short, flat causeway to Carlow Island, its thick hemlock shapes marching down to the water; they crossed in a few moments.

"You don't have to be nearby," he said before she could voice her next objection: that if Campbell were outside her house with an eavesdropping device, someone would notice.

Pierce himself had been monitoring from the backyard, so Campbell couldn't have been there. "You get something better than a baby monitor, you can target a phone from anywhere," Pierce continued. "Just key in the phone number. Stuff's expensive, and illegal, too, but your pal's not worried about that, probably."

Yeah. Probably not. Or you, either, she thought at Pierce. "So if you didn't think anyone was watching, why the stealth act just now? Making me turn out the car's dome light and so on?"

"No sense taking unnecessary chances." *Like you're doing,* he didn't add. But she heard it in his voice.

Or maybe it was in her own head. "Yeah, well, if you were listening to me, then you know that I'm supposed to go alone."

"Uh-huh. To the solar house, that big million-dollar baby out on the Jiminy Point road."

So he had heard. For a while, every tradesman in the county had known about the Jiminy Point house; it had been a gold mine for carpenters, plumbers, drywallers, and electricians. But when it was finished, everybody forgot about it, including the owners who now came around only once or twice a summer.

Sitting there empty at the end of a dirt road, as a hideout it was just about perfect. "How come you didn't call the cops?" Pierce asked.

She slowed for the posted thirty-five-mile-per-hour zone through the Passamaquoddy reservation at Pleasant Point. Now was no time to get snared in a speed trap.

"About the call? Why didn't you?" she turned the question around. "Call Bob Arnold, tell him all about—"

(the screaming, please stop the . . .)

Sweat made the steering wheel feel greasy under her hands; she bit her lip and tasted blood. As they crested the next hill, the black-and-white Tribal Police squad car sat motionless under the lights in front of the Pleasant Point municipal building.

"I would've, but if I stick around to explain, Bob Arnold's got to pull me in and book me for assault," Pierce answered. The squad car didn't move as they passed. "He's got no other option, what with that kid still in the hospital."

Pierce laughed humorlessly. "Timmy Barnard. Jeeze, what a complete waste of space on earth. He's lucky traction's all I put him in. Pine box would've been my first choice."

At Route 1 she turned left and crossed the bridge past the Perry Farmer's Union building. "And if I didn't stick around to explain things to Bob," he went on, "you'd just deny it all, say you hadn't had any call from anyone, then go ahead on your own. To meet whoever it is out here."

"You've got that much right." After what she'd been through, it wouldn't be hard convincing Bob that the only place she meant to go anymore tonight was upstairs to bed.

The rank, muddy smell of the river seeped in through the closed car window. A hopeful thought hit her; after all, he'd set up the security camera. "Did you record it? The call?"

"No. Only reason I had the baby monitor was because it was in my truck; I'd fixed it and had it out there already, to bring back to the customer. All the rest of my stuff is in the house, and I didn't want to risk that."

The blacktop curved uphill between thick stands of spruce and hackmatack crowded up close to the edge of the road. "As it was, I nearly got spotted by one of the state boys while I was getting the tape from the camera. Had to hotfoot it."

The scream echoed in her head. "Still, if Campbell wasn't watching the house, how'd he know to call right *after* Bob Arnold and Wade left? How could he, unless he–"

Pierce cut in. "Think about it. Bob uses the radio in his squad car."

He stopped, waiting for her to get it. After a moment she did, unsure at first whether it made her feel better or worse. "Scanner," she said, remembering the one at Hoke Sturdevant's. "Bob's radio calls . . . and the helicopter, ready to take Wade and the mechanic back out to the ship."

"Uh-huh. I'm just guessing, but by covering your phone and local radio traffic a fellow could pretty much keep current on what everyone's doing. Where they are, when they're leaving . . ."

He leaned over the seat to look at her, his expression puzzled. "But what I don't get is–I mean you know who this guy is, right? The guy you're going to meet? And you must've told him before that you *wouldn't* meet with him, so that's why he's making you do it, why he's got to make you, by–"

The scream on the phone had risen to a shriek, then trailed off. She shifted uncomfortably behind the wheel. "I know him. But he's never asked for any meeting before. I have no idea what he wants. So I don't understand any more than you do why–"

"Watch it," he cut in. "It's coming up on the left."

The driveway was a pale cut in the dark undergrowth, barely visible until the car's lights hit it. "We're early."

"Yeah, okay," he said. "Drive on, then, why don't you, you can turn around down at Shore Road or on Gin Cove."

The road straightened along a bluff overlooking the bay. In the distance twinkled the Canadian tourist town of St. Andrews; beyond that lay the hazy glow of St. George and the intermittent strobing of the Cherry Island light, slicing through the night.

"Is Jerrilyn okay?" he asked.

Jake slowed for a family of skunks crossing the road single file, hit the brakes once more as a striped straggler hurried to catch up. Then without warning she felt her determination falter.

"Jerrilyn was okay when I saw her," she said. "Or as okay as she could be. But . . . look, maybe we *should* call Bob Arnold. Or go get him. We could explain the situation to him so he understands, tell him no one can use their phones or radios, either, so—"

Pierce's answering laugh was a short, sharp bark. "That'll work," he replied sarcastically. "How long you think it'll take before one of the good ol' boys breaks radio silence? Calls his wife to let her know he'll be out a while longer?"

When they reached Shore Road she made a U-turn in the deserted intersection, then stopped to let him get into the front seat. Pierce was correct that the cops couldn't function without phones or radios; except for Bob, they couldn't even be summoned without them. And if they went back to get Bob, they'd miss the agreed-upon appointment time with Campbell—she glanced down at her watch—twenty minutes from now.

Not that Bob would do any of this without more cop backup, anyway, because what if it went wrong? If it did, and Bob hadn't told anyone, it would be his job on the line. Meanwhile, though, now that she'd begun having second thoughts, she couldn't stop.

"So I guess we're stuck with this, then," she said, keeping her eyes on the road. "Just the two of us."

"Uh-huh." They drove in silence for a few more miles. But a new idea had occurred to her, not a happy one: that if he'd heard the call the way he said, why hadn't he mentioned the screaming?

"Helen doesn't like me much," he said. "Doesn't like all the outdoor stuff I make her do and learn. Survival stuff, first aid and water safety—she thinks I'm too tough on her."

"Are you?"

He stared straight ahead, watching the road. "Maybe I am. But that's all right. She'll learn later on what I've been trying to make happen."

"Which is?"

"Keep her alive, for one thing. You live around here, get back in the woods or on the water with somebody . . . Did you know that kid Helen was seeing has got a boat?"

Maybe he hadn't heard it. The scream . . . maybe Pierce had been told what Campbell's guy would say on the phone. Time, place . . . but the scream could've been improvised on the spot, not planned, and in that case no one would've mentioned it to Pierce.

Thought about who might be helping? Bob had asked. *Somebody local, giving this guy the lay of the land . . .* On top of that, who better for Campbell to get snooping equipment from than Pierce?

A radio scanner, for instance, and a phone-eavesdropping device. Suddenly it all fit together.

She wished she hadn't told him she had the gun. "Kid's so dumb," he was saying, "I'd be surprised if he could chew gum and keep his eyes focused, but they let him run a boat."

He sighed, turning to her in the dim passenger compartment. "Anyway, things happen. Accidents, all kinds of things. And most girls, they get to be fifteen or so, they'll turn around and tell you to shove it, but Helen hasn't, yet, and I just want her to be able to handle 'em if bad things happen to her, that's all."

It sounded believable, Jake had to admit to herself. But now that one of the bad things had happened to Helen, Pierce didn't seem disturbed enough. And the scream on the phone, so horrific it had driven her out here to meet Campbell . . .

Pierce still wasn't saying anything about it. "So what's his story, anyway?" Pierce asked. "This guy doing all this?"

In as few words as possible, she told him. Maybe Pierce knew all about Campbell already. Maybe he'd heard the whole story—Jake's mother, her long-ago murder, and the upcoming trial—from Campbell himself.

But if he had, she didn't want him knowing that she was onto him. "All I can think of is that something in my victim's impact statement set him off," she finished. "But I don't know why. The only detail in it isn't the kind of thing that could hurt him, things like what my mom wore that night. Her hair ribbon, black velvet. Her dress: flowered, silky material. And . . ."

The ruby earrings, bloodred in the firelight. She let her voice trail off as the old, familiar lump invaded her throat. "I don't see why he'd care," she finished. "It doesn't make sense."

She slowed the car, drove it onto the sandy shoulder. She could pull the .22, but if his intentions were bad he'd probably try to go for it; he was bigger than she was, after all, and he'd already put a local kid in the hospital with his fists.

On the other hand . . . oh, the heck with it. If he got grabby it was his funeral. She aimed the .22 at him. "Get out."

His eyes widened; he hadn't been watching for this. Women like her didn't point guns at people.

"Sorry. I had to let you in the car when I thought he was watching. But he isn't, you've convinced me. So if you're on the level, I apologize. If not–"

His lips pursed ruefully. "Listen, this having a gun aimed at me is kind of . . ."

Startling; that was the idea. Be forceful, or be forced; she wasn't sure if she'd learned it first as a financial whiz in an office in Manhattan, or years earlier in a small candlelit room in a house in Greenwich Village, seeing her mother strangled.

Either way, it seemed to be working now. "I can't trust you. So I need to unload you." If she could get him out of the car she could drive in ahead of him, get to the house alone.

"Okay. I understand," he said. "But here's the thing: Either you shoot me now, or I'm going in. I'm here to get Helen back and I mean to do that, with you or without you."

He looked at her. "Your choice. But make it snappy, because we haven't got all night." He glanced down at his own watch. "In fact, we've only got about fifteen minutes now. And . . ."

"What?" she demanded.

"Well," Pierce replied, "first of all, when I get Helen out of there I'm going to give her that new iPod she's been fussing at me for. Already ordered it, rush-express, so it ought to get here soon . . ."

He spoke earnestly. "I mean a girl deserves some foolishness once in a while. Don't you think? And not for nothing," he added, "but if you can't trust me you're better off keeping me in sight. No offense, but your only other option really is to shoot me, and I just don't think you're going to. You're not the type."

Nice try, she thought, though the part about the iPod had been very persuasive. "You have no idea what type I am. And when you find out, it might be too late. Now, why don't you–"

"Nice job on Hoke's deck step," he said suddenly. "Canoe, too. Though at the time I thought you'd never leave."

That closed hallway door at Hoke's, she recalled. The old man had said it was to hide his sloppy housekeeping, but now she realized: He'd been hiding Pierce. And *that* meant . . .

If Hoke had needed help, he could've told Jake so. While she and the old man were out by the canoe, or while they'd worked on the deck repair together.

And he hadn't. "I could've ambushed you in your driveway," Pierce added, "if I wanted."

But by now she'd made her decision: He could have taken the gun from her, too. She lowered it.

"Christ." He let a breath out, rubbed his palms on his pants legs. "Never had one pointed right at my head like that, before. Just out of curiosity, what convinced you?"

She told him. "Hoke trusted you. And . . . the iPod. Because if it were my son, Sam, that'd been taken, that's what I'd be . . ."

Thinking. Praying. That I'd get the chance to surprise him with some silly gift. Pierce nodded solemnly. "Yeah. What you'll do for them, huh?"

"Anything," she agreed, noticing for the first time that he was dressed in fall hunting camouflage, green and brown mottled canvas jacket and pants, sturdy black lace-up boots on his feet. Slowly he produced his own weapon, a Glock 9mm, small and pricey.

She'd seen them at gun shows, recalled now the good rifles in the gun case at his house. "Semiauto," she said, unable to keep the appreciation from her voice.

She let the car roll back onto the road; soon the pale dirt driveway to the Jiminy Point house showed once more between the evergreens. He tucked the gun away. "Beats a twenty-two pistol for firepower, with not much more size and weight. And if you don't mind my saying so, I've got a better idea than you do, too," he added.

As the car pulled to a stop he shoved the car door open and got out. *Smart-ass,* she thought, absorbing the mine's-bigger-than-yours jab. But then she heard the rest of what he'd said.

"Hey." She rolled the window down. It hadn't occurred to her that *he* might go in without *her.*

"Nose the car into the trees," he called back softly. "You leave it in the road, it'll be pretty obvious to anyone who–"

Headlights appeared behind them. Hastily she got the car in gear, eased it forward, and doused the lights. A truck roared by without slowing, its muffler clanking as it disappeared uphill.

When it was gone, Pierce leaned in. "Here. You carry this." He shoved a flashlight at her. "Are you okay?"

"No," she said furiously, pulling off her seat belt. "And this wasn't the plan. I'm supposed to see Campbell, to get him to let the girls go. I don't want you to . . ."

Screw things up. Brief chuckle from Pierce; what she wanted or didn't want wasn't entering into his calculations at all.

Never had. "They'll see your light, focus on that, and with any luck not think to look for anyone else," he said.

The two guys from the security tape, he meant, who'd taken Helen and Lee. Assuming that was who they'd be confronting, the operative phrase here being "with any luck."

"By the time you get spotted, I'll have gotten behind them," he went on. "I'll drop one of them real quiet-like, and . . ."

His tone chilled down to the bone-cracking temperature of a February night. "We'll see about the other one," he finished.

Wrong, she thought as he turned and walked away from her. This was all going wrong; she never should've let him . . .

Just as he was about to disappear among the trees, he turned back. "Jake. I know what he wants."

This bossy little prick thought he knew it all, didn't he? Her fists clenched. Even if she could trust him, even if he had as good a reason to be out here as she did, he was still way more trouble than he was . . .

"What who wants, Campbell? That's ridiculous, how could you possibly know what he—"

"You. Think about it. All he wants is you."

He vanished into the woods.

The dirt driveway, Pierce informed her as they started down it, was about two miles long; he'd been here before, to put in an intercom system when the Jiminy Point house was being built.

"But the path through the woods is better for us," he said, striding into what looked like a puckerbrush thicket but was in fact two massive cedars growing up out of a single root.

They'd gone a hundred yards in silence when he stopped and pulled a flask from his pocket. "Snort?" he offered. "We're still a few minutes ahead of ourselves."

I am, she thought clearly, *out here in the woods late at night with a guy I don't know, getting ready to sneak up on some other guys who I definitely don't.*

And ambush them. Which had emphatically not been part of her plan. . . . The stuff in the flask was Allen's; swallowing some, she made a face.

"Coffee brandy, cures what ails you," he said. "Did you know that of the ten best-selling alcoholic beverages in the state of Maine, Allen's is four of 'em?"

He had another gulp, offered it to her again. She tipped it; in her opinion, the taste was right up there with the smell of burning rubber, but the warmth it produced was welcome.

"'Cause there's four different bottle sizes is why. You gotta watch it, though," he added. "Calories. Some folks call the stuff 'Fat Ass in a Glass.'"

It was unbelievably dark in these woods. "You're just full of fascinating information, aren't you? But don't you think we should be quiet?" She found a big rock by feeling around for it, lowered herself onto it.

"On account of them?" he answered. "Don't worry, they're not out here, yet. I'd hear 'em. They're up at the house; neither one of 'em's any good at rompin' around in the forest."

"You sound awfully sure of things," she said. *Not the least of them being yourself,* she added silently.

"Saw 'em on the tape," Pierce explained. "Before I slipped in an' dropped it on Bob Arnold's desk while all the lawmen"–he gave the word a sardonic twist–"were over at the Waco Diner for coffee, I had a look at it."

He drank from the flask again. "That camp on the Shore Road I got the boys jobs cleanin' out an' paintin's got a VCR in it. That's how I know both our pals, here, are dumber'n flounder."

He held out the flask; this time she shook her head. For one thing, after a couple of swigs, Allen's brandy had improved; now it just tasted like old coffee grounds soaked in cough syrup. Besides, warm and energized was one thing; drunk and stupid was another.

"In a minute you'll get on the driveway with that lamp," he said. "Start walking. I'll stay on the path, get ahead of you."

She got to her feet. "What'd you mean before, about Campbell wanting me?"

He shrugged. "Obvious, isn't it? I mean, why didn't this guy just offer to make some kind of a trade on the phone with you?

Say what he wants?" He tucked the flask away. "Whatever it is, he knows you'd do it. It's why he picked 'em, the little girl Helen was taking care of, especially. He's done his homework on you."

They began moving forward together. "That's why I think the deal was just the carrot, you see. And the scream . . ."

So he had heard that, too. Faint light showed ahead.

". . . the scream was the stick." At the gleam from between the trees he put out a silencing hand, stopping her sharply, and in the next instant he was gone, slipping away into the forest.

The light went out.

Chapter 10

*When replacing a broken lamp
switch, replace the cord
and plug, too.*
—Tiptree's Tips

Helen Nevelson stumbled like a sleepwalker through the dark, cold night, barely knowing what she was doing, much less in what direction she was managing to keep going.

Her head hurt and her mouth was still agonizing. Scary, too; bleeding. Every so often it filled with hot, coppery blood, and she opened it just barely enough to spit. Anything more made her injured head feel as if it might split wide open, while her safe, cheerful home, her family, and her warm, safe bed all seemed like things that might have existed, once, on some other planet in the distant past.

Or in a dream. Here, though, all she knew was that if she gave in and lay down on the cold ground as she desperately longed to do, she would die.

Move. Walk. Don't give up.

Never. Helen kept reciting this to herself as well as she could, which was not very well. Somebody kept hitting her in the side of the head with an enormous hammer; somebody else pushed her down, giggling each time she struggled up again.

After a long while, through a window of lucidity she slammed shut in a reflex bolt of terror almost immediately, she knew that the madly giggling person was herself. *Losing it, I'm starting to* . . . Unwilling, or possibly by this time unable, to admit that she already had.

Suddenly, lights snapped on all around her, blinding her and making her cry out in terror. Huge, yellowish lights like the ones at an airport or jail yard flared mercilessly from . . . She put her hands to her face, peered squintingly through her fingers—

A cabin. Small and shaped like a child's drawing of a house, two square windows and a door, pointy roof and crooked chimney; she moaned at the sight of it. Scrambling toward it, falling and getting up again, she struggled on bare, wounded feet that stuck bloodily to the stones in the dirt road.

"Help," she whispered, because the men who'd done this to her might still be out here somewhere. "Help, please."

Staggering onto the deck that stuck out plain and unpainted from the plain wooden front door, she fell once more, caught the doorknob in one hand and gripped it. "Please . . ."

But it was locked, and now she realized that no one was here.

The yard lights had been set up to go on automatically, triggered by motion detectors. They illuminated a small shed, a rack with a pair of kayaks chained to it, and a white stone path leading down alongside the locked cabin to a dock.

The locked cabin . . . Helen began to cry. With her hand still clutching the unmoving doorknob she felt what little fight she had left go streaming out of her; it wasn't fair, after all she'd just been through, it wasn't fair at all.

When she was done crying, though, mostly because it hurt too much, the door still didn't open. *It doesn't care,* she thought in her wretchedness, gazing around wildly for help but not seeing any as she contemplated this dreadful notion. *The door doesn't care, the trees don't care, the sky doesn't care, the water down there at the end of the dock doesn't care. . . .*

Water, she thought. She could cry until her eyes bled and it wouldn't do her any good. But–

Water . . . and kayaks. Probably they were locked, too. Anyone who put so much effort into security lights would probably lock the boats. It was why they'd been chained there, instead of just left stacked down by the dock.

Slapping her other hand around the first one on the doorknob, she hauled herself up. Just standing took most of what she could muster, and the bright glare from the yard lights made her head feel like it was being attacked by a bag of rocks.

But the cabin didn't only have a door. It had windows, and windows were made of glass. Stepping off the deck, she lost her balance and fell hard into a pile of rough, stripped tree bark, wood splinters, and a few old logs too knotty and gnarly to be usable for firewood.

When her head hit one of the logs, she saw stars. But then she saw something else: Next to them stood a chopping block, a broad stump where the cabin owner propped good logs on end so he could split them, either by swinging an axe down hard if the log wasn't too big, or by driving a splitting wedge and sledge-hammer into it.

On the block lay a splitting wedge, a heavy length of cast iron forged into a blade shape at the business end and a broad, flattish shape at the other, to slam the hammer down onto. The part of her mouth that could still move twisted into a painful smile at the sight of it.

The thought she'd had earlier about water and boats still flit-ted around in her head. But she didn't want to look at it too clearly now because of what the idea implied:

Darkness, cold, and the possibility of drowning. But never mind; all that could come later. Tentatively, she reached up and grasped the metallic solidness of the cast-iron splitting wedge.

Then she did smile, feeling but not paying any attention to the fresh gout of blood slipping over her lower lip and down her chin as she hefted the simple tool.

Heavy, but not too heavy. Even in her weakened condition she could probably manage it. Clambering up again, she stag-gered toward the cabin with the wedge cradled in her hands, holding it out in front of her like an offering.

Windows, she thought, stumbling onto the white pebbled path that ran along the cabin's side. The cabin was locked but it had windows. Made of—

Standing on the deck with her feet planted apart she hurled the splitting wedge: closing her eyes, swinging her body around, and remembering to let go at the very last possible instant before the big plate-glass window overlooking the lake exploded.

Lee, Helen thought as it shattered. She was still shivering hard, her teeth chattering hideously, her breath coming in short, uncontrollable gasps. *I've got to stay alive. And I've got to get out of here, find Jody, and tell him about the guys who took Lee.*

He'd know what to do. It was why she'd stuck with him for so long, going on outings with him long after other girls would've quit; because even when she was mad at him, she knew in her bones the one thing that made it all worthwhile:

He loved her. He really did. If he hadn't, he'd never have taken so much backtalk from her, or taught her to swim, or sent her out alone in the canoe in a windstorm, the black, terrifying waves as solid as buildings looming higher than her head.

So that nowadays, she wouldn't deliberately go out in a wind like that. But if she got caught in one, at least she wouldn't do something stupid just on account of her panic. Thinking this, she climbed through the cabin's window frame, trying to avoid gashing herself on the glass daggers at the edges of it and mostly succeeding.

Inside the cabin it was pitch dark, and the next thing she did was fall over a low table. As she pitched forward her hand slammed down onto something hard, solid and plastic-feeling . . .

A flashlight. She wrapped her fingers around it. Dear God, thank you, it was a—

Nothing. Shuddering, she snapped the switch back and forth frantically but nothing happened. Cold, she was so cold, and the batteries in the flashlight were probably cold, too.

So maybe they'd gone dead. She probably would've sobbed over it, but she felt pretty sure that, as Jody would say, she was running on fumes now. Too hurt, too cold, too scared . . .

She was conscious and able to move. But a calm, unkind voice inside her head remarked coolly that she wouldn't be for long. No one was going to help her, and she could still die here, easy as falling off a log.

"No," she whimpered, crouched with the useless flashlight in her hands, but the sound of her own voice scared her pretty badly, too. It sounded like the girls in the horror movies she'd seen.

And those girls never made it out alive. "No," she repeated, more strongly this time.

Because she wasn't one of them . . . was she? Slowly and very carefully, because it was so dark in here that she could slam her head into something, Helen began to crawl.

She wasn't like the girls in the scary movies . . . but they never thought they were either, did they? Not until it was too late. No one ever believed she was one until—

No. Just shut up, now. Just stop telling that silly stuff to yourself.

Trembling, she leaned on one arm and waved the other out blindly. Wall . . . chair . . . table legs . . . a wooden post. It was how a lot of these lakeside cabins were built, one big room with posts holding the beams up, all pretty much the same layout.

At last she came up against the woodstove, its cool, gritty shape unmistakable under her fingers. Rising into a crouch, she found the stove's door and opened it, and felt around inside. And then she really did begin to weep, never mind how much it hurt, because someone had laid a fire in there, she could feel it, the newspapers and kindling and the split-log pieces set crosswise on top. So next time whoever it was visited the cabin, all he had to do was strike a match.

But she didn't have one. Or a lighter. Sobbing, she let her body fall sideways against the wooden post, lowering her swollen face into one hand, flailing out blindly with the other, because it was too much. It was just . . .

Her hand struck the flashlight she'd abandoned. It rolled across the floor, its plastic case striking the post with a sharp *smack!* The flashlight went on, sending a bright, unwavering beam of pale yellow across the cabin's linoleum floor.

• • •

Here goes nothing. Entirely against her better judgment, Jake pushed through a stand of poplar and low huckleberry bushes to the driveway, snapped the flashlight on, and began walking.

"Jody." She said it softly. No response. But that was to be expected; by now he should be far out ahead of her.

Dark, quiet. It might work, what Pierce had planned. No meeting; instead getting behind the men unseen, disabling one or both of them, getting the girls out. Assuming they were here . . .

She still wished Pierce hadn't come at all. Her own idea seemed better and safer. But there wasn't much she could do about it now; making her way through the pitch darkness, she kept the flashlight up high so the men who had Helen and Lee would see it and think Jake was following their instructions.

Huge trees loomed around her, smelling of rain-soaked pines. Living things, each grown from a single seed long ago . . .

Without warning, the memories came once more: her mother's hair, tied back by a velvet ribbon, her dress softly perfumed and silky-feeling, patterned with flowers. The two ruby earrings, red as heart's blood, just out of Jake's childish reach . . .

But no. That was muzzle flash, ahead in the trees.

And the flat *pop-pop* of a pair of gunshots.

Helen found the matches in a box by the propane cookstove, in the kitchen area by the pitcher pump. Next to the pump was a jug of store-bought spring water; if you wanted to get sick, Jody always said, just drink water out of a beaver-inhabited lake. It was how you got what the old-timers called beaver fever, which would either kill you or make you wish you were dead.

She struck one of the stick matches on the side of the wood-stove, stuck it inside. The paper flared up at once, igniting the pale yellow strips of kindling wood and sending flames roaring up the metal flue, which began radiating heat almost immediately.   .

Still shivering, she scuttled back to crouch by the stove, feeling its blazing warmth make her muscles start unclenching a little and her clothes begin drying. On the floor by the stove, a knife lay where somebody had dropped it; examining the thing, she accidentally pressed the button on the grooved ebony handle and the blade sprang out, wickedly long and sharp.

It glittered at her redly and somehow suggestively by the light of the open stove door, but she had no immediate need for it. Closing the blade she put the knife absently aside and turned her mind to more pressing matters. *Drink something hot,* she could practically hear Jody saying, so as soon as she was able to pry herself away from the stove's blessed heat, she put a kettle on the propane burner in the kitchen area, and set about figuring out how to light it with another match. Rummaging further, she found a container of tea bags, and some saltines in a tin box.

I could stay here, she thought as she dipped a saltine into hot tea, then placed a soggy piece of it carefully into her sore mouth. It hurt horribly, but the cracker piece went down.

No one would blame me. I could stay here until morning, she thought, breaking another cracker into sections.

Because for one thing, there was really no good way to get out. Walking wouldn't work; she didn't even know which direction the paved road lay in. And although she hadn't tried searching for one yet, she was sure the shed she'd seen outside wasn't big enough for an ATV or other motorized vehicle.

She put the rest of the second cracker into her mouth and winced as a broiler-hot bolt of anguish erupted from one of her broken teeth. Outside, the yard lights had gone off. So even if those guys were still lurking around out there, no light would alert them. A whiff of wood smoke . . . well, she wasn't sure they'd figure out the reason behind that. Neither one of them seemed very outdoorsy.

So she was probably safe here. On the other hand . . .

On the other hand, those bastards have still got Lee.

Thinking this, she got up and lit some candles she found in another tin box in the kitchen area, placing them around so she could get a good view of the whole cabin.

Two dark blue overstuffed chairs and a purple velveteen sofa filled one corner of the pine-paneled room. A square wooden table with a red-checked plastic tablecloth stood in the other corner, four wooden chairs pulled up to it. A bookcase held board games, a pair of binoculars, and old copies of *Reader's Digest*.

The curtains were red-checked gingham, except for the drapes in front of the big broken plate glass window, which were made of more dark blue, very heavy and fortunately breeze-proof velveteen material. Helen pulled one drapery panel back a little.

Dark. Thick, black, impenetrable dark, except for—

There. Across the lake, a red beacon winked on and off. The radio tower, she realized, the big one on the community college campus. . . . Suddenly, she knew where she must be. Straight across the lake from here was Roughy Hill Road, which led to Route 1 and civilization.

Nothing in these woods was really very far from help, Jody said. It was just that you could get all turned around so easily, lost beyond hope of finding yourself when you were really just a few hundred yards—or even less—from a main road.

But now that she knew the right direction . . . sorrowfully, she sank into one of the wooden chairs at the table. Now that she did know, she had little excuse for staying. Because those kayaks were there, and unless she missed her guess the key for them was probably on a hook in that shed, with the life jackets.

That's where Jody would've put them. It was, she realized to her surprise, where she would've decided to store them, too. Much to her amazement now, she'd actually learned a few things while tagging along behind her stepfather, whining and com- plaining.

Even more amazing to her was that she seemed to have come to an unwelcome decision. Hurt, scared, lost, cold—but she wasn't any of those things anymore. Or anyway not so much. And the road was right over there, straight out across that lake.

A mile or so, maybe a little more. She would need warmer clothes. . . . Moving gingerly around the cabin she found a chest of drawers containing men's sweaters, long underwear, and a few old sweatshirts.

Pulling them on hurt like hell, but the next thing she knew she was wearing a bunch of them. She found the switchblade she'd put aside and slipped it into a sweater pocket, just in case.

Next, *Eat something more,* a voice in her head commanded. And for the first time it wasn't Jody's. It was her own. *Do the right thing, the smart thing,* she instructed herself, whether she felt like it or not, so that with any luck she could end up at home, warm and safe instead of alone out here bleeding and crying.

Her own voice . . . Helen might have spent a little more time wondering at this, but instead located chocolate pieces, fig bars, and a can of syrupy fruit with a pull top, in one of the kitchen cabinets. She didn't feel hungry, but she put them into her mouth one after another nevertheless, mushing them around in there with sips of warm tea.

After that, she found a switch that kept the yard lights on, bashed the lock off the shed with the splitting wedge—this took a long time, and it hurt—and got the kayaks unlocked. She found herself a life jacket that fit, put it on, and pulled the straps tight around her chest.

Finally she dragged one of the kayaks to the dock and was about to push it in when the first nauseating wave of dizziness washed over her. Dropping to her knees, she splashed lake water onto her face. But that brought on chills and when she opened her eyes again, her mouth was bleeding onto the dock's pale wood.

Suddenly the blinking red light on the other side of the lake looked very far away, the sky unimaginably dark and uncaring overhead and the water so cold.

But she could do it. She could. And she had to. There were houses on the road over there, and the people in them would help her.

And . . . *Forget about Jody for a minute,* she told herself, this new thought more amazing to her than any before. *Jody's who you want. But right now, he's not who you need.* When she got back to Eastport, she decided very firmly for herself, it was Bob Arnold she needed to find, to tell him who the men who'd taken Lee away were: what they looked like, the kind of car they drove, and . . .

And where they were going. The memory popped suddenly into her head as if triggered by the splash of cold lake water. A big cliff hanging way out over the water . . .

Bridge to nowhere, the other guy had replied, not caring if she heard. They'd planned for her to be dead. But—

I know that place, she thought. The scariest, most dangerous spot on the island . . . *That's where they're going.* Fresh urgency seized her; grimly she shoved the kayak into the water.

If she just kept her eyes on the red beacon and paddled, she would be all right. Not comfortable; not for a while, yet. But . . .

Eyes on the prize, Jody would've told her. But somehow what Jody would say wasn't important anymore.

Which, she understood now, was what he had wanted all along. *Because I can say it. I can say it myself.*

Grabbing the paddle she swung herself off the dock and into the kayak's seat, stuck the paddle's blade into the water—

Her head jerked back suddenly, very hard. Such anguish as she had never before experienced nor even imagined shot through her jaw. Something yanked her head around and up.

A man crouched on the dock. Pale hair, squinty eyes, and a walrus mustache were all she could see of him. He had a battery lantern in one hand and her long braid wrapped around the other hand like a dog's leash.

"What the hell d'you think you're doing?" he demanded, and Helen tried to answer. She opened her mouth, sucked in a breath, and formed words, ready and eager to speak them. But then . . . she couldn't help it, she tried, but she really couldn't— her jaw locked up with a horrible, agonizing *crunch!* and she passed out.

Afterward, when rough hands had come out of the darkness to seize Jake and snatch the little gun and the flashlight away from her, she understood why Pierce hadn't mentioned the screaming on the phone until he had to do it, to make his point.

It was because he couldn't bear to. Her, either; it was what had brought them both out here, she realized as the men hustled her roughly along. To do something about it; anything.

Anything at all. *Stupid,* she berated herself bitterly.

But it was too late for that, too. Night-vision goggles on thick, black rubber straps obscured the men's faces. They passed Pierce's body lying spread-eagled on the driveway, motionless.

Blood stained the gravel. Maybe he'd seen them heading away from the house and decided to forget about ambushing them, just get in there while he had the chance. It was what she'd have done, too, found Helen and Lee if she could and rescued them.

If they were there. But the men must've turned and spotted him. Craning her neck, she gazed back as they pushed and pulled her up the steps—pausing to search her pockets again, find her phone, and hurl it into the woods—and into the house.

"Are you going to let me help him?" she demanded.

Inside, the place smelled of cooking and cordite. "Or is it going to be murder you both end up getting charged with on top of everything else?"

No Lee in sight anywhere; no Helen, either. And no Campbell, or anyway not as far as she could tell . . . Her knees trembled, and the gun smell in here was very worrisome. But people did scary things all the time, she reminded herself; Wade climbing the rope ladder, Ellie on an airplane, Bella marrying Jake's dad.

Sam not drinking. And if she behaved like a victim, these guys would turn her into one; she could smell the sour, sweaty reek of casual violence coming off them in waves.

"He'll die. Is that what you want? So far it's been fun and games, a sharp lawyer could bargain it down for you, but—"

"Shut the freak up." The harsh, slightly nasal Jersey accent came from behind her; she turned.

The second man was small, compactly built, with dark, curly hair, red lips, and a cruelly amused expression on a face that could've been handsome if it weren't so depraved, as if something inside him were deeply and permanently broken, human-being-wise.

He wore designer jeans, a white T-shirt with blood spattered

on it, and a black leather jacket that was a half-size too big for
him and a little too shiny. Fat gold chains hung around his neck,
and he had a gun.

Two of them, actually. Her own, and—"I could shoot you
right now, you know that?" he smirked.

The gun he had was a snub-nosed .38-caliber Police Special;
Wade had one in his shop. It crossed her mind fleetingly that not
being scared of guns was a point in her favor.

A slim point. "I'm supposed to meet Campbell," she said. "So
where is he?" But the guy wasn't listening.

"Why couldn't you just follow the freakin' instructions?" he
demanded peevishly. "What, it wasn't simple enough? The
'alone' part? But no, you had to bring somebody. Dumb freakin'
broad."

"Marky, maybe we should try helping—" the tall one began
nervously.

"Shut up!" yelled Marky. "What're you, a freakin' Red Cross
nurse now? Who cares about him?"

He turned back to Jake. "Get in there," he said, waving her
down a short hall.

At the entrance to the living area she paused. It ran almost
the length of the house, with sliding glass doors facing where the
water must be on the long side, a fireplace and sitting area at one
end, to the right, and the dining area at the other.

One of the long glass door panels was broken, glass pellets
scattered on the shiny prefinished wooden floor nearby. It was
the first broken thing she'd seen here; after her own old house,
the smooth unmarred surfaces and level floors in this one
seemed almost too perfect to be real.

No expense had been spared, she saw by the terra-cotta tile
and brushed aluminum appliances past the archway leading into
the kitchen. And although the owners only came here in one sea-

son, the house had been built to be livable in all four, so the glass doors had storm sliders, one closed to cover the broken section.

"Sit," Marky ordered coldly. The taller one stood watching from the kitchen archway, still looking frightened.

He's not into this, she thought. *Or . . . no, something's wrong. He doesn't want to say what it is. Something Marky doesn't—*

In the kitchen a cabinet door edged silently open. Bottom cabinet on the right . . . Jake's heart stopped. *Please, let it be—*

"Aunty Jake!" yelled Lee, tumbling out of the cabinet. As Lee scrambled toward her, the taller guy's face went slack with relief. Then the child was in her arms, warm and real and . . .

Alive, she thought gratefully as Lee's arms clasped tightly around her neck. "Hi, baby," she whispered, breathing in the warm sweet scent of the child's hair and trying not to weep. "I'm so glad to see you. Are you okay?"

Lee seemed uninjured, and her silky blond head nodded *yes*. But: "I losted my dolly," she whimpered desolately. "And I losted Aunty Helen . . ."

"Ssh, that's okay. I found your doll; it's at home. You can have her as soon as we get there. And we'll find Aunt Helen, too," Jake promised, wondering if it was true.

Across the room, the one the taller guy called Marky turned impatiently to sorting among some equipment on the dining table. The goggles they'd worn, a spotting scope, a cell phone, and . . . a tape machine. A small, old-fashioned . . .

An old cassette machine; seeing it, she knew how she'd been tricked. *That scream . . .*

Faked. Lee snuggled closer in her arms as, abandoning the gear, Marky began yanking the chain-switch of a floor lamp that stood near the table, harder each time but without any result.

The tall guy in the kitchen watched anxiously. He was in his early twenties, still wearing the Jersey Devils jacket she'd seen in the VCR tape over a sweatshirt and dungarees, with a long, sallow face and a big, beaky nose that he hadn't yet quite grown into. His arm was bleeding, inexpertly bandaged with what looked like a torn strip of sheet.

"I can fix that lamp," she said, nodding her head at the one Marky fumed over. Because she needed an angle, any angle at all, and anyway, it would help her to be working on something. Just . . .

It just would, that was all. "Marky. Listen up a minute. She says she can—" ventured the taller guy.

"Oh, yeah?" Marky glared. "Get over here, then," he ordered belligerently. "You, too," he added to the tall one. "*Anthony*," he added sarcastically.

Go with what you know, said Ellie White softly in Jake's head. Ellie, Lee's mother and Jake's dearest friend . . .

Ellie, sweet and delicate as a fairy-tale princess on the outside, was tough as tree bark when push came to shove. As it had now, Jake thought; if she put Lee down on one of the sofas, she decided, when she got near Marky with that lamp in her hands she could swing it.

"I'll hold the kid," said Anthony, stepping forward to lift Lee from Jake's arms. "Don't," he added in lower tones, "make any of this worse." His gaze met hers impassively.

Damn. "Do you have any tools?" she asked. "A screwdriver or something?"

Marky spoke again. "Oh, yeah. We got the freakin' Snap-on tools guy comin' in here twice a week. What are you, stupid?"

He checked his wristwatch, a large, many-dialed monstrosity that would've looked more like a Rolex if the gold paint around the bezel hadn't been wearing off. "Okay, let 'er fix the damn thing," he told Anthony. "But that's it. When the time comes . . ."

He looked straight at her, drew a finger across his throat. "That's it. I guess that's why they call it a freakin' deadline."

He chuckled, a dry, unpleasant sound like sharp knives clattering together in a drawer.

Yeah. Maybe that's why, she thought.

A few minutes later she had the lamp unplugged and the bulb removed. It was a high intensity fluorescent bulb, its slender tube wound in a spiral shape; staring at it, she wondered for a dazed instant if wiring fluorescent fixtures might be different somehow.

But no. The bulbs were interchangeable so the wiring scheme must be, too. Anthony produced an imitation Swiss Army knife with a minuscule screwdriver attachment and grudgingly handed it over; she used the flimsy nippers on it to seize and unscrew the nut at the base of the bulb receptacle while Anthony went outdoors. In his absence she considered gripping the knife handle in her fist and plunging the screwdriver's blade into Marky, if she got the chance. A fast sideways punch should do it. . . .

But he kept dancing out of range. "Come on," he demanded, stepping briefly nearer to peer over her shoulder. "What's the problem? I thought you said . . ."

He didn't need the lamp. It just made him angry when things wouldn't do what he wanted them to. Objects, people—they were all the same to him; they obeyed or he destroyed them. She'd met his type often, back in the city, where very few of her money-management clients had resembled Mother Teresa.

Mostly they'd been more like Marky, but with better clothes and more expensive haircuts. And a little better impulse control, maybe. With the bulb receptacle pulled apart she took the brass wire off one of the tiny screws in the switch unit; the silvery wire had already separated from the other screw.

So that was the problem: a broken circuit in the switch. But as she'd hoped, it was easily repaired; she twisted each wire's strands together tightly, then bent a small hook into the end of each one, pulled on the switch's chain again to make sure there were no problems there. Finally she hooked the wires back over their own screws again, brass to brass and silver to silver. She was screwing the bulb's receptacle back onto the lamp base and tightening the lock nut once more when Anthony returned, raising his hands in a What-can-I-do? gesture at Marky's querying glance.

"Freakin' guy," Anthony said, and she took this to mean that Jody Pierce was refusing to die. So there was hope; if she could get that cell phone, or if she could put even one of these guys out of action . . .

"Awright," Marky said disgustedly, with the air of someone stepping manfully up to a chore no one else had the stomach for. He pulled the gun from his inside jacket pocket. "Lemme go out there, then, for freak's sake. I'll take care of–"

"Wait." A feeling of unreality swept over her as with shaky fingers she slid the switch casing into its base until it locked.

The feeling, she realized with a stab of panic, was one step away from not being able to do anything about any of this, so why even try? Why not just give up, give in, get it over with?

Just one step, one stray thought, one panicked feeling. But that way lay disaster. "I've got it," she managed through lips that had suddenly gone papery-dry. "Don't you want to see it go on?"

Praying that the loose wire really had been the trouble, she glanced up at Anthony. She had a feeling he knew perfectly well what she was up to: keeping his pal Marky from going outside and finding Pierce, still lying there in the driveway, and finishing him off as easily as clipping a pesky hangnail.

"Okay," Marky allowed grudgingly. *Thank God,* she thought in a brief burst of optimism, *for short attention spans.* And when the lamp snapped obligingly on, "Big deal, I could've done that," he said, turning away.

Eyes narrowed, he stood with his arms folded as if waiting for something. Anthony gave him a "What?" look.

"The knife, you schmuck. Or were you gonna let her keep it? Maybe I should give her the gun, too? Moron," Marky added.

"Hey, it was worth a try," she said, attempting a light tone as she relinquished it. But at her words, alarm filled Anthony's face and in the next instant, Marky's hands were on her throat.

"Don't," he uttered viciously as his thumbs dug into her voice box. "Don't freakin' try *anything.* Keep your mouth shut and do what I say, you got it?"

He let go. Her eyes prickled with black stars. "You, too," he added to Anthony as she dragged in a harsh breath.

See? Anthony's look said. *See what I'm dealing with, here?*

Silently he followed his partner out to the kitchen, leaving her in the pool of light shed by the newly repaired lamp.

She crossed the room, gathered Lee up, and held her. *Yes,* she thought as the child moved fretfully in her arms, then settled. *I do see. You're so far up the creek that your chances of getting down again are just about zero.*

Like mine, she realized with sad certainty. And the chances of the man lying out there in the driveway were even slimmer.

If he was still alive at all.

"Damn kids," **the** walrus-mustached man raged, glaring at Helen Nevelson before seizing her and yanking her up out of the kayak. In the darkness he couldn't see that she was injured.

Or maybe he didn't care, too angry at the destruction she'd

caused. "Alla you, got no respect for people's property. Come out here, throw your pot parties and booze parties and I don't know what all."

The smell of his breath said he'd been having a party of his own recently. He pushed her ahead of him up the pebbled path alongside the cabin, shoving her when she faltered.

"Kids stole all the kayaks, so I locked 'em up," he ranted. "Now you come along and smash the shed lock, break the windows."

She knew him, she realized dimly. His name was Hank Harriman and he lived across the lake on Roughy Hill Road where she'd been heading; he went hunting and fishing sometimes with Jody.

But not often; Jody hadn't cared for Mr. Harriman's habit of getting loaded, even before he got into the woods. And the one time Mr. Harriman had seen Helen, she was much younger and he'd been half in the bag, as Jody had put it.

As he was this minute; more than half, even. Way more, so Mr. Harriman didn't know her now.

"Teach you a damn lesson," he slurred. *Lesshun.* The motion detectors on the yard lights must've set off an alarm over at his house across the lake, so he'd come to check. Jody had probably hooked the alarm up; it was the kind of thing Jody was good at, and everyone around here knew it.

"Throwin' around beer cans, trashing the whole area. Why'n the hell a man can't have a place to himself 'thout a buncha you little brats comin' in an'—Git along, there," he said, shoving her angrily again.

She tried to speak, but by now her broken mouth was so badly swollen that all she could produce was a sort of *baa*ing sound as he hustled her out to his pickup truck. It was an old GMC beater with a plow mount on the front, a trailer hitch on the back, and a two-way radio with a Radio Shack microphone wired into the dashboard, probably also by Jody—*he's your friend,* she tried and failed again to croak out—some time or another.

He'd even stopped by to see her mother not too long ago, she recalled, to get a book that had been put aside for him. But he hadn't seen Helen; she wished now she'd gone in from the screened porch to speak to him, but—

He yanked the cab's passenger door open. "Get in there," he snarled. "You and your trashy ways. Stole clothes, too, I see," he added, spying the sneakers she'd found in the cabin, and the old sweaters.

When she faltered at the high running-board step, he grabbed her and hoisted her up one-handed, sending her sprawling.

"Now you just sit there," he growled. She was crying again and couldn't stop, gasping and sobbing with pain and renewed fear. Most of the people you ran into around the lakes were like Jody, good-hearted and easygoing.

But not this guy. "Little bawl-baby," he growled. "Guess your scummy pals must've put a pretty decent beating on you, on top of everything else. Teach you to hang around with 'em."

She scrambled upright as he leaned into the truck cab to survey her in disgust. "Buncha losers," he spat contemptuously, backing out again and slamming the door.

In the yard lights she watched his stocky form stomping into the cabin. Shudderingly, she battled to get back some composure, to stop crying and figure out something to make him understand—

There. On the dashboard, a notebook black with finger marks, and a stubby pencil clipped to it. Relief flooded her; of course, she could write him a note.

Opening the notebook she flipped rapidly through a dozen

or more pages of symbols and numbers with counting marks lined up alongside them, four upright marks and a diagonal line indicating five of something. A counting system, maybe for plow jobs so he'd know how much to bill people. But why not write their names down?

She didn't bother wondering any more about it, though, just kept flipping until she came to a blank page. On it, she printed her name, Jody's name, the word *daughter,* and three more words: *Help Me Please.* When he came back, she waited until he was all the way in but with the door still hanging open and the dome light still on, then thrust the notebook at him.

"What the—?" He scowled at her, his eyes full of angry contempt and . . . something else. Fear, she realized. But of what?

Fear and . . . shame. Too late, she understood why.

"What the hell is this?" he demanded, shaking the notebook at her. "It ain't enough you kids come out here trespassin' and ruinin' my stuff, now you gotta screw up my job book?"

He flung it at her, started the truck up, and jammed it into gear. Jouncing down the dirt road, they passed through an open gate; he jumped down from the cab, swung it shut, and locked it behind them, then climbed back in and accelerated again, heedless of the way the truck clanked and rattled over the bumps.

He couldn't read. That's why her writing in the notebook had made him angry; he couldn't, and he was embarrassed about it. He had stopped by the house to get materials for something about the reading lessons her mother gave; that's what the book he'd gotten was, another part of the lesson material.

So the note she had written him wasn't just useless. It had made things worse.

"Fasten your damn belt," he growled when they got out to the main road, Route 1 a ribbon of darkness in the larger dark.

While she was out cold her jaw had released. "Please," she

managed to whisper. It came out "bleh." But he understood, as they sat there waiting for an eighteen-wheeler to pass by.

"Oh, sure," he said scathingly. "Now you're scared. You've had your fun, paid for it, too, you thought, with the clobberin' they put on you. Well, you're gonna pay more," he went on with vindictive relish. "I'll teach you a lesson you'll never forget."

She didn't like the sound of that one bit. Behind the truck came a poky little subcompact, too slow and underpowered to pass on the downhills and too scared, probably, to try it on the ups. Mr. Harriman waited angrily for the slowpoke; she didn't like the sodden gleam in his eye, either, as he sat contemplating whatever it was that he was planning to do with her.

The subcompact was *very* slow. He'd miscalculated in waiting for it and now he fumed impatiently while it struggled up the hill behind the truck. Helen unbuckled her seat belt stealthily.

"You're gonna learn," he recited. "Oh, yeah. Think you know it all?" His mustache twitched damply in anticipation, big hands tightening on the wheel.

Helen's mind worked frantically. She wasn't afraid of jail, or the cops. By now, they must know she was missing and she'd be able to communicate with them. So they would help her.

And she hurt, oh, God, she still hurt so bad; more than almost anything in the world, she wanted to pour her story out to the police, and then lie down and let people take care of her.

Mr. Harriman was still talking. If you could call it that: "Kids nowadays, buncha little whining, grabby parasites, got no respect at all for other people's hard-earned . . ."

Tuning him out, she struggled to remember what it was she had to tell someone. A name? An address, a phone number, or—

No. None of those things. The answer went through her like an electric shock: *she knew where they were going.*

"But first, you're gonna gimme all the names of everyone

who was out there at my place with you, drinkin' and dopin' and—"

Carrying on, Mr. Harriman would've finished, but she didn't hear him because she was already out of the truck, flinging the door open in the last instant before he roared out onto Route 1.

"Hey!" he yelled furiously as she hurled herself out of the truck's cab into the roadside gravel. Clambering up, she tripped and fell headlong into a ditch full of icy rainwater, then hauled herself desperately hand-over-hand up and out the other side.

"I'll get you, you little—" But before he could chase her, Mr. Harriman was still sober enough to realize, he had to back the pickup truck out of the travel lane and put the parking brake on. And by the time he'd done that, Helen was in the trees.

The cliffs, they were taking Lee to the . . . Gagging at the pain rocketing through her, Helen struggled through thick brush. Behind her, Mr. Harriman yelled for her to stop and fought his way into the brush, too. But pretty soon, he gave up.

Hadn't he? Or maybe he was sneaking up on her. Shivering, she crouched in the mucky hollow between a rock and an old stump. If she moved even a muscle he might hear it and pounce on her . . .

But in a few minutes she heard his truck start, then peel out onto the highway with a clattering of its old engine. So he was gone. She struggled achingly upright.

He could drive up and down the road scanning for her, and he might. So she'd have to keep out of sight; meanwhile, Eastport was twenty miles south of here; no way she'd be able to walk that far, but she could get herself away from where Mr. Harriman might be on the hunt for her. If she could find an old trail or logging road paralleling the highway, she could stay even better hidden.

He wouldn't call the cops. His boozy outrage wouldn't help

him with them, especially since he was driving. And he would know that; drunk guys generally did.

So she was on her own. A motorcycle sped by in the dark, its insect whine rising to a roar and fading again. If she could flag down one of those . . .

Her feet were so swollen that even in the too-big, stolen shoes, they felt like a pair of blood-blisters. The ringing in her ears was a lot louder now than it had been, and she had a bad feeling that the darkness all around her wasn't entirely on account of the endless-seeming night.

That *she* was fading in and out. Clumsily she blundered into a patch of stinging nettle, backed out of its fiery clutches, and altered her course a fraction. After another unmeasurable stretch of slow going, she stumbled onto a track. Two ruts, humped down the middle and padded with grass at the sides . . .

Every so often a car sped past nearby, so she knew she was close to the road. There were things about what she was doing that didn't make sense. But she knew one thing:

She had to get back to Eastport, find Bob Arnold, and tell him about the awful men who'd taken Lee, and . . . God, what was the other thing she'd known about them only a minute ago?

Fright stabbed her as she wondered if the memory, whatever it was, would ever come back. But—

Keep moving. Keep the paved road on your left. Put one foot in front of the other.

With these words echoing in her head, she tripped hard into a mess of vines and fell sprawling into them, hauled herself to her knees and sat back, panting, then fought the rest of the way up. A hoarse snort from somewhere very nearby froze her blood for a moment. But from the rustling and crunching that came with it, Helen realized it must be another moose.

At her next step, a snake slithered thickly from under her

right foot; jumping back with a shriek she slammed her head into a tree trunk. The impact sent stars rocketing around behind her eyes; staggering, she lost the road, and for a while didn't know where she was at all.

But then just by luck she heard cars going by once more, and another truck. Faint with relief, she left the trail, angling her steps closer to Route 1 so she wouldn't lose it again. *Make sure I can hear it, maybe even see headlights, because if I get lost out here again . . .* She put a foot out blindly, expecting it to come down on rough earth, fallen branches, and uneven stones.

But instead she stepped off an embankment, plummeting with a breathy shriek of surprise. Tumbling and bouncing, she felt her skull smack something hard at the bottom.

Oh, she thought mildly. A car went by, and another. But the ditch at the foot of the embankment was too deep for them to see her where she lay, half in and half out of a drainage culvert.

From somewhere above her came a slow *plonk-plonk* of dripping water, like a dull gong being struck. She rolled over to get her face out of a puddle.

But that was as far as she could go. She wanted to go on, but she couldn't. Maybe she could stay here a minute, and rest.

Sleepy. Just for a minute . . . As Helen lay there, it started to rain again, a steady, soaking downpour that fell off the ledge in foamy runnels, streaming down the embankment.

After a while, the culvert began filling.

Chapter 11

*Prepare a small engine for
winter storage by cleaning it,
draining the fuel from it, and
taping a brand-new spark plug
and fuel filter (for use next
spring!) to its handle.*
—Tiptree's Tips

At the Jiminy Point house, Jake sat waiting in the living room under the newly repaired lamp. Outside, it was beginning to get light; Lee lay peacefully in her arms, asleep.

A squall swept over the bay, rain hitting the windows in fat spatters and slashes. It paused, then poured straight down for a while before ceasing altogether.

The men were out in the kitchen, Marky in charge of

whatever they were doing together there, his voice hectoring, criticizing and complaining. She wondered how Anthony stood it, especially when the sound of a slap rang out and no protest followed.

"Do you hafta question every little thing?" Marky demanded. "For freak's sake, I don't *know* why we gotta do it this way. We just do, that's all. Maybe," he concluded, " 'cause by now all the roads are full of cops. You ever think a' that?"

Her leg was asleep. She tried moving Lee, but at the tiniest change in position the little girl's eyelids flickered warningly. And under the circumstances, Lee asleep was best; for the moment, anyway, and the present moment seemed all that Jake could manage.

"Why do I have to do all the thinkin' around here?" Marky demanded.

Jake wondered again what they were doing, decided it didn't matter as much as finding a way to escape them. The deck outside the sliding glass doors, she'd already discovered, was twenty feet off the ground; even alone, she wouldn't have tried jumping. But with Lee in her arms there'd be no sense to it at all; from that height, it was a cinch neither one of them was exactly going to hit the ground running.

And running was what she needed. Now that she had Lee, there was no point to seeing Campbell. Getting away was her best chance to save Jody Pierce, too—if he was still alive—and to find Helen Nevelson. But the men out in the kitchen had a clear view of the only other exit whose location she knew.

"Get up, we're going," said Anthony, coming into the living room. Pain and fatigue marred his face, while in the hall, Marky hauled something heavy.

"Where?" she asked. Lee turned in her arms, whimpering.

"Never mind. We're going, that's all. You want to make him

mad?" He raised his bloody arm toward Marky's complaining voice.

"He's pretty hard on you," she ventured. And when that got no reaction: "Look, before we go you might just want to let me do something about that bandage. It's—"

"Shut up." He didn't look at her. "You'd better be on your feet when he gets in here."

Then Lee woke, whining uncomfortably. "Hey, baby," Jake crooned, smiling down into the child's flushed face. Then with a spike of alarm she took in the perspiration beading the little girl's hairline.

"What did you give her?" she demanded of Anthony, suspicion piercing her suddenly.

Anthony looked away again. "Nothing," he mumbled. But even allowing for her exhaustion, Lee had fallen asleep too easily and deeply, as if she'd been . . .

"Tincture of opium," Anthony admitted, his guard dropping briefly. Astonishing, she thought; he wants to be *liked*. "It's okay, though, Marky got it from a pharmacist he knows back in—"

But then he crumpled with a cry. Behind him stood Marky, who'd slugged him in the kidney. Anthony straightened, grimacing.

"I got a freakin' schedule to keep," said Marky. "Starting now, anyone who gets in the way of it gets a bullet." He punched Anthony again, this time in the shoulder of his bloody arm. "You got that, you worthless little sack of—"

He kicked Anthony. "Answer me, you freakin' idiot, you're so friendly, gettin' ready to tell Little Miss Moron here all about where we're from and what we're all about. Do. You. Got. That?"

He delivered another kick, harder. "Yeah," Anthony gasped. "I got it, Marky."

"Good." He pulled his gun from his jacket. "Now let's just cut the crap and get out of here."

"Where?" Jake repeated. Lee had fallen asleep again. Or lost consciousness. Marky regarded her coldly.

"You'll find out when we get there," he said.

Anthony hoped his kidney wasn't ruptured. Maybe it was only bruised. Either way, too bad; now Marky wanted him to haul the little outboard engine from where they'd found it in the utility room, so Anthony went outside.

The rain had stopped, and the outboard sat on the steps where Marky had dragged it. But when Anthony tried to lift it his wounded arm screamed in protest, warm blood coursing down it.

He flipped a switch by the garage door. As he'd hoped, light flooded the driveway; at the edge of it he spied a large garden cart someone had left tipped up against a pile of dirt. Ignoring the man's body still lying there motionless where it had fallen earlier, Anthony dragged the cart to the house, manhandled the engine into it despite shrieks of agony from his arm, and began muscling the loaded cart clumsily downhill toward the water.

The pistol he'd taken from the guy in the driveway was in his waistband, tucked in against the small of his back. Marky didn't even know it existed because Anthony had gotten to the guy after Marky shot him, and snatched it before Marky noticed.

Lucky, he thought; and lucky, too, that its hiding place had escaped Marky's kicking foot. But that was all the good fortune Anthony expected. The rest he would have to arrange for himself.

At the foot of the hill a short, sharp drop led down to some flat boulders. He got in front of the cart, holding it back with his weight, and held the engine steady while the cart bumped down hard. Finally he was on the beach, his bleeding arm pulsing like a gangbanger's boom box, thumping with pain.

The gun bit into his back as he worked to get the cart over the stony beach to where the boat lay rocking in the small waves. Marky wanted him to put the engine on the boat, too.

Sure, Anthony thought bitterly, even though he'd never done it and wasn't sure he could figure out how. But try telling that to Marky, right? Talking sense to that guy was like talking to a wall, with the added attraction that when you were done, the wall would drop a few of its bricks on you.

To hurt you, because it could. Because it liked to. That, he realized as he pondered the problem of getting the outboard onto the boat, was the good part of all this for Marky. Not the money, although of course Marky wanted some of that, too.

But hurting people and making them take it was what Marky got off on. And probably just some of the money wasn't what he was after, either. In fact, it was dawning on Anthony that no matter what happened, he probably wouldn't be riding back to New Jersey with Marky in the Monte.

That instead, Anthony and the fishes swimming around out there in the water would be getting acquainted. Thinking this, he finished hauling the cart, then examined the engine once more. He guessed the propeller must hang out over the outside of the boat—*Wow*, he heard Marky commenting sarcastically in his head, *what an Einstein*—and there were a pair of C-clamps he imagined must get tightened at the back, there, to clamp the engine on.

A cord with a handle on it hung off the engine, which he knew must be to start the thing. There was a choke lever, too, and a throttle on the handle.

In the gathering gray light he could make out white notched

lines on the handle, for speed, forward, and reverse. Drop it to idle, probably, to shift gears. Ignoring the pain it cost him, he muscled the engine around, set the clamps properly—he hoped—and began tightening the screws down.

But in the midst of this he stopped, something about his surroundings making the outboard engine seem wrong, maybe even dangerous. Calm, silent, the sky now very slowly changing from slate gray to a rich, dark blue, the heavily saturated color of brand-new blue jeans . . .

He'd washed new jeans with his underwear at the laundromat, once, and gotten a load of blue skivvies as a result. But this mistake, whatever it was, was going to be a lot worse if he didn't figure out what the hell was bothering him so much—and then suddenly he had it:

The silence. It was morning now, so early that even the people around here weren't up yet, most of them. The ones who were, though, would know as naturally as breathing what went on, out on this water. The daily routine: who went where, who they went with, what they were doing and why.

Like cops, knowing the usual on their beat. And the outboard engine in the silence . . . it was going to be loud.

Across the water, a few more lights had gone on even as he stood there, like eyes opening one by one in the dark. Probably they couldn't see him yet, but they would soon, if he gave them any reason to look.

But if he told Marky so, Marky would reject the idea just because it was Anthony's. Then Anthony would be screwed.

Which he was anyway; as far as he could see now, the only way to not get killed by Marky was to kill Marky first. And out on the water was the place to do it, definitely. Hit him in the head, dump him over the side.

The water was calmer than it had been the last time Anthony was down here, but he could see from the small moving ripples on top that it still ran fast, speeding one way hours earlier when the tide was coming in, the other way now, when it was going out.

Which meant Marky's body would float away somewhere, carried by the current. Too bad about the money, of course; if he got rid of Marky, Anthony would never get any of that. But just like with the girl in the woods, earlier, he had no choice.

What he would do about the woman and kid, he wasn't sure. But right now, the swift current was giving him yet another idea: that the outboard shouldn't start until Anthony wanted it to, a situation he thought he could arrange without much trouble.

Because air-conditioner repair wasn't the only trade they'd tried teaching him, back in the juvie home. They'd thought he might be good at lawn care, too: cutting grass, blowing leaves, crap jobs like that. So he'd worked a summer edging sidewalks in the public parks in Parsippany, which was how he'd learned in the ninety-degree heat while running a gas-powered trimmer that spewed foul smoke and stalled every five minutes that he'd rather earn his pay biting the heads off live chickens.

And how he'd happened to learn about spark plugs.

Choking, Helen Nevelson lurched up. Her head hit something above her that rang with a dull clang. Spewing water from her nose and mouth, she realized she was lying in it, and that she was in a tunnel. A metal tunnel . . .

Confused, she scrabbled painfully on hands and knees until she spotted the culvert opening, a round hole of not-quite-pitch-black. Then she remembered; she'd fallen, and crawled in here to hide. But from what? The opening she could see was far away, and there wasn't room enough inside the culvert to turn around so she backed out, trying to keep her head down.

She smacked it again, anyway, but the pain hardly penetrated through the other pains now awakening, too, her jaw throbbing massively like a sledgehammer with a spotlight attached, thudding and flaring with her pulse. She'd turned her ankle, and the gash in her arm from the glass at that awful guy's camp—

She froze at the thought. Then the rest of it came back in a rush: the men, the kidnapping, thinking that one guy was going to shoot her, finding the cabin, then jumping out of the truck . . .

And Lee. She turned her head suddenly to the side, vomited. Lee was with the men, and only Helen knew where they were going: to the cliffs. And why would terrible men take a little girl like Lee to the cliffs, unless . . .

She pushed herself up as another eighteen-wheeler roared by, its running lights turning the gathering dawn fiery orange and its tires spewing water that flew sideways, drenching her again. But she was up now, and she mustn't go back down.

Slowly, gripping one handful of grass after another, Helen hauled herself up the embankment toward the edge of the pavement. When she got there, she stood swaying, thinking about something Jody had told her.

She remembered it well; they'd been setting out on the first truly long paddle she'd ever taken, right after he'd made her capsize in the kayak so she'd be safe. She'd been wearing a ball cap, sunglasses, a life jacket, a long-sleeved cotton shirt over her swimming suit, and flip-flops.

Also, she'd been coated with enough suntan lotion and bug repellent to choke a moose; the combined stink, like cheap perfume mixed with weed killer, made her feel sick to her stomach. And on top of it all, she didn't want to go.

It was just too much. He was always doing things like this, making her try things that got her scared, and even when she got through them she always ended up with sore muscles and blisters, when she could've been doing things with her own friends or even just doing nothing. And even if nothing terrible happened on its own, he'd make something happen, set some obstacle up she would have to overcome, just so she could learn some new stupid lesson. So she'd begun to cry, sitting there in the kayak looking across at the far side of the lake, several miles distant.

"It's too far," she'd complained, sobbing. "Don't you get it yet? I hate this," she'd screamed at him, not caring who else was on the lake, listening. She hurled the kayak paddle at him.

"I hate it, it's too far, it's too hard, I can't do it."

Because she'd thought he might give up, that maybe a tantrum of that size would convince him. That he would let her out of the kayak, load her into the truck, and take her home, never to try making an outdoorswoman out of her ever again.

That she would be rid of him. But Jody had only maneuvered his own kayak to her thrown paddle, returned it, then leaned in toward her. "Helen, you stick that damned paddle in the water and take one stroke. After that, you can quit if you want to."

So she had, and the one stroke had felt silly, so she took another. And then one more . . .

It took nearly two hours to complete just half of the kayak trip. On the way they saw a beaver working on his lodge, swimming toward it with a yellow-white peeled birch log in his teeth. A bald eagle flew over, so low she could hear the heavy whoosh of its enormous wings. On the far shore they ate a lunch of salami, homemade bread, pickles, and beer.

It was delicious. The whole day was, and all because of that one stroke. Now she put her hand up to wipe the truck-sluice from her face, her fingers in the growing light coming away dark with blood.

Dizziness swept over her. *It's too far. I can't do it.* But Lee was out there in the cold, rainy dawn with the bad men, and only Helen knew where.

And only Bob Arnold, she felt sure, would believe her about it. *He's nuts,* her stepfather had once said about Bob, who looked like the Pillsbury Doughboy much more than he resembled a law officer: plump, balding, and pink-faced, with so much heavy cop gear always dangling from his belt you'd think he'd get pulled down just from the weight of it.

Clearly he was not meant to be a police officer at all, much less a chief. A high school teacher, maybe, or a vacuum cleaner salesman. Something mild-mannered. Not a guy with a gun, who was sworn to use it. But cop was what he'd wanted, so he'd done it.

That's a good nuts, Jody had told her. *Guy sets his eyes on the prize and goes for it, nine times outta ten he's a person you can trust. Like you,* he'd added surprisingly, clapping her on the shoulder in what was for him an unusual display of affection.

Hoping it was true, she turned south on the gravel shoulder by the side of the dark road, steadying herself against the near-overwhelming waves of dizziness that were coming more often, now.

Oftener and worse. But she didn't have to walk the whole way at one time, did she? Or maybe not the whole way at all. A single step, and then maybe another one if she felt like it . . .

I will begin, she decided unsteadily, *with the first one and see how it goes.* Because you never knew; maybe Jody was right.

Maybe she was good nuts, too.

• • •

Jake's heart lifted briefly at the sight of the tiny motor mounted on the skiff's wooden transom, on the beach at Juniper Point. Small as it was, the engine's sound might still manage to draw attention.

But gloom overtook her again as she realized that even so, further investigation was unlikely. Plenty of people weren't even up yet, and the ones who were had their own morning routines to attend to. And it wasn't unheard of for someone to be out here at this hour; seals swimming here liked fish breakfasts, and that meant men out guarding their weirs, the strong, handmade standing nets they had propped up on constructions of long, thin sticks.

Herring fishermen weren't supposed to shoot marauding seals, which were protected by law. But some did anyway, and everyone knew it. So even a gunshot wouldn't sound too out of place, if—As if summoned by her thought, a single shot sounded from up in front of the house. The pair of thugs holding her captive had muscled her down here, Anthony gripping her elbow as she descended the steep slope with Lee in her arms. But then Anthony had gone off somewhere . . .

Jody, she thought sorrowfully as her other captor returned, skidding clumsily down the slope. He'd gone back and finished Jody Pierce off, hadn't he? A shooting star streaked greenish yellow across the paling blue sky, her angry tears blurring it to flashing sparks until she blinked them away.

"So?" Marky demanded petulantly as Anthony handed him back his weapon. "You do it, or what?"

Anthony shrugged. "What d'you want me to say?"

Marky eyed Anthony narrowly. "I want you to tell me that

you done what I told you, you freakin' punk. You think we're freakin' around here? Is that what you think?"

"No, Marky," Anthony replied. His face impassive, he reached around to the back of his sweatshirt and scratched at something. "I don't think that. I did it just like you said."

Killed Jody, he meant. Still carrying Lee, she let the unwelcome knowledge flood her as Anthony waited for Marky to tell him what else to do. *Like me,* she thought, trying to stop her teeth from chattering.

The chilly dampness had taken all night to settle in; now the cold, wet stones on the beach felt like ice cubes through the bottoms of her boots. Stones too uneven and slippery to run on even if there were any good places to run to . . .

Which there weren't; to the south at the end of the beach, a massive shoulder of granite rose from the waves, cutting off any escape. To the north, half a mile of round, slippery stones lay; if Jake tried running on them she'd be down in only a few steps.

And the first thing Marky had done when he hit the beach was hurl her beloved .22 as far as he could out into the waves. No chance she'd get it back. So her only option right now was going along with what these two wanted, and watching for her chance. "Get the oars in," Marky told Anthony. "And pull that engine up; if you drag it across the stones like that it'll break the propeller."

It wouldn't, actually. The cotter pin that held the prop on the shaft would break first—it was designed to do so—and the pins were replaceable. Probably there was a little cardboard box around here somewhere, containing the extras; in the low lean-to on the shore, or maybe up in the house.

But she wasn't going to tell Marky so. "You ever run a boat before?" Anthony asked as he tossed the life jackets in. Two of them, Jacobia noticed. Not four.

Marky shot a dark look at his partner. "'Course I have," he snarled insultedly. "'Course I've run one. What, you think I'm stupid?"

Anthony knew better than to hesitate. "No. I just wondered."

"Yeah, well, don't wonder anymore, okay? You're gettin' on my freakin' nerves. Push the boat in the water, for freak's sake, what d'you think, we're gonna start it while it's sittin' there on the rocks?"

Anthony bent to shove the wooden craft into the shallows. It would've been much better, Jake thought, to swing it around so the transom was in deeper water, eliminating the need for rowing before starting the engine. But Marky with all his experience at boating would figure that out.

Sure he would, she thought sarcastically. The only boating he'd ever done was on a kiddy pond; she could tell by the way he eyed the skiff so tentatively while Anthony leaned on it, putting his back into the task of readying it for their departure.

Tentative, she thought as she watched Marky, when he should have been rejecting the idea of setting off in it altogether, and if he'd known anything about the waters around here he would've been. Big waves, fast currents, granite ledges that poked up like teeth in the unexpected shallows . . . and that ridiculous outboard, a tiny two-and-a-half-horse Evinrude.

The boat, she guessed, was intended for puttering around near shore, a toy for the summer people. "Get in," Marky snapped.

On the horizon the sky began changing from deep, marine blue to light aquamarine. A rose-red line appeared behind the hills, thickening rapidly.

"Hurry up," he said. "It's time, we don't wanna be late."

Late for delivering me. Because that still had to be what this was about, for these two: Do a job, get the money. They'd taken Lee to use as bait and now they were finishing the task.

She wished she understood why they had to do it by boat. She wished Marky weren't so jumpy and irritable, too, all hopped up on the excitement of doing this right, as if it were an achievement test.

And she wished she knew where Helen was, and where Pierce's gun had gotten to. On his body, maybe, up there in the driveway? Should she be running now, trying to get to it before . . . ?

But no. Because if it wasn't there, they might do something to Lee, to punish Jake for the attempt. Still carrying the child, she made her way carefully over the slick stones to the water's edge.

"C'mon, c'mon," Marky urged, waving her on impatiently. The boat had three flat seats: a sailing thwart in the bow, a rowing thwart at the center, and a rear seat back by the transom, right in front of the engine. Metal oarlocks with oars in them flanked the rowing thwart.

Jake waded in, struggling to keep her footing as the icy current swirled around her legs. The water was so cold it made her hips ache, though at this time of day it was only knee-deep; later, the tide would bring it up nearly twenty feet. Reaching the gunwale she gripped it one-handed, settling Lee in her arm, and hesitated. "Where?"

Marky let out a sigh of strained patience, as if just being around her were way more than a normal person could bear. "In the front, there, for creep's sake. The pointed end. What, you think maybe I'm gonna let you steer?"

"Okay." The bow, he meant. She paused, regarding the little vessel and trying to remember how Sam had taught her to do this; Sam, who was so agile on the water he practically had gills. *Here goes nothing . . .*

She placed Lee, wrapped in a blanket, on the rowing thwart.

Once safely in Jake's arms the child had succumbed to exhaustion, and was now sound asleep, her face still flushed with fever. Next Jake swung a leg over the rail, then shifted her weight, leaning as far as she could stretch out over the flat wooden seat to keep the boat from rocking too much.

Almost there . . . Pivoting on the seat with Lee once more in her arms she faced the bow, stood, did a one-eighty while taking care not to lean one way or the other, and sat.

"Now you," Marky ordered Anthony. "Get on out there and keep the boat steady so I can get in."

Anthony obeyed, holding the boat still as well as he could while Marky cursed and complained about the cold water, fumbled his way over the rail, and finally settled himself on the transom seat in the stern.

"We're all wet, now," Anthony pointed out unhappily. Even his Devils jacket was soaking.

"Yeah, well, suck it up," Marky retorted. "There's plenty dry clothes where we're going. You check the fuel on this?" he asked as Anthony swung a leg over and hopped in, moving gracefully and swiftly despite his injured arm.

But at the question he froze. "No. You didn't tell me to . . ."

Marky leaned forward. "Hey, Anthony? Have I gotta tell you to breathe? Are you really that dumb, or is it all a big act to make me think you're freakin' harmless? Turn around, you punk."

Anthony did. Marky reached out and grabbed a handful of the Devils jacket's neckline, bunching it up tight. "Listen to me," he grated softly. "I don't think you're harmless. I know things about you. So don't mess with me, tryin' to make me think maybe you are. Got it?"

Anthony nodded as well as he could while trying to breathe through Marky's grip. "Okay," he choked out.

Marky let go, shoving Anthony as he did so. "Creep's sake, I gotta think of everything," he said, then found the fuel tank cap and opened it. There was enough daylight now for him to see in; satisfied, he screwed the cap back on while Jake thought about people who left tanks of gas sitting around for months on end.

She wondered how much gunk was in the bottom of the tank by now, ready to get sucked up the fuel line and clog the filter, and whether or not the outboard would start. She wondered if it would stall later, the way Wade's crippled freighter had, making the vessel impossible to control.

Marky peered doubtfully at the throttle arm, frowning at the words printed on it. But he wasn't about to admit his doubts, and anyway, puzzling out the procedure wasn't difficult; locating the Start position on the sleeve, he turned it and gave the rope a mighty pull.

The engine spun briefly and clanked to a stop. A stream of profanity issued from Marky's mouth as he pulled again, with the same result, then looked up to see Anthony watching curiously.

"What're you lookin' at? You think this is easy?"

"No, Marky," Anthony replied patiently. A breeze sprang up, riffling his hair. "Try it again, though. If it's anything like a lawn mower," he added helpfully, "sometimes they take a little loosening up."

"Oh, loosening up," Marky repeated mockingly. "So you're the expert, now? Start rowing," he ordered, so Anthony did, seizing the wooden grips in a way that made Jake think he knew more about rowing than Marky did about engines. For one thing, Marky hadn't checked the spark plug or the fuel line, two main things Sam had emphasized to her about troubleshooting balky outboards.

In the reddening dawn, the skiff pulled away from the rocky

shore, bouncing in the chop that had come up with the breeze. A hundred feet out the bow eye dipped sharply and the boat's nose swung suddenly south, caught by the current, the limply trailing painter suddenly slapping itself against the skiff's side.

"Hey!" Marky objected. He'd been caught off guard when the bow swung to starboard and nearly gone over the rail. "What the hell you doin'?"

"Nothing," Anthony grunted. "It wants to go that way." He bent to the oars, trying to change course but unable to make the skiff obey.

Jake watched him struggle, knowing he would have no luck. Even an oarsman with two good arms would have trouble out here; this was no sweet, meandering current, though it might resemble one from a distance. These tides rose and fell twenty-plus feet twice a day, the resulting cascade like Niagara Falls only without the vertical drop.

Unless you counted the one that took you down to what Sam called Davy Jones's locker room . . . Jake gripped the seat with one hand and held Lee tight with the other. The current shot straight south toward the rocky Narrows at Lubec, eight miles distant.

Which—especially if you were engineless—was bad enough. But between here and there swirled something worse, that made the Narrows look as trivial as your average golf-course water hazard: Old Sow, the largest whirlpool in the Western Hemisphere.

Twice a day when the tide ran hardest, billions of gallons of water surged through it, over channels, ledges, and granite spurs, into abysses so cold and black that the creatures in them resembled science-fiction animals, eyeless and strange. Combined with the massive tides, that hidden geology dropped the bottom out of the water or sent it surging, swirling it into spouts and sinkholes that swallowed boats or tossed them heedlessly, broken and spinning. Ferries had been lost there, and schooners, not to mention the occasional unwary pleasure boat.

But these two guys wouldn't know anything about the hazards. Why should they? And that, she thought as the boat's bow jerked stubbornly from Anthony's control again, was very likely her only chance.

Because Marky being moody was the least of it. Worse, he was hard. Hard as hinges, as Bella Diamond would say, and he didn't mean Jake to live much past her usefulness to him, she felt sure. For one thing, she'd seen his face, and no matter what Campbell had told Marky to do or not do, money and witnesses were the two things a fellow like Marky never left on the table.

Maybe Campbell thought he'd been employing a hired gun when he signed Marky up for this. But he'd gotten a loose cannon and sooner or later it would fire, and to hell with how well Campbell thought he was controlling the situation.

Glancing down, she spotted the pair of life jackets lying behind her in the well of the bow. Cautiously, she snagged one of them, covering the action with Lee's blanket.

Marky paid no attention, fiddling with the engine's choke lever. Not that a two-and-a-half-horse outboard would do them any good in the Old Sow, but he didn't know that, either, did he?

To him, one engine was as useful as another. Besides, now that daylight had come up a little more, she realized that this one wasn't going to start at all, because what jumped out at her now was that there wasn't any spark plug in it.

The socket where the plug belonged was empty, the short wire with the electrical contact on it dangling. But nobody left gas in a boat's tank and then took the spark plug out of the engine; if you were careless enough to leave one, you left the other.

Ipso fatso, as Sam would've put it. Which meant . . .

It meant that maybe Anthony had the spark plug. She hoisted the life jacket up under the blanket. The jacket was too big for Lee, but if Jake overlapped the front panels and ran the straps a couple of times through the armpits before tying them, she thought she could make it stay on.

Just in case . . . Lee barely moved, lying there in Jake's lap, and the redness of her cheeks was now way past the rosy pink of health and into the flush of fever. *Just a little longer,* she promised the child silently as the rolling, pitching vessel they were trapped on wallowed farther out into the bay.

But she still didn't know how or whether her promise would be kept. As they struck open water, the cold breeze blowing out of the north stiffened miserably, sending icy slaps of salt water off the oars' blades each time Anthony lifted them. Blood soaked his sloppy bandage and a low grunt of pain escaped him with each stroke; she wondered how he kept on rowing at all, much less so steadily and determinedly.

Fear, she supposed. Fear of Marky, and the kind of youthful energy that Sam still had; boundless, seemingly inexhaustible. As larger waves began smacking the boat's sides, bullying the tiny craft this way and that and hurling spray up in foamy gouts, she thought again about what Anthony could be planning.

The way they were seated, Marky in the stern still furiously struggling with the outboard and Anthony a few feet from him on the rowing thwart, facing his partner, she didn't see how Anthony could do anything without Marky noticing. Meanwhile Anthony rowed on, helped by the rushing current.

Even now the retreating shore lay only a few hundred yards distant. But in this forty-degree water, she reflected, it didn't matter if you could swim at all, much less how well.

And anyway, Marky would shoot her if she tried it. Cradling Lee, she hoarded the scant warmth they shared. A spark plug, the dead, perhaps deliberately crippled engine . . . what was Anthony up to?

"Cripes, Anthony," Marky's nasal voice cut into her thought, "what the freak are you doing? Get us out of this, can't you?"

Anthony didn't answer, too busy handling the boat. He had wisely decided to let the water's massive power have its way for now; the current hurtling them along was going in the direction they wanted, apparently. If not, surely Marky would already be yammering about it in that buzz-saw voice of his; Jake made a mental note to slap the taste right out of that boy's mouth, as Bella Diamond would've put it, if she ever got the chance.

But the satisfaction she took in this imaginary comeuppance was short-lived, as an unwelcome sensation invaded her stomach all of a sudden. *Seasick* . . .

"Oh, hell," she muttered miserably, the wind snatching her voice away. The lurchingly unsettling movements of the boat had gotten to her. Queasily she leaned over the rail . . . but then Sam's voice sounded in her head: *Look at the horizon. Find it, and keep your eyes fixed on it.*

Gasping, she straightened. Despite Anthony's efforts the boat had come around on its own in a swirling eddy: deep green, glassy-looking, and foam-topped. She cast her gaze past it.

The water tower at Pleasant Point loomed dead ahead. After that came Carryingplace Cove, Walker's Landing, and the summer-cottage-sprinkled green mound of Kendall's Head.

Just beyond them lay Gleason's Cove and above it Dog Island with its high, grassy bluffs, clusters of birch, mountain ash and raspberry cane, and a miniature red-and-white lighthouse perched at the edge of them among the masses of beach roses.

As the pale yellow dry grass of the highlands came in sight, she had a moment of hope; from them, it would be an easy walk to town, to people and help. But between her and any such refuge still boiled the Old Sow, turning and churning with chaotically tossing whitecaps. Anthony bent forward and pulled on the oars again, the skiff juddering as its prow struck the higher wave tops.

"Anthony," Marky began hectoring again. His nagging sounded panicked, though she could tell he was still trying to hide his fright.

"I'll get us out when we need to get out," Anthony panted in reply, leaning into his work.

And then she saw it: Jody Pierce's gun, the Glock he'd shown her. Its dull black grip peeked from the back of Anthony's waistband when his shirt hiked up; he must've taken it from Pierce's body back in the driveway of the house on Jiminy Point, she thought. Now the weapon was so close, she could almost reach out and—

Marky looked up. She yanked her hand back. "So you're some kind of freakin' navigator, now?" he inquired evilly of Anthony.

He had straightened from fiddling with the uncooperative outboard and was in an even more foul mood than before; he hadn't noticed the empty spark plug socket.

"We get down there," he went on, "this damn current, it's gonna carry us under the damn bridge, right out into the freakin' ocean."

And for once he was at least half right. If they didn't run aground by the concrete bridge pilings and get pounded to death by the waves there, or smash to smithereens on the rocks around them, they would end up adrift in the Gulf of Maine.

Which would not be a good outcome. "Hey. Switch places with me," Marky told her suddenly, giving up on the outboard at last.

Half a mile distant, the Deer Island ferry set out on its first run of the day, three cars and a handful of tourists with bicycles and backpacks on board. Pairs of porpoises played in the ferry's wake, their slick green backs reflecting the rising sun. But the ferry was too far off to be of help; at this distance, no one on it would even notice the skiff.

"These gas fumes are makin' me sick." Marky had his own gun out and was waving it sharply at her. "Anthony, get those damn oars in. Now. I mean it."

He half stood, staggered unsteadily, then began making his way forward past Anthony to change places with her, heedless of the way the boat pitched dangerously under his uncentered weight. "Keep it steady, you punk," he spat as he went by.

"Jesus, Marky," Anthony protested, hastily hauling the oars in to get them out of his partner's way. But that made the little boat even less manageable; it heeled over, green water shipping the rail in a thick, sloshing surge.

Jake snatched the other life jacket from under the seat as Marky lost his balance. Pitching forward, he saved himself from toppling into the waves only by gripping the rail with one hand and Anthony's hurt shoulder with the other.

Marky's gun clattered down. Now, she thought, aiming her foot at it. But quick as a lizard his arm came up hard to smack her leg away, then swooped down to grab the weapon back.

Anthony's face went still, his hands on the shipped oars as a stray current turned the boat in a half-circle, then swung it back. *Marky might do anything,* Anthony's look said. But Marky was more interested in being seated again than in punishing her for the weapon-grabbing attempt.

"Funny," he said humorlessly, settling on the sailing thwart she'd vacated while she made her unsteady way to the transom. "You a comedian?"

"No," she replied flatly. *Stay in the center, no fast moves, go where you're going and sit,* said Sam from inside her head.

By following these instructions while holding her breath and praying hard to whatever gods took care of blithering idiots, she reached the transom seat by the outboard engine successfully and sat on it. But now that they'd switched places, Marky would spot Jody Pierce's Glock in Anthony's waistband as soon as Anthony began rowing again.

"Hey." Marky leaned forward, poked Anthony in the shoulder. "Hey, you moron, I said get us out of this freakin' current. You hear me? And hurry up, we're goin' in soon. Right over there."

She followed his gesture out to the rocky tip of Dog Island, where a narrow, sandy inlet lay at the foot of a set of granite cliffs, dark gray and fissured by eons of heaving and weathering. The Knife Edge, it was called by kids who went trespassing there, close to town but out of sight of any houses, to party and dare each other to venture onto the promontory soaring into thin air.

Sam had done it once, reporting unfazed afterward that at its narrowest, the Knife Edge was about two feet across, and very unstable. And when she got done reading the riot act to him about that, he'd told her further that the view from the Knife Edge was amazing, all water and sky. Like you could float right up into it, he'd said, highly pleased with himself and, as ever, utterly fearless.

And of course Campbell would pick a dramatic spot . . . Because maybe it was about money for the two yo-yos in the boat with her, she thought, but for Campbell this was about *him.* His loss, his pain . . . even the ruby earring he still wore like some twisted red badge of devotion.

The question was, what *else* was it about, she wondered as the shore—and whatever Campbell planned to have happen there—drew nearer. "Anthony," she ventured softly. "Where's Helen? The other girl you guys took, where is she?"

If she didn't find out soon, she might never know. And she owed it to Jody Pierce to try to find out. Not that it was likely she'd be able to do much about it, but . . .

Anthony looked up. She'd been wrong about him, she realized; seen close up, it was clear he wasn't in very good shape at all. His eyes had the dull, beaten glaze of a wounded animal, his face slack and a cut on his left cheek gaping raggedly. "Why should I tell you?" he asked.

Not "What girl?" or even simply "I don't know," either of which answers would have been much better, more self-protective for him. So either he was just too hurt and tired to be able to think straight or he didn't care anymore.

And neither of those things boded well for her and Lee, she thought with an inward shiver. But his next remark surprised her so much, she nearly fell out of the boat herself.

"Guy's nuts about you."

"Who, Marky?"

"Nah. Other guy. One we're going to see."

Behind Anthony, Marky leaned over the rail and lost whatever he'd eaten recently. So she wasn't the only one prey to what Sam called the green monster; good, it would keep Marky busy, while Sam's antiseasickness tip had cleared her own nausea completely.

Like old-house repair, she thought with the little part of her mind that wasn't scared absolutely witless. Just learn the tricks and tips of the trade, and use them. . . .

"What're you talking about?" she demanded. "How could you possibly know that about him?"   ·

Anthony glanced over his shoulder to check on his progress; they were near enough to shore now that the red blobs of the rose hips showed against the deep green foliage tumbling down the edge of the cliffs.

"Carries your picture," Anthony said, looking back at the approaching beach, too.

Now she could see the steel cable that ran from the shore to the survey marker, a squat concrete pyramid sunk in a concrete foundation blasted into an offshore boulder. If she could reach it, she could use it to . . .

Carefully, Jake eased her arms into the straps of the second life jacket. "But . . . I don't understand. You've met him? He showed you some picture of me that he had?"

Still following Anthony's gaze toward land, she recalled the photograph these two were supposed to have shown Tom Godley, in Wadsworth's Hardware Store. But seeing the cliffs massed against the shore triggered another memory, too: that near the beach was a set of caves.

Each opened from the rear of the previous one, their ancient depths hollowed out by hammering water over millions of years. From out here you couldn't see them, or from the top of the cliffs, either. But they were there. And they might make a good hiding place, should that turn out to be necessary . . .

Or possible. "Nope. Got a look at him a few times is all," said Anthony. "In that bar of his. And I saw the picture Marky got from him."

Hastily she buckled the final life jacket strap just as Marky peered around suspiciously. He looked almost as ghastly as his partner, but he was getting his wind back, his face less greenish and his eyes hard and unwavering.

Anthony frowned again at the rapidly approaching shoreline, then turned to face her once more. "Your hair was different in it.

Longer, and you were wearing earrings. The guy's got one just like 'em. Wears it, too."

Buoyed by the promise of dry land, his voice strengthened. "Carries the picture in his wallet, the guy does. Marky said so."

With her mind racing, she turned sideways enough to get the outboard's tiller arm into her peripheral vision. Below it, on the floor nearly under her seat, lay a green plastic tackle box.

"Part of the earring," Anthony corrected himself. The second wind he'd gotten was making him chatty. "The round part, not the dangly part like you had on in the picture."

But by now she was barely listening to him, because in that tackle box were the cotter pins for the outboard's propeller, she was almost certain. That was where they kept extras in case one broke, not back in the house.

It was the way Sam did it in his boat, too. Plus—please— maybe an extra spark plug. Given the way they'd left gas in the tank to get all sludgy, she figured there was only about a fifty-fifty chance this boat's owners had done something so sensible as put a spare plug in the box. But . . .

She forced her mind back to what Anthony was saying; by now he was looking oddly at her, and she didn't want him to see any further hint of a plan in her face.

Crazy and unlikely to work, but the only plan she had. She would just have to worry about Helen later. "I don't get this," she began. "I've never worn the earrings you're describing."

Because her mother's ruby earrings were clearly what Anthony was talking about, but that didn't make sense. Her dad wore one, and the other—

Campbell had it. A gift of love, he'd always insisted, claiming Jake's mother had given the earring to him long before her murder; it was how he explained how it came to him.

And then it hit Jake, whose photo Campbell must be carrying: not hers, but her mother's. The thought made her shudder, but just then the wind shifted, slamming them broadside; the skiff heeled over hard again and threatened to swamp as Marky cursed loudly, then leaned helplessly over the rail in renewed wretchedness.

Good, she thought, but now was no time for entertainment. "Pull hard on the left oar, get the bow into the wind," she told Anthony, who obeyed without question; the skiff settled. Now if she could only get the engine started, get the tackle box open and find a spark plug in it—

"Hey." Marky's voice was flat, his eyes blackly glittering as he pushed himself up from the rail, his face smooth with the realization of Anthony's betrayal.

He'd spotted the Glock. And whatever else the awareness of his partner's hidden weapon had done, it had definitely cured his seasickness. "Don't you move a freakin' inch, you little punk." He plucked the gun from Anthony's waistband.

Not much time . . . "Sorry, kiddo," she whispered to Lee as she slid the child's unresisting body onto the boat bottom, fumbled the box open—no lock, thank heavens, just a plastic latch— and found—

A white, cylindrical spark plug. "You punk," Marky repeated. Gripping the Glock in one hand and his own gun in the other, he had no eyes for anyone but Anthony.

Hurry . . . Desperately she sank the spark plug into its socket and turned it down tight, found the ignition wire and attached it, and seized the pull-rope's spray-slick grip—

Seeming suddenly to understand how big a disaster had just befallen him, Anthony dropped the oars with a clatter, turned in a smooth, catlike maneuver that surprised her with its ease and grace, and leapt at Marky in a fluid pouncing motion.

She pulled the starter cord. The engine coughed once, died

with a metallic clatter just as Marky stuck his weapon like some short-bladed cutting tool deep into Anthony's ribs and fired. But with an already uncertain footing, the recoil was enough to knock Marky off-balance, and then the boat lurched really hard.

Start, damn you. Jake cursed silently at the outboard as, seemingly in slow motion, Marky began falling, put his hand out to catch himself, and missed. He fired once more on the way down, his second shot going wild as his head hit the skiff's rail with a sound like a melon splitting, the gun flying from his right hand in a shining, end-over-end arc out into the waves.

Just then the outboard caught and died again, as Marky's left hand came up still holding the weapon he'd had all along, the .38.

"Punk," he said thickly again as she braced her left hand on the outboard's chassis and with her right gave the mightiest pull of her life.

"Freakin' punk." He seemed half stunned, his eyes slightly unfocused and his speech thickened. But his hand still worked and his finger tightened suddenly as Anthony grabbed for the .38.

Again . . . The engine caught, howling; Jake fell on the throttle arm, twisted the sleeve, shoved the tiller as hard as she could to the right. In response the wooden craft veered obediently toward Old Sow, whose wide, green whorls with the tide running hard now took on a knifelike edge.

You want a boat ride? she thought grimly at the men still struggling over the weapon. *I'll give you a boat ride.* And then, irrelevantly, *I wonder what Sam would say if he could see me?*

Seizing the .38, Anthony fell on his partner and punched him, just as the skiff hit the first of the Old Sow's innocent-appearing ripples. While she'd been working on starting the engine and the men had been busy fighting, they'd drifted away from shore again. Gripping the tiller, she swung away from the seductive swirl of the sinkhole at the monster's vortex; the skiff's bow whipsawed wildly.

"Anthony, do this," the taller man recited as he hit Marky again. "Anthony, do *that*."

Without warning another slowly rotating depression opened up in the water, a good two feet deep with a blackish-green spot at the center of it, the color of a bruise. The bow dropped before she could steer away from it; the stern rose up abruptly and the prop screamed, lifting out of the water still spinning.

Lee's blanket-wrapped body slid forward on the wet boat bottom, stopping only when Jake slammed her heel down onto the corner of the fabric. At the hard thump near her head, Lee's eyes drifted open; groggily, she looked around.

"Mama," she whimpered, trying to escape the blanket.

"Oh, baby, don't do that," Jake begged. She couldn't let go of the tiller or the whirlpool would swallow them; she'd gotten them in too far and now the water surged and pummeled them with a force that was purely geological, uncaring and blind. If she stopped steering for an instant or the engine failed, it would suck them down into its netherworld. Forever and ever . . .

Anthony hit Marky again. He'd been doing so for some time now, Jake realized belatedly. His fist made a wet, pulpy-sounding smack on what had been Marky's mouth. "Punk? I'm a *punk*?"

Marky made an answering sound. It was by no stretch of the imagination a word, or anything like one. Nor did there seem to be any meaning behind it. It was just one of the sounds a human body could make when it had not yet finished dying.

Not quite. A sudden upsurge hit the skiff amidships, heeling it over with a vicious lurch and popping the bow up out of the sucking hole in the water. Jake dropped the tiller and snatched

Lee's sleeve just as the child was about to go over the nearly hor-
izontal rail. And then . . .

Then the real thing was upon them. Eerily silent, dead ahead
and devoid of mercy, the Old Sow turned majestically, its surface
mirror-bright. A bit of flotsam bobbled toward it like a leaf in a
storm drain, popped under like something being yanked hard
from below, and vanished with a small wet *thup!*

Anthony slammed his bloodied fist a final time into Marky's
limp form and straightened, just as Lee escaped Jake's grasping
hand and began crawling determinedly toward him under the
rowing thwart.

Anthony turned, steadying himself on the heaving rail with
the .38 still in his other hand and his face deathly pale, as if in the
aftermath of some terrible seizure. His glance fell on Lee, and on
the life jacket still wrapped tightly around her.

"No!" Jake cried, and dropped the throttle to idle for the
barest instant before cranking it again hard, shooting the skiff
forward and knocking Anthony sprawling.

The gun flew; she leaned down and snatched it before it hit
the puddle of water pooling freshly in the boat's bottom—Where
had *that* come from? she wondered for an instant—then grabbed
up the tackle box, popped the weapon inside, and snapped the
box shut.

"Give it to me." Anthony pulled himself halfway up onto the
rowing thwart. Behind him in the bow lay Marky, unconscious.

Or dead. Jake kicked the tackle box behind her under the
seat. "No, Anthony. I'm not giving it to you. It's over, don't you
see? If we don't want to drown, we've got to try to—"

She waved at the devouring monster ahead. Even despite the
remarkably helpful little two-and-a-half-horse Evinrude, the
wooden skiff had begun turning, sucked inexorably toward that
green mouth.

"Anthony," she began again, but then the obvious dawned on her: Water. In the boat. She looked down; the puddle was already an inch deep, and at the center of it a fountain bubbled merrily.

Marky's second shot had gone wild, all right.

Just not quite wild enough. He'd blown a hole in the bottom of the boat.

And now they were sinking.

For a moment everything was quiet. Calm before storm, Jake thought as the whirlpool crept steadily nearer like a predator sneaking confidently up on its prey.

She met Anthony's gaze. "Unless you want to die," she told him, "sit down and shut up."

He looked at the leak, and at her again, and in his eyes she saw Marky's .38 dropping suddenly from his wish list.

Now he wanted her life jacket. "Come near me or Lee and this boat's going down," she warned him, meanwhile watching the water for the slightest hint that the whirlpool might be drifting away slightly. Because it did, sometimes; here one minute, there the next. The wind, the currents and tides changing so swiftly . . .

It could move a quarter mile in an instant. That, Sam had warned her, was what made it so treacherous. If it did, that was her cue to cut hard in the other direction. But it had to happen, first.

And it had to happen before they sank. "Hang on," she said, pushing the tiller to the left as she cranked the throttle again, engine howling as the prop spun foam, then dug in with a guttural moan. *Come on, baby, I'm begging you now.* A hundred yards off, a seagull sailed over with pink dawn shimmering in its wingtips.

Come *on* . . . The engine gurgled, giving out a sick groan, hit an air pocket and screamed briefly, bit in again with a chug. But it wasn't enough, they couldn't escape it, and—

Something rattled under the seat: a coffee can. She kicked it at Anthony. "Bail, damn you." Three inches deep, then four, the leak was lowering the skiff's transom very rapidly. Soon the bow would tip up, the transom would swamp, and—

Marky sat up, swaying. "Anthony," he garbled hideously.

He struggled to his knees, caught sight through swollen eyes of the heavy oar inches from his hand. "Anthony," she warned.

But he didn't hear, and the whirlpool was still a sucking monstrosity in the water, one that was apparently not going away until it swallowed them and took them on what Sam would've called the voyage to see what's on the bottom.

Meanwhile, the only thing she could remember about getting out of a rip tide—which was all that a whirlpool was, really, except its current went around in a circle instead of parallel to the shore—was the old advice everyone knew: Go with it. Relax and let it carry you along, until—

And suddenly she had it. Scary, like letting a riptide have its way with you. But it was their only chance.

Gently, she angled the tiller again, this time easing it to the right. The prow slipped toward the sinkhole, the boat's wild bouncing and juddering gone calm all of a sudden as its battle to escape quieted, the water sliding easily along its sides.

All the way around: Dog Island, the distant Narrows and the bridge, the nearer shores of Campobello all whirled, faster and faster as the engine and the current together sped them along . . .

Faster, until they'd gone all the way around and the wooden boat's prow aimed like a compass needle at Dog Island again—

Now. Straightening the tiller and cranking the throttle a final time, she charged straight at the Old Sow's devouring edge.

A final time, because this was it; the boat's gathered momentum would either shoot them from the whirlpool's clutches or capsize them, to be dragged under and drowned.

As the prow hit the first edge-ripples like a fist hitting a concrete wall and the Evinrude howled miserably in agonized protest, the sun creeping up behind Campobello's green hilltops rose redly at last, its sudden brilliance near-blinding on water turned abruptly the color of Anthony's shirtfront.

The color of blood.

Chapter 12

*For removing big areas of old
concrete, hiring a person with a
jackhammer beats doing it
yourself with a sledgehammer
every single time.*
—**Tiptree's Tips**

W hat the hell happened to you?" The woman in
the purple car slowed alongside Helen Nevelson on Route 1 in
the gathering dawn.

It was cold, and Helen understood in a numb distant way
that she was hurt and wet. She'd managed to limp only a few
hundred yards since she'd begun walking again.

If that. Part of the way, she'd crawled. "Nothing."

Nugh-ugh. She put one foot in front of the other. The woman pulled the car closer to the side of the road, inching along to keep pace with Helen, and leaned farther toward the open window.

"Hey. Hey, listen. Get in the car, I'll take you where you want to go. Come on, you can't–"

An eighteen-wheeler blitzed by in the other direction. The driver's face appeared whitely in the high windshield, peering down curiously; then he was gone.

The woman pulled the car to a stop and got out, hurrying to catch up with Helen and move in front of her, blocking the way.

"Hey," she said again, standing with her feet planted apart and her hands on her hips. "Look at me."

The woman was forty or so, a big, pretty brunette with dark eyes and a lot of red lipstick, wearing wire-rimmed glasses. "Listen," the woman said. "You can't stay out here, you'll catch your death."

Helen wanted to laugh, but if she did she was sure that she wouldn't be able to stop. Then they would take her to what Jody called the laughing academy, and lock her in a room and she would never get out again, just laughing and laughing.

Or crying. She didn't remember waking up, or how she got out of the culvert. She was pretty sure she was dying, but before she did that, she had to find Bob Arnold and tell him–

"I've got a thermos," wheedled the woman. "Hot coffee, with plenty of cream and sugar. Look," her voice turned pleading, "you can sit in the car and drink it. I'll turn off the ignition, you can leave the door open so if you want to get out, you can–"

"No." Helen turned suddenly toward the purple car. Inside it a radio was playing. "Don't turn it off." Because trying to walk just wasn't working. "I need to get to . . ."

Before Helen could finish, the woman was all smiles. "Good. Come on, get in, then, and we'll go."

Under other circumstances, Helen thought she might like the woman, even trust her. She didn't think she'd ever be doing that again, though. Or anyway not for a long time.

If she lived. Carefully she got into the car. The heater was running, and what looked like a doctor's bag sat on the backseat by a pair of white shoes. An ironed white smock hung neatly on a hanger in one of the rear passenger windows.

"Well, all right then," the woman said heartily, as if they were off on some enjoyable day trip. But Helen could still feel the woman's eyes on her, and hear the clinical note in her voice.

Deftly the woman twisted the top off the thermos with one hand, while driving very fast with the other. "Here. Try to get some of this into you. Don't worry about spilling."

Warm vapor drifted from the open thermos. Helen lifted the bottle shakily to her mouth, winced as the hot liquid touched her lips. But she got some of the sweet, milky stuff onto her tongue and just let it sit there, heedless of the pain, before managing to swallow it.

It tasted good. "Thank you," she whispered, but a sob came out with the words so she shut her mouth angrily again.

"You're welcome." Helen had never ridden with a woman who drove so fast before, handling the car briskly and without the slightest hint that slowing down a bit might be a fine idea.

Good, Helen thought. *If I get there in time I can still* . . . Panic seized her; she couldn't remember, again. Everything kept fading in and out: bigger and smaller, lighter and darker. Awake and not-quite . . . She drank some more of the sweet, hot stuff in the thermos and tried to stay focused, without success.

She jerked back into awareness as the woman began talking again. Outside, the sky went on filling with pearly light.

"Look, I don't know what happened to you. But I've seen some badly beat-up women in my life and you look like one of them. Do you want to go back to Calais, go to the hospital and get checked out and maybe talk to the police?"

She glanced over at Helen. "I'll stay with you if you do," she added kindly, slowing the car as if to begin turning around.

"No!" Helen lurched forward, nearly dropping the thermos as she flailed for the door handle. She dimly recalled having jumped out of one vehicle already; she could do it again.

"Okay, okay," the woman said hastily. "Forget it, you don't have to. I won't try to make you do anything you don't want to."

Good, Helen thought. *You'd better not.* Because sitting back again, she'd felt something poking her in the ribs, and when she stuck her hand in the pocket of the old sweater she'd stolen, she found the knife she'd taken from the awful man's camp.

He's lucky I didn't remember it then, Helen thought. *When I was in his truck.* Because it was dawning on her now that she'd have used it.

That she still would. She let her hand close around it, her thumb on the button that made the long, sharp blade spring out. The sky to the east was red, trees lining the blacktop like scissored outlines against it. "Eastport," she mumbled, her mouth feeling like broken glass and hot coals jumbled together.

"Eastport it is," the woman said mildly. But she had other plans. Doing the right thing, the helpful thing, was important to this woman, Helen could tell. And the right thing now was medical attention.

But Helen still had the knife, and even though she couldn't quite remember just at the moment what she had to do instead of seeing a doctor, she would recall it again soon.

Surely she would. Meanwhile, though, the heat in the car was beginning to be overpowering; woozily, Helen felt the dark armies of unconsciousness getting ready to overtake her once more.

Suddenly and without any warning her mouth began bleeding again, a hot rush pouring down the front of the stolen sweater. Helen leaned forward, one hand gripping the car's center console, meaning to tell the whole story so even if she passed out, the woman could still find Bob Arnold and tell him . . .

What? A sob escaped her, along with another bright red gush. The woman at the wheel looked far away, though Helen could still smell her shampoo and the faint, sweet scent of her perfume.

A whine like the sound of a dentist's drill heard through a fog of anesthetic filled her head; as the woman's alarmed face loomed suddenly over her, she felt the car swerve sharply to the side of the road.

Panicked, she pulled the knife.

Jake felt the outboard lurch purposefully, the tiller calm and the boat's wild thrash subsiding to a gentle bounce. And then they were out: of the whirlpool, the danger, the—

"Oh, baby." Lee still sat on the boat's bottom. "We're going home."

Directly ahead lay Dog Island, not far from the cliffs and the beach. Behind Lee lay Marky and Anthony, blessedly still; in the last instant before the current whipsawed them out of the Old Sow, Marky had managed to hit Anthony in the head with one of the oars, knocking him out, then lost consciousness again himself.

So the two men were out of action and they were all nearly on shore, now, though the water leaking through the boat bottom was still getting deeper, fast. *Surely there's a fix for that* . . .

With one hand still on the tiller she got the tackle box out again, found a bobber made of a cork lying among some fish hooks in it, and after carving the cork smaller with the cheap, fake Swiss Army knife she leaned over and fished out of Anthony's back pocket, stuck it into the bubbling hole and stepped on it.

Presto, one ex-leak.

Next she got Marky's .38 from the tackle box, felt it over briefly, and snapped it back in again. The sun at her back climbed fast, warming and sweetening the breeze and setting the waves flashing cheerily as if they hadn't just been trying to kill her.

Steadying the tiller, she aimed the skiff at Eastport's breakwater, a mile or so distant, keeping in close to shore just in case that cork popped out. Once they got there she could hand these two jerks over to Bob Arnold, and then go . . .

Home. But as they passed under the high, granite cliffs of Dog Island's precipitous drop-off, the treacherous Knife Edge jutting out like a bony finger over the rocks below, a new worry struck her: Was Campbell up there, watching? Cursing his luck, perhaps, still trying to think of some other way to get at her? Reflexively she sent the skiff veering away from the cliffs, out of the shallow water, and was instantly and without warning caught up in another current, its force whipping the tiller from her unprepared grip and startling an oath from her. Lee's head bumped the side of the boat, hard; she began wailing.

"Sorry, baby, oh, I'm so—" Busy, actually, was what she was all of a sudden. The water, so deceptively calm only a moment earlier, was perilous and confusing again: steer straight at the waves rucking up between here and shore and the skiff might flip. Parallel the waves, and they'd swamp for sure.

But she'd escaped the current once; surely she could do it again, now when they were so near safety that she could see the downtown pier's tall pilings, thick as tree trunks. Wielding the tiller like a club, she was very slowly winning over the water's stubborn power until Anthony reared up suddenly.

His gaze focused and found her. Bellowing, he threw himself at her. "No!" she shouted at him as behind her the skiff's wooden transom sank under his sudden weight. Fully submerged, the engine burbled and died; in the next instant they were all in the water.

Struggling and choking, Anthony flailed his arms and looked around for help. But there wasn't any. He went under, surfacing at last with a raw, whooping gasp that went like fire into his lungs, his hands grabbing uselessly for something, anything to help him stay afloat.

But there wasn't any of that, either, until something jabbed his leg. Sharp and jagged-feeling . . . desperately he shoved his foot down at it. The water was so cold that his legs were already numb, but his shoe hit a solid something.

And then another something. Rocks. He wedged himself against them, heedless of the massively booming pain in his head and arm, until he was braced between two boulders against the icy, rushing current.

It wanted to try to shove him off. But for now at least he wasn't inhaling ice-cold salt water, which to him was one hundred percent solid improvement.

He was still about chest-deep in icy slush, though, or that was what it felt like. So something else would have to be tried soon. But not yet.

No. Absolutely not now, he thought, gazing in frozen terror at the green maelstrom between himself and the shore. It looked to be only about fifty yards or so, but that was plenty. Later, maybe, he would surrender his grip on the rocks. When the water got warmer.

Or when hell froze over, whichever came first. As he thought this, one of the bright orange life jackets floated by, wrapped around the little kid. She was howling her guts out.

Anthony reached out and, balancing himself precariously for an instant, grabbed the life jacket. Sorry, kid, he thought as he fumbled one-handed with the straps. But they were tied too many times for him to undo them with only one hand, and if he let go of the rock with his left hand he would get washed off.

And his knife was missing, he realized when he felt in his pocket for it. Opening her eyes, the kid glared balefully at him as if she knew what he'd been thinking, and howled even louder. Shut up, he wanted to say. But he couldn't, his teeth chattering so hard and uncontrollably he thought they might break off.

And then he had it: He could use the life-jacket-wrapped kid as a float. Hold her out in front of himself, kick his legs hard, make it to shore that way. Because it was a cinch he wasn't going to last much longer here, wasn't it?

As for the kid, well, it probably wouldn't be good for her. Too bad; he liked her, and ordinarily he wouldn't do anything deliberately to harm her. He wasn't that kind of person; he'd shown that, hadn't he, with the other girl back in the woods?

By not shooting her. By risking his own neck in generously giving her a chance to survive. Because that's the kind of guy he was, bighearted to a fault, not like the others he'd been in juvie with. Only it was push-comes-to-shove time now, and at the end of all this, he meant to be the one still shoving.

Satisfied with his ethical situation, Anthony gripped the life jacket with the child in it and prepared to push off. But a familiar voice stopped him.

"Freakin' punk," said Marky. Turning his head very slowly,

Anthony stared in disbelief. Only a dozen feet away, Marky clung one-handed to a stout steel cable over his head. Dimly, Anthony recalled seeing the cable from up on the bluffs; it ran from the shore to a rock jutting up behind him.

Next, the tackle box that had been in the boat came bobbing by, its lid hanging open. As Anthony watched, a wave swamped it.

"Thought I was dead, huh? You wish," said Marky bitterly. Another wave drenched him, tossing him around in the water, but he didn't let go of the cable. Marky's mouth was bleeding, and his eyes were like ripe plums, purple and swollen.

But he could still see out of them. Or well enough anyway to be aiming his .38 at Anthony's head. Marky must've snatched it from the tackle box before the box sank. Just my luck, Anthony thought.

"Get over here, you punk," said Marky through a mouthful of broken teeth. "Bring that kid, too. And when you get here, just grab on this way . . ."

As well as he could, Marky angled his head up at the stout steel cable running tautly over his head, his hand wrapped around it so tightly that it might as well have been welded there. Maybe Marky really was some kind of a weird creature, Anthony thought, the kind you could only kill by putting a stake through its heart.

Or a bullet in its head. Slowly he began making his way over the submerged rocks, towing the floating kid by one of the life jacket straps. A few times he actually did find himself swimming, the kid yelling and choking out there ahead of him.

Then when he reached the cable at last and grabbed onto it, Marky stuck the gun in his ear.

"Don't worry, punk, you won't drown. I'll blow your brains out, first," said Marky. "Now, hurry up and get us to dry land."

. . .

Somebody kicked her. "Put the clothes on, Jake. That's your name, right?"

She woke with a gasp and was halfway to her feet when a blow to the side of her chest sat her down again hard.

"I said, put the *clothes* on."

She opened her eyes to find Marky standing over her, rubbing his knuckles. He'd punched her, and if she lived she was going to have a bruise on her ribcage.

If. The smell all around was of cold, wet stones, sand and seaweed, and a whiff of rotting fish. Overhead hung the low stone ceiling of one of the caves at the foot of Dog Island; dimly she recalled hitting the frigid water, flailing and gagging, and then the awful doomed feeling of going under and not being able to find the surface again. After that . . .

Panic seized her until in the bluish gloom of the cave's interior she spotted Lee a few feet away, sitting on the damp sand with the orange life jacket still tied to her body, drenched and dazed-looking.

"What's wrong with you?" Marky mumbled. There was something wrong with his mouth. "Can't you freakin' follow instructions?"

He waved at a heap of dry clothing piled on the sand nearby. Her own drenched things clung clammily to her, and she'd been in the water too long; if she didn't warm up soon hypothermia would get to her. Still, she hesitated.

"You want us to turn our backs? Anthony, turn your freakin' back," Marky said.

Despite his teeth all being broken, he still sounded alert. But then he reeled unsteadily a few steps and his eyes rolled whitely up; he was out cold even before he hit the cave floor.

Anthony plucked the gun from his partner's limp hand. "I'm not turning my back," said Anthony flatly, looking as if a car had run over him. Bruised eyes, bleeding arm . . .

She wondered if the .38 had been in the water and if it would still fire, decided this might not be the time to try to find out. "Fine," she said. "I'll turn mine."

Stripping her wet clothes off she dressed hastily in what had been provided: a long-sleeved cotton undershirt and pants, a crimson hooded sweatshirt with the word MAINE lettered in white on the front, green cotton trousers with a drawstring waist.

Socks and sneakers, too, all new and in the right size; she didn't like thinking about what that meant. A detail guy, Sandy O'Neill had said of Ozzie Campbell.

Yeah, no kidding. Pushing her arms into the sweatshirt, she winced as sharp pain in her shoulder triggered a sudden memory of being hauled, gasping and with her arm yanked back unmercifully, through the ice-cold water. But she couldn't recall more.

Marky snored wetly. "Get the dry stuff on her, too," said Anthony, waving the gun at Lee.

Outside, a breeze gusted fitfully around the cave's bright mouth, sending bits of sea lavender and dried seaweed tumbling. Lee sang tunelessly as Jake crouched in front of her.

"Honey? Hey, it's me, Aunty Jake." The child's skin and lips were blue, her chubby fingers reddened with cold and her eyes wide and staring. "What, you couldn't even get her out of her wet things?" Jake demanded furiously of Anthony.

"Not my job. Go on," he waved the gun again. "Hurry up, it's almost time."

"Ain't you forgotten something, you freakin' moron?" Marky raised himself up on one elbow, leering like something out of a horror movie at them, all bloody and grinning.

"How're we gettin' away from here?" he demanded. "Freakin' boat's gone, we got no car—"

Anthony half turned in surprise. "You're awake," he said. And then: "I'll get us a car," he added smoothly. "As soon as we deliver them I'll go find a parked car and poke the ignition . . ."

He put a hand on his back pocket, remembered his knife, and turned a speculative eye on Jake. Bending to the wet clothes she had discarded, he fished among them.

"Cute," he said to her, coming up with the knife. "I'll poke the ignition with this," he finished, turning to Marky again, "and bring the car here. Then when we're done we'll go get our own car and put the stolen one back where it was, so nobody'll—"

Marky's nose leaked bright red. "Yeah? I'm gonna sit here waitin'?" He hoisted himself up, took a moist, hitching breath.

"Go now, you moron," he ordered thickly. "Get a car, we'll hand these two over to the guy, get our money and split. Got it?"

"Sure, Marky," Anthony said, again so easily that she knew he must be lying. Marky knew it, too, or suspected.

"You'd better not freakin' leave me here," he threatened. "You hear me? You better not run."

"Marky," Anthony said reassuringly, "you know I wouldn't do that. After how good you've been to me?"

Cold-eyed, Anthony watched without expression as his partner slowly drifted back into semiconsciousness. But he flinched when Marky's eyes snapped suddenly open again.

"Your mother . . ." Marky muttered venomously. He was talking out of his head.

"Hey, Marky? Shut up about my mother, okay?"

Anthony spoke lightly but Marky's eyes brightened, unfooled. "Your freakin' mother. You think nobody knows about her and you?"

A spasm went through him; a seizure, it looked like, limbs

trembling, heels drumming. But when it was over he still wouldn't quit. "Never seen the ocean," he slurred mockingly.

"Marky, cut it out." Anthony's tone was cautioning, now. But Marky either ignored it or didn't hear it.

"Yeah, 'cause your ma kept you locked up in a closet," he said. His voice sounded stronger.

But under the circumstances, that didn't mean much. Waxing and waning consciousness, Jake knew from her long-ago stint as a brain surgeon's wife, was a bad sign.

A very bad sign. "I seen your file from the juvie home, An-tho-nee. I got a buddy works there; before I brought you in on this thing here, I went an' had a real good look at your record."

A strange expression spread over Anthony's face as Marky went on babbling. "She burned you with cigarettes, gave you dog food to eat. Hey, you were lucky to be in juvie, you know? 'Cause when you got big enough, your loser mom would'a rented you out to any stinking, no-good bunch of—"

"Shut up, Marky," said Anthony. But Marky didn't.

"—freaks and weirdos . . ."

Anthony looked down, aimed the gun at close range, and shot Marky in the head. Marky's body jerked like a fish trying to flip itself off a hook as Jake scrambled Lee into her arms and cradled her. "Don't hurt her," she said, looking up at Anthony.

He'd committed a murder right there in front of her, so he would have to shoot her; from his point of view, he had no choice but to eliminate the only eyewitness.

But he didn't have to kill Lee. A three-year-old couldn't . . .

A three-year-old couldn't identify anyone.

Hold that thought, she told herself as she began stripping wet clothes off the child's body, hastily dressing her in the dry ones. As if that could stop Anthony, as if just one normal thing after another could—

"No," he said, but not to Jake. To himself, maybe, looking around at the low cave as if unsure how he'd gotten there.

"No, I'm done, now." He dropped the gun, turned, and walked out, crouching briefly at the mouth of the cave because he was tall.

Then he was gone and sudden urgency flooded her as she tried to stuff Lee's limp, uncooperative arm into the sweater, gave up, and buttoned the garment around her. Swiftly she wrapped the wet life jacket atop the sweater and tied it again, not so tightly as before.

That way, she could wear Lee like a backpack and keep her hands free. Grabbing the .38 and sticking it into the pocket of the loose trousers she wore, she scrambled to the entrance of the cave and peeked out of it, scanning for Anthony.

Nowhere in sight, but Campbell was around here some-where; he must be. That's what all this was about. So they had to run, but from atop the cliffs the grassy bluffs of Dog Island were visible for their whole expanse. If he was there, he need only wait until she clambered up to him.

Along the beach, then. It would be slippery and difficult, but at least they wouldn't be sitting ducks. Lee coughed weakly, her lungs spasming with a congested sound Jake didn't like.

"Okay, baby," she whispered over her shoulder. "Hang on."

Heart thudding, she crept out into the sudden brightness. A seagull cried distantly. Small waves slopped on the stony beach. A plane drew an expanding white arrow overhead on the blue sky.

"Hang on," she repeated, uttering it like a mantra. "Aunty Jake is taking you—"

"Oh, leaving so soon?" called a voice from high above; a *fa-miliar* voice, raspy and harsh even at this distance.

"I think not, actually," Ozzie Campbell said. From atop the

path that ran up beside the sheer cliff he gazed confidently down at them both, smiling and holding a high-powered rifle.

Jake stared dry-mouthed. The sudden sight of him after all this time was like an unexpected gut-punch, knocking the breath out of her and turning her knees to water. Sparse, sandy hair; round, red cheeks ravaged by years of weather—a construction worker, Sandy O'Neill had told her; a steel man in his prime— and that nose of his, once hawkish but now purple and crumpled like a piece of rotten fruit pressed to his face.

A big, powerful-appearing man with broad shoulders and wide chest, he didn't look at all like she remembered him, except . . .

Except for the earring, the ruby stud glimmering in his left ear. She'd last seen it shining with its twin, on the night her mother died.

Unbidden, Jake's hand rose in a reaching gesture as Anthony appeared beside Campbell. "Get the child, please," Campbell said. And when Anthony hesitated: "Or I could shoot you, have your body disposed of by this fellow I know, he owns a cat food company."

I have a gun, she thought clearly. To her surprise, her shock at seeing Campbell again had dispersed as suddenly as it came. *So go ahead. Try taking her.*

Just try it. Campbell twitched the rifle. "Oh, and Jacobia," he called, "before I forget. Please drop the weapon my careless young friend, here, accidentally left with you."

He must have heard the shot that killed Marky, she realized, then intercepted Anthony trying to get away across the bluffs. And since Anthony didn't have the weapon, Campbell had known—

"Drop it where I can see it and then step away from it," he added, as Anthony started down.

"You're going to hell for this," Jake told him when he got to her and picked up the gun.

The oar mark on the side of his face was a mess, and his lip was freshly split. The dry shirt he'd changed into in the cave shone with fresh blood, the front saturated and the sleeve oozing brightly. The only thing keeping him upright was his youth.

And even that wouldn't help him for much longer. "Hell," he repeated with a bitter laugh, then turned her and shoved her.

"Don't worry, I'm not planning to harm the child," Campbell called down. "Not unless you resist my friend Anthony, here."

Of course he would say that. Maybe it was even true. One thing was for sure, though; Anthony wasn't the problem anymore. At this point, a light breeze could've tipped him over.

Campbell was, and she had no chance of doing anything about him unless she got closer to him. *Mano a mano*, as Sam would have put it, but jokingly; he'd never been much of a fighter. She wondered distantly if she would ever see her son again.

"Okay," she called up to Campbell. "You want me, you've got me. But leave this kid out of it, okay? I'm here, now, you don't need her anymore."

A new thought hit her. "Listen, why not let Anthony take her into town, to the clinic? She's getting sick, she needs a doctor, and he's not in such great shape, either—"

"Oh, please cut the crap," Campbell interrupted. "Who do I look like here, Florence Nightingale? If I gave a rat's ass for that punk's health I'd call him an ambulance."

He shifted the rifle impatiently. "Now get up here, or the only place that precious kid's going is in the water."

Anthony took the child from her while Campbell held the gun on all of them. Lee put up limply with being handed over, her eyes glassy again and her breathing harsh as he carried her away.

The path turned back sharply upon itself several times as it ascended the slope flanking the cliffs, the handholds on it few and crumbly and the sandy soil slipping under her feet. Gasping, she hauled herself hand over hand the last few yards.

At the top stood Anthony, sucking in ragged breaths. Lee was already in Campbell's arms as he strode away. Without looking, he unslung the rifle from his shoulder and hurled it over the edge.

He didn't need it anymore. He had the .38—and Lee. "Hey!" she called after him, but he didn't look back. Which made no sense; there was nothing ahead of him but the cliffs and—

The Knife Edge. Stark, forbidding, and in places vanishingly narrow, it stuck out over the water like a diving board out of a height-phobic's bad dream. Ozzie Campbell stepped out onto it as if casually visiting somebody's stone patio, and kept going.

"Wait," she cried, but he didn't. "You wanted to—"

At its far end the long, narrow promontory widened minimally to a tablelike platform, four feet square and a hundred feet at least above the waves churning around the jagged rocks below. He reached the platform and turned.

Crumbs of loose shale rattled away beneath his feet. A gull sailed past him, nearly brushing his head with its wing tip. Lee looked half-conscious, one small hand dangling as she hung from beneath his arm like a parcel he'd forgotten he was carrying.

Jake reached the edge of the cliff. Campbell smiled serenely.

"So. We meet again."

She crept a few feet out onto the promontory, stopped as a wave of dizziness swept over her. "What do you want?"

No reply. The ruby stud in his ear flashed brilliantly. "You know I can't hurt you with that statement I sent in. No one cares what a three-year-old saw all those years ago."

She crept forward another foot or so. From a distance the Knife Edge had appeared hopelessly narrow, but now that she was out on it a small rational part of her mind noted that it was in fact about three feet wide.

Like my front walk. As wide as a sidewalk. Anyone can make it down a sidewalk.

"So you've figured that out, have you?" Campbell said, then turned toward Anthony. "Go get that car, like you meant to," he called out, and as the wounded youth turned to obey, added:

"Don't think, Anthony, okay? Punk like you starts trying to think independently?" Campbell glanced down at the beach where in one of the caves, Marky's body still lay.

"Nothing but trouble," said Campbell softly. Anthony stood still, absorbing the veiled threat: that Anthony was the one who had committed murder. He'd better do as he was told.

"Yeah," Anthony muttered, then limped off painfully through the tall grass to do as he was bidden. He'd find a car to steal, Jake estimated, in only a few minutes. Then he would be back.

And against the two of them she had no chance . . . Shakily she got to her feet on the Knife Edge. Sidewalk's width or no, it was still a precarious spot, and its sturdiness was not precisely a reassuring feature, either. Out at its middle, halfway between the bluff where it began and the pinnacle where it ended, the ancient stone bridge to nowhere was only a few inches thick.

A chunk plummeted from it, then another. Eons old, battered and worn, like even the most durable geological entities the Knife Edge had its allotted life span, its beginning and end in time as well as in space.

And now its physical end had begun. Another big chunk of it dropped out as Campbell watched Jake with avid interest.

With an effort she dragged her gaze up to meet his. He was enjoying this, she saw from his mocking grin. He'd planned it all right down to the last detail, and now he was doing it; how he'd readied himself for a hop-skip-and-jump right out to the end of a suicidal drop-off, she couldn't imagine.

But somehow, Ozzie Campbell had done that, too. "Whatever it is you want, it doesn't matter to me," she told him. "I'll do it. Just . . . give me the little girl."

"Really?" The smile on the face of the tiger had nothing on the one that spread toothily over Campbell's face now, the bloodred earring in his ear flashing wickedly as he replied.

"Good. I'm glad we understand one another, then." He thrust Lee out over the yawning emptiness below. "Just—"

"What?" she demanded. If Lee's clothes tore, if a wind gust hit him or he just got dizzy . . . "Tell me what you want, you . . ."

What? A wave of unreality washed over her: There he was, the man who'd killed her mother, who'd haunted her dreams, driven her father into hiding and made her, in effect, an orphan. Yet facing him now she felt . . .

Nothing. Zero. All this time she'd believed that if only he were caught and punished, if he were locked up where people even worse than he was might hurt him even worse than he'd hurt her . . .

Vengeance. She'd wanted it; yearned for it. But nothing in her life anymore was about what he'd done.

A pang of regret pierced her for all the time she'd wasted thinking about him, and then . . . *gone.* Like a wisp of smoke. "What do you want?" she demanded again. "Why won't you give her back to me?"

His smile widened. Tauntingly, he swung Lee's body back and forth. "Give her back? Oh, no. That would be too easy. That, my dear Jacobia, wouldn't achieve my goal at all."

The smile vanished. "No, I have a plan for you, and I want to be sure you understand that you will cooperate in every way. I want to be sure you know how serious I am . . . and will remain."

He swung Lee like a rag doll. "That's what all this has been about, you see. The detail, the complexity—that you *believe* me, that you know I can do what I say I will, no matter what."

His voice and his gestures were growing more grandiose. He'd won—or so he believed. "So you can have her back," he finished in a mock-reasonable, smarmily obnoxious tone, "just as soon as I'm convinced you understand your end of the bargain."

She crouched again, trying to catch her breath as she clung there listening to him, taking one deep breath after another in an effort not to throw up. Her heart raced, her hands on the narrow stone bridge suddenly sweat-slick and prickling with fright.

"And to prove that you do," Campbell finished, "I want you to come right out here to me and get her . . . now."

Chapter 13

*An ounce of help cures
a pound of desperation.*
—Tiptree's Tips

T his might still turn out to be his lucky day after all, Anthony thought. Hurting and bleeding, black spots floating in front of his eyes . . . but he could hang in a little longer.

Absolutely, he could. Long enough to run away. He had the feeling that overall, he might not be thinking very clearly. But he was clear on the running part. Screw the money; he'd murdered Marky and now it was time to get out, to run so far and fast that even the bedbugs from his old place wouldn't be able to find him.

Almost immediately, he came upon a big white mommy-van parked at a haphazard angle in a yard so full of scattered toys and other assorted crap, you could hardly see the house. The garage with its door hanging open was crammed with junk, too, stuff they just threw in there and forgot about. Build a garage and park the car out on the lawn, he thought scornfully; at least in the juvie home, they'd taught him to keep his things in order.

The few he'd had. Inside the van was also wall-to-wall chaos and naturally the keys hung from the ignition where somebody had left them. He sat in the driver's seat, surrounded by half-empty organic juice bottles, abandoned clothes, and the other dirty or ruined belongings of these foolish people.

Anthony considered entering their place and teaching them a few things about how carelessness could lead to disaster; the key ring had a house key on it, for creep's sake. But screw them; let them learn it from someone else.

Someone worse. A weedy-looking little dweeb with a wispy tan goatee, still wearing his striped pajamas, ran out onto the front porch of the house as Anthony drove away. Little pot belly, this guy had, pooching out from underneath his flapping pajama top.

"Hey," the guy yelled, raising his fist. "Come back here!"

Ooh, Anthony thought, grinning widely through his pain with the pleasure of gunning the van down the early morning street. Sticking his hand out, he flipped the little dweeb the bird, at which the dweeb hopped up and down in impotent outrage.

Ooh, come back here, Anthony thought, laughing aloud. *Yeah, sure I will. Go on back in and finish your Cheerios, or whatever it is dweebs eat.* In the rearview, the dweeb's bare foot came down on a plastic toy, and that made him even madder.

The last time Anthony looked, the dweeb was still out there waving and shouting.

Jake was no natural athlete. Sam had inherited his physical agility from his father, she felt quite certain. Still, once she got to her feet again, walking on the Knife Edge wasn't quite as bad as she'd feared. *Just don't look down,* Sam always told her. *One foot in front of the other.*

But halfway out another wave of vertigo hit her; she dropped to one knee and clung there, breathing shallowly. *Don't look to the left or right,* Sam would've instructed. Desperately, she tried listening to him while the world turned and tilted and the narrow stone bridge seemed to be trying to buck her off.

"I know," Campbell said. "You're very angry with me, aren't you? But look at it from my side for a minute."

She crept forward a few more inches. "You despise me," he went on, "and yet I need you very badly. I need you to retract your victim's impact statement, Jacobia. You *must* do it for me."

Oh, really? she retorted silently. *Then how come you're trying so hard to kill me?*

But he wasn't, she realized. For some reason she hadn't yet quite figured out, being out here like this was easy for him, and he had no imagination for other people, their feelings and fears.

Only for his own. She dared another quick glance at him; at least Lee still had the life jacket. If she fell, there was the barest chance she might hit water, might miss those rocks jutting up like teeth.

But they'd be hard to avoid. Another gull swooped in boldly, curious to see whether any of the unusual activity around here might promise food, nearly brushing Campbell's head with its muscular wing as it went by. At the unexpected movement his feet shifted uncertainly, all the brash confidence vanishing from his face for an instant.

"No!" she gasped, scrambling forward as more stone fell away beneath her, bits of it bouncing and tumbling.

"Calm down," Campbell advised, regaining his equilibrium. "That's the trouble with you, you get so upset over everything. Just come on out, it's as wide as a sidewalk, for Christ's sake."

I'll give you something to be upset over, she thought. And then: *If I could get out there, maybe I could give* him *something to worry about, for a change.* But before she could complete this thought, two things happened:

Lee began waking up. Or regaining consciousness. Whichever: the cool breeze, her discomfort at being clamped under Campbell's arm, or just her own childish recuperative powers—kids spiked fevers all the time; they didn't necessarily mean serious illness—one or all of these things together made Lee begin whining and squirming, kicking and waving her arms angrily.

Campbell frowned, shifting his stance to keep his grip and his balance and barely succeeding, just as another big chunk of granite fell, exploding in a burst of shards on the rocks below.

Where it had been, a jagged crack opened up, widened alarmingly.

The Knife Edge was collapsing.

". . . Jesus," **Bob Arnold** exhaled wonderingly.

Helen Nevelson opened her eyes. The Eastport police chief's pink, plump face hovered over her, delight and concern mingling in it. His blue eyes widened vexedly. "Christ, she's bleeding."

His face receded, a balloon bobbing away. *No,* she thought. *No, come back, I have to tell you . . .*

"—call Town Hall, tell 'em get the good ambulance running

and get it over to my office, pronto," she heard him say. "We got a hospital run to make. And while you're at it, call the feds and the county guys, ask them to get over to me ay-sap. And you know what? Get somebody to Wallace Warfield's place, too; he called a minute ago to say his van got stolen."

There was a silence while he listened. Then: "Yeah, I know. Wonder he can even tell it's gone. Run down there anyway, though, or . . . yeah. Yeah, he is kind of a little—"

Pissant, Helen thought clearly. She baby-sat the Warfields' kids, and Bob was going to say that Wally Warfield was a—

"Okay. Thanks," Bob finished. Then he returned. "Hey, Helen. Hey, girl, you know how hard we've all been lookin' for you? Your ma's gonna be tickled pink."

A shadow crossed his face; there was something Bob wasn't saying. But it couldn't be as important as . . .

She tried struggling up but somehow her head wouldn't rise from the headrest, in the front seat of the purple car that she'd gotten into somehow, hours or days earlier.

But before that, what had happened? She wasn't sure; had she been hit by a car? Or had someone attacked her?

Maybe, she realized dizzily. Whatever it was, it felt like a ton of bricks had been dropped on her from a great height. Then the woman who'd saved her—

. . . the knife, Helen thought, what happened to the . . .

—began speaking.

"I wanted to take her to the clinic," the woman said, "and I tried, but she was so absolutely insistent about talking to you first, and she looks awful but her vital signs seem okay, so—"

Helen's eyes rolled, focused again. *Don't tell them that I pulled a knife on you,* she begged silently. *Please don't.* If the woman said that, they'd think Helen was the one who'd . . .

But no one was talking about a knife. An ambulance

screamed up to where the purple car woman had taken Helen, outside what Jody always called the cop shop . . .

Jody. Suddenly she remembered him and felt frightened for him, though she didn't know why. Something was happening; he was here but he wasn't here . . .

"Helen? Come on, now, stay awake for me a minute. Your mom will be here shortly. Helen, do you remember what happened?"

Again Bob turned away. "Hey, get that FBI crew on the horn, will you? Tell 'em we got one of 'em back. Yeah, the big one."

He leaned over her. "Helen, where's Lee? Was she with you?"

She could smell the Juicy Fruit on his breath. "Helen, do you know where Lee is? Do you know what happened to her?"

Lee . . . they'd taken her. But how long ago, and where? Pain came slam-banging back into her head as Helen struggled to stay awake, to remember—

Suddenly, the woman held out the switchblade. Helen's heart sank. "She pulled this, in the car," the woman said reluctantly. "I'm sure she wouldn't have hurt me, but . . ."

Bob looked at Helen, at the knife, and then at Helen once more. She could practically see him thinking with his cop mind: who Helen was, who her friends were, where they went and what they did there. The parties they all went to at night in summer, for instance, at the gravel pit or . . . out on the cliffs.

"Knife. The Knife Edge," he said.

"You know, Jacobia, when I look back on it I have to admit that almost all of it was really about your father."

"Get to the point." Astonishing, she thought, that she could summon the breath to speak, now when the terror she felt made all other fears fade. The stone bridge out over the rocks and water had cracked all the way through, and any instant now it could . . .

Oh, screw it. Just . . . She got up and took a step.

Act as if, Sam's AA pals told him. Fake it till you make it. Pretend you've beat the bottle, that you don't want a drink. That you're fine. That you're not, as he would've suggested, flat-out shared skitless.

Another step, and then another. Campbell stood only six feet away, now, Lee still trapped under his left arm. She'd stopped struggling, and from the look on her face she was thinking about something, turning the pros and cons of it over in her head.

"He was a lot smarter than me, your dad," Campbell went on. "Better looking, too. Better all the way around. He had a home, a wife and a kid."

He shook his head ruefully. "Just . . . better." Behind him the water spread brilliant blue, with the long strip of green that was the island of Campobello dividing it from the sky.

"Not that he ever made me feel that way deliberately. He was too good for that, too."

Sour twist on the word *good.* A sailboat motored tranquilly out past the Cherry Island Light. Fixing her gaze on the horizon made Jake feel better, but then a breeze riffled her hair, set her heart hammering again inside the fragile cage of her ribs.

"Did you know they never spent a penny on themselves?" he asked. "Your mom and dad? On you, the things you needed, sure."

He laughed for some reason only he knew, sparking a long-ago vivid memory of his voice from a nearby room where her parents sat happily with him, eating a meal and drinking wine, while she lay warm in her bed drowsily listening to grown-up laughter. A laugh from another life. "Otherwise they gave fifty here, a hundred there," he recalled. "Anonymous, gave it to people in the neighborhood who they knew needed it."

Because everyone there had known everything about everyone, just like here. She put her foot forward again. "What's that got to do with me?"

Back then, he'd been a young man with thick hair, a wolfish grin that both delighted and terrified her, bright white teeth and gleaming eyes . . . Even to the child she had been, Ozzie Campbell had been a handsome man. But now he looked like what he was, some guy from New Jersey who used to work construction and owned a bar and was in trouble with the law. If she'd passed him on the street today, she wouldn't have recognized him.

"I just wanted you to know," he said. "Why I loved her. Both of them, really. He was my friend, and she—"

"Fine, I get that. Cut to the chase, though, will you? Tell me exactly what you need me to change in that statement. I'll do it, no problem. Just give me the kid."

He blinked in surprise. "But . . . I thought you knew. The DA's guy didn't tell you? That Sandy guy, he works for—"

"Told me what? They haven't said anything." *If,* she added impatiently to herself, *there was anything to tell.* Campbell was desperate about something, or he wouldn't have done all this. But guys who walked into shopping malls and began firing at random were desperate, too; just not about anything coherent.

He spoke again. "There's new forensic evidence."

She stopped dead. "What?" Sandy O'Neill had mentioned it, that all the evidence from the original crime scene still existed and was being examined again, in case it might turn up something new. And his message last night . . .

Call me. There've been developments. A change in plans.

Campbell's ravaged face took on a dreamy expression. "The dress she wore, remember that flowered, silky one she had on? I didn't. But you described it perfectly in your victim's impact statement. And that black velvet ribbon in her hair. The soft shoes she always wore, like ballet slippers . . ."

He met her gaze. "They found them; even back then they were good enough to find things like that. Traces of them, what was left after the fire."

He hitched Lee tighter up under his arm. "They're in the new report. It's all there. Everything but . . ."

She understood. "The earring," she finished for him. The one he was wearing now, the one he'd always said Jake's mom had given to him, days before she died . . .

But on that night Jake had seen both of them. "I described it, didn't I? Seeing the two earrings, not just one—"

Dangling before her as she lay under the quilt, her mother leaning over to murmur loving words, kiss her good night. The ruby earrings, flashing by the light of the scented candles her mother had enjoyed, and later by the larger fire's savage brilliance . . . "That must've been how the fire got started," she said. "The candles must've overturned." *In the struggle,* she didn't add; it would've been pointless.

But it was so. "Maybe," he said, even now admitting nothing. "But here's the thing," he went on, his voice suddenly brisk with purpose. "The new forensics tests confirm your whole description of her that night. Clothes, shoes, hair ribbon—all accurate in every detail. So . . ."

At his words, what Sam would've called a knowledge-bomb went off in her head. "So because I'm proven right about the rest," she said slowly, "a jury will believe me about the earrings, too?"

She couldn't keep the triumph out of her voice. "They will, won't they? That she wore both of them that night so she couldn't have given one of them to you, days earlier. Before . . ."

Her whole body trembled as her understanding of what this meant went on expanding. "They'll know you lied. She didn't give it to you, not for love or any other reason. She never would've. And there's no other motive for you to have lied, is there?"

Her throat closed convulsively. "They'll know you must have gotten it while you were . . ."

While you were strangling her. And with that, she realized, she wasn't just a long-ago murder victim's survivor anymore, her story no longer a heartrending but ultimately irrelevant tale of childhood tragedy. Instead, she was what she'd yearned to be:

The prosecution's slam-dunk. Campbell nodded, confirming it. "Sandy O'Neill's boss Larry Trotta is revising his trial strategy as we speak, I would imagine. With you as the star witness and him as the political scene's brand-new golden boy."

That, she realized, was what Sandy's last message must have been about: He and Larry Trotta had already decided what to do. Now they were letting her in on their plan. Which Ozzie Campbell and *his* attorney would have figured out, also. . . .

"But you couldn't just kill me," she said, still staring at him, "to shut me up. Because if anything happened to me, you'd be the obvious suspect. So first, you sent people to watch me."

He'd saved her, she realized abruptly. She didn't remember, but that's how she'd wound up on the beach. Campbell must have gone out, hand over hand on that steel cable to the rocks near where she'd floundered, and dragged her ashore before she drowned. Because he needed her to live. . . .

Lee looked up and smiled purposefully, as if she, too, had

come to some realization. Jake stepped out to the midpoint of the promontory, and past it. The height, the wind . . . they still buffeted her, still scared her.

Just not like before. Inside her head, everything had gone calm. "You wanted to know where I went, what I did. You wanted to learn what I cared for the most. Who," she finished, "I loved."

His face said she'd gotten it almost right. Her Achilles' heel, her weakest point, where he could best attack her. But—

"That's why I felt followed and watched, not because I was being paranoid but because you really did have someone here."

Though even now she couldn't have said who. "And then . . ."

He shook his head. "Not someone. Me. Hanging around, playing the tourist. Oh, don't look so surprised," he added. "You barely recognize me now. And people here," he went on, "are friendly. So *chatty*," he pronounced scornfully. "If you approach them right."

Not if you behaved like the thugs had in Wadsworth's, asking a lot of nosy questions right off the bat. But if your curiosity stayed low-key and you never got too pushy or intrusive . . .

"Anyway," he said, "I found you and I wanted to make a deal. But if I'd asked, would you have met with me? Of course not," he answered before she could. "Why would you?"

She faced him wordlessly. "That's why I fixed it so you'd have to agree to see me," he went on, "to hear what I had to say whether you liked it or not. Lured you, teased you. And now . . ."

He smiled beatifically as the day brightened around him, all the water and sky filling steadily with the rich, golden light of a Maine island summer. "And now here you are."

"They'll never believe me," she objected. "If I just change my story for no good reason–"

"You don't have to change it. Just say . . . you're not so sure anymore. About the clothes and so on, fine. But not the earring. Hey," he added, "it's not like eyewitnesses don't go sour on the prosecution all the time. Don't worry, you won't be the first."

Small comfort. And slinging that kind of thing past Sandy O'Neill and Larry Trotta wouldn't be any cakewalk, either. Still, it could be done; better no witness than a poor one, the two of them would be thinking. If they couldn't use her, they couldn't. Whether *they* liked it or not.

"But how do you know I won't cheat?"

Because he must have thought of it, too, that his deal made no sense. Once she got Lee back, it didn't matter what she'd told him; there was no way for him to guarantee she'd keep her word to him. But he had an answer for that, also.

"I already told you." He waved his free arm; she caught her breath as he teetered, caught his balance again. "It's why I had to get you way up here, do it all the way I did. So you'll know, so you'll *believe* . . ."

He looked gloatingly down at Lee. ". . . that I'll do anything. And . . . that I *can*."

His plan, conceived and executed in only a few weeks, had been from the start a shaky, Rube Goldberg–like contraption of tight scheduling and obsessive preparation, so detailed and full of opportunities for failure that only a madman would attempt it.

But it had succeeded. He'd done it. She was here.

"I'm not going to jail," he said flatly. "After all I've been through . . . I'm just not, that's all, no matter what. So either you promise to change your statement or I'll drop this kid right now. Break your promise later, though," he added, "and . . ."

He extended his arm, dangling Lee over the precipice. "I'll come back. She'll never be safe—I swear," he finished obscenely, "on your mother's grave."

There was no grave. The fire, and the resulting explosion, had made sure of that. "You'd be in jail," she responded dully.

"You're sure? So confident that even with your testimony they wouldn't convict me on lesser charges, or even not at all?"

Again correct: In a jury trial, anything could happen. And even if he did go to jail, or if he died . . . he'd hired thugs once. He could hire more, even from the grave. She felt her old money-management know-how kicking in, ticking off the steps: set up a trust, fund it, leave instructions with a crooked lawyer . . .

Probably Ozzie Campbell would have no trouble finding one of those. "All right," she gave in. "I promise. Bring her in now."

"No. I told you before, you come out here."

"But—" The drop from the Knife Edge yawned emptily at her.

"Don't argue with me," he snapped. "Your mother . . . she'd have come with me, you know," he added slyly, trying to goad her.

Or maybe he couldn't help himself; maybe he believed it. Maybe that was what he'd been telling himself all this time. "She loved me; she'd have left him for me. She just wouldn't leave *you.*"

That was it; he really did believe it. The sheer narcissism of it took her breath away—that he blamed *her.* "She would never have left my dad," Jake said before she could stop herself.

His eyes narrowed; after all, she'd just contradicted what *he* wanted to believe . . . but then his focus returned. "Come and get her," he repeated. "Or I'll drop her just to get this over with."

Lee gazed around mildly, unaware of her peril. But

Campbell could still lose his grip on her at any moment. Or he might just let go deliberately—*to torture me,* Jake realized.

Because the way she'd felt about Campbell was how he'd felt about her, too, she understood now. Blame, bitterness, fantasies of revenge . . .

Unsteadily, she steeled herself; once she got all the way out to where he stood, maybe she *could* grab Lee, make it back off the cliff before it crumbled or she fell.

Maybe. "That's right," he crooned avidly. In the distance a siren howled, rising and falling, but nothing anyone else did now was going to help her.

Nobody but me. Another chunk of old granite broke off and fell away. Lee blinked sleepily as if waking from a nap, frowned as she turned her head.

Campbell's grin widened loathsomely. Abruptly, he hoisted Lee up against his shoulder. The child looked around as if seeing her chance for something, her bright gaze lighting suddenly on—

Uh-oh, Jake thought. But it was already too late. The little blond girl with the Dutch-boy haircut opened her mouth very wide, then snapped it shut again.

On Campbell's ear.

"Lee, no!" Jake cried as he howled, staggering. Gripping the child's body in both hands he shoved frantically at her, but she'd clamped down on him like a bear trap; he stumbled on the shale still crumbling from beneath him.

"Jump toward me," Jake urged him as more rock broke off and plummeted. But he wouldn't or couldn't, and the gap fast opening between them now was already a good two feet wide, whole sections of it splitting off and vanishing while Lee's jaws went on making angry chewing motions.

Like the hole in the sidewalk, Jake thought grimly of the gap in the stone bridge, readying herself to leap. *No bigger than that.* But as she tensed for it Campbell saw his peril at last and began plowing forward at her, trying to get off before the whole thing collapsed.

Straight at her, like some out-of-control engine, a big one, and no way would she be able to catch him safely. He was nearly twice her size, while the stone surface he charged across was too narrow, the gap he approached already too wide. If his weight wasn't perfectly centered when he hit her—and how could it be?—he would send all three of them hurtling off the . . .

But then without warning a memory popped into her head: Sam on a ladder, scrambling up the rungs with the confident agility of a monkey in the jungle.

"See, Ma?" he was telling her, fresh from an AA meeting and still artificially cheery from it. "Don't do it deliberately. In fact, don't think at all. Just let your own momentum carry you."

Give up, in other words. As he had. Let go and *believe* . . .

Campbell leapt the gap, his hands still clamped furiously to his small attacker's wriggling body. Jake let him come, praying that Sam was right, that Campbell's forward-toppling weight on the fast-diminishing width of the Knife Edge would carry them . . .

The part of the stone bridge that lay behind her was plenty wide enough, despite the chunks still dropping out of it; if it were on solid ground, she told herself, she wouldn't even be worrying about it. *Don't think.* . . . She put one foot back fast as Campbell half fell toward her, then caught him by the shoulders and embraced him, smelled hair oil and cigars.

Lee was close enough to grab now, too, clamped between his neck and Jake's arms. But the little girl still gripping his ear between her teeth could be carried sideways or backward just as easily as forward, and if his weight shifted—but she mustn't let that happen, even though it felt as if she were dancing with a huge, half-trained circus bear. . . .

Dancing on a high wire. Still moving back as fast as she dared, she felt loose stones under her feet and beneath them the larger rocks cracking and sliding dangerously. She let Campbell's bulk go on falling toward her, and kept retreating from him.

Please, let this work. . . . Each time she stepped back she knew utterly in her heart that it would be into thin air, until her foot struck hard stone again and it wasn't. Again, blindly, each step an act of faith until her searching boot heel struck a clump of weeds and stuck there.

Backpedaling in the soft earth, she fell rump-first onto the grassy bluff and scrabbled wildly for a better handhold. Fingers gripping scrubby dry grass stalks, she hauled Ozzie Campbell and his small, still-biting tormentor toward safety, inch by inch—

Seeming to understand that she was trying to help him, he swung his leg up. But as he did so, the biggest chunk of stone so far broke abruptly from beneath him and he slid away, small stones streaming and rattling and his feet dangling in air while his body wormed helplessly and his eyes implored her.

If it hadn't been for Lee, she might simply have put a foot in his face and pushed. Instead, with what felt like her last bit of strength, she seized his collar and hauled yet again, her hurt shoulder exploding in pain and her breath coming in harsh gulps, reddish-black dots blooming in her vision as she dragged him back up the last few agonizing inches.

And with him, the little girl. . . . As if knowing it, too, Lee smiled widely, blood streaking her teeth. But as Jake let go of him and he climbed up over the edge on his own, Campbell managed to get his breath back as well.

"Why, you little . . ." *He's got a bad temper,* Sandy O'Neill's warning echoed in Jake's head. But before she could do anything to stop him he'd seized Lee again, raising her with both hands and flinging her away into the tall grass.

The lighthouse, Jake thought. *That miniature wooden . . .*

Lee's eyes widened startledly as she sailed in a high arc, her arms spread wide and her blond hair shining in the dawn light. She hit the low-angled side of the squat wooden structure with a hideous thump, bounced off, and landed out of sight, yards away in a goldenrod thicket.

Blood still streaming from his ear, Campbell knelt, gasping. And grinning, because he'd heard that sick thump, too, and the deathly silence afterward. And he was loving it.

He looked up at her. "Our deal still stands, Jacobia. This makes no difference. Any kid," he finished coldly, "will do."

Staring at him, she thought of the high-powered rifle he'd had—if she betrayed him, how easy it would be for him to get another, use it to target some child on a street somewhere, or in a schoolyard, with no thought for anything but himself and how she would feel when she learned about it—and believed him completely.

Plans upon plans . . . The bottom line was, he'd won and there was nothing she or anyone else could do about it. As long as he lived—frozenly, she realized she couldn't even tell anyone.

He got to his feet while she sat in stunned horror, hoping against hope for the sound of Lee's outraged wail. But it didn't come. Nearby, a finch chirped. Patrolling gulls still soared serenely, and the air still smelled sweetly of cold salt water, rank weeds, and sun-drenched grass.

He began walking. Any minute, Anthony would show up with the stolen car and they'd be off the island, getting away . . .

She struggled to her feet. Striding unsteadily after him, she heard Wade in her head, calling out to Sam from the sidelines of the only high school football game Sam had ever played in: *Hit him low. Hit him low, take him down . . .*

Hurling herself at Campbell's knees, she felt him fall and heard the breath get knocked out of him with a grunt. Groaning, he rolled over to try fighting her but she was already straddling him, battering him with her fists.

"You killed her," she wept. Her knuckles split; she barely noticed. The pain in her arm was stunning; she ignored that, too. "You killed her, you—"

Monster. You didn't have to be strong to kill a person with your hands, or even particularly evil. You just had to hit him hard enough, often enough. *Again—*

"Jake." The voice came from somewhere behind her as Campbell went limp. His cheekbone shattered under her fist; then his nose fractured, the cartilage slipping sideways mushily. A tooth stuck in her knuckle; she flung it away, hit him again.

Again. Hands gripped her shoulders, dragging her backward as she remembered the gun that Campbell must still have; sobbing, she scrabbled furiously at him, meaning to find it and aim it and—

"*Jake.*" She fell back, weeping. Bob Arnold loomed over her, one hand on his own service weapon. But in his other arm he held a little blond girl with a reddening bump on her forehead. She was squirming to get down, and after another moment he let her.

"Hi, Aunty Jake," Lee said, toddling forward. She touched her bruised forehead briefly, then sat down and coughed.

"Hey, baby," Jake managed through her tears. "How are you?"

Alive . . . "She's okay, I think," said Bob. "Took a little head-bonk, but my kids do that all the time."

He looked down at Campbell's sprawled form. "Who's he? That is, other than someone I think I'll take into custody, pronto?"

She told him, and was about to go on. But then Lee coughed once more, harder this time, and an odd look came into her eyes. "Come here, sweetie," said Jake. "What's the matter?"

Lee's lips moved testingly on something. "I hope she didn't break a tooth, too," said Jake, reluctantly readying a finger for the still-perilous task of investigating the child's mouth.

But that turned out not to be necessary. "Yuck," said Lee, spitting the offending thing into Jake's hand: the earring that Campbell had worn, and with it a chunk of earlobe.

Jake brushed the bloody bit of flesh away, cringing, and looked down at Lee. "Why, you little devil," she said, unable to keep the congratulatory tone from her voice.

But Lee didn't hear, relaxed in Jake's arms. She'd had a long day and night, but all the excitement was over now, so . . .

Now she was fast asleep.

Jesus. I killed Marky, Anthony thought in astonishment.

The van drove like a loaf of bread, and Route 9 headed south toward Bangor and I–95 was the worst possible place for it. The two-lane highway widened occasionally so the rampaging eighteen-wheelers could charge onward without flattening too many of the passenger vehicles skittering nervously in between.

The cars were mostly of two kinds: perfectly maintained, practically antique small sedans with little old ladies gripping the steering wheels in undisguised terror, and junkers driven by wild men whose maniacal speed made Anthony's own lead foot seem more like Styrofoam.

I shot him. I shot him in the head.

Every so often it hit him again that he'd done it, and for a while the world went unreal, like the tires weren't even touching the road, just floating along. And the view, all the mountainous scenery and trees and so on, went two-dimensional as if it were being projected on a screen.

A thin screen, and any minute he might punch through it. He didn't even want to think about what might be on the other side. Marky, maybe, grinning and gibbering at him. Mad as hell.

Anthony jumped, jerked back to alertness by the blare of a horn coming up on him from behind. Blood slimed the front of his shirt; the other driver, holding up a furious middle finger as he went by, stared suddenly at the sight of it. Without realizing it, Anthony had been halfway across the yellow line.

Jesus, he thought again, although he doubted that particular entity was going to have very much useful to say, any time in the near future. *Going down,* most likely, was all he would say to Anthony when he did meet him.

Like some cosmic elevator operator, he thought, telling you your destination. *Going down; next stop will be the furnace room. Pitchforks, hot coals, asbestos underwear . . .*

Get a grip, he scolded himself. But he couldn't shake the memory of the way the gun had felt in his hand, the crazy heat of it and the way it had jumped when he'd pulled the trigger.

The way Marky had jumped when the bullet hit his head and all the signals in there suddenly went haywire . . .

Some sick stuff, Anthony thought, trying to talk sense into himself. *Ugly, no freakin' doubt.* It was nothing to do with him, though, what the human body did when it was—*Jesus!*

A big brown moving shape loomed suddenly in the windshield. Wrenching the steering wheel desperately to the right, he hit the brakes with both feet so as not to plow into it, then hung on as the van ker-whanged out of control, tires shrieking, horn blares around him clashing into a hellish, last-thing-you're-ever-gonna-hear falsetto while the van hit the shoulder and rolled. He got one upside-down glimpse of the big buck deer he'd just managed to avoid hitting, those antlers and the way it looked back wild-eyed at him as it bounded the rest of the way across the road.

Then it was all metal crunching and glass exploding, the van slamming a tree, bouncing off. It rolled in the other direction, Anthony feeling the seat belt ratchet tight like a prizefighter's punch in his left shoulder, while something very unpleasant that he would worry about later went on with his right.

The steering wheel came loose, smacking him in the chest before dropping into his lap while he waited for it all to stop.

Which it didn't, at first. It went on for freakin' *forever*. But eventually the tumbling and crashing and exploding got done with and he hung stunned there, upside down in the seat belt, staring dazedly at the blood puddling on the ceiling.

Wisps of smoke rose from beneath the crumpled hood. A bright tongue of flame licked up through them as if wondering what fresh air might taste like. What *Anthony* might taste like . . .

"Help! Help, somebody—"

A hand reached in, popped the seat belt. He dropped, limp as an empty sack, into the blood.

"Okay, buddy." A guy with a sandy mustache and a black cap stenciled in orange script peered in. The guy's professional way of doing this alerted Anthony at once.

"Hang on, I'm a cop, there's an ambulance coming, we'll get you some—"

Help, the cop had been about to say. But then a bell seemed to go off in his head as he made some coplike mental connection.

The stolen van, maybe, or Anthony's description; the dweeb might've gotten a better look than he'd thought. The cop reached in, grabbed Anthony's hair, and pulled. The sudden torque on his neck sent pain rocketing through him; he screamed hoarsely.

"You son of a bitch, where are they?" the cop snarled. "You tell me, you murdering bastard, or I'll leave you here to roast."

Anthony tried speaking but couldn't. The cop pulled harder. "You hear that?" he demanded, angling his head at the van's hood.

Anthony did. It was the crackling sound of fire devouring the engine compartment, thick, black, oily smoke spiraling up out of it with a stink like a burning trash barrel.

The passenger compartment would burn next. Already it was getting warmer . . . Anthony opened his mouth, tasting his own blood.

"What?" the cop snarled. "Say it again, punk. What?"

Punk. As if Marky were still here. A crackle of flames drew nearer . . . *going down!*

They sounded like Marky, too. If Anthony told the cop what he wanted to know, they would find Marky's body in the cave and hook Anthony into it, for sure. But now the smoke thickened fast, choking him and making his eyes run.

"—the cliffs," he wept, but from the look on the cop's face he realized he hadn't said it aloud. He tried again but with no better success: "They're at a place called—"

Flames exploded into the passenger compartment.

Chapter 14

For a while they were all in the hospital together:

Helen Nevelson, awaiting a transfer to Bangor for surgery on the compound fracture of her jaw, with associated hemorrhage.

Lee Valentine-White, for antibiotics against what turned out to be a budding pneumonia.

Anthony Colapietro, for a cracked collarbone, second-degree

burns to the face and hands, a gunshot wound, and a patch of torn-off scalp.

Jody Pierce, found by a search party looking for Lee and Helen, to remove what remained of his bullet-obliterated left kidney, and for blood transfusions.

Marky Larson, awaiting official transport to the morgue at the state medical examiner's office in Augusta.

And Jake Tiptree, to have—as her family and friends said exasperatedly—her head examined. Or anyway all but Lee's mother and father, Ellie White and George Valentine, expressed this.

"I don't know how to thank you," said Ellie. She sat by Jake's hospital bed, still wearing the clothes she'd departed in.

"You don't have to. You know that. There's no way I could possibly have—"

Let someone else do it. Sat at home waiting. All the things smart, sensible people would have advised.

"I was just a stand-in, anyway," Jake said. "For her mom."

And for my own, she added silently. She hadn't mentioned the Knife Edge. No mother's mind needed that kind of memory in it.

Anxious and drawn-looking, her red hair shockingly bright on her pale, narrow face, Ellie managed a smile. "George thinks she never would have made it through alive without you."

Without me, she'd never have been in all that trouble in the first place. But that was water under the bridge, too, Jake told herself again determinedly as Sam rushed in.

"Mom," he said, his forehead creased with worry. With his dark, curly hair, long lashes, and lantern jaw, he was the very image of his late father, handsome and troubled. "You all right?"

The question is, are you? But he looked sober, smelled that way, too, and his hands were steady as he reached out to hug her.

"This place," said Bella Diamond as she came in behind Sam and began peering suspiciously around the assertively clean room, "is probably swarming with germs."

Well, of course it was. Hospitals were full of sick people. But that wasn't the main reason Jake wanted out of it as soon as possible.

Home, she thought yearningly. *I want to go—*

"There, there, old girl," said Jake's father, slinging an arm around Bella. His injured foot was still in its big cast but it wasn't slowing him down any. "Pretty soon, you can scrub to your heart's content," he assured his new wife.

"I left," Jake said guiltily, "a sinkful of dirty dishes."

She'd meant to do them before Bella returned. She'd meant to finish sanding the glob of architectural putty she'd pressed into the mantelpiece, too.

And she'd meant to complete the sidewalk repair. She opened her mouth to say something about it, but her father spoke first.

"There'll be a backhoe over to the house tomorrow morning, get the drainage taken care of," he reported to Jake as if he'd been hired as a foreman on the job. "You need a culvert, not just gravel. And for the rest of it, Sam can go up on a ladder."

For the gutters, he meant, because Sam up on a ladder was so natural and confident you'd think he'd been born on one, instead of in—almost; there'd been at least two minutes to spare—the cramped backseat of a speeding New York taxi.

Momentum, she thought, smiling up at her son. He'd gotten his physical agility from his dad, she still felt sure, along with the awkwardness he always displayed in moments of feeling.

She closed her eyes contentedly. Because they were all here, and she was alive and Helen and Lee were, too. Even Jody Pierce had just come out of emergency surgery and was expected to live.

Or almost all of them were here. One was still missing–

And then he wasn't. Wade strode in, shedding his jacket and wrapping his arms around her in one smooth enveloping motion.

"Oh," he exhaled into her hair. "Oh, don't ever do this to me again. I'm not kidding, Jake, my heart can't take it."

He smelled of the harsh soap they used on the boats and of the bag balm he used to keep his hands from cracking in the cold salt air. She pressed her cheek to the sandpaper of his jawline.

"Where is this Ozzie Campbell person, anyway?" Ellie asked. She'd seen Lee and been reassured by the pediatricians that the child would be just fine. Now she examined her prettily polished nails, which if Campbell had been here she'd have used to remove numerous layers of his skin plus other important portions of his anatomy.

Wade looked up alertly at the mention of Campbell's name. "Yeah, I'd like to have a word with him, too," he said evenly. Just then George Valentine came back from the pediatrics ward where he'd been sitting with Lee. A compactly built man with a small, stubborn chin, dark grease lines permanently etched into his work-hardened hands, and the pale white skin that ran in some of the old down-east Maine families, he looked exhausted.

And he had news. "I just talked to Bob Arnold," he said. "Ozzie Campbell woke up in custody, got away and tried to run after Bob gave him over to the federal guys. Surprised the hell out of them, they said; the guy made as if he was pulling a gun on them."

The .38, she realized, the one that Marky had been carrying. But . . . "What happened?"

"They shot him. He's dead. They'd searched his place first, though," George went on, "last night. And . . ."

So Trotta had lost his high-profile murder trial, and with it his run for attorney general, probably. And Campbell wasn't holding any random children as his unknowing hostages anymore.

"Can they do that?" Ellie asked. "Just go in and–"

"They can if they had a warrant, which Sandy O'Neill arranged on account of events here," Bob replied, coming in right behind George. "Seems he took your concerns a little bit more seriously than you thought, Jake."

Of course, she realized; *because I was the slam dunk, and he and Trotta already knew it.* Bob seated himself in the remaining chair, his cop gear jingling on his belt.

"And when they went through Campbell's place, they found he had backup plans. Fake passport, a plane ticket, fake ID. Lot of electronic equipment," Bob added, "eavesdropping gadgets and so on, cameras and recorders. And cash."

Wade frowned. "I don't get it. He must've been crazy to do all this. Set it up, take the risks . . ."

"Maybe he was." Bob looked at Jake again. "Seems this trial he was scheduled for was just the tip of the iceberg. His wife passed on, not long ago. And he had money troubles, doctor and lawyer bills. His bar was going downhill, fast."

Bob sighed heavily. "Lot of his customers had legal problems themselves. And they didn't like hanging out in a place where the owner was under indictment for murder. Wrong kind of attention."

Campbell's voice echoed in her head: *After all I've been through* . . . She tried imagining the pressure on him, couldn't.

"The cash he had hidden, that was probably all he could get his hands on," the Eastport police chief finished. "Guy was dead broke."

So no one else would be coming after her . . . "Bob, what about the gun?" she asked. "How did he—"

"He didn't." Bob met her gaze. She'd never mentioned the .38 Campbell had had on him out there on the bluffs. She hadn't had the chance.

"I found it and took it off him after I—that is, after you apprehended him," Bob explained. "He just wanted the officers he turned on to *think* he was armed."

So they'd be forced to shoot him: Campbell's final backup plan, she supposed. The one he'd saved for if he didn't win.

Plans within plans . . . "He made it all look so easy," she began, then stopped. Ellie was still listening alertly.

Bob caught Jake's eye. "What, his tightrope act out on the Knife Edge? Yeah, I saw part of that."

He turned to Ellie. "The guy led Jake in a little song-and-dance routine out onto the Knife Edge," he said smoothly.

Thank you, Jake thought at him. "As for making it look easy, for him it was," Bob went on.

"Because," he explained, looking around the room, "it turns out the construction work Campbell used to do wasn't the hammer-and-nails kind. They found an old union card and a lot of other papers among his things when they went in."

He got up and looked out the window to the hospital parking lot. "He was an ironworker, all right, back in his youth. But not in a factory."

Bob turned back to the room. "On skyscrapers."

"Oh," Jake breathed comprehendingly. "The kind who—"

"Yup. The kind of guy who walks along those high beams, puts the fasteners in. Eats lunch up there, a hundred stories in the air. 'Course, those guys all wear safety harnesses," he added. "But if you're afraid of heights, you don't have that kind of job in the first place, I guess."

No kidding, she thought, feeling again that awful yawning emptiness at the edge of the precipice. "Wait a minute, the federal marshals told you all this?"

Bob looked wise. "Well, not all of it. Week or so ago I got in touch with that Sandy O'Neill fellow. Nice enough guy, and just for fun I figured I'd fatten up my knowledge base in the Ozzie Campbell department."

Ten percent doing, ninety percent knowing . . .

"And Sandy was very helpful," Bob added. "Once I convinced him I'd go down there and drop-kick his butt right into the East River if he wasn't."

"I see," she said evenly, wishing she'd been a fly on the wall for that conversation; Sandy helped his boss chase big-time criminals for a living, and was not precisely a pushover.

"Well, however you did it, it's a good thing you showed up when you did and caught him, isn't it?"

Or I might have killed him myself, she added silently, and from his answering look she saw that Bob understood that, too. The question of exactly who'd saved whom from whom might never be fully settled, she thought. But maybe it didn't have to be.

"Guess so," he agreed. "Even better thing, that little girl was never in a position to have to be out there with him."

There was a small silence in the room, everyone thinking of what might've happened and hadn't. In her mind's eye Campbell's face appeared once more, but transparent, now, like an apparition glimpsed briefly in the window of some old, long-empty house.

Bob headed for the door. "Okay, then. Guess it's time I went an' had another confab with the feds, the state guys, the county guys, my guys—best we get all our ducks right out in a row for the news conference later."

Alarm pierced her. "Bob, can you keep me—?"

"Out of it? Oh, you bet," he assured her. "I doubt the feds and the state boys'll mind soaking up all the credit, do you?"

"No. Thanks, Bob," she said, and when he'd gone she sank back stiffly against the pillows. Every part of her was sore despite the painkillers they'd given her; by tomorrow she'd be in a world of pain. She didn't like staying in the hospital overnight, but the doctors insisted. Exhaustion, dehydration, and her inability to keep even the smallest amount of food or water down—nerves, she supposed, though she hated admitting it—had made them adamant.

But for now . . . She settled more comfortably as the others began gathering themselves to leave. "See you later," Wade said, bending to kiss her. "Get some rest. I'll be back soon."

"Later," Sam echoed from the door. Behind him stood Bella, running a finger disapprovingly along a length of woodwork.

"I'll bring a dust rag," she promised, ignoring the insulted look of a nurse passing by in the hall. Her new husband had already stumped away toward the orthopedics department, bent on getting that cast off, finally. "And," Bella added, "Lysol."

Ellie leaned down to hug Jake. Her hair still smelled like the interior of an airplane but Jake inhaled it gratefully before releasing her friend. Then it was George's turn.

"I don't know what to say," he told her, holding his cap in front of him awkwardly in both hands. "You got her back for us. Thanks don't seem like enough."

"They are, though, George. More than enough. And . . . you're welcome," she told him and then he went out, too, leaving her to rest in this calm, quiet place.

She wanted to go home, but tomorrow would be soon enough.

Tomorrow . . . her eyes drifted shut.

•   •   •

Helen Nevelson sat in a wheelchair just inside the ambulance bay, pressing a towel-wrapped ice pack to her face and waiting for her mother to return with a suitcase full of the things Helen would need in the next few days.

Around her, aides and nurses in hospital uniforms bustled purposefully, carrying thick charts, pushing medical equipment on wheels, or escorting patients. She'd already had one surgery to stop the bleeding; next, an oral surgeon in Bangor would fix her jaw.

Nervously, she wondered if it would hurt much. A tear leaked down her face, a hot, stinging runnel through the cold numbness of the ice pack. "Hey, there," someone behind her said.

It was the purple-car woman, smiling and carrying something in one hand that she kept tucked a little behind herself so Helen couldn't see what it was.

Now wearing the white smock that Helen had last seen hanging in the purple car, the woman had pinned her dark brown hair back tightly and refreshed her red lipstick. She crouched in front of Helen and took her hand reassuringly.

"Don't try to talk. I work here," she added, her voice low and gentle as if she knew just about anything might terrify Helen at the moment. "That's why I can barge right in anywhere."

She put a pink zippered bag into Helen's hands. "I thought you might want a few treats like this for later," she said. "For after surgery, when . . ."

Slowly, Helen unzipped the bag. In it were a dozen or so small, pretty samples of expensive cosmetics whose labels she'd seen in magazines: Lipsticks, soft pointy colored crayons for her eyes, a mascara wand and a mirrored compact containing pale pink blush powder and a lush, soft makeup brush . . .

And a flat disk of pancake makeup with a sponge applicator. Helen looked up.

"You'll have bruising," said the woman matter-of-factly. "So you might want some cover-up for it. And anyway," she added, "you deserve a little something to make you feel better."

Thank you, Helen tried to say. "Now," the woman went on as if not noticing Helen's fresh tears. "There's someone who'd like to get a look at you, before your next adventure."

Without asking permission she seized the wheelchair handles and began rolling Helen from the waiting area. "Don't worry, they won't leave without you," she said.

They rolled through the hospital lobby, down a corridor full of beeping EKG machines and empty gurneys, and into a room with a bed in it. Jody was in the bed, lying very still and surrounded by IVs that dripped clear fluids of various pale colors into him, covered to his neck by a white sheet. One arm lay exposed.

His eyes were open. When he caught sight of Helen he smiled weakly and tried to speak. She was halfway out of the chair when the woman caught her.

"Hey, hey, give him a break. He's just waking up from big-time surgery."

He wiggled his fingers at her, unable to speak past the tube still in his throat. "Hi," she whispered, and he nodded faintly.

"We can't stay," the woman said. "He needs to sleep, and you need to travel. But there's something else for you, and he wanted to give it to you, so . . ."

On Jody's bedside table lay a box with the stylized outline of an apple on it. "Go on. He told your mother that he wants you to open it right away."

So Helen did, while Jody watched her through eyes that kept drifting shut. "Oh," she said when she had the packaging removed.

It was an iPod, exactly the one she'd wanted forever, just to have because it felt special, luxurious and so . . . well, she'd just wanted it, that was all. But from Jody she'd heard again and again that it was silly, too expensive, too . . .

Biting her lip, she met his gaze. *Thank you,* she mouthed as well as she could, and felt he understood. But there was more she had to tell him, and on the bedside table also was a small white notepad. She leaned over and grabbed it, and the pen with it.

Music. Good for canoe trips, she wrote. *Long trips.* She held the pad up; his eyes smiled happily. Proudly.

Then they fell closed once more. Helen turned, frightened.

"It's okay," said the woman. She sounded as if she knew what she was talking about; Helen relaxed. "He's full of anesthesia, still. He'll sleep now, and by the time he really wakes up you'll have had your own surgery, and we can tell him you're fine."

Urgently, Helen wrote again. *His* daughter. *Tell my* dad *that his* daughter *is fine.*

The woman smiled. Helen wondered if after this, she would ever see the woman again.

Maybe. Maybe not. "I will. I'll be sure to tell him his daughter wants her father to know she's come through with flying colors. Again," she added lightly.

Content, Helen let herself be wheeled away, not noticing the pair of eyes from one of the other rooms they passed fastening upon her as she went by, narrowing with recognition at the sight of the bright braid piled atop her head.

Recognition, and the beginnings of a plan.

• • •

Bad dream . . . **Jake** woke suddenly to the choked, smothering feeling of a hand clamped to her mouth. Hot, sour breath gusted into her face.

"You're not gonna freakin' testify against me about Marky."

That voice—her eyes snapped open in disbelief.

Anthony Colapietro's bruised, bloody face loomed over her, his expression murderous. "The girl's alive. I didn't kill her. And I didn't kill the guy in the driveway, neither. I was s'posed to, but I—"

His hands closed around her throat. She couldn't *breathe* . . .

"They say three minutes is all it takes, you know? Hey, you were hurt worse than they thought. So you stopped breathing. They should've checked you better, is what they'll think."

It wasn't. They wouldn't. Autopsy evidence would show she'd been strangled, and he'd be the obvious suspect. But he was just a dumb punk who didn't know anything except how to kill. . . .

She tried throwing him off, tried reaching the call button, knocking the telephone off the bedside table so its crash might summon someone—all useless. And he'd closed the door.

Stars swarmed in her vision, bright pricklings in the encroaching blackness. Suddenly a ripe *thump!* sounded nearby. As Anthony toppled away, she surged up, gasping, sucking in air. When her vision cleared her father stood there, gripping a heavy white plastic molded cast shaped like a foot.

Groaning, Anthony Colapietro shifted and tried to get up. Her father looked down at the bandaged, hospital-gowned form with its orange antiseptic stains and bloody trailing IV tubes.

"Don't you move," Jacob Tiptree told Anthony. He reached out to lean on the wall-mounted emergency button.

"Don't you move, goddamn it, or I swear I'll stand here and bash all the rest of your brains out."

Whereupon Anthony Colapietro, seeming to understand the deep sincerity of this promise, didn't budge.

Three days later, Jake sat at the oilcloth-covered table in the kitchen of her big old ramshackle house in Eastport, Maine, sipping a cup of tea. At the antique soapstone sink, Bella Diamond filled a bucket with hot water and soapsuds, all ready to begin scrubbing the back porch after the most recent onslaught of visitors and well-wishers.

Too bad she couldn't scrub away the current one. "Jake, I'm so sorry," said Billie Whitson, pushing back her strawlike hair with her red-tipped claws. "This was my fault. If I hadn't shown him around . . ."

Because that, it turned out, was how Campbell had gotten the lay of the land; he'd found Billie's real estate Web site, come to her and faked interest, and let her drive him around looking at places—including the Jiminy Point house, whose owners she'd talked into listing "just in case there was a great offer."

She'd even rented him a small cabin on her own property on the mainland, at the end of a driveway nearly as long as the one at Jiminy Point. In it, Bob Arnold had found the ruby pendant to the earring Campbell had worn; recognizing what it must be, he'd neither mentioned it nor hesitated before slipping the thing into his own pocket, later handing it over to Jake's father.

"Anyone asks, Campbell gave it to Jake," Bob had said. Bob already had what he called a quiet word with the fellow who was supposed to have been guarding Anthony Colapietro in the hospital, and who instead had been chatting up one of the nurses.

Although Jake suspected it had actually been more than one

word, and that quite a number of them had been profane. Just because Colapietro had appeared to be unconscious . . . well, Jake didn't envy the guard.

Now Billie Whitson went on apologizing profusely: "If I'd had any idea who he was, I'd never have–"

"It's okay, Billie. You couldn't have known."

Instantly the real estate maven brightened, glancing around greedily; she'd been wanting to get in here for ages. "You know, this room would photograph beautifully as a 'before' picture . . ."

Bella, who had put down her bucket and pulled a broom from the closet, yanked Billie's chair out hard with Billie still in it. Shoving the broom under the table she found Billie's sandal-clad toes while energetically pursuing nonexistent crumbs. Yelping, Billie took the hint and fled, after which Bella went back to preparing her mop bucket.

"Now, that there's a woman who'd sell her dead grand-mother right out of her coffin if she thought she could make a buck on it," Bella remarked. "Coffin, too. She'd tell folks it was a studio apartment."

Apahtment–the Maine way of saying it. And although Jake couldn't responsibly endorse Bella's methods for getting rid of pestiferous persons, she had to admit the result made her feel as if some henna-haired, bony-faced, super-hygienic cross between a housekeeper and a fairy godmother had granted her dearest wish.

Stepmother, she realized, gazing with gratitude at the dour, ropy-armed woman in the cotton housedress, a bib-style red apron trimmed up with black rickrack tied around her skinny waist and her hair skinned harshly back into a fraying elastic.

Bella's rawboned hand cranked off the hot water faucet. The sudden act rattled every pipe and radiator in the house.

"Anyway, she's the end of all the company for today," Bella

declared, which was a notion Jake absolutely could get behind, as Sam would've put it. She felt hollowed out with exhaustion, like a radiator that had just had all the water drained out of it.

And not just by Billie; already this morning there'd been half a dozen kinds of cops needing to do interviews so they could finish their paperwork. Reporters had found the house, too; it hadn't been as easy as Bob Arnold thought, heading them off. But now that they were gone and Anthony Colapietro had been sent to a jail hospital in New Jersey, Jake hoped to begin feeling normal again soon.

Bella hustled out to the porch just as Jake's dad came in, looking troubled. "Hoped I'd find you here," he said. "Couple of things I wanted to say to you."

"It's okay, Dad," she began, but he sat anyway.

"You did fine, you know," he said, resting his hands on the table. "And . . . well. It's time for you to have these."

He opened his right hand. Two earrings lay in it. "Sometimes we all need something to hold onto. And Bella's been awfully good about me wearing one, but . . ."

She let him drop them into her palm, closed her fingers on them. "Thank you," she said. It wasn't all Jacob had come for, however.

"Ozzie could be a fine fellow when he wanted to be," he said. "But he had another side to him, one that I should've paid more attention to."

"Dad. None of it was your fault. I don't—"

"He always had a way of figuring out what to say or do to hurt you," her father went on. "I know because he was my friend, once, and I knew him very well. Just not . . ."

Not well enough. "Anyway, I thought maybe he might've said something ugly to you about your mother and me. It would've been just like him."

Tears filled Jake's throat; she blurted the truth. "He said I made her stay with you, that if it weren't for me she'd have– Dad, was I the reason? Was she in love with him, is that why . . . ?"

"Why he thought she might leave me?" He shook his head. "We both loved her, yes. There wasn't a man alive who wouldn't. But not like . . . we'd laughed about it, the three of us together. How devoted he was, how at her service."

He paused, remembering. "Sir Galahad, we'd started calling him. Foolish, I guess. But it's hard to explain, now, how happy we were. Like nothing could ever go wrong. We were young, that's all. We just didn't know."

They sat in silence for a moment. "I wanted to straighten it out with him but she said no, she'd talk to him herself. And she did, she sat him down and told him, the day before . . ."

His voice trailed off; he got control of it again. "She told him that what he wanted would never happen, there wasn't a chance and that even if there were, that she'd never leave you. Or take you from me," he added.

His eyes glistened. "Afterward, she said that he seemed to understand, that she thought it would be okay. But . . ."

"But he came back," Jake whispered.

He nodded. "The very next day. I was busy in the kitchen. He must've slipped in past me. Other people saw him come in."

The explosion had blown both her father and his visitor out the door, leveled a city block. Later he'd found the earring in the rubble. "I stuck around," he went on, "and kept out of sight until I was sure you were both . . ."

Dead. In the pandemonium he'd managed to escape notice.

Jake recalled being dug from beneath a warped piece of sheet metal in the yard, hours after the event; recalled the astonished face of the young cop who'd found her.

Recalled being lifted, carried away. "She was so beautiful," Jake said.

"Yes, she was." He got up and crossed to the window.

In the yard both dogs rested in the shade of a pointed fir tree, happy to be back home where the only thing either one of them ever had to retrieve was a Frisbee. "Your ma would've put the screws to Ozzie just the way you did," he said. "That woman had more guts'n anyone I ever knew."

He turned and met Jake's gaze. "Except maybe her daughter. So, is there anything else you want to ask me?"

"No. I know all I need to now."

He regarded her. "All right. Any questions, though . . ." He tapped his chest with an index finger. "You know where I'll be."

With that he went out to oversee the backhoe work for the broken sidewalk. After a while Bella came in and went upstairs to turn on the vacuum cleaner, just as another chunk of old gutter crashed past the hall window.

"Big doings out there," Wade observed, descending from his shop. He was cleaning the .22 Marky Larson had hurled into the water off Jiminy Point; that morning at slack tide, Sam had gotten up very early, put on a drysuit, and gone down there and found it.

"Mmm," Jake replied, fingering the earrings once more before closing her hand around them. Wade leaned over and kissed her.

"Life goes on, then, huh?" he murmured before heading back upstairs to work a little longer.

Yes, she thought. If you were lucky and you remembered what people who loved you had taught you, sometimes it did.

She placed the silver stem of one of the earrings into her ear just as another, louder crash sounded from the front of the house, followed by laughter.

Getting up, she paused at the hall mirror to put in the other earring, feeling the pair of them as a sweet, solid weight, the color of heart's blood. Then she turned from her reflection and hurried outside to see what all the commotion was.

About the Author

SARAH GRAVES lives with her husband in Eastport, Maine, where her mystery novels are set. She is currently working on her thirteenth *Home Repair Is Homicide* novel.